"Enticing!"—*Seattle Post-Intelligencer*
"Spicy!"—*Library Journal*
"Heart-stopping!"—*Publishers Weekly*
"Highly charged!"—*Rendezvous*

Praise for *New York Times* and *USA Today* bestselling
author **CHERRY ADAIR** and her irresistible
romantic suspense novels

BLACK MAGIC

"Adair keeps the pace brisk and the action vivid. This
book should appeal to readers who like bickering
protagonists, plenty of sex, and a hero who always comes
to the rescue."

—*Publishers Weekly*

"Adair's version of wizards and magic makes a much-
welcomed return in a hot new adventure that brings
estranged lovers back into contact."

—*Romantic Times*

NIGHT SHADOW

"Smoothly blends sensuality and espionage. . . ."

—*Publishers Weekly*

"Pulse-pounding . . . all the danger, treachery, and
romance a reader could wish for. . . . Exceptional."

—*Romantic Times*

HIDE AND SEEK

"Cherry Adair stokes up the heat and intrigue in her adventurous thriller."

—Romantic Times

"Wow, it's gripping, sexy as all get out, and the characters will send you into orbit in steam heat . . . enough chills to keep you on an adrenaline high for the duration of the story."

—The Belles and Beaux of Romance

"Full of highly charged sensuality and violence."

—Rendezvous

"Outsize protagonists, super-nasty villains, and earthy sex scenes."

—Publishers Weekly

"A reason to stay up way too late."

—The Romance Journal

KISS AND TELL

"A sexy, snappy roller-coaster ride!"

—*New York Times* bestselling author Susan Andersen

"A true keeper."

—Romantic Times

This title is also available as an eBook

Also by Cherry Adair

Black Magic

Available from Pocket Star Books

CHERRY ADAIR

HUSH

POCKET STAR BOOKS

New York   London   Toronto   Sydney

Pocket Star Books
A Division of Simon & Schuster, Inc.
1230 Avenue of the Americas
New York, NY 10020

This book is a work of fiction. Names, characters, places, and incidents either are products of the author's imagination or are used fictitiously. Any resemblance to actual events or locales or persons, living or dead, is entirely coincidental.

First Pocket Star Books paperback edition May 2011

POCKET STAR BOOKS and colophon are registered trademarks of Simon & Schuster, Inc.

For information about special discounts for bulk purchases, please contact Simon & Schuster Special Sales at 1-866-506-1949 or business@simonandschuster.com.

The Simon & Schuster Speakers Bureau can bring authors to your live event. For more information or to book an event contact the Simon & Schuster Speakers Bureau at 1-866-248-3049 or visit our website at www.simonspeakers.com.

Cover design by Lisa Litwack
Cover illustration by Craig White

Manufactured in the United States of America

10 9 8 7 6 5 4 3 2 1

ISBN 978-1-4391-5382-6
ISBN 978-1-4391-6711-3 (ebook)

ACKNOWLEDGMENTS

TO K.S., FOR YOUR awesome firsthand tales of BASE jumping. Thank you for offering, but the answer is still a firm and resounding no. Never!

To Tara F., for your assistance with the translations. You went the extra mile. My bad guys should have their mouths washed out with soap. Good for you.

To Yoselin and Elvis Rojas, for your help with all things Venezuelan. No, I don't think my readers would each pay you even one dollar for my safe return. But it was sweet of you to suggest sharing the ransom.

Any mistakes in this work are mine. (Except for that one thing, *that* was not my fault. But you know who you are!)

HUSH

~ ONE ~

Venezuela
Tuesday
5:33 A.M.

Three things happened simultaneously: the soft, warm curve of a woman's bare ass tucked enticingly against Zakary Stark's good-morning-happy-to-feel-you erection, the familiar gut-wrenching realization that she was the *wrong* woman, and the cold hard metal of a gun barrel pressed to his temple.

The tantalizing fragrance of fresh, jasmine-scented female, coupled with the erotic base note of last night's sex, was obliterated by the sour stench of stale male sweat.

Fuckit. Hell of a way to start the day.

Zak's heartbeat ratcheted up a notch, and his entire body stiffened in reaction to the threat.

"¡No te muevas!" Pure menace infused the instruction to remain still; the words, spoken in the local dialect and punctuated by another motivational jab a millimeter from his eye, got Zak's head back in the game.

Zak spoke fluent Spanish, but he wasn't going to show his hand until he knew what the guy wanted. His gut urged him to get the hell off the swaybacked mattress. Fast. But he wasn't going to be speedy enough to beat the man's finger on that trigger.

He processed the situation. While he was all for taking crazy risks in an attempt at kick-starting a spark of giving a shit about life in general, he wasn't alone. *He* might not give a flying fuck if he died one way or the other, but Zak suspected the woman probably didn't hold the same disregard for *her* life as he did for *his*.

He was no goddamn hero. Pissed him off to be put in a position where he had to accept that he was going to be responsible either for another woman's death or, worse, for ensuring that she stayed alive.

Hero or coward. It was a toss-up which would kill him quicker.

The bed was shoved against the wall, and *she* lay between him and the man with the gun. God damn it. He *hated* guns. Kathy? Christy? . . . the American he'd met in the bar the night before went from limp to tense between one heartbeat and the next as she realized they weren't alone.

Zak cracked open the eye not pressed into the fragrant curve of her neck and looked through a mass of corn silk blond hair. Fuckit. Not just *one* intruder. In the murky light of dawn he made out three silhouettes, and heard the shuffle of several more pairs of boots out of his line of sight.

Fatigues. Boots. Weapons. More than an audience. A whole fucking predawn party.

Military? Locals? Guerrillas?

Three crappy choices.

Lips against the woman's ear, Zak whispered, "Stay still," and felt the uneven thud of her accelerated heartbeat beneath the hand cupped around her breast. She let out a small shuddering breath and froze as he spoke more loudly to the guy with the gun. "I'm unarmed."

She *unfroze*. "*¡Él no tener una arma!*" she translated urgently in bad Spanish.

Jesus. "He got it the first time," Zak snarled. "Don't move, don't talk." Don't be so fucking *conspicuous*. Impossible. Her lush body was displayed like a delectable smorgasbord, ripe for the taking and within easy reach, on the sex-tangled sheet. Christ, there was nothing more than a sheen of sweat gluing their entwined limbs together.

Hardly bulletproof.

As if determined to be the independent woman he damned well didn't need her to be right now, she turned her head so their lips were mere inches apart and said in a furious undertone, "I don't want to get shot because he doesn't unders—"

The barrel of the gun gouged a deeper dent in Zak's temple. "Lady," he managed between gritted teeth, "shut the fuck up." He squeezed her breast in warning.

Her entire body bristled. "How dare y—"

"Six of them. Six weapons. Us? Naked. Worth it to you to make a point?"

Zak could practically hear her brain turning over in the brief pause before she whispered tightly, *"Fine,"* and faced forward again, body rigid.

"Callate." The guy standing beside the bed was wearing some sort of pseudomilitary uniform, camo pants tucked into heavy boots. A man of few words, clearly, willing to let his gun do the talking. Zak recognized a Russian-made Uzi when he saw one. In full-auto mode, the weapon was designed to put a lot of lead into a small area very quickly. It also had a strip of electrical tape over the grip safety to prevent a sweaty hand from sliding off the rear of the grip assembly and leaving the shooter with a locked piece. The language the weapon spoke was universal: Obey or die.

Despite the erratic *thwap-thwap . . . thwap* of the ancient ceiling fan, the room was hothouse stuffy from the jungle heat of the previous day, and ominously quiet. Everyone staying at the small, seedy hostel-type hotel was probably asleep at this hour. Frankly, he doubted anyone other than his brother would respond to gunfire or yelling. Small-town people in this neck of Venezuela's woods tended to mind their own business for good reason. No one would come running to aid a couple of gringos and risk getting killed. Chances were they were waiting for their own payout from the takedown.

He carefully uncurled his fingers from the smooth, warm globe cupped in his palm, then slowly raised his hand to show that he was unarmed and compliant. He whispered close to her ear, "Stay quiet, and wait for me to tell you what to do. Then fucking *do* it. Got it?"

Fine tremors shook her body, but she gave a small nod, which dragged a filament of jasmine-scented silk across his cheek.

Zak suspected *he* was the one who'd endangered them both, but his task would be a hell of a lot easier and less complicated if she weren't sex appeal personified— weren't there in the goddamned hotel room with *him*.

As far as he knew, there were only three Americans staying in this fleabag hotel just inside Canaima National Park. Himself; his brother, Gideon; and the blonde.

Her bad luck.

Wrong place. Wrong time. Wrong man.

The men had been in the room for approximately two minutes. Long enough to kill them, take them, or rob them. None of which had happened. Yet.

This was too organized to be random. There were more extremely-well-armed men than they'd need if their objective were merely to rob him. No, not a robbery. And he and the woman weren't dead yet, so, not a homicide either. They weren't here for the blonde, no matter how good she was at stripping or whatever her dance of choice was. They were here for the Stark brothers. He wondered if Gideon was in the same predicament right now. Zak considered another option.

Kidnapping.

Big business in Venezuela.

The fact that they wanted him lying down indicated they felt safer with him flat on his back. Naked was a bonus, meant he was even more vulnerable.

The fact that he was still alive told him that they

didn't *want* to kill him, at least not now; always reassuring.

The fact that they weren't doing much of anything meant they were waiting for someone else to arrive. He had to act fast. He knew the odds *now.* Any second those odds would change. And he'd bet his Rolex they wouldn't improve any.

Hell, might as well kiss his Rolex good-bye.

He heard the shuffle of booted feet changing position out of his line of sight. The ultimate goal was to get himself and the woman away from those weapons alive. He was at a distinct disadvantage, though, lying there with an armful of fragrant, interfering, naked female blocking his exit from the bed. First things first.

The plan of action was to be on his feet for whatever was coming down the pike. "Look," he said in a reasonable tone, addressing the man's groin, since it filled his field of vision. "Whatever you want, we can work it out. Let the woman go. She's got nothing to do with this." The gun barrel drilled harder into his temple.

"*Que te calles, coño,*" the man growled. Loosely translated, "Shut the fuck up."

Think faster.

What the hell could he do with her that wouldn't get them both killed in the next minute? Zak was used to thinking on his feet. He was a risk taker, a daredevil, a master thrill-seeker. But that was *him.* Now he had another life to consider. Been there, failed at that.

What else you got, Stark?

"You want money?" He eased his leg from between

hers very slowly, and inexplicably felt his dick respond to the silky glide of her firm, smooth thighs clasped around his. Jesus fucking hell, not *now*. "I'll give it to you. Just back off. Let me grab my clothe-"

"*¡Date prisa, cabrón!*" the guerrilla shouted, no longer bothering to keep his voice down. Not a good sign in the quiet of the small hotel. The Uzi never wavered in his grip as he stepped far enough away from the bed for Zak to see greasy perspiration glistening on his upper lip and in the creases of his thick neck. Big barrel of a guy. Buzzed black hair. Camo gear. Handgun in holster on utility belt. KA-BAR knife strapped to his thigh. Not military.

Not officially, anyway.

Guerrillas. Well-funded.

Christ, what a clusterfuck. The Uzi was pointed at Zak, but it was the woman who had the man's avid attention. "Hey, buddy"—he got the guy's eyes back on him—"plenty of dollars and *bolos* in my wallet. Over there, in my pants." Which he'd practically ripped off before tumbling the blonde onto the bed the night before.

"*¡Me hables una vez más y te corto la verga!*" the man shouted, face mottled. He leaned forward, reached out with one meaty hand, grabbed the woman by the wrist, and yanked her unceremoniously off the bed. She screamed like a fucking banshee as she staggered to regain her balance. The guy backhanded her and the scream was cut off mid-decibel.

"Don't let them—*please!*" she begged Zak through

lips gone white and stiff with terror. The wild tangle of her long blond hair tumbled around her shoulders as she stood there, not sure which way to go. What to do next. Her skin looked pearlescent in the half-light as she gave him a pleading look from tear-drenched eyes. Without breaking eye contact, she whispered, "*Do* something."

Still lying on the goddamn bed with a gun aimed at his head, he shot her a hot stare in return. Sympathy wasn't going to help. *Buck up, Barbie. It's gonna get a helluva lot worse.* "Any suggestions, considering the odds?"

"Y-yes, I——" She dragged in a jerky breath and held it. "I can give th——"

"*¡Cállate la jeta, traga leche!*" The annoyed guerrilla swung her away from him. Zak winced as she crashed into a nearby chair, fell against the wall, then slid to the floor. It happened so fast, he could see by her bewildered blink when she lifted her head that she hadn't processed what was happening yet. Two men raced to her side, grabbed her upper arms, and hauled her roughly to her feet, groping her everywhere they could in the process.

Everything in him wanted to haul ass across the room and beat the shit out of both of them. But there were four weapons trained on him, two on her, all at close range—he'd be no damn good to either of them dead.

"Easy," he said calmly, sitting up and raising his arms, palms out. When he wasn't immediately drilled full of holes, he swung his feet to the gritty floor. "No need to hurt her. She has nothing of value. Just let her leave, she won't be any trouble."

"Right. I won't be any trouble at all," she assured

them fervently, her eyes darting from man to man, then back to him. She dragged in a shaky breath. "Look. I don't want . . . Just take . . . Damn it. All I wanted was one night of—" She blushed. *She goddamn blushed.* "Which was great—but I don't think I deserve to get the hell beat out of me because I made a bad choice. Not that you were bad," she hastened to add, "but, well, this situation is . . ."

She shot him an annoyed glance. "*They* don't appear to speak much English, and *you* don't speak Spanish, so . . ." She turned to one of the men and said in halting, Rosetta Stone Spanish, *"Si vas a disparar, me gustar morir con mi dignidad. Y con la ropa encima."* *If you're going to shoot me, then I'd really like to die with my dignity. And fully clothed.* She motioned with her chin to her clothes scattered on the floor.

He'd ripped the scrap of dress off her in his haste to get her naked the second the door closed behind them the night before, and it wasn't going to do much to cover her even if they let her have it. *"Es aquí mis cosas. ¿Yo poder . . . ?"*

"Lady? Last time. Shut the fuck up," Zak repeated, coldly, ear cocked for his brother. Where was Gideon? His brother was a light sleeper. He must've heard the scream if nothing else. Fuckit. *Had* the men dealt with Gid before coming here?

"I talk when I'm nervous. Which you might agree I'm justified in being," she snapped. Apparently, realizing she wasn't going to be able to do anything about her nudity, she behaved like the emperor with his new clothes. Just stood there haughty as hell and as if she were fully dressed. Her chin rose as she gave him a hot look. "The circumstances notwithstanding, stop telling me to shut up. This is my room, and I can say whatever I damn well like in it. You don't like me chatting? Take a hike."

Unbelievable. Bare-ass naked and surrounded by military grade hardware, and she still had a mouth on her. He'd liked it last night, but then again, they hadn't exactly been talking. Standing there sleek and naked, blond hair wild and just-been-fucked sexy, she was escalating an already volatile situation just by looking the way she looked.

"For fuck's sake. They hold all the cards." And it would be worse for her if they decided to shoot him and take her. Any way, anywhere, they wanted.

She gave him a fulminating look and snapped her mouth closed. Zak could almost read her thoughts in a word bubble over her head. Fear radiated off her in waves. One of the men holding on to her shifted to hook his arm across her throat. Her pearly skin gleamed in the semi-darkness as she struggled to remain on her feet while the two men tugged her this way and that, which they found vastly entertaining as she fought uselessly to get free.

Two dogs with one bone might work after all . . . at the least, she'd keep them distracted.

He kept his arms up: *Patience.* His mother used to say, "You wait until your father gets home. He'll deal with you." This was like waiting for the shoe to drop, and for his father to mete out the usual punishment when he eventually got home——be it at seven that night or a week later. The only difference was the amount of blood this shoe was going to take with it.

"Well?" He kept his tone fairly civil. All things considered. "Take what you want, and go. We won't call the authorities."

The man closest to him laughed. Besides eye-watering BO, he stank of a several-pack-a-day cigarette habit. "We don't need your permission, *pendejo*," the guerrilla in charge said in slow, deliberate English. "We take what we want." He jerked his chin to indicate the two men searching the room. One pocketed Zak's wallet from the bedside table, another helped himself to his watch. The Rolex had sentimental value, but Zak wasn't prepared to die for it.

The woman cried out indignantly as one of her captors grabbed her breast. Zak decided he'd kill that son of a bitch first. He was stunned that she wasn't already in full-blown hysterics, but knew it was just a matter of time. "Take it easy. Let the lady go." He rubbed his fingers together in a universal gesture for money. "I have more money in the safe downst—"

The man shoved her in Zak's direction, with an obscene suggestion he didn't dare acknowledge. *"No hay bolos suficientes aquí, marica."*

Zak jumped to his feet just in time to catch her up in one arm. Her entire body quaked with terror. Nothing he could do about it. He kept his voice impersonal. "Pull yourself together. They're feeding off your fear."

"I can't . . ." She wilted against him.

"Jesus. Are you going to faint? Don't faint, for Christ's sake!"

"*¡Ya basta con la puta charla!*" the guy in charge snarled, not enjoying the chitchat. He raised the barrel of the Uzi to cover them both.

Zak let her go, but she remained glued to his side. "Get it together and do it fast." As women usually did, she was exacerbating the situation without even trying.

The guerrilla motioned with his weapon for them to separate. Her nails dug into Zak's waist as she clung to him like a baby monkey. The man motioned to the two guys. Blue Bandana and Gold Tooth looked like equally butt-ugly identical twins. They peeled her off him.

Cursing *him*, she fought them with everything she had, blond hair flying, spitting disjointed words in a mixture of bad Spanish and English. They shoved her into a corner and held her there at gunpoint.

ACADIA GRAY PRESSED HER naked back against the cold cement wall as she accidentally made eye contact with one of the men who'd cornered her. Leering, he licked his lips and rubbed his crotch suggestively. Bile rose in the back of her throat as she saw every sick fantasy he was entertaining play out in his eyes.

She looked around wildly, struggling not to hyperventilate as she tried to decide whom to offer her freaking lottery winnings to. Because dollars to doughnuts, *that* was why they were in her room. Somehow they'd read or heard about her lottery windfall, and they'd come to collect. Although how they'd known to come *here*, so far from Kansas, was a mystery she didn't have time to figure out.

Her fellow captive was trying—*unsuccessfully!*—to negotiate their release. In *English*, for God's sake! One would think he'd at least make an effort to learn the language of the country he was visiting. The men clearly understood but a few of the words he was saying. But he was pigheaded enough not to let her try to talk to the soldiers in their own language, which she'd been practicing for weeks.

His ego was going to get them both killed. Or worse. Acadia stopped hoping he'd save the day and get them both out of this alive. He wasn't doing . . . *anything* useful, just standing there naked with his hands in the air.

Trying to think when she was scared out of her mind was no easy task. Heartbeat manic, she stiffened her muscles, willing her body to stop shaking.

It didn't work.

Uncharacteristically, she'd made a series of extremely bad choices in the past twenty-four hours, and they were all culminating right here in this tiny room. Damn it, she was going to die before her long-awaited big adventure really began.

Her muscles, especially in her legs, felt as weak and unsubstantial as tapioca pudding, and the erratic pounding of her heart throbbed loudly in her ears. Locking her knees, she told herself to think hard and smart.

She was *good* at thinking. At preparing. She just had to get the fear untangled from the process. Breathing deeply, and several stages beyond abject terror, she considered the facts. Waking to find herself in a living nightmare was bad enough. Waking up naked in front of all these men was beyond unacceptable and took humiliation to a whole new level. Though the travel agent had said to expect unusual customs in Venezuela, Acadia doubted he'd been talking about *this*.

Oh, she'd been warned that there were military types, but she certainly hadn't expected them to be crotch-to-face with her in her own damn hotel room first thing in the morning, waving guns about, forcing her to stand there naked in front of them.

Leering at her. Touching her.

She struggled uselessly to break the soldier's grip on her arm while her one-night stand—stood there doing absolutely *nothing*. Zakary Stark was hot in bed, but he was piss-poor at hero stuff. He looked shockingly bored and disinterested—he might as well be sunbathing on a nude beach on the French Riviera, for all he was doing.

Without warning, the man let go of her arm to jam a hand between her legs. She let out a wild, choked-off scream, grabbing his wrist and digging her nails into the sinew and bone with all her strength. For all the effect it had. He jammed his hand against her harder.

"Whoa, whoa," Zak protested. Too little too late.

It was the man in charge whose sharp warning made the soldier slowly withdraw his questing fingers from between her legs. He grinned lasciviously, his eyes promising worse to come.

Panting, light-headed with dread, and holding back hysteria by sheer determination, Acadia fell back against the wall. Her skin crawled, and bile refluxed in the back of her throat.

"*¡Ponte de pie nojoda!*" The barrel pressed hard against Zak's throat. Raising his hands higher, he appeared completely relaxed as he kept his attention on the guy in front of him. God. How could he be so calm? Acadia was trying not to blubber like a baby; her breathing was so erratic she felt dizzy enough to pass out.

Pull yourself together? she thought furiously, incensed by his dictatorial attitude that so far had done absolutely nothing to help *either* of them. Clearly unconcerned by his nudity—well, sure, because none of the men seemed interested in *his* spectacular physique—he just stood there, big and bold and naked. Even the fully armed soldiers didn't seem to give him pause. Acadia envied him his sangfroid.

She'd never felt so exposed, or so vulnerable, in her life.

And this on the advent of one of the biggest life-changing things she'd ever done. Only she could be so unlucky as to wake up to a roomful of armed men days before embarking on what she'd thought, until now, was the ballsiest thing she'd ever done in her life.

Somehow, enrolling in architectural school at her age didn't seem so daunting anymore. She'd spent most of her life with constraints that hadn't allowed her to move forward. This trip was supposed to jump-start her "new normal." But the men holding her weren't going to let them go. They weren't going to stop leering. No point drawing any more attention, or hands, to herself than necessary. She had to calm down, had to start thinking rationally and methodically. There was a way out of the situation; there was *always* a way out. Letting her brain run around like a rat in a maze was counterproductive. Acadia drew in a calming breath and let it out slowly. Keeping her attention on Zak, she blocked out everyone else.

She knew his features by feel and taste better than by sight. He wasn't *that* good-looking, she thought, eyeing him critically. His hair was dark, a little long, and shaggy. His face was a little too rugged, his mouth bracketed by lines that could have come from a grim life, or long-hidden dimples—though he didn't give the impression he was a man who smiled much. He had plenty of scars. One dark brow was bisected by a thin line, while another, a good two inches long, slashed his left temple near the corner of his eye. He had a puckered scar high on his right shoulder, and another on his left hip. She'd kissed all of them last night.

Acadia couldn't see the color of his eyes in the meager light, but she remembered staring into them across a candlelit table in the cantina the night before: dark and heavy-lashed. Sexy. Hypnotic. Zakary Stark was unlike the men she usually dated. Different enough that he was exactly what she'd needed last night to kick off her grand adventure.

Clearly a lover, not a fighter. Unfortunately, she needed a different kind of man right now. Preferably one who was well armed and willing to kick some butt.

"I get that we're waiting." Zak's voice cut the unnerving quiet in the people-filled room as he spoke with mind-blowing, *annoying* calm to the leader. *Waiting* was news to Acadia. Had she missed something? "While we're just hanging around, why don't I go ahead and get dressed? Save you all some time?"

"Waiting for what, exactly?" Acadia couldn't keep the sarcasm out of her voice.

Zak ignored her.

His broad chest was lightly covered with crisp dark hair arrowing down his belly to . . . Oh, Lord. He wasn't aroused, but his penis lay against his well-muscled thigh, and it was— *Wow.* Acadia swallowed. It took some concentrated efforts to disengage her attention and draw her gaze back up his body.

Just looking at the ripple of muscle and satin-bronzed skin on the way up made her brain conjure the feel of his mouth between her legs, and the rasp of his callused hands as he—

She blushed from her head to her toes. Every man in the room was suddenly staring at her as if he too were imagining what had happened right on that very bed hours before.

A whole new wave of fear-fueled adrenaline zoomed through her system with nowhere to go and layered with the sudden surge of lust, making her so woozy that she swayed. She was standing there with two thugs gripping her upper arms, their dirty fingers leaving streaks on her bare skin, and she couldn't stop staring at Zak's package? What the hell was wrong with her?

On the other hand, it was a diversion from relentless terror.

Zak turned his head slightly, as if he could feel her

focus fixed on him like a tractor beam. Intense dark eyes clashed with hers across the twelve feet separating them in a brief and all-encompassing look. Acadia's gaze skittered away like spit on a griddle.

She had absolutely no idea how to interpret the look he'd just given her. *Run? Stay where you are? Dive for the floor? Drop dead?* In books and movies, the helpless heroine always knew exactly what her hero's silent stares meant. Hell, those heroines could read a whole chapter into a single glance. In real life—not so much.

Long strands of her hair stuck to the sweat on her face and throat as she gave the man on her left a cool look. "I'm getting dressed now." She made a move toward the scattered clothes she'd put out the night before, which were now on the floor. The man on her left blocked her with the barrel of his gun, warning her to stay put. To hell with that.

The room was like an oven. They were all sweating, and God—they smelled so rank her eyes stung. She made another useless move to break free, but the men beside her restrained her. Acadia screamed her fury and tried to kick them as she fought to break their hold.

The guy in charge turned to see what the commotion was and shouted, "*¡Compañeros, ya basta de rumba! Pueden jugar con ella más tarde.*"

She understood Spanish much better than she spoke it, and knowing there'd *be* a later was good news. Good news she had to get across to her seemingly disinterested lover before—

Without warning, Zak exploded, taking advantage of

the soldier's inattention. He grabbed the barrel of the Uzi, ramming the stock hard against the man's chest and driving him against the wall beside the bed. The mattress went one way, the metal frame the other, as the man was slammed against the cement wall with a bone-jarring thud.

"Get down! Get down!"

Acadia didn't need to be told twice. Her two captors let go of her to reposition their weapons, and she dropped to the floor and rolled against the wall, trying to make herself as small as possible.

Still grasping the barrel in his bare hand—was the man *insane?*—Zak ripped it out of the guerrilla's hand. The following explosion was deafening, and the bad guy's shirt erupted in a surreal blossom of red.

The retort of the discharged bullet must've been loud enough to wake people in far-off Caracas. Half the plaster crashed from the ceiling to the filthy floor in a shower of masonry and choking dust. More shots echoed in the chaos as the men swung their weapons around looking for something, someone, to shoot.

Acadia stared uncomprehendingly at the gaping, bloody hole in the middle of the soldier's chest and curled her arms over her head. Like that would stop a bullet. There was nowhere to hide, nowhere to take cover, and the door leading out into the hallway was still blocked by two men who looked as though they were rooted in position, guns pointing into the center of the room.

Not waiting for the debris to settle, her newly minted

hero swung the gun around and pulled the trigger as another man lunged. The Uzi clicked uselessly, and Zak dropped it in one smooth motion as he went in fast and low from the cloud of plaster dust while the soldiers tried to regroup. Using his shoulder, he rammed the closest man in the belly, driving him across the room. They crashed into the wall, so close to her that Acadia heard the soldier's breath escape in a strangled *whoosh* as his spine made contact with the unyielding wall. She winced. Zak didn't let up for a second, lashing out with a swift undercut to the man's unshaven jaw. Unconscious, the soldier slid to the floor beside her.

"Two down, four to go," she said, unaware that she was speaking out loud. Where the hell were her clothes? They'd been on the chair . . . She found one boot and clutched it to her chest as she looked for something a little more concealing.

She glanced at the men blocking the only exit. If they'd go and help their pals . . . but no. They were still there, weapons fixed on the moving target of the naked guy without shooting. Considering the size of the small room, maybe they realized that a stray bullet could hit any one of them.

With a metallic jangle and the scream of metal grating on the wall, the bedsprings flipped end over end, coming to rest against the wall. Zak, bare-assed and suddenly proactive, grabbing anything he could get his hands on, now wielded it as a weapon. One of the soldiers came up behind him, locking his arm across Zak's throat in a wicked choke hold. Acadia lurched to her feet.

Without consciously making the decision, she drew back her arm and let her boot fly. It missed her intended target, but hit another man smack in the nose. Blood spurted; he made a garbled shriek-y kind of yell, then dropped like a rock and lay still.

"Three left," she yelled, looking for another weapon. The man she'd beaned still had his Uzi in his slack hand. She crouched down and started across the room.

The soldier she'd aimed at and missed tightened the bend of his elbow against Zak's throat as he fought to get free. With superhuman strength, he half twisted his body, enough to bring a bent arm up in a lightning-fast move, and put his full weight behind it. Fingers spread, Zak jammed the heel of his hand up under the guy's chin and dug his fingers into his opponent's eye sockets. The bruising blow to the chin made the soldier's hold loosen, while blood spurted from his bitten tongue. Zak grabbed him by the hair and gave him a swift knee to the balls. With a shriek, the man dropped to writhe on the floor. Whimpering, he clutched his hands between his legs.

"Two to go." Picking up the Uzi, Acadia realized it was heavier than the shotguns and rifles she'd handled at the sporting goods store where she worked. She knew the basics, though she'd never fired an automatic weapon, but it didn't take an action hero to know which end to point in which direction.

"Great. A naked blonde with an automatic," Zak drawled. "You're giving these guys their fondest wet dream."

"Help or shut the hell up," she snapped. She didn't

make eye contact—with any of them—as she swung the business end of the Uzi from man to man. At this range she couldn't miss, and they knew it.

Suddenly someone grabbed both bare breasts from behind. Hauled off her feet, she was slammed against the wall face-first. The Uzi went flying, clattering to the floor across the room as the man pressed his entire body weight against her and pinned her to the wall.

Sound was obliterated by the hard drumbeat of her own terrified blood racing through her veins and the ringing in her ears. Face smashed against the wall, Acadia's vision darkened around the edges. *Don't faint don't faint don't faint.*

Choking on her tears and the black rage pouring through her, Acadia reached behind her, digging her short nails into the man's hand, which was wedged between them.

Nothing was going to stop what was about to happen. She knew that. And yet she kept fighting, finding more hidden strength when she was sure she couldn't find one more drop.

Somewhere, over the din of her own fear, she heard shouts, but they were meaningless. Her survival instinct filled every atom of consciousness.

The loud crack of a gunshot, from very close range, made her world stand still.

The hot, sweaty weight of the man slid in grotesque slow motion down her bare back; then he crumpled to the floor behind her with a heavy thud. Acadia couldn't breathe. Couldn't move. Couldn't think. But her internal organs shrank as something warm, wet, and too horrific for her brain to identify dripped slowly down her naked back.

Afraid to turn around and see what had just happened, Acadia was relieved by what had *not* happened.

"Porqué está desnuda esa puta?" (*Why is the whore naked?*) an authoritative gravelly voice ground out in rapid-fire Spanish.

⤚ TWO ⤙

Acadia had no idea who he was, but whether it was the newcomer or Zak who'd . . . gotten rid of . . . the soldier, she was profoundly grateful. She knew she had to turn around and face whatever was about to happen. But God—she couldn't move. She was aware of scuffling, of thumps and groans, but it was as if someone had hit the Mute button.

She needed a moment—a lifetime, or an all-inclusive therapy session—to center herself. It took everything she had to lever her shell-shocked, blood-splattered body off the wall. Feeling a thousand years old and as fragile as glass, Acadia turned around and numbly observed that the room now contained more armed men than there'd been moments before.

A tall, skinny guy in cargo fatigues lowered his gun to his side as he surveyed the room with clear displeasure. *"Porqué lleva tanto tiempo?"* No, not a man at all. A woman, with a low, rough voice that rang through the small room and stopped everyone in their tracks more effectively than the last gunshot had.

After a brief pause, all the men started talking at

once, their voices tumbling over one another in an unintelligible babble. The woman stopped *that* by firing a round into the ceiling. The other half of the ceiling rained down on their heads. Everyone shut up.

Acadia's gaze found Zak. He was sprawled facedown on the floor, hands behind his head, a soldier's booted foot on his bare, straining back.

"Let her—"

The woman strode across the room to deliver a vicious kick to his ribs. She hefted her gun like a club. *"Hombre,"* she said, "she's the least of your problems."

Acadia winced as the butt of the woman's gun connected with Zak's head with a dull, painful-sounding thump.

"Get them dressed, and in the truck." She spoke heavily accented English. *"¡Apúrate!"* She paused, eyes flashing as she surveyed her men. "The next man to touch her dies like Santos, *¿vale?*"

Acadia leaped to grab a T-shirt first, cheeks burning as the men watched her scramble to yank it over her head and over her bare breasts. No one stopped her. She quickly shrugged into a sleeveless vest, schooling herself not to betray how heavy the garment really was. The vest had a million hidden pockets. If Acadia managed nothing else, she'd be taken *with* her stuff. She wriggled into the matching, multipocketed cargo pants, unable to keep from blushing fiercely as a man whistled mockingly as she yanked them over her bare bottom.

A guerrilla threw her boots at her. She bit back a cry as a heavy hiking boot ricocheted off her instep.

"Be quick," snarled the man she'd hit with the same boot earlier. Acadia was gratified to see that his nose appeared to be broken, and that he was already sporting two black eyes. *Good*, she thought with relish, as she hurriedly finished dressing.

ACADIA WAS TREMBLING, HER heart pounding so hard she was afraid she'd throw up any second. Sweaty and ice-cold at the same time, she braced her hands beside her hips to counter the motion of the swiftly moving vehicle. The ancient, windowless—some kind of delivery van, she suspected—stank of sweat and cigarettes. The van had no shocks, and each bump and turn made itself felt as they bounced over pockmarked roads at suicidal speeds.

She and the unconscious Zak had been unceremoniously tossed into the back of the vehicle with another man about fifteen minutes before. The doors had been slammed shut and locked; then they'd taken off with a screech of bald tires as if the hounds of hell were after them. The second guy had a large, painful-looking bump on his temple in almost the same location as Zak's.

She studied the men in the dim light, noticing their similar coloring and builds. The second man's long, dark hair was tangled around his face and shoulders; Zak's was a bit shorter, brushing his collar. Even unconscious, the two men looked unkempt and vaguely dangerous. Zak's bad-boy looks had been appealing the night before, but seeing him now, Acadia wondered if she'd lost her mind and all her good sense in taking the guy back to her room. Kidnapping could've been the least of her problems.

She pushed those thoughts out of her head. He hadn't killed her, or worse. Her aches and pains proved she was alive, and unfortunately, she couldn't blame him for their kidnapping either. But what if her kidnapping had nothing to do with her lottery winnings? Acadia's brain went a little manic when she considered the ramifications of her—their—kidnapping.

The three of them could be held for ransom. She had money in a savings account, which she'd happily hand over in exchange for her freedom and that of the two men.

Or they could be killed.

Or they could all three be sold into slavery. Not as far-fetched as she'd like to think—it was a very real possibility. She'd read all about the sex slave trade. Women weren't the only victims, and both Zak and the other man were strong and fit, and fairly good-looking.

There was nothing for her to hold on to in the bare metal box. No way to see where they were being taken, and no way to escape. The ceiling was high enough for her to stand, and she'd tried pulling, kicking, and screaming at the doors, which were locked from the outside. The most she'd done was to make a dent in the metal with her boot heel. She sat back against the hot wall, the van jarring every bone in her body as it lurched along its trajectory.

She'd always felt a faint disdain for women who needed a man to rescue them, but she'd be freaking ecstatic if either of the men sprawled on the rusted floor would wake the hell up and *do* something. *Anything*.

They were not going to be happy when they discovered they'd been kidnapped because of her. But when she gave them all the kidnapping statistics, they'd see that even without her lottery winnings, there was an excellent chance that they would've suffered the same fate. Still, she was going to have to talk fast—presuming they'd have a chance to talk once they arrived at their destination. She shivered despite the heat building up inside the tin can on wheels.

After the next pothole almost put her spine through the top of her head, she rearranged her clothing to give herself more padding between her behind and the unyielding metal of the floor, then dug a small box of mints out of one of the hidden pockets in her brand-new SCOTTeVEST gear. Dressed from head to toe in khaki, she looked ready for a safari—or a trek through the jungle. When she'd bought the vest and pants, the twenty-eight hidden pockets they boasted had amused her. Now, she mentally patted herself on the back for having splurged on the outfit.

She shook out two of the tiny mints and popped them in her mouth. "Ha. That's living on the wild side."

Hearing her own voice was small comfort. This sustained terror was a freaky thing. Having someone else to share her concerns with "would be nice," she finished out loud as she stuck the small plastic container back into the same pocket as the Swiss Army Knife and a small first-aid kit. She'd considered trying her Army knife on the doors, but the tools were so small they wouldn't make a dent. The soldiers had taken her watch, her St. Christopher medal, and her bag, but they hadn't bothered to pat her down as they'd done with Zak.

Lucky her. Because she'd spent considerable time the day before carefully packing *all* of the hidden pockets in her breathable cotton SCOTTeVEST and pants with everything she could think of in preparation for her five-day jungle adventure. The extra eighteen pounds had seemed overly cautious yesterday, even for her, but now she was grateful she'd had the foresight to be so prepared.

The female soldier who'd shot the man attacking her hadn't voiced her reasons for ordering the men to keep their hands off Acadia. The tires bounced over a series of violent bumps that made her bite her tongue, twice. She winced sympathetically as the men's heads thumped on the ribbed metal floor.

"At the risk of being politically incorrect," she muttered, crawling between them on her hands and knees, "aren't you the ones supposed to be saving *me*?" She carefully lifted Zak's head, then maneuvered her body so that his head and neck were supported by her thigh. He wore the same lightweight khaki pants and pale blue dress shirt he'd tossed on the floor before ravishing her . . . and a spectacular and noteworthy ravish it had been. Acadia blushed at the vivid memory, then bit her lip because there was blood on his shirt from his head wound and this was no time to relive the pornographic memories.

She wasn't strong enough to drag the other man closer, so she spread her legs out and, with a lot of huffing and puffing in the heat, she was able to get his head off the floor and braced on her opposite thigh.

If her friends could see her now, she thought as she stretched her back. Safe and cautious Acadia Gray trapped in the back of a speeding van driven by kidnappers with not just one good-looking man sprawled all over her, but two.

She inspected Zak's stubbled jaw and closed eyes as she undid the Velcro on the pocket over her left breast and took out a sealed pack of antiseptic wipes. She had to clean the blood from his face so she could assess his injuries. It was stifling inside the van, and she had to stop what she was doing to catch her breath. Since she was hardly qualified to treat any injury more severe than a splinter, his unconscious state was for the best, she thought as she gently wiped around the gash.

Qualified—ha! Being the only conscious person in the back of the van practically made her a doctor.

Cupping Zak's bristly jaw in her palm, she inspected him at close quarters in the sliver of hot white sunlight seeping through the doors. Most people looked vulnerable when they slept. Not this guy. He looked tougher. Edgier. What in God's name had she been *thinking* last night? He was no tame house cat to pet, he was a wild exotic jungle animal.

Strong, stubborn jaw, blade of a nose. All those scars. . . . A fighter. Because she couldn't help herself, Acadia traced a gentle finger across the wide expanse of his chest, through his thin blue cotton shirt. Internal muscles she'd only recently discovered contracted in response.

"What's your last name, soldier?" she whispered, tracing his hard, thin slash of a mouth, which was set firmly, as if he were fighting even in his dreams. Maybe he was.

Given the way he'd handled himself in the hotel room, maybe he was all too used to brawling with strangers in dangerous places.

Acadia had a Technicolor memory of kissing and licking her way down the crisp hair on his chest and following the arrow all the way down to . . . Her cheeks turned fiery hot.

So much for her prediction that he'd leave her room while she slept, after they'd made love. So much for her certainty that she'd never, *never* see him again. Wasn't that what one-night-stand guys *did*?

There was that whole be-careful-what-you-wish-for thing that she'd never appreciated the irony of until now. She carefully wiped around the bump and worked carefully at the crusted blood on his temple with the pungent wipe. The bleeding had stopped. That was a good thing. But he was still unconscious after all this time—a bad thing.

"Dirt roads, armed men, jungle," she said briskly. What she wanted was the magic button she could press to reanimate these guys. "They are not taking us to a fiesta, boys, so can you please wake up sooner than later and help me figure out what we're going to do when we finally stop? I would really, really like to have a plan."

Acadia did not like chaos or uncertainty. Life went much more smoothly when things were anticipated and planned for. She made lists of her lists; she anticipated, strategized, and planned ahead. Boring, her friends insisted. But Acadia knew that the way she did things left no room for horrible surprises.

The smorgasbord of current possible "surprises" made her heart pound. She tried to keep track of when they turned and when they went straight. Hard to do without visual clues. She made a mental note of the condition of the roads they traveled, which kept her mind occupied and her dwindling hopes up as her mind filled with "ifs": if they could escape; if they could make it to a road; if they were actually able to walk and able to backtrack.

Her heart skittered as the bald tires of the van bumped off a paved road and turned left onto something rougher and a lot more ominous. God . . . a dirt road could go anywhere. *Be* anywhere.

She finished thoroughly cleaning Zak's head wound, then used a clean edge to wash several smudges off his face. He still looked dangerous. She whipped out another wipe and went to work on the other guy. Good-looking, with shoulder-length dark hair. Not as interesting a face as her lover's, but nice enough. "At least you don't have to listen to me talking to myself," she told them as she finished up the triage. "I tend to get overly chatty when I'm nervous. And this situation is tying my stomach in knots."

She did something else when she was extremely nervous: she lied through her teeth. She knew she was doing it, but couldn't seem to stop herself. Staff Sergeant Dad used to warn her that her fibbing would get her into serious trouble one day. Last night had clearly been that day.

She'd fibbed to Zak about being a dancer—when the least of it was, she had two left feet—the exotic, erotic kind was implied when he'd approached her in the dimly lit, very loud cantina the night before. As fibs went, it was pretty much a white one. The whole evening had been a surreal, exciting, out-of-body experience. The small . . . *untruth* had enhanced her first one-night stand.

Talk about Murphy's Law. Her first one-night stand couldn't have turned into a worse nightmare. She wasn't used to standing around bare-ass naked and surrounded by burglars, or felons of some sort, being . . . eye-fucked. Oh God. That was the very first time she'd ever used *that* word, even in her head, but there wasn't really any other way to put it.

Apparently she wasn't cut out for adventure. She shouldn't have come to Venezuela a day earlier than her friends to get acclimatized. She sure as hell shouldn't have picked up a dangerous stranger, should not have brought him to her room, should not have had wild monkey sex with him, and should not be traveling at the speed of fright to an undisclosed second location.

The Lover She Never Wanted to See Again was supposed to have gone off this morning at dawn for his Angel Falls BASE jump. She, to do a river trip to *see* those falls. Which pretty much highlighted their different life views as far as she was concerned. He was a doer. She was a watcher.

The reason the sex had been so incredible—so mind-bendingly *amazing*—was because she'd believed it was a one-time-only deal, so she'd checked her inhibitions at the door. A one-night stand, she thought, annoyed, should be just that. One damned night.

Her entire body blushed with mortification. She'd done things, had things done to her, that she couldn't even *think* about in the daylight. She'd never done anything remotely like what they'd done the night before.

Acadia wiped the sweat dripping down her temples on the shoulder of her T-shirt. She couldn't imagine looking into the eyes of the short-term lover who knew what she'd done the night before. He had been a hot, sweaty adventure that she'd never forget. She didn't need the knowledge in his eyes to remind her of just how adventurous she'd been. She let out a little moan of embarrassment. All she'd damn well wanted was an *adventure* before her thirtieth birthday. To live a little. To step outside her small box in Junction City, Kansas, and experience what she'd only read about. She'd wanted to taste a hot arepa fresh from the oven, pick a sun-warmed passion fruit straight off the vine, feel the tropical sun on her face and the splash of the Akanan River against her skin as she and her friends went on their crazy adventure to see Angel Falls.

She'd wanted a fun-filled vacation before she packed up her neat little life and took her first steps into a brand-new world; wanted to say good-bye to her friends in style, give herself memories to savor when she moved away to start her new education in a new city.

Had that been too much to ask? Clearly, yes. The universe, not known for its sense of humor, had granted her wish. Her father, retired army staff sergeant Corey Gray, had frequently warned her to be careful what she wished for. Maybe she'd wished too big, Acadia thought, as the van slewed around a corner and threw her back against the hot metal wall once more. The guys' heads rolled, and she anchored them with a hand on each forehead.

She'd wanted to live, and instead could very well die in the jungle where no one would ever find her.

ZAK CAME TO WITH a blinding headache, his head pillowed on the woman's leg, the smell of antiseptic and hot female overpowering the unwashed stink of the van. Tuning in to his brother's steady breaths, Zak asked, "You awake?"

"Oh! Yes, I—"

"Yeah," Gideon answered over the woman, his voice laced with amusement.

Much as he'd have liked to lie on her thighs all day, Zak forced himself to sit up. The interior of the vehicle swam in his vision.

Her slender hands supporting his back, she said in a worried voice, "You probably have a concussion."

He waited for the black snow to fade. "I don't."

"You don't know that for sure."

"I know the difference." He squinted until his brother, also sitting up, solidified. "Had it before."

"Many, many times," Gid added, scraping his long hair back and securing it with the leather thong he kept on his wrist. He looked like hell, probably felt worse, but smiled as he returned Zak's searching look. "You look like shit."

"Feel excellent," Zak assured him, turning his head to look at the woman. Her shoulder-length streaky blond hair was disheveled, and her Persian-cat-gray eyes looked as serious as the situation warranted. Her hands were still on his back, braced on either side of his spine. Right where her heels had pressed just hours before.

He was relieved to see that she was dressed. Not in the little bit of nothing she'd worn the night before, which had consisted of about a yard of pale yellow silk, her blond hair curled enticingly around her lightly tanned shoulders, eyes smoky, smell mouthwatering. Now she wore sand-colored cargo pants and a sleeveless zippered vest over a pink T-shirt, last night's makeup smudged beneath her eyes. Her hair was disheveled, and dirt streaked her face—tear tracks, he realized with a twist of his gut. But she didn't seem to have any injuries. She'd been lucky, no thanks to him. Fury raced through him, startling him with its savagery. Those assholes had abused her, nearly raped her, and he'd been helpless to prevent any of it. He reined in his anger, because losing his temper when the object of his rage wasn't around was a waste of time. It was going to take him a while to get over feeling so goddamned helpless. Again. He'd pack the new guilt on top of the boatload he was already carrying.

Tempted to touch her to make sure she was okay, Zak resisted the urge and kept his hands to himself. Besides, sympathy would probably make her fall apart. "How you holding up, Barbie?"

Her hands dropped away from the back of his shirt and she squared her shoulders as she said fiercely, "*Acadia.*" Her pale cheeks went a little pink. "Acadia Gray." Scissoring her legs closed, she curled them under her and leaned against the wall, looking up at him as he staggered to his feet. "And to answer your rather obvious question, I'm fine. I always enjoy a hot sauna."

Good. She was going to need that sense of humor. "Stop looking at me like I'm going to find some fucking magic carpet and fly us out of here," Zak told her, annoyed as hell at seeing the hopeful look she was giving him. "In case you haven't got it yet, this is not going to end well."

"Zak—" Gideon cautioned.

"Oh, for— You have the emotional range of a freaking teaspoon, you know that?! Just because I'm blond doesn't mean I'm stupid," she said with asperity, talking over his brother. "And the way I'm looking at you is because I'm concerned about the severity of your concussion, and if you'll be able to defend yourself when we eventually stop. Because *I'm* going to do whatever it takes to get away from these people before they—" She rubbed her throat as she swallowed, gave him a flinty look, and repeated, "*Whatever* it takes."

His brother was watching him with narrowed eyes and a belligerent expression, which meant he wanted to say something that tasted bad. "Don't say it," Zak told him, then glanced back at Barbie. "Whatever it takes?"

"My father was a soldier." Her chin tilted pugnaciously. *"Whatever it takes."*

Zak looked at her slender body, her mass of messy blond hair, her slender hands. Her big, soft gray eyes. "Trained you, did he?"

She looked him in the eye. "Yes. He did."

If Zak hadn't been watching her so closely he would've missed her pupils dilating. It had taken him years to learn the tells when a beautiful woman lied to him. But he'd finally gotten it. Too late, but he'd learned.

Eventually. He hated liars almost as much as he hated having anyone—male or female—depending on him. *Especially* a female.

"Good," he told her. "I'll keep you in the loop."

She crossed her arms at her waist and gave him a level look. "Do that."

Zak's jaw hurt from clenching it so hard. Christ, it had been so long since he'd wanted to laugh that for a moment he didn't recognize the ache in his chest. Most women would have curled into a fetal ball and stayed that way for the duration. She was practically coming out swinging. Warrior Barbie.

"Don't tar her with the same brush as Jennifer," Gideon warned, while he examined the wall that was between the cab and the rear of the van. He had to duck his head to move about.

"No tar and no fucking brush." Zak's mild amusement evaporated. "It's a nonissue."

She looked from one to the other. "What are you talking about?"

He shot her a cold look. "None of your business."

"*Everything* is my business. We're in this together."

"Just because we're in the same geographical space doesn't mean we're together."

"Maybe they can shoot you first, and put us *all* out of our misery," Acadia told him tartly. Then she immediately shut her eyes and dragged in a shaky breath. "Sorry . . ." Her eyes were still stormy when she opened them. "I don't want anyone to get hurt. Even you. But we don't stand a chance if we're already fighting among ourselves."

Braced stiff-armed against the erratic movement of the vehicle, Zak's hand splayed over her head for balance. They were only a foot apart. Her pupils dilated as he stared into her eyes for a moment longer than was polite for strangers, because despite what they'd done in the early hours of that morning, they were still strangers. Intimate strangers, but strangers nonetheless. He knew more about this woman's body than he knew about her.

"We're not 'fighting,' we're not buddies, and we're not together. We just had sex." It *hadn't* been "just sex." But the fact that he'd felt alive for the first time in years was none of her damned business. He didn't want her clinging. Didn't want her feeling needy and dependent because they'd slept together. Didn't—damn it all to hell—want to feel anything seeing the tear tracks on her face.

Fortunately, he didn't feel a damned thing right then other than irritation.

"Fine," she told him sweetly. "Can we both agree you're an ass?"

"I've been called worse." Zak turned away as his brother moved from the front of the van to the back, but he heard the small expulsion of air as the blonde let out the breath she'd been holding.

"What we got?" he asked Gideon, who was trying the doors.

His brother turned to look at him. "A blind man who never saw what was right in front of his nose."

Ah, shit. "Not this old refrain again. You want to speak ill of the dead *now?*"

Gideon gave him a dead-eyed snake look. "Couldn't speak when she was alive. Can't speak when she's . . . not. When *will* be the right time, Zakary?"

"How about fucking never? This is hardly the time or the place."

"Got somewhere you gotta be?" Gideon leaned a shoulder against the doors. He needed a shave, and with his hair scraped back off his face he looked like a pirate. Or—hell—a hero. The role suited him.

Zak touched a finger to the bump on his temple. "None of your damned business. Told you then, repeating it now. Leave it the hell alone once and for all."

"Was not your fault."

He had heard this verse and chorus before. About a hundred times in the last two years. "I'll keep that in mind," he said to pacify his older brother, as he always did when Gideon tried to convince him that he couldn't have done anything to prevent Jennifer's death.

Gideon ran his hand over his mouth in a familiar gesture of frustration. "I wish I could believe that."

Zak's jaw hurt from clenching his teeth, which didn't help the hellish headache pounding through his skull. "And I wish you'd stop flogging a dead horse."

Gideon, damn him, never would back down, and now wasn't the exception. "Funny how quickly you forgot afterward that it hadn't been working for a whi—"

"Shut up, Gideon. I mean it. I won't lis—"

"While it's vastly entertaining to hear you two bickering back and forth like two premenstrual schoolgirls," the blonde said with annoyance, "maybe you could shelve the argument to concentrate on the here and now. We just turned off onto a different-surfaced road. What are you guys going to do when we stop?"

Gid, who still wore his metaphorical superhero merit badge, gave the seam between the doors a hard kick, then glanced over to smile reassuringly at her. "Strategize until they open the doors."

"Then I suggest," she told him, "we do just that, and *quickly*."

It was a given that they'd have to erupt out of the van and use the element of surprise to take their captors unawares.

He looked down at her. "Did you walk out of the roach motel under your own steam?" Zak hoped like hell they hadn't knocked her out as they had him, while she was naked, and . . .

She nodded. "There are five soldiers in front. Maybe more."

Doable. If there were only that many when they got there.

Gideon rubbed the back of his neck as he looked around the empty space. Like Zak, he'd already ascertained there was nothing they could use as a weapon. "This make and model carries six passengers in the cab."

Zak nodded. "Then we wait." He slid down the hot metal wall to sit, knees drawn up, a few feet away from her. Gideon sat nearby. "Uzis," Zak told his brother. "KA-BARs. Various handguns. More brawn than brain."

"Yeah. Saw when they grabbed me on my way to see what all the screaming was about."

Barbie screaming. Zak would have that earworm with him for a while. If he'd kept his dick in his pants, she wouldn't be here right now. So, whether he liked it or not, he was stuck being responsible for her for the duration. And he was going to be responsible for her death unless some fucking miracle presented itself PDQ.

A sheen of perspiration made her skin glow. She absentmindedly used the short sleeve of her T-shirt to wipe the sweat from her face. The smudged makeup beneath her eyes made them appear even larger and a lot more vulnerable. Her lips were the same color as her nipples, a soft defenseless rose color. Her mouth hadn't felt helpless surrounding his—

Zak wrenched his gaze from her mouth, from his visceral memory of where it had been the night before. Damn it to hell. Just looking at it was evocative and a turn-on.

He noted that she had a scratch on her upper arm. Another small one on her wrist. A fingerprint-shaped bruise on her wrist. They'd marked her. Zak's temple throbbed, and he had to consciously ungrit his teeth.

"Stop looking at *me* like that!" she told him crossly, the pulse at her throat, damp with perspiration, throbbing in time with his own rapid heartbeat. "I wonder where we are. They could've driven us in circles for the past three hours, although I—"

"No circles," Zak said shortly. "If it's been almost three hours, at an average of fifty miles per, we've gone about a hundred and fifty miles."

"You've been *awake* this whole time?"

"Not all," he told her honestly, because she was clearly annoyed at what he was sure was some perceived moral infraction.

"Actually," she said, looking quite pleased with herself, "you and your friend were unconscious for the start of this little road trip, and I believe we were going a little faster when we headed out of town. We only slowed down when we hit the country roads about, oh, maybe two hours ago? So I think we—"

"My brother, Gideon." Jesus. What a sanctimonious little thing his fellow captive was. "And approximately twenty minutes works. We're certainly still within Canaima National Park."

Situated in southeastern Venezuela, the park ran along the border with Guyana and Brazil. The vast area was mostly unpopulated and consisted of rolling savanna, dense jungle, palm groves, and sheer cliffs as well as steep, flat-topped mountains. They hadn't done any climbing; that just left them somewhere within a three-million-hectare area. Approximately the size of Maryland, most of it dense jungle.

Underbrush had been striking the sides of the vehicle for several minutes. This wasn't merely a dirt road; they were penetrating jungle. Fuckit.

She got to her feet, stumbled, grabbed his shirtfront, pulled away as if burned, then spread her boots for balance. It took a moment as she swayed, trying to find her center of gravity in the moving vehicle; then she gave him an earnest look.

Christ, she had pretty eyes. Big and soft with long dark lashes. Eyes that trusted him to keep her safe. He had news for her: he'd already failed that test. *I'm the last fucking man you should trust*, Zak thought savagely. Payback was a bitch. It was his own personal hell that had thrown them together, because Zakary Stark couldn't protect any woman. He knew it. His brother, despite his protests and excuses, knew it, and she was going to learn it soon enough. The hard way.

"I think if we put our minds to it we could figure it out exactly." She frowned in concentration. "Give me a minute."

He dragged in a breath, got a hint of hot jasmine, and blew it out. "I appreciate your confi—" The sound of the engine changed as the van slowed down. He met his brother's eyes and indicated he'd go left. Gideon nodded and moved into position on the right of the doors.

"Go crouch in back," Zak told her. Nowhere to take cover. No way he and Gid could mitigate what was about to go down. "Keep your head down."

Her chin jerked up and her soft eyes got flinty. "That's ridiculous. I can help y—"

"Barbie, unless you have a death wish, a secret skill, or a SAM hidden in a pocket, go back there and make yourself inconspicuous." Zak didn't wait to see if she did what he ordered. He moved into position beside the sealed doors as the van shuddered to a stop.

Zak counted off. One . . . two . . . three . . . four . . .

A metallic scrape . . .

The doors were flung open, letting in a flood of

white-hot sunlight and exposing three armed guerrillas who stood in a row, blocking their way. With wild cries, Zak and Gideon leaped from the back of the van like unexpected ninja jack-in-the-boxes.

Zak took down the two on the left, Gid the guy on the right. It wasn't neat, and it wasn't finessed, but the element of surprise was damned effective. Zak knocked out the taller guy, who was wearing a blue bandana. The second man, shorter and stockier, was the guy who'd held him down for the knockout blow back at the hotel. A bonus.

As they scrabbled in the long grass, the guy struggled against the twisted strap of his Uzi and kicked and shouted invectives as Zak beat the shit out of him. Zak staggered to his feet, the guy's camo shirtfront clutched in his fist. The guerrilla was still yelling, still struggling to untangle himself from the webbed strap slung diagonally across his body. Zak grabbed the son of a bitch around his bull neck and brought up his knee in a swift move that broke his nose with a satisfying crunch. It was a twofer. The man fell into the long grass unconscious.

He and Gideon shot each other a grin, then split up to go around the van to see who else they had to deal with.

"Shit." Zak stopped dead in his tracks, his way blocked by the butch commando guerrilla from the hotel.

"*Sí.*" She looked Zak up and down; her unpleasant smile didn't reach her black eyes. "On your knees."

Since he'd seen how accurate she was with the H & K when she'd blown a man's head off point-blank in the hotel room, he sank to his knees.

The vividly green vegetation, mostly grasses, closed around his thighs and came almost to his waist. The ground was spongy and damp, and smelled swampy.

On the other side of the van, his brother's loud curse was abruptly cut off, and the sound of a scuffle followed. Seconds later, Gideon was herded around the front of the van, Uzis pointed at his spine, ahead of two more guys dressed in camo.

"Loida—"

"*¡Héctor! Joder chamo, que tonto eres.*" Clearly not happy that her man had used her name, the woman cursed him fluidly in rapid Spanish as he brought Gideon to stand beside a kneeling Zak.

Apologetically the man mumbled, *"Lo siento, lo siento, lo siento."* Shoving Gideon to his knees, he sent a nervous glance in the direction of his leader and asked tentatively, "Piñero?"

"*¡Húevon!*" Loida Piñero slugged him in the jaw with her elbow for using her either of her names, knocking the hulking guy on his ass. He got up, giving her a hot look.

She pointed the business end of the Heckler & Koch at him. "*¡Ya basta!*"

He put up a hand, still nursing his jaw. *"Sí, jefa, sí."*

As they said in the local vernacular, she was the "goat who pissed the most." The boss. Clearly the one in charge, clearly the one whom the men had been waiting for at the hotel, and just as clearly the one they were all afraid of. She'd taken out the man attacking Acadia without a moment's hesitation, without a blink. She looked like one scary dude, with a bandolier of bullets slashing across her flat chest, a wicked-looking KA-BAR knife in the scarred scabbard strapped to her thigh, and an H & K G3K assault rifle held like an extension of her arm.

As Héctor used the side of the van to pull himself to his feet, the woman glanced coldly at the men watching from the sidelines. They too were armed to the teeth. She did not look happy as she shot fulminating glares at them. "I will deal with you later," she snapped in low Spanish, clearly pissed about something. "Morales. Goito. López. *Asegure los presos.*"

She was okay about broadcasting *their* names.

Zak counted heads, weapons, and attitudes. The odds of breaking free of this lot were slim to none; bound, their odds plummeted. Shit. Where was Barbie? Still in the van?

He and his brother had their wrists bound with plastic restraints in front of them. Amateurs. Pros would've made sure their hands were secured behind them. It was almost a reassuring thought. The sheer size of this operation was grounds for concern, amateur or not. At least a dozen men milled about the vehicle. Nobody was going anywhere. He and Gid shared a quick speaking glance before the woman indicated they should clasp their bound hands on top of their heads. They both did so.

She had sharp, ferretlike features and soulless black eyes, and a crew cut of greasy black hair. Up close and personal, she stank just as bad as her men.

She cradled the H & K as if it were as light as a handbag over her arm as she addressed him. "*¿Hablas español?*"

Zak gave her a blank look.

"You come to my country," the guerrilla leader said scathingly, taking a menacing step forward so her combat boots were inches from his knees. "You Americans! So arrogant. So—*American*. You come to my country, and you cannot be bothered to learn my language?"

"A distinct oversight, under the circumstances," Zak agreed. Beside him, Gid's breathing sounded labored. He was hurt. How badly? Zak wondered, knowing this fiesta was just getting started.

⊷ THREE ⊶

Zak surreptitiously took in their surroundings. Small clearing. A patch of low underbrush surrounded on three sides by massive trees, vines, and thick vegetation. No road to get to wherever the hell they were. Behind the tires of the van, nothing more than flattened undergrowth. In days, if not hours, the jungle would take even that back, and there'd be no sign that humans had ever been there.

Piñero snapped her fingers. One of the men came up beside her, handing her two American passports. One-handed, she flipped each open, fanning them so their photographs were exposed. She didn't even glance down, but maintained eye contact with Zak. "Zakary and Gideon Stark. ¿Sí?"

Something told him she'd known who they were already.

"We'll pay to ensure our safe return to a city or town close by. No questions asked," Gideon said, using the deep, calm, rational voice that usually pissed Zak off. Today, he could have kissed him. "Take us to a bank and we'll—"

"Your ransom is twenty million. *Each*."

"Fine," Zak interjected sharply, concerned by Gideon's labored breathing and the gray tinge to his skin. Had his older brother suffered internal injuries when they'd captured him? Had Gideon been stabbed by one of those KA-BAR blades and the son of a bitch was too stubborn to tell him in case the knowledge skewed Zak's focus? Because, yeah, that'd do it.

Maybe throwing money at this problem *would* make it go away. Maybe. "Whatever it takes," Zak added. Under normal circumstances—whatever the hell *those* were—Zak wouldn't sweeten the pot. Not yet. A good player knew when to reveal what was in his wallet without adding that he had shitloads of money shoved in his jockstrap too. But this was now about Gid's and the woman's survival, and that trumped anything else.

"Zak," Gid warned quietly, but Piñero's thin lips tightened into a grim little smile as she said swiftly, "Cash. American dollars."

Yeah. They'd known *exactly* whom they'd kidnapped. "Fine. Obviously we don't carry that kind of cash on us," Zak told her. "We came to BASE-jump Angel Falls, not make a business deal. As my brother said, take us to a bank in Caracas—"

"You will be held until the ransom is paid."

It would be a fucking long time. Zak and Gideon, much to the concern of their partner at ZAG Search, frequently visited countries that had cottage industries in kidnapping. That, Zak understood grimly, was only the start of the cost of a damned good adrenaline fix. Which was why he, Gideon, and Buck had that *no negotiating* clause in their insurance policies.

They had a nonnegotiable, ironclad stipulation in place that no ransom would be paid in the event they were ever kidnapped.

Didn't mean they couldn't negotiate their way out of this, given half a chance. They hadn't parlayed a small business into one of the leading search engine companies in the world by sitting around waiting for someone else to make the first move.

Zak was half-tempted to inform her she was as shit out of luck as they were. Gid beat him to it.

"Contact Anthony Buckner," he said, and rattled off Buck's private number at ZAG's corporate office in Seattle. Buck knew where they were. Fortunately, though as a company they refused to be blackmailed into paying ransom, that didn't mean they had no provision for such an eventuality.

The guerrilla didn't write the number down, merely cocked her hip and stared down at them with those cold black eyes that absorbed light, her scarred fingers loose on the assault rifle.

"If I do not have forty million dollars cash in three days," she told them, tone chillingly expressionless, "I will start sending body parts back to your families."

Handy. All the family the Stark brothers had was right here, kneeling on the jungle floor with a dozen weapons trained at their heads. Other than a handful of friends and a user base numbering in the anonymous millions, no one would give a flying fuck if they disappeared for good. Buck was too pragmatic to let the death of his partners affect the bottom line. He'd do everything in his not inconsiderable power to find them. But if and when he didn't, it would be business as usual at ZAG Search.

Zak gritted his teeth as a sharp scream from inside the van was accompanied by loud scuffling. The commotion was followed by a cut-off cry. Seconds later Acadia was brought to the party and shoved down unceremoniously beside him.

Her face was dead white and dirt-streaked. As she sank to her knees, the grasses almost obscured her smaller frame.

"Watch out for snakes," she warned under her breath, her eyes darting not to the two-legged variety, but as if searching the thick vegetation surrounding them. "There are over seventy species here, and most are poi—"

"Quiet." Piñero was not entertained by her captive's chatty observation. "I talk." She gave the blonde an unfriendly look. "You listen. ¿Entender?"

Barbie nodded. Her hair fell in a tangled mess around her shoulders, but matted and sweat-dampened as it was, it still gave off the faint fragrance of jasmine. That pleasant aroma was obliterated when Loida Piñero stepped forward.

"I have some money," the blonde interrupted, voice shaking, breathing panic-mode rapid as she looked up at the other woman.

Guerrilla Bitch's black eyes flicked to her. "Twenty million for you, too, *perra*."

"T-twenty million what? *Dollars?* I don't have *nearly* that much."

"This is unfortunate, *¿sí?*" Piñero's attention slid back to Zak and Gideon as she dismissed the other woman as easily as one would a pesky fly. "And to be— how you say?" Piñero cocked her head, and her dead eyes bored into Zak's. "Humane? *¿Sí?* I will start with the woman." She fingered the wicked machete on her hip. "She has pretty hands, yes? Such elegant fingers. We will play . . . *¿como se dice?* This little piggy?"

Jesus.

"My daddy is head of the CIA," Acadia said in a cool, surprisingly calm voice. "He'll pay whatever you ask, but if you hurt us, he'll kill every friend and relative you have, and then he'll hunt you down until you don't have anywhere to hide."

The ice in her tone made Zak's narrow-eyed gaze slide sideways.

"I love him, but he is not—" She shuddered. "My father is a cruel man. He killed my mother in cold blood because she just *looked* at the president of the United States at a *dinner party*."

She'd just managed to convey a powerful father, great wealth, and a presidential connection all in one breath. Bullshit. But impressive. Her bluff might protect her. For a while.

"*Asegúrese bien de que están atados.*" Unimpressed, Piñero told her men to secure them well. "*Vamos al campo.*" She turned on her heel and stalked off, leaving her men to haul the captives roughly to their feet and encourage them—with an unnecessary and vicious prod from the barrel of one of the Uzis—to follow her to the tree line.

Zak staggered forward in Piñero's wake. *"Wie stark bist du verletzt?"* he whispered to Gid as they walked side by side through the dense grass and lush foliage, the sun beating a hot brand on the crown of his unprotected head.

It was unlikely that the two men behind or the three in front understood German, but he kept his voice just loud enough for his brother to hear him.

"Ribs geknackt." Ribs cracked. Gid slanted him a look that tried to catalog every ache Zak wasn't acknowledging himself. *"Du?"*

"Ich bin gut." Barring a few bruises, anyway. It wasn't anything a damn long soak in a hot tub wouldn't soothe. More important, he needed to know how badly that cracked rib was going to hamper them. *"Kannst du laufen?"*

If Gid wasn't able to run, they were going to have to start thinking about a plan B, C, *and* D. Because Zak suspected there weren't going to be that many chances to make a break for it before these goons realized there was no ransom money coming.

"Ja," his brother assured him. *"Sprechen das wort."* Say the word.

He got the point. As the less injured of the two—and not counting Barbie—he'd have to be the one to give the word to roll out. Zak hoped like hell it wouldn't be the *last* fucking word he ever said.

He watched the guards closely, but they didn't seem too worried that the prisoners would bolt. Why should they? There was nothing for thousands of miles but jungle, flat-topped mountains, and rivers. Stepping off the rudimentary path meant death.

Every now and then the guards in back fell behind to have a smoke, and Gideon, who'd taken the lead, let more and more space open up between himself and the guys ahead. Zak kept one close eye on them, and one on the suddenly all-too-silent blonde between them.

Her clever little fingers dipped into another pocket, and she reached forward awkwardly to hand Gideon several aspirin. Zak did his best to block the motion from the guards behind them with his body, and frowned as Gideon chewed the bitter pills dry. That was enough to tell Zak that his brother's ribs were hurting more than he was letting on.

Serious problem. The more deeply they penetrated the jungle, the more dire their situation became. Making a break for it now, no matter how inattentive their captors were, wouldn't exactly be optimal, Zak knew. But given the circumstances, he'd act on whatever opportunity arose.

He was in the best shape he'd been in his life. So was Gideon, but not with that injury. And Barbie, as valiant as she was, was already flagging. Over the last hour her steps had become slower and slower.

And the guards, now realizing how much space had opened between them, closed in again. There went any chance for making a break for it. Catching his brother's eye, he used their own form of sign language and waited for Gid's nod of acknowledgment. *Later.* The unique brand of sign they'd learned and developed over the years had saved their asses almost as often as it had allowed them to commit mischief growing up. Barely a year separated them in age. They were as close as twins. People frequently said they looked like twins. But Zak couldn't see himself in his brother other than a facial similarity. Gid was charming and compassionate, and had a hero complex. Zak was and had none of the above. They were opposite sides of a coin. But there wasn't a person alive whom Zak loved and respected more than he did Gideon.

He'd die for his brother. He just hoped like hell it wouldn't come to that.

He and Gideon exchanged subtle hand signals until they agreed on a plan; it was half-assed, but it was the only one they had. Zak fell back, angling behind Acadia once more.

They couldn't account for every contingency, and most of it would depend on their surroundings at the time, but it would work. It had to work. Failure was not an option he wanted to entertain, not again. Not when it meant the blonde's terrified gray eyes pleading with him to stop Guerrilla Bitch and her machete from chopping off her fingers one by one.

He'd already proven to one woman he was no hero, so protecting both this one *and* his brother from what was about to happen was a tall fucking order.

THE PLANT LIFE LOOKED nothing like her poor, half-dead *Dieffenbachia* at home, Acadia thought, glancing around nervously as she pushed her way through the under-growth. She tried not to let her imagination run away with her. Since she wasn't usually an alarmist, or that imaginative, she was surprised by the detour her mind took, thinking that if the leaves were this big, then the inhabitants of the jungle were also supersized. She braced herself to be jumped on by something that bit. Maybe a giant snake, or a spider the size of a dinner plate. She shuddered.

Somewhere in the thick wall of foliage to her left, something snapped. She flinched as a flurry of dry, rasp-ing sounds skittered and moved behind a woven tangle of vines.

Don't picture it, she told herself silently, and bit back a groan as a slinky, fanged creature filled her imagina-tion. Catlike. Glittering yellow eyes. Hungry, salivating, stalking—*Stop it, Acadia!*

Her wrists were bound with plastic handcuffs. Not tightly, but it was uncomfortable to walk with her hands hobbled in front of her, and her shoulders had stiffened into aggravated knots an hour ago. The rough ride in the van had left bruises in interesting places, and the long, difficult walk through thick trees was making exhaustion and pain mingle into a steady beat pounding from her forehead to her leaden feet.

She studied her surroundings as they marched through the trees in the hope that, given an opportunity, she could backtrack. But she knew that would be next to impossible. One tree, one tangle of vines, one freaking Jurassic-size leaf, looked pretty much like the last. The lush jungle foliage was a thousand variations on vivid green, the giant leaves unrecognizable as the common houseplants they were related to. It was surreal tromping through a tropical forest. Even though Acadia had planned this trip to the last detail, even though she'd had mental dress rehearsals every day for a month, she'd never actually pictured herself here for real.

"That was a good save," Zak said abruptly from behind her. He hadn't spoken to her in probably half an hour or more. She jumped, heart hammering, as his voice pierced the thick silence. "Keep her on her toes for a while. So which is it? Is your father CIA or military?"

"He was a staff sergeant, in the army." Acadia told him, chest aching. "He died a few months ago." He'd died not knowing who she was as she'd held his hand in that soulless, sterile hospital room. Early-onset Alzheimer's. Her father hadn't known who she was for the last six years of his life. She'd always been a daddy's girl. They'd moved every two years from base to base, like clockwork. She'd lost her mother in her early teens, so it had always been she and her father. She'd adapted to the constant upheaval, and the task of making new friends in new cities. But the slow, terrible way he'd started getting sicker and sicker had hit her hard. They'd stayed in Junction City after his diagnosis. She'd remained at his side, even when it meant forgoing her dreams of a degree in architecture, and Acadia had never regretted putting her life on hold to care for him. She'd treasured every moment. No matter how seeing him like that had torn at her heart.

Knowing that he didn't realize who took care of him day in and day out had just about killed her.

Something must have shown on her face, because Zak moved in closer to drop his voice. "You all right?" His gaze was on her mouth, and he was practically on top of her. His breath moved her hair against her sweaty cheek.

"If by *all right*, you mean happy to still be alive, then yes. I'm most excellent." Her exposed skin itched, from sweat and the bugs that were feasting on her as though she were a long-awaited banquet. She didn't scratch. There was no point. She did her best to ignore everything. Ignoring the man beside her wasn't quite as easy.

"Is your name really Acadia? You told me 'Candy' last night."

Lovely. He'd done things to her she didn't even want to think about, and he didn't even know her name. "Acadia," she told him stiffly. His brother paced several yards ahead. Zak stuck close beside her. Far too close for comfort, and frankly no easy feat, considering the space restraints on the hacked-out path through the dense foliage.

He shot her a glance. He had very nice eyes when he wasn't looking at her as though he wished she'd go somewhere else. A wish they both shared. His eyes were dark-lashed, and a brooding hazel—sometimes green, sometimes a tawny brown that ate the light. And unfriendly.

Sweat stained the front of his once-crisply-ironed shirt, and he'd rolled the sleeves up over his muscled forearms for relief from the unrelenting humidity.

Because of the way the sunlight fell through the trees, Acadia noticed a previously unseen hair-thin scar on the corner of his upper lip, and another high on his right cheek. The cut above his right eye was definitely going to give him another scar. If he lived long enough for the wound to heal.

"So, which is it? Candy or . . . ?"

"You obviously didn't hear me." Some of her friends occasionally called her *Cady*. But that wasn't often. She wasn't a nickname type of person. The pet name had sounded appealing in the bar the night before. He was not, she didn't need reminding, her *friend* by any stretch of the imagination.

"Last night you didn't even know your *own* name when we were practically having sex all the way up the stairs, down the corridor and—" She sucked in a hot, humid breath. He'd been there. She didn't need to do a verbal reenactment. Besides, his brother was not even three feet away, listening in. She blushed again despite the heat.

"My name," she reminded him, trying for sophisticated nonchalance, "is Acadia Gray."

She could smell him even through the lush, wet scent of the jungle. Hot, sweaty male. Not sweaty like the soldiers. His scent was clean and earthy and brought back every vivid memory of every place on his body she'd kissed and tasted the night before . . . Her heartbeat sped up, and all her girl parts seemed to have antennae tuned in to him.

She waved her bound hands in front of her face and

tried to move ahead of him. It gave her a little comfort being sandwiched between two big, strong guys.

Pinhead-tiny black bugs swarmed in lazy circles inches in front of her nose. Pulling out her insect repellent now would only get her gear confiscated, or worse, subject her to a more thorough search. A large red-and-green-striped leaf sprang out into her path, and she used her knee to push it aside, then scratched an itch on her cheek as something bit her.

"You don't look like the type who'd BASE-jump the falls," Zak said, sounding annoyed, as if her presence there was an affront to him personally. "What the hell are you doing in Venezuela?"

Acadia resented the implication that she wasn't the bold, daring type. "Looks can be deceiving," she told him mockingly. Hoping like hell she didn't—"What else would I be doing here?"—lie. *Nerves, damn it.*

"You were going to jump the falls?" He sounded insultingly disbelieving, but she didn't glance back to see his expression.

"I was waiting for my guide. He was picking me up later this morning. Now, I suppose." God. She wished she'd stop doing that. It was a ridiculous defense mechanism she'd thought she'd outgrown, from when she was an insecure kid. Apparently not. Zakary Stark brought out the worst in her. Which was unfortunate as hell, since she was stuck with him for the duration.

"Is that right? Venezuela's a damned dangerous place for a woman to visit alone."

"That's very unenlightened of you. Isn't Venezuela a

dangerous place for a man to come to alone?" Judging by the scars on his body, he'd been to some very dangerous places already.

"Yeah. It is. And as I recall, I didn't *come* alone." Heat rushed to her cheeks at his oh-so-obvious double entendre. But he saved her the embarrassment of floundering for a response as he added, "As it so happens, I traveled here with my brother."

She cleared her throat. "Well, I was expecting five friends to fly in later this morning. I wasn't planning on—" *Don't say it!* "—being alone for long. They're going to freak out when they arrive and I'm not there."

An understatement. Shelli, Sharon, Julia, Amber, and Natasha were going to be *frantic*. They'd practically strong-armed her onto the plane because Acadia hadn't wanted to be *this* daring. Sure, she'd reluctantly agreed to step out of her comfort zone, but she'd imagined they'd all go to New York, or maybe be wild and crazy and take a trip to Aruba and be served umbrella drinks at the pool by tanned cabana boys.

Sharon, the boldest of her friends, had dared the group to go to Venezuela. The next thing Acadia knew, she was paying a fortune for the tickets and accepting the itinerary from well-organized Julia. She'd known before her brand-new Cypress Ion WPi waterproof hiking boots touched the ground in Caracas yesterday morning that she was having a mid-something crisis and way in over her head. But by then it was too late to chicken out and turn back.

Zak shrugged, powerful shoulders moving in her peripheral vision. "Your friends will put two and two together and go to the authorities."

Nice of him to sound half-assed confident, but Acadia was pretty sure that wouldn't achieve anything. The police in Venezuela were pretty much as corrupt as the plethora of kidnappers in the country. They'd go to the American embassy and hope someone there could help. Then they'd run out of money and options and return home to see what they could do from there.

She fell silent, concentrating on putting one foot in front of the other in the knee-high grass. As it got hotter, moisture on the foliage evaporated into a steamy hothouse fog that caught in her lungs and made sweat pour down her face. She felt around in one of the pockets on the outside of her pants, checked on the position of the guards—Zak met her eyes as she glanced behind her, and shifted subtly to block their view of her—and surreptitiously pulled out a flat packet of moist towelettes.

"Thanks," she murmured. Plucking one wipe out of the package, she carefully restuck the seal and shoved it back into the hidden pocket, her mind returning once more to her friends as she wiped her face and throat. They would blame themselves, she knew. They'd go to the police first. Then they'd freak. Natasha's father had served with Acadia's dad at Fort Riley. When Natasha realized there was no trace of her friend, she'd call in the cavalry. Literally.

"Perhaps they'll think you went off with some local guy," Zak offered after too long a silence.

Acadia choked back a laugh. "Not in a trillion years." It wouldn't even cross their minds that she might be with some handsome Latin American man having a wild adventure. Going off with strange men wasn't who Acadia Alyssa Gray *was*. She was the leave-the-kids-with-Acadia-on-Friday-night kind of friend. She was predictable, reliable, and, she hated to admit, boring.

"Not that far from the truth," he corrected, which annoyed the hell out of her.

"You don't have to sound so smug about it," she retorted waspishly. "It was hardly a red-letter day on my calendar."

"Really? You pick up men in bars all the time, do you?"

"Isn't that like asking someone if they've stopped beating their wife?"

He chuckled.

Gideon gave a muffled snort of laughter too. His white T-shirt was sweat-stained and blotched green from the leaves they were pushing through.

"Great, so happy I can amuse you guys." She applied the now warm, moist cloth to her hot cheeks. The mild antiseptic stung the abrasions on her skin, but it smelled fresh. She used it on her hands and as far up her arms as she could maneuver her bound wrists. She wished she could wash the blood off her skin, then pulled her thoughts back from the abyss. Blood splatter on her back was the least of her problems right now.

She tucked the used wipe into another pocket. No littering for Acadia Gray. Even while being kidnapped. *Follow the rules. Do the right thing.* Acadia felt a giggle bubble up in her chest, and ruthlessly tamped down the urge. This was no laughing matter, and she wasn't entirely sure that she'd be able to stop laughing if she started.

"What else do you have in those hidden pockets?" Zak asked.

The whole point of hidden pockets was that they were freaking *hidden*. None of the soldiers had bothered to pat her down, thanks to their scary boss. If he talked about what she was carrying, someone was sure to want to see exactly what it was. "How do you know I have pockets?"

"Unless you're a magician planning on pulling a rabbit out of your ass, I'm presuming the aspirin from earlier and that wipe were secreted in that outfit you're wearing. What else is in there? Cough everything up, Miss Gray. Our lives might depend on whatever you're carrying."

"You want me to dump everything on the ground right now?" Acadia was rapidly discovering a hidden talent for sarcasm just as pointed as his.

"No. But once it makes sense, I want to inventory everything you brought." He paused. "How heavy are your clothes?"

"An extra eighteen pounds, that's all." Although, after walking for what seemed like days, the weight seemed to be increasing with every step. "I have just about everything we might need," she admitted, sotto voce. "Except, unfortunately, a weapon."

He came up right beside her, his arm brushing hers. "You'd be surprised what can be made into one."

"I know how to make a shiv." How hard could it be?

His smile widened. It didn't reach his eyes, but he showed his white teeth and a dent of a dimple in his lean right cheek. "Ah. Learned no doubt while you were incarcerated for your life of crime."

"I'm a quick study." *Make of that what you like, smart-ass.*

"I'm starting to think you just might have hidden depths," he said dryly.

They walked for about five minutes while she mulled that over, then she blurted, "I don't. Have any hidden depths, that is." Honest to God, she could keep lying, but in this scenario it wasn't in her best interests to mislead him. She had no idea what—if anything—he was planning, but making him think her capable of things she was incapable of doing would be not only stupid but hellishly dangerous as well. "Look, I'm not exactly what you think I am—"

"A pretty woman way the hell out of her depth?"

"Yes. That." He thought she was pretty? "Wait, no, I *am* exactly that. Out of my depth, I mean," she admitted. "I wasn't exactly honest last night. I'm not an exotic dancer. I work at Jim's Sporting Goods store in Junction City, Kans—"

"*Kansas?*" His laugh sounded rusty, and he stopped to stare at her. His eyes looked very green and were deceptively filled with laughter. Clearly a trick of the light.

Acadia scowled. "Yes, Kansas. What's so funny?"

He started walking again before the guards could prod him. "Keep moving. Nothing, Dorothy."

Infuriating man. "You weren't held as a baby, were you?"

"I have pictures."

Acadia made a rude noise. "Obviously Photoshopped."

Gideon chuckled as he shoved enormous, leathery leaves out of his way, then held them so she could pass. "Zak was born sparring."

He'd clearly had plenty of practice. Acadia changed the subject. "Kidnapping is a pervasive problem in Venezuela, were you aware of that when you came?" She'd read about it, but of course had thought it wouldn't apply to her. For God's sake, she had no idea how she could have ignored the compelling statistics and the probability of being kidnapped herself. In for a penny, in for a pound. "I don't want to sound like I'm lecturing you or anything," she added, "but it's good to know some facts. Caracas has one of the highest per capita homicide rates in the world."

"Fortunately," Zak murmured, his voice Sahara dry, "we're not *in* Caracas at the moment."

"And it's even *higher* in outlying areas where there's no pretense of law and order."

"Aren't you a font of information." He didn't sound like a fan.

"I am, actually," she replied, unperturbed. "They even have a National Counter Kidnapping Commission. In fact—" Now she remembered the data, anyway— "In fact, kidnappings have increased from forty to over *sixty* percent in the last year alone. And that's just the ones reported to the police. Most aren't." Because, reported or not, the kidnappers were rarely caught, and even then, rarely charged.

Zak said nothing as he dropped a step behind her, so she continued hopefully, "It's unlikely that they'd walk us all this way just to kill us later, right?" Pointless to mention that the guerrillas could do worse than kill them. He'd know that.

"I imagine they'll hold us until the ransom is paid."

"Hold" didn't mean *gently*. The way the one called Eloy had been looking at her when he shoved her out of the van didn't bode well. "About that . . ." Now would probably be a good time to tell him just why he and his brother were being dragged willy-nilly through the jungle with her.

"Don't worry about it," he said, using his bound hands to brush a small green lizard off his shoulder. "Gideon and I will figure something out."

"There are *three* of us involved here," she pointed out. "But in the interest of full disclosure, I have to tell you why we're here. It's because—"

"Save it."

Acadia understood the situation wasn't optimal, but did he have to be so rude? She rubbed her cheek on her shoulder, retorting, "For what? Candles and dinner?"

"Until we're alone or can't be overheard. Get Gideon's attention for me."

They were walking single file. With her hands bound at the wrist, Acadia used her fingertips to poke Gideon

Stark in the back, but he turned around so fast, and with such fury in his eyes, she fell back a step and bumped into Zak's chest.

"Easy," Zak said, steadying her with his forearm against her shoulder.

"Sorry," she told Gideon. He wasn't looking at her, but rather at his brother, who was right over her shoulder. Acadia could feel the tension coming off the two men in waves. Like her they were stressed; she just hoped they didn't do anything stupid in this volatile situation.

"Look. Don't engage these people, okay? I'll just tell them how to access the money, and I'm sure"—*Not in a zillion years*—"that they'll let us go."

"How could you . . . *What* money?" Gideon Stark scowled, then continued walking. A flying insect the size of Acadia's fist landed on his back. The iridescent blackish green bug was a millimeter from the exposed skin of his neck. She shuddered.

"There's a Godzilla-size insect on your—Yes. There—okay. It's gone. That's what I've been trying to tell you guys for the past *hour*." She hadn't, but she should have. "*I'm* the reason they grabbed you. I'm really, really sorry."

"*You're* the reason?" Zak asked, sounding incredulous. "Who are you? Head of State? Rock star . . . Not an actress."

"I work— Why *not* an actress?"

"Because you can't act worth a damn."

"Funny," Acadia said lightly, "that's not what Spielberg said."

His lips twitched. "Steven Spielberg?"

"Who else?" Well, Michael Spielberg, her eighth-grade math teacher, who could never tell when she was fibbing, even when he knew she was. It hadn't been a compliment as much as a statement about him.

Acadia lowered her voice and slowed her steps so he could hear her. She hoped her voice wouldn't carry. Though the kidnappers must have a pretty good idea how much she was worth; otherwise why bother kidnapping her? "I won five hundred thousand in the Kansas lottery two months ago."

"Ah," Zak responded. A lot less interested, or relieved, than she'd expected.

"I still have most of it," Acadia assured him quickly, just in case he was worried she couldn't pay at least a portion of what the kidnappers were asking. "I paid for this trip of course, for myself and five of my friends, and—"

"This isn't about you."

She tromped through a thicket of leaves and vines to give that a moment to sink in. A toucan high on an overhead branch tilted its yellow head to watch them pass. She stepped over a pile of branches and leaves that the men up ahead had sliced to clear the path. "Wow," she finally said, surprised. "That's pretty rude considering the circumstances. I know kidnapping is the national pastime here, but I suspect they knew who I was when they burst into *my* room instead of yours. Do *you* guys have half a million dollars?" she added sarcastically.

Gideon chuckled and continued walking.

"Gid and I own ZAG," Zak informed her.

It took her a moment. *ZAG?* The multigazillion-dollar online search engine? "Oh." Here she was, feeling guilty as hell, and all the time *she* was the one who'd been inadvertently scooped up in *their* kidnapping. "Then I guess *you* owe *me* an apology."

"At this point, your lotto score is pretty worthless. As you say, kidnapping is big business in South America. They've already set a ransom demand at forty mil for me and my brother, and they don't care that you're just collateral damage. Loida Piñero set the same price on your head."

"Forty *million?*" That was so far above what she *now* thought of as her meager winnings that it didn't even seem real.

"Wait a minute . . . Loida Piñero? I presume that's the name of Cruella de Vil, scary leader of the pack? How do you know her name?" Acadia demanded, sidetracked.

"She told us."

"That's not good. She doesn't care that the three of us have seen her face and those of her men, and she told you her name? That doesn't bode well for our chances of survival."

"Don't worry about it. They'll contact our people to make their demand."

"*Don't worry about it?* I'm blond, not Pollyanna. I'm plenty worried. With just cause." Blondes might have more fun, but she should've told her hairdresser to give her screaming red kick-butt hair instead of foils. Right now she needed the courage of a redhead and the sophistication of a brunette. She was *feeling* her mousy hair right now.

"We'll be out of here as soon as the ransom's paid."

"Liar," she said without heat. She tamped down the fear bubbling up inside her. Freaking out and panicking weren't productive. This situation needed a clear head, and some ingenuity. And while she hoped Zak and Gideon Stark could come up with a viable plan to get them safely out of the jungle, Acadia was too used to taking care of business to trust her life to two men she didn't know. "As soon as they get the money, we'll be redundant, won't we?"

And then it clicked. From somewhere in the vast filing cabinet of her brain, she remembered the headlines. The outcry, even brief as it was in the never-ending run of bad news that filled the media every day.

In stark, bold letters, the headline flashed across her memory: ZAG OWNER LOSES WIFE IN TRAGIC ACCIDENT.

The brothers' argument in the van now made a bit more sense. It had barely registered as a blip on her radar at the time. So, Zak Stark had lost his wife. Tragic. But why did his brother have strong issues about it? Jennifer Stark had been an investigative reporter for CNN; if Acadia remembered the news correctly, she'd been killed in some war-torn country a couple of years ago. Acadia tried to remember what she'd read, desperately rifling through what few facts she'd gleaned at the time, but she didn't recall more than a few headlines.

"Redundant or not," Zak said evenly, "Gideon and I will get you out of here."

She hoped he could. But just in case that didn't happen, Acadia was trying to come up with an escape plan of her own. Planning, practicality, and adaptation were her strengths. They were attributes she'd needed when she'd continually changed schools. New teachers, new kids to make friends with, new everything. She'd had to draw on those same strengths when she'd had to deal with her father's diminishing capacity.

If she could just sit down somewhere cool and quiet for a while, she knew she would come up with some sort of plan. Too bad cool, quiet, and seated were out of the question for the moment. So be it. She had several ideas. None of them feasible. Yet.

"How does sitting behind a computer monitor at your fancy Internet company qualify you to liberate us from armed kidnappers?" She kept the sarcasm out of her voice with effort.

"You'd better hope we have something up our sleeves," Zak answered, not exactly forthcoming.

Gideon paused until she was practically right on top of him. "We've accumulated some skills in the years we've been doing extreme sports," he told her quietly. "Trust us, this isn't that much different than the Mount Kilimanjaro climb we did a few years back, right, Zak?"

"Right. Hostile natives, and an even more hostile environment."

They both sounded as confident as she didn't feel. Climbing a mountain, while certainly dangerous, didn't quite compare to trekking into dense jungle surrounded by Uzi-carrying guerrillas. "Armed kidnappers?"

Gideon glanced over his shoulder with a grim smile. "Armed *terrorists*. They all have shitty attitudes and consider violence a conversation starter. Don't worry, honey. We're working on i—"

"*Manténgase en movimiento!*" one of the men yelled from behind them.

Acadia gave Gideon a little shove with her bound hands. "He wants us to keep moving."

"We both speak Spanish fluently," Zak informed her, his voice low. He was right on her heels, and the closeness of his voice made her start so that she almost walked right into a thick clump of bright red flowering vines hanging like a garland right in front of her. The twenty-foot vines, covered in flowers, were alive and moving with buzzing insects.

She walked around the clump, swatting the bugs away from her face. "Then why didn't you—"

"Because pretending *not* to understand the language gives us an edge."

"How did you know what I was goi—"

"Going to say? Barbie, you're an open book."

A drop of sweat trickled down her temple, making her skin itch. Acadia bit her tongue. There was no point in engaging him in an exchange. There wouldn't be a winner, and arguing would just irritate them both.

Acadia put one foot in front of the other and kept her gaze on the middle of Gideon Stark's sweat-stained back. Three small capuchin monkeys swung from branch to branch at eye level, sweet little white faces turned to watch the humans' progress, black eyes curious.

"Look," she said calmly after about fifteen minutes of human silence, "I don't know you. I'm sure you mean well, but don't make promises you can't possibly keep. We all know that when they have what they want, they'll kill—"

"Zakary."

Acadia glanced up at Gideon's warning tone, expecting to come eye to eye with some large man-eating animal or, worse, the lead kidnapper, gun in hand, murder in her eyes. Instead she saw a clearing in the jungle, foliage hacked back and wide-open space filled with a dozen or more armed men. Waiting for them.

This was it, then. The end of the road.

❧ FOUR ❧

The compound, comprised of a handful of small cement and stone buildings, squatted in a large clearing hacked out of the living walls of the jungle. Piñero and another half dozen camo-dressed, well-armed men were their welcoming committee as they emerged from the trees. A baker's dozen.

Zak knew the odds—shitty before—were now considerably worse. Piñero berated the men for taking so long, and got them to hustle the prisoners into their jail cells with customary guerrilla flair.

There was no use fighting the shove of the gun butts as the three of them were herded between piles of rudimentary building materials. They passed cinder blocks, bags of cement, tools, a large water tank, a cookhouse, and a building large enough, Zak imagined, to house at least half the men. All the comforts of home.

Men. Guns. Tools to entrench, and enough supplies to sustain the guerrillas for—how long? he wondered. It was obvious their kidnappers were part of a well-organized, well-funded group. Funded by whom? Certainly not Loida Piñero. Her men feared her, sure. But it couldn't be as simple as that, not with this setup. Zak bet it was more likely some fat cat with seemingly clean hands, sitting in a big office in Caracas. He'd find out who after he got the three of them out.

Because even though the situation was dire, Zak knew, between them, he and Gideon *would* make it out alive. How depended entirely on the plan they'd concocted out of thin air.

Two smaller mud brick buildings faced each other, several hundred yards apart and covered almost completely by a thick tangle of big-leafed vines. They were clearly older than the rest. Zak was already examining them for weaknesses that could be exploited as the guards opened the doors.

He and Acadia were shoved into a six-foot cube of a cell. The ceiling was so low, he couldn't quite stand upright. Leafy vines clung to the interior walls, making the space appear even smaller. The door was slammed shut and the key turned in the lock. Through the rusty bars filling the door frame, he watched Gideon being led to the other small building. Divide and conquer.

He counted off the men. The twins, Blue Bandana and Gold Tooth . . . Thick Neck . . . Shorty . . . Pug Face. A new guy staggered by, muscles bulging, arms straining under the weight of the cement blocks piled haphazardly in the wheelbarrow he was shoving through the trampled-flat undergrowth.

Wearing a Yankees baseball cap, Loida Piñero walked into view, smoking what looked like a Cuban cigar as she gestured to the wheelbarrow and cement blocks nearby.

Who knew what the hell the older mud brick buildings had originally been used for—a drug hideout? Gun running? A co-op for kidnappers? Whatever it had been, their hostess was beefing up security. Judging by the bars already fitted into the window openings, another, slightly bigger jail was being constructed a few hundred feet south of them. She finished giving instructions and turned as two men handed her the jail keys.

She glanced between the two buildings. Zak knew she was deciding which of the Stark brothers to hassle first. Whichever she chose, it was going to be like pulling teeth.

Which wasn't entirely out of the question, either.

She turned and strode through the weeds toward him. Lucky him. As he stood at the barred door, he watched one of her men trot after her like a well-trained puppy. Several yards back, Héctor gave Zak a shit-eating grin before turning away to go off with another man. Piñero pushed the brim of her cap back off her face, then snapped her fingers. The guerrilla beside her handed her a small, expensive digital camera. She snapped a quick succession of pictures of Zak through the bars. "I will contact your people."

And the second Buck got that picture, he'd mobilize whatever resources necessary to look for them, but he sure as shit wouldn't be sending her forty mil. But neither would matter. Because Zak suspected that Piñero would kill all three of them. Soon.

"The woman requires food and water," Zak told Guerrilla Bitch. The sun burned directly overhead, an eye-watering spotlight making it that much harder to peg their exact location. For all he knew, they could be in Brazil. Or, as he suspected, damn close to the border.

Loida Piñero gave him a tight, malicious smile that didn't reach her black eyes. "This is not American soil, Mr. Stark. Here are *my* rules, not Geneva's. The only reason you are still breathing is because your people might require additional proof of life. Twenty-four hours. You do not need food." She snapped her fingers again and instructed the man beside her to bring each prisoner a cup of water.

"What a vile woman," Acadia muttered as Piñero strode off. Several of her men jogged to catch up with her when she snapped her fingers for them to follow.

"Be grateful she wants us alive."

"Trust me, I . . . am." Her gaze followed a capybara; the ratlike creature with reddish-brown fur was the size of a large house cat, and it scurried from its hiding place beneath a cement ledge running the length of the back wall. The squeaking animal slipped between them, wiggled through the bars, and disappeared into the underbrush outside.

Acadia shuddered, but to her credit, she didn't say anything. Her butter-honey hair was tangled, her skin was dewy with perspiration, and her cheeks were flushed attractively from the heat. Without makeup she looked as fresh and wholesome as the girl next door.

Zak tracked the sweat trickling slowly down her throat and was gripped with the sudden, insane urge to lunge over there, sprawl her on her back, and sink into her wet heat until he couldn't think anymore. His body clenched in memory, and for a moment he tasted the earthy sweetness of her secret flesh on his tongue.

He'd lost his goddamn mind.

"Don't get too close to the vines," he told her. "They're full of spiders." He turned away to observe the men outside. He was actually fucking impressed that she hadn't broken down. Yet. It would come, of that he had no doubt. Anyone like her—normal, touristy people—would break down in a situation like this. He, on the other hand, thrived on the element of high risk, which was why he was so into extreme sports. Take the situation he was in now; it was a test to see what the participant was made of and how far he could take himself. But this wasn't surfing a tsunami, or rock climbing without ropes. This wasn't a situation for which he had meticulously planned and researched every possible outcome. Those risks were different.

And he wasn't here alone.

He'd once told a reporter that he did what he did because varied, novel, complex, and intense sensations and experiences were his drug of choice. They'd called him an adrenaline junkie. And that was before Jennifer's death. After he'd buried his wife, Gideon accused him of having a death wish, which was bullshit.

Adrenaline junkie or not, Zak had to admit this situation had taken a turn he didn't like. But for now he was grateful he didn't have to deal with a hysterical woman as well as everything else.

"God, aren't you thirsty?" Acadia asked, standing in

the middle of the cell. Which meant if he reached out he could touch her damp skin. "They won't bring us water, will they?"

"Don't think about it. Piñero just left camp." Zak watched the foliage close in behind her and two of her men. They would also, God damn it, be taking the van. It was going to be a long walk back to civilization.

He turned to give the cell a cursory glance. Barely big enough for one, let alone two. Mud brick walls absorbed the sun, making it slightly cooler inside than out. But not by much. There were no windows in the blackened, mold-stained walls. The only fresh air came through the door, which was nothing more than a worm-eaten wooden frame and thick, rusted metal rebar.

Not much of a deterrent. One good kick, Zak estimated, and he'd have the frame off its hinges, no sweat. Then he'd have to go through the scrimmage of ten guards who looked like they had nothing better to do than beat down a couple of gringos just because they could. Then they'd go for the pretty blonde. And this time there'd be no Loida Piñero to stop them.

Zak dangled his bound wrists on a crossbar of the door and signed to his brother. After a moment, Gideon signed back.

"What was that about?" She had good eyes.

"With Piñero gone, we have to take the opportunity to make a run for it in the next hour. She could be back any time, and even if she isn't, it would be suicidal to take off through the jungle after dark. I have a fairly good sense of direction." He tipped his head toward one pocked wall. "I know *that* way is the river, probably some sort of a settlement where we can get help getting back to Caracas or one of the big villages. But I've neither a map nor a compass." There was a GPS on his watch. If he could get that back . . . A whiff of flowers interrupted the thought. She stood much too damned close as she tried to look outside.

A second man with a loaded wheelbarrow made the trek across the clearing. Acadia's eyes tracked him as he passed by the bars. How the hell, after walking for more than four hours, and everything else she'd endured, did she still smell of flowers?

"Um, I have—"

"We need every hour of light we can get." He frowned at her. "What's the matter? You have to pee? Don't be shy. You aren't getting a hall pass to the ladies' room. Go back there and take care of it. I won't look."

Amazing how cool a pair of warm gray eyes could become. "Every now and then I start to like you," she told him crossly. "Then I'm reminded why I don't. *Listen* for a second, hotshot. I have a GPS."

Zak stared at her for a moment, stunned. "You have a GPS?"

"I'm visiting a foreign country. Of *course* I have a GPS. It's not very big, and it might not be accurate, considering where we are . . ."

He could have kissed her hot, sweaty, beautiful face. Could have, and thought better of it. He stayed right where he was, already too close for comfort. "Hand it over, Barbie."

"Please may I have your GPS, Acadia?" she suggested, eyes still cool. "That was amazingly forward thinking of you to *bring* it, *carry* it, and not keep it for your own selfish flight from a fate worse than death."

He snapped his fingers like Piñero. "Give."

"Only if you stop calling me *Barbie* in that annoying, condescending tone." Fake cheer slid into a scowl as she glared at him.

"Fine, what do your friends call you?"

"Acadia."

"Ah. Cady?" That's the name her alter ego had used in the cantina what seemed like a lifetime ago.

Her chin came up. "Nobody calls me that."

He had. Last night while they'd been fucking their brains out.

He turned back to observe their captors. The men had gathered in a loose group in the shade of the largest building. They were playing cards and drinking from a shared bottle. Turning from the temptation he damn well didn't need to remember, Zak counted heads. All ten of them. "So. Cady or Barbie?" If he and Gideon could get a couple of guns, they could round up the guerrillas. Lock them in the cells . . . from which he'd already ascertained that it'd be child's play to escape.

So, on to plan B.

Kill them. He and his brother wouldn't enjoy it, but it was the guerrillas or them. He picked them.

"Try 'Acadia.'" She turned slightly, giving him access to her left hip. "Third pocket. Help yourself."

Zak found and withdrew the GPS without pausing to fondle the taut cheeks of her ass. She was right, the device was small. But it worked when he turned it on; better yet, it was backlit. Quickly, before the guerrillas could see it, he shoved it into his back pocket. "Good job. What else do you have in those magic pockets of yours?"

"Actually, a lot. There are twenty-eight pockets in all. It's the store's best-selling . . . never mind that. They wouldn't lock us in here if they were planning on killing us, right?" Acadia moved back to his side, her shoulder snug against his arm as she peered between the bars.

Hot jasmine. Above every stink there was, he smelled her skin. And smelling her skin reminded him of what her skin tasted like, and it had been hot, smooth, and sweet, like crème brûlée against his tongue.

It was going to be problematic as hell attempting to run for his life through the jungle with a cockstand. "You're crowding me. Why don't you go sit down?"

· "Why don't I not?" she returned politely, watching the men pass around the bottle. "There's at least a little bit of air right here," she pointed out. "If you feel crowded, you go and sit down."

"Your mouth must get you into a lot of trouble."

"Only in Venezuela," she said sweetly. He instantly imagined her mouth exactly where he wanted it now.

Damn it to hell. "Are you stupid, or completely fearless?"

Her eyes widened at his provocative tone. "How did you build a successful company talking to people that way?" She shook her head with clear disgust as she pulled a small plastic container from one of her magic pockets and shook out a mint. He couldn't wait to find out what else she had hidden in all those secret places. "Your brother has got to be the front man for ZAG Search. *You'd* scare people with that pissy attitude. Cut it out." She popped the mint into her mouth. "I'm not your freaking enemy. We're stuck in this together. So give the big bad-ass attitude a rest, okay?"

She shook out another mint, and before he could say anything, she stuck it into his open mouth. The cool bite of spearmint on his tongue and the smell of it helped distract him some. Her finger, wet from her own mouth, made his dick levitate.

"They're well organized," she said into the silence. "But I bet Cruella won't like them drinking on the job."

"No shit. But it'll suit us just fine." To walk away from the annoyingly provocative scent of her skin and hair meant he'd have to go to the other side of the cell. Hotter, and with no scenic view. Going way the hell across the continent was completely out of the question. For the moment.

Zak figured he'd put up with a lot worse, and as he leaned his shoulder against the stained, pockmarked wall beside the door, a leaf brushed his throat. He pretended to inspect the inch-thick construction rebar while he kept an eye on the men. The bars were rusted and crumbling in sections along their length. Shit just didn't hold up in the constant humidity. Too bad they didn't have months to wait for nature to do the hard work for them.

Zak held out his bound hands. "Got anything in your pockets to cut through these ties?"

"A Swiss Army Knife."

Jesus, he thought, stunned and impressed by her ingenuity. She was a regular Girl Scout. "Let's have that, too." Acadia twisted to get at it. Her contortions weren't helping him not think about her naked body and wild, hot sex. He damn well better try. "Which pocket?"

"Since I know you're having a hard time vocalizing your undying gratitude for my forethought"—she turned around—"left butt."

Great. Zak felt for the pocket, found the knife, and removed it. "You first." She obediently held out her wrists so he could cut through the thick plastic with the tiny hacksaw. It would've taken a lot longer for him to gnaw through the tie with his teeth.

"Hold on to that," he directed when the edges parted and the tie fell away. "We want them to think we're still secure."

He held out his wrists and she took the knife from him, efficiently sawing through the thick plastic tie. It took her a little longer than it had taken for him to saw through hers, but she got the job done.

She was holding up well, but they needed water to replace what they'd sweated out. Strands of honey-blond hair stuck to the sweat on her face and neck, her cheeks gleamed with hectic color, and her gray eyes were shadowed. When a person got that exhausted, fear was damn near impossible to hide.

As if reading his mind, her eyes met his. "You must be as thirsty as I am." She glanced outside to make sure no one was looking, then rummaged around in yet another hidden pocket on the thigh of her voluminous cargo pants. This one revealed a flip-top plastic container.

"Got a cold beer in there?" Christ. Wouldn't surprise him. If he hadn't been familiar with the SCOTTeVEST outfit she wore, he would've sworn she didn't even have a pocket on her.

"The alcohol wouldn't be good for us in this heat, even if I had a six-pack stashed in my pants. Besides," she added, "I've seen you after a few drinks. You need all your common sense, sorry."

His gut clenched. She'd seen a lot more of him than somewhat drunk. "Jesus," he said flatly. "Is it always about sex with you? I thought the pole dancer shit was BS."

Her eyes, so velvety and gray that any idiot would want to wrap himself in their warmth, opened wide. "You really *do* have sex on the brain, don't you?" She sighed, like some kind of put-upon schoolteacher. "It's the tropical climate, don't worry. I'm sure you'll have plenty of other issues to fill your every waking moment soon. Like staying alive."

She held out the container. "Another mint? Three's our limit until we know . . . until we get out there and know what we're dealing with."

"Sure, General." Zak held out his hand, filthy and still bleeding from the paper-cut-like lacerations he'd sustained from the sharp grasses and leaves en route.

So were hers. But she hadn't said a word. She would, soon enough. Oh, she wouldn't whine, he figured. The smart ones rarely did. Jennifer had used to have fainting down to an art form. She'd "fainted" to get them a room at a fully booked hotel in Peru, and pretended she was pregnant when she wanted to get into the shade the time they'd gone sand-boarding in Gharb Soheil. The situation hadn't even had to be dire. If Jen wanted something, she used theatrics to get it. Zak had never known what was real and what was faked. He'd eventually stopped trying.

He knew unequivocally that Acadia would eventually pull the weaker-sex card in ways that would tie a man up six ways from Sunday, and with such innocence he'd convince himself he was a fucking abusive brute. Fortunately for him, the blinders had come off years ago. "Fool me once" and all that crap. Been there, done that.

She shook a tiny mint onto his palm. Zak put it in his mouth. "They didn't search you?" he asked around the cooling tab.

She wiggled her eyebrows. "I'm blond and female in a male-dominated country. Who *wouldn't* trust this face?" She opened her eyes wide and batted her long lashes.

Same crap Jen used to pull, Zak thought with knee-jerk irritation. Depending on her femininity and beauty to pay her way. The difference was that there was humor behind Acadia's statement. Jennifer had had no sense of humor—it had taken him years to realize that.

Looking at Acadia's angelic features, soft blond hair and smokin' hot body, anyone would trust her. Until they saw the devil in those soft gray eyes. Just like he'd done the night before. Despite her stripper claims and the wild implications that she was a hell of a lot more experienced than she had actually turned out to be, he'd been intrigued enough to test the boundaries.

He had to admit, it had been so worth it. Right up until morning, when real life had come crashing right back down around his ears.

And hers, this time.

Acadia curled her slender fingers around one of the bars. In the same way as she'd wrapped them around his—

Zak pulled his mind back from that visceral memory and glanced over at the shack where Gideon was being held. He couldn't see him; he'd probably gone to lie down on that hard cement ledge. Smart move, but atypical of his brother, who never sat down if he could stand, never stood if he could run. The extreme sports they both loved had conditioned them for pretty much any contingency, be it bad weather, bad food, or dangerous people. The places they frequented meant they were *always* prepared for the worst. Some of their best adventures had been when they'd bested all the elements that kept sane people from attempting a particular sport in a particular location.

The Stark brothers knew how to survive against overwhelming odds. Gideon's conserving his strength for what was coming indicated that he was hurt worse than he'd admitted to.

Fuckit.

They'd traveled at least three hours in the van, which meant approximately a hundred miles and change. Then they'd trekked through the jungle for another four. He figured it was barely noon, given the sun's zenith.

There was *maybe* enough daylight to get back to civilization, but night came *fast* in the jungle. Which meant so did the predators.

It was damned strange that they'd been transported so far away from the pickup point. The kidnappers would demand ransom, sure. Then kill them. The thing that bothered him was that they could have done that in someone's backyard. Christ, this kind of operation frequently did. It wasn't necessary to take them way the hell deep into the jungle just to hold them for a while.

Most of the local kidnapping operations were known as *secuestro express*, or express-kidnappings. It was a grab and hold kind of job; they kept the victim until the ransom was paid. Less than forty-eight hours. Those kidnappers were known to keep their victims prisoner in someone's house, or even the trunk of a car, not transport them hundreds of miles into the jungle. Not to a secret location that looked like it had been built, or was in the process of being built, for the express purpose of detaining victims.

"Not that I'm complaining, but why didn't they just kill us somewhere closer to the hotel?" Acadia asked, keeping her voice low, although no one was taking any notice of them.

Again, it was as if she was tuned in to his frequency, a feeling Zak didn't like. Still, it wasn't *her* fault she'd been swept up in this.

"They probably figured it would be easier to secure us away from civilization." The mint was gone. A sweet memory.

She plopped down on the filthy cement ledge that had probably been a bed at some point, lifted her ass to adjust something in her clothing, then settled back, one foot on the ledge, arm around her updrawn leg. She rested her chin on her knee.

"What do you think they are going to do to us when they figure out nobody is going to pay our ransom?" he asked sharply.

"Of course someone will pay—"

"Who has access to your bank account?"

"Nobo—"

"Right. *Nobody*. What were you planning to do? Give her your PIN number?"

"If that's what it takes for her to release us, God yes," she said fervently. "In a heartbeat."

He rolled his eyes. "She won't thank you for it. She'll order you killed. Just like Gideon and myself."

"You don't *know* that."

"Grow up, Barbie," he shot back. "This is the real world, and people aren't as friendly as they are in Junction City."

"Isn't that the truth?" She gave him a pointed look. "But . . . I must admit," she continued, voice softening, "even though you're extremely cranky and uncommunicative, I'm glad they put us in here together."

He wasn't. "There are only two cells," Zak pointed out, turning back to the guerrillas. They were laughing and shooting the breeze, money in the pot, bottle still making the rounds, weapons on the ground beside each man, close at hand. New weapons. Plenty of ammo.

"And they weren't going to put you and your brother together so you could figure out a way to get out of here," she finished logically.

"Yeah. That too."

"Too?"

"They found us in bed." Zak paused, then turned his head to give her a cool look. "In bed. Bare-ass naked. They put us together so they'd have something to entertain them later."

"Good God. Watch *us*, you mean?" She grimaced, then opened a flap over her left breast, removed a tangled knot of rubber bands, chose one, and stuffed the rest back inside the pocket. "Surely they don't think we'd have sex . . . in *here*?" She stretched out her arms, her fingertips brushing the walls.

"I presume they don't have Wii or TV reception way the hell and gone out here." He pointed to a peephole in the wall about eye level behind her. Acadia gave him an even look as she scooped her hair into a haphazard ponytail on top of her head and off her neck. As she messed with her hair, her vest, heavy with all those damned pockets, parted, exposing the soft curve of her belly. It looked smooth and vulnerable, velvety soft. He'd rubbed his face there last night, nuzzled his lips against her fragrant heat.

She'd look just like that after a shower, glistening, with damp tendrils of hair the color of honey streaked with butter clinging to her neck and shoulders and curling over her breasts. Pebbled apricot nipples——

Zak let his forehead thump against the rough, rusted bars. The small pain jolted his brain. Fuckit. She was just a pretty girl. Nothing extraordinary, nothing special. Just one of a million available blondes out there.

"I hope you have a plan to get out of here sooner than later." She looked at the card-playing, booze-swilling guards, then back at him. "*Do* we have a plan? Or are we going to wing it?"

A drop of sweat rolled slowly down his temple, stinging like hell as it hit the slash beside his eye. Appropriate. Obviously he hadn't paid enough attention, with the first injury so close to his eyes. He needed a second for the lesson to really sink in. "Wing it." Mostly. The plan he and Gideon had come with relied on fast thinking as the opportunity arose.

"Okay. Just give me a few minutes' heads-up." Apparently their daring, insanely dangerous escape was as simple as that.

She rummaged around in another breast pocket and took out a flat packet of something or other.

He should hang the woman upside down and shake her, Zak thought, half baffled, half amused, and all so damned horny he couldn't see straight. He'd like to start by sliding his hand into that pocket and cupping her——

She jumped off the ledge and came to stand beside him. "Since we seem to have the time, would you do me a favor?"

"You want sex?"

"Um . . ." She pretended to consider it, then rolled her eyes, "No." She pulled a moist towelette from the pack in her hands. "Would you mind cleaning the um . . . the b-blood off my back?" Her voice shook, suddenly not nearly so calm or composed. "It doesn't bother me— blood, I mean. Not usually, I'm pretty tough that way. Sort of. Kinda. Most of the time. But that was just . . ." She walked back to the shelf, where there was at least an ounce more privacy, and turned her back. She waved the cloth over her shoulder. "Please?"

There was no blood on her clothing because she'd been naked when the rapist had been shot by Piñero. Zak stood at the bars and realized he'd gripped one in each tense fist as she waited, her back presented like an offering.

"Zak?" She still had her back to him, but it was obvious by the way her elbows and shoulders moved that she was unzipping her vest.

He'd rather have faced a thick-necked psychotic guerrilla with an Uzi and a shit attitude than Acadia's pale, slender, *naked* back right now. There was something about her that was insanely appealing. He didn't understand what her draw was. But whatever it was, he was being sucked into some sort of sexual vortex and he wasn't sure why her, why now.

She slipped off the vest, tossing it onto the ledge, then crossed her arms and pulled her T-shirt up around her neck, exposing her back. Her skin was pale where the tropical sun hadn't turned it red, and as fine-grained as a baby's. The dried brown blood splatter was an obscenity, and the sight of it on her made Zak want to put his fist through something.

Like maybe the brick wall. Or every single leering face of every single asshole *hombre* who had looked at her slender naked body. The ones who'd touched her he'd shoot. God Almighty, and he was a man who *abhorred* guns.

"Could you hurry?"

Oh, Jesus. While he'd fought and she had nearly been raped, while he and his brother had rested their unconscious heads on her thighs . . . Fuckit, she'd been wearing someone else's blood on her back like some kind of brutal warpaint.

"Yeah," he said, because he didn't know what else to do. He walked up behind her, deliberately blocking her body from view, and took the wet cloth from her. "Let's get this over with." He ignored the vulnerable nape of her neck. Ignored the smooth line of her vertebrae, like little stepping stones trailing down the pale silken skin of her back.

Ignored all of it. Unfortunately, his brain connected what her skin looked like to what it had *felt* like under his hands the night before. Baby soft, smooth, silky. It wasn't a leap to remember how she'd responded when he'd kissed the tender skin at the juncture of her thigh, or how sensitive and responsive her nipples were when he rolled one on his tongue—

She dropped her head, holding her T-shirt out of the way. "Just on my back."

The problem with jasmine, Zak thought, feeling savage and out of sorts and generally pissed off, was that the soft flowery scent smelled like innocence. Like things he didn't want to think of: joy, and hope. He efficiently ran the wet wipe across her shoulder blades and frowned at the stubborn, rust-colored flakes. "It's dried," he muttered, voice gruff. "I have to scrub if you want it off."

Oh, God, she wanted it off. Acadia felt each individual fleck and speck of blood as if it had stuck to her skin and fastened like some kind of grotesque tick. She shuddered. "As hard as you like. Please."

Making a rough sound she couldn't identify—probably disgust that she was so squeamish under the circumstances—Zak did as she asked—a little more vigorously than Acadia was prepared for. His steadying hand tightened on her shoulder as she staggered under the sudden pressure, but she braced her feet, not saying a word as he briskly applied the wipe to her skin.

She'd rather be rubbed raw than carry that man's blood on her for a second longer.

"Done." He yanked down her T-shirt to cover her, and she heard the scuff of his boots as he stepped away.

"Thank you," she said with feeling as she slipped her arms into the armholes of the vest hurriedly. She turned around. "Give me the . . . that." She wiggled her fingers, and he handed her the blood-smeared wipe. "I can put it to good use."

When he only cocked his head, scarred eyebrow twitching inquisitively, Acadia kneeled on the cement ledge and stuffed the cloth into the peephole.

His lips twitched, but he didn't smile as she returned to his side. "They can look in through the door."

"Where I'll see them." She went to stand next to him. The bump on his temple was a painful shade of purple. "I have more aspirin if you'd like some." She reached up to touch the bruise, and he jerked away.

"Don't pet me. I don't do touchy-feely."

"Really? I would never have guessed," she told him tartly. "I love being petted." She loved no such thing. No one had ever done it, and it wasn't something she was used to. But under the circumstances she felt the urge to needle him. "I don't suppose you'd consider giving me a hug— No? Okay. Never mind." She disguised her smile at his annoyed expression by digging into her pocket for the aspirin. "You must have a terrible headache; here, take a couple of these."

"I don't." He gave her a brief glance, his eyes unreadable as she stuck the flat pack back in her pocket. A muscle jerked in his jaw as he held the severed ends of the plastic handcuffs. He had very large hands, which she'd noticed last night, but up close she saw that his fingers were long and almost elegant, like a piano player's.

Her gaze flickered to his face. "Do you play? I had

lessons when I was little, but my parents lost interest almost before I did. I was terrible—"

"What the hell are you talking about?" His head turned a few beats before he made eye contact.

"Do you have absolutely no social skills?" Acadia demanded crossly. "We're stuck in this confined space because of *you*, we're probably going to die because of *you*. You don't appear to have a viable plan to get us out of here, do you? No, apparently no—"

"What do you want from me?" His eyes glittered, and the skin was pulled taut over his cheekbones.

"The answer to that seems obvious. Get me out of here alive."

"Do I *look* like a fucking hero to you?"

"Don't swear at me just because you're scared too," Acadia said furiously. "You *look* like a man whose money and position got me where I am right now. You *look* like a man who doesn't have a plan. You also *look* like a big, strong guy who *should* be able to outsmart ten drunk guerrillas who are *half asleep*. I don't give a hoot if you're a hero or a freaking antihero. If nothing else, help me formulate a plan that'll work before we all *die* in here." Acadia was stunned to realize that she was absolutely furious, and worse, she was yelling.

She lowered her voice with considerable effort. "And the very least you could do in our last hours on this earth is *talk* to me in complete sentences." She punched him in the arm. His brow rose. No one was more shocked than she was. There wasn't a violent bone in her body. Or at least there never had been before she'd met Zakary Stark, almost been raped, been kidnapped, and been thrown into isolation with a monosyllabic pacifist.

She punched him again.

He didn't blink. "Feel better?"

"How old are you?" she demanded, jaw aching because she was gritting her teeth so hard.

"Why?"

"I'm stunned that someone bigger and stronger than me hasn't killed you by now."

Totally unconcerned, he was staring outside at the men drinking and playing cards in the shade. "Not for lack of trying."

"My father taught me seventeen ways to kill a man that'll look like an accident. Why don't I give it a shot?" she offered sweetly. Her heart was manic, her palms damp with perspiration. She'd never lost her temper this way. Ever. The man was infuriating.

Still looking at the soldiers, he leaned a shoulder against the wall. "What happened to him?"

"He died three months ago. Early-onset Alzheimer's. Trust me, I've lived with an uncommunicative, socially awkward man for most of my life, and you take the prize."

"That why you talk enough for two people?"

She was so scared she was afraid to blink, so hot she was sweating out every drop of moisture in her body, and so blindly furious with Zakary Stark she wanted to do some sort of atypical violence to his person until he begged for mercy.

"If I were you," Acadia told him, brimming with

temper, "I'd talk to me nicely, and apologize a *lot*. I have things with me that can make you and your brother's last few hours a lot less unpleasant." Her voice rose. "And things that will make your last few hours a living hell!"

He reached out, gripped her wrist, and a second later had her arm twisted painfully behind her back. "I can take whatever the fuck I want from you, *and* I won't have to listen to your inane chatter afterward. How's *that* for a give-and-take conversation, Miss Gray?"

He held on to her for another second or two, then shoved her not so gently out of reach. Acadia rubbed her wrist, even though he hadn't hurt her. Her heart was pounding painfully in her chest, and her breathing was erratic. "Bastard."

"Bitch," he returned without heat, his attention on the scene outside. Suddenly, he straightened. "Gideon just gave me the signal. We're going to take the men now. The combo of this heat and all the booze . . . While we deal with the situation, stay right here, where I know how to find you."

Like she'd just sit here waiting for him to do his thing. "I'll be halfway to Caracas the second your Neanderthal back is turned," she told him furiously.

"As soon as we're done, I'll come and get you," he said, as if she hadn't said a word. "We'll head back the way we came. Follow the track we made coming in."

He was an infuriating dictator. Weighing the odds, Acadia glanced through the bars and assessed what was happening outside. The place was crawling with uniformed, armed guerrillas. She scowled at him. "Three of us are going to take out ten armed men?"

"*Two* of us," he corrected. "The alternative is, *they* decide the when and the how of whatever they have planned for us. Gideon's ribs are cracked, if not broken. We can't wait."

"I agree. But I'd feel a lot more confident if we had a cohesive plan before you raced out of here unprepared." *Come on, Acadia, think.* He might've gotten her into this mess, but she wasn't willing to bet her life that he could or would get them out safely. She had to participate in this escape plan if it had a hope in hell of working.

She'd kill for pen and paper so she could write down her thoughts and see if there was some sort of escape plan that didn't involve people getting shot in the back as they ran.

She went through her mental inventory of the pockets, then she felt down to the calf of her left leg, opened the pocket there, and took out a bottle of Visine. *Thank you, boring Saturday nights with the Internet.* She held the tiny bottle out to Zak. "Use this."

Zak gave her one of those looks men had perfected since they'd clubbed their dinner, the I-have-important-business-don't-bother me-little-lady look, and said impatiently, "I don't need eyedrops."

"How would you like to take out those men, and keep them incapacitated for at least six or seven hours, without even one shot being fired?"

"Obviously the answer to that is, hell yeah."

"Put this in that brand-new bottle of whatever they just opened," she told him with exaggerated patience. Really, didn't the man read? "It doesn't really cause diarrhea. That's an urban myth. But the active ingredient, tetrahydrozoline, has much more serious consequences when ingested."

He gave the small bottle a dubious glance. "You sure it works?"

"Difficulty breathing will incapacitate them plenty," Acadia assured him. "But it also causes severe headaches, muscle weakness, seizures, and possibly coma."

"Jesus. You are one dangerous woman, Acadia Gray."

She gave him a wicked smile. "I've been trying to tell you that all day."

∽e FIVE e∼

L ie down like you're about to pass out."

"That's not far from the truth." Acadia crossed the tiny cell to stretch out obediently on the filthy slab, repositioning the plastic handcuffs to look as though she was still restrained. Heart pounding with both fear and anticipation, she tried to unclench her muscles.

"Okay. Just alerted Gid. Relax. You look like you've been embalmed," Zak said dryly, adjusting the plastic cuffs over his own wrists. "I just want you to look faint, not dead."

For several beats she felt a prickle of awareness travel through her body like an electrical current as his hot gaze swept over her like the caress of possessive hands.

Was he remembering last night? Apparently not. From his grim expression, she could tell sex with her was the last thing on his mind. *Get a grip, Acadia.*

She shut her eyes and went limp. "Better?" It was hard to regulate her erratic breathing. Fear. It was fear. And the images of . . . She held her breath until she thought maybe, just maybe, she could inhale without getting a potent rush of memories of exactly what those hands could do.

Unaffected by the tangible sexual current she felt between them, Zak yelled through the bars. "Hey! Get over here. The woman passed out, she needs water! Hurry!" The panic in his voice was startling; the man was a good actor. "She's not moving!" Then under his breath. "Five. Four. Three. Two."

Her lips twitched. He was so damn cocky and confident, utterly convinced everything would go according to his plans. Except they were *her* plans. She'd remind him of that. If they made it out alive.

The sound of voices got closer, Spanish too fast to translate. Resisting the urge to stiffen, she remained wilted, mentally bracing herself for a confrontation.

It was obvious from the way Zak and Gideon were able to come up with a diversion without a single spoken word between them that they'd been in tight places before. And survived. Being brothers was part of it, but Acadia sensed a deeper bond than that. They trusted one another implicitly.

She couldn't fathom what that would be like. There'd never been anyone but herself to rely on.

Zak shouted for the guards again, urging them to hurry. Acadia heard their slightly slurred comments as they neared the shack. They were already tipsy. But even so, they suspected a trap.

It was hard to tell just how many men crowded inside.

A whole damned herd by the sound and smell of them. The stink was overpowering.

"She needs water and medical care," Zak told them, letting his voice trail off. The unspoken words to finish off *that* sentence were clearly "or do you want her to die?" Which would've been redundant, even for them.

The guerrillas discussed the situation in rapid-fire Spanish. They'd just divulged that Loida Piñero would return before nightfall, and she'd be pissed. God—if they'd waited even a few more hours to do this—

She peeked through the screen of her lashes as one of the twins—Gold Tooth—came very close to lean over her. Acadia smelled the rancid stink of sour body odor before she heard his booted feet. His breath, moist and fetid, washed over her face, and she had to dig her short nails into her waist to prevent herself from gagging. *Hurry, Zak.*

In her slitted vision, she watched Zak step behind the men, as if to give them room. She let her eyes flutter fully open and whispered weakly, *"N-necesito a-agua, por favor."*

She caught a glimmer of silver on the soldier's dirty neck and recognized the chain that held her St. Christopher medal. Acadia wanted to reach out and grab it off him, and it took everything in her to maintain the ruse. The medallion and chain had been the last present her father had given her before he'd forgotten her name. He'd laughed as he had clasped it around her neck and said, "So you can travel safely to all those exciting places you're always reading about, Cady girl."

God. She wanted her medallion back. Now.

But instead of lunging upward and blowing their entire escape plan, Acadia paid attention to what was happening just outside the door.

In a sliver of space between the men, she glimpsed Zak and his brother. Then Gideon was gone. She let out a shaky breath of relief. Almost there. The soldier wearing her necklace slapped her cheeks, and she opened her eyes fully, lest he break her jaw.

He started to turn from her, so Acadia gasped for air and broke into choking coughs so that he would focus on her and not realize Zak was just slipping back inside the hut.

She could've wept with relief as Zak, his tone uncompromising and angry, said, "If your leader hears that you didn't do what she told you, she's going to be pissed. Each of us is worth twenty million American dollars to her. Which of you wants to tell her that a prisoner died because you didn't follow her instructions?"

The men were silent, trading loaded glares.

Zak gestured with his seemingly bound hands. "If that happens on your watch, she's going do more than kick your ass. She told you an hour ago to bring us water. Do it already."

Acadia reached out, then let her hands drop weakly. *"Por favor, señor. Agua."*

The men left, locking the flimsy door behind them.

Acadia sat up tailor fashion, resting her elbows on her knees. She stared at her hands blankly as her mind raced.

They'd taken her medallion back at the hotel. All right, so she'd resigned herself to never seeing it again. But now she had, and she damn well wanted it back. She hoped the eyedrops affected Gold Tooth first. And hardest.

The only problem now, she realized, was that they'd made such an issue about getting water that it was all she could think about. She'd talked herself out of acknowledging her parched mouth and the thirst that had dogged her since the early hours of the morning, but now the possibility of quenching her thirst was front and center in her mind.

Would the men poison themselves before they got her water? God, she hoped not.

"Piñero will be back tonight." She addressed Zak's broad back. Perspiration stained his blue shirt, and his dark hair curled against his strong, tanned neck. It seemed like a lifetime ago when she'd kissed the sensitive nape. Laughing, he'd rolled her over and gently bitten her in return, his strong white teeth scraping the sensitive skin between her neck and shoulder—

"I hea—" He frowned, and his voice roughened. "Don't look at me like that."

God, he'd turned just in time to see her *lusting*. Her cheeks got hotter. She blinked him into focus. Large, unhappy male. She sucked in a deep breath. "Maybe we should hang out in the trees until she gets back to camp," she whispered. "Take the van . . ."

Zak turned back to the door. "Unless she's delayed, or changes her mind. We need daylight for this to work."

"We need *transportation* for this to work," Acadia told him, annoyed with him for thinking he was in charge, and with herself for forgetting she didn't like him.

Stockholm syndrome, she told herself firmly. That was the only thing that made rational sense. Was it the right syndrome? Technically, Zak wasn't her captor, but—hell, she'd take any excuse she could get for her inexplicable response to him.

"Who exactly made you boss of me, anyway?" she demanded. "I don't remember casting my vote. And just as a refresher, *I* was the one who cleaned your wounds while you were unconscious, gave your brother aspirin for his headache, had the tool to cut off our cuffs, *and* gave us a way to incapacitate all those men out there without firing a shot."

He glanced over his shoulder and gave her a cold, dismissive, arrogant glance. "If it works." He turned back to look outside, his long, elegant fingers clamped around the bars. "Fine. We'll take a fucking vote. Hope like hell your poisoning plot takes down the guerrillas. Follow our trail in back out, *and* stick around our entry point to wait for Piñero to return."

"That has my vote."

"And if she decides to wait until tomorrow?" he countered.

It was like he was testing her, which ticked her off even more, considering she'd been the resourceful one in this situation. "We follow her tracks and walk to the nearest town."

"On the road?" he said, with a slight mocking tone.

"Yes."

"In broad daylight?" This time his sarcasm came through loud and clear, and her temperature spiked for a whole different reason.

"I haven't thought it through," she said through her teeth. "But yes, why not?"

"Because more than half the population in these parts are criminals of one sort or the other; because three Americans, one of them a light-eyed blond *woman*, and another *injured*, will be picked off like they have targets on their backs. Because we have no idea where the fuck the nearest village is, and Piñero could drive up right behind us, and the next time she kidnaps us she won't be so nice about it. That enough reason for you?"

She sagged back against the wall, feeling like a punctured balloon. "We aren't going to follow the road?"

"Did you *see* a road?"

"No, but we got here, at least part of the way, on a paved road. I think I remember the turns—"

"*Or*," Zak cut in, "your fiendish plot works, the men are out of action, and we take a short walk through the jungle until we hit the river. Hire a boat and have a late steak dinner in Caracas tonight. Let me know when you're ready to cast your vote."

She was starting to really hate him. "How far's the river? Do you even know which way it is? What if it's a really long walk?"

"*Walking* won't kill us. What's out there hunting at night will. We have a narrow window of opportunity before dark. Lie down; they're coming back."

Fuming, Acadia stretched out on the slab. She didn't bother closing her eyes. Every time she thought Zakary Stark was a nice guy, he did or said something obnoxious to change her mind. The fact that he was all kinds of sexy, and turned her on without trying to, was the irritating icing on the cake.

Gold Tooth shoved a plastic cup through the bars at Zak. He made a crude suggestion that Acadia only vaguely understood, but her whole body flushed with fiery humiliation.

A big fat steak dinner accompanied by about a gallon of ice water, in Caracas, *alone*, sounded more and more appealing.

THE GUERRILLAS WERE DROPPING like flies, which surprised the hell out of Zak. He would have thought the eyedrop thing was an urban legend, but damned if it wasn't working.

Gideon had emptied the whole container of drops into their guards' new bottle of rum. Within an hour, most of the men were puking their guts out, two were unconscious, and the rest seemed to be confused and lethargic as they staggered into the trees clutching their bellies. A bloodless coup.

"I can take some of the crap in your pockets, lighten the load some," Zak offered, glancing at Acadia over his shoulder.

She gave him a cool look. "The weight's evenly distributed." The woman went from hot to cold and back again on a dime. He didn't even try to figure her out. The way she'd pulled up her hair made her look like a sexy girl-next-door.

Which was, as any red-blooded man knew, the most dangerous and subversive kind of female. He turned away from her smooth skin and the drugging fragrance of jasmine.

Blue Bandana was trying to give his brother water. And failing. Gold Tooth couldn't hold the cup. Water splashed into the grass at his feet. Blue Bandana went back for more. "Don't be so fucking stubborn," Zak told Acadia as he tracked the last holdout, now carrying the almost-empty rum bottle, back to his twin. *Finish it, asshole.* "You're going to have to run."

"And I will. How long?"

Whatever. "Blue Bandana's the holdout. He wasn't drinking as much as the others. We'll give him another fifteen minutes to catch up."

She lay back, closed her eyes. "Wake me when it's time to go."

She was taking a nap? *Now?* Well, at least she'd shut up for a while.

Zak turned back to observe the goings-on outside. Gold Tooth was out cold. His twin chugged the remainder of the drugged rum and looked around, clearly worried and confused as hell. A man stumbled out of the tree line, made it two yards, and collapsed.

Zak knew for sure which direction they wouldn't go:

toward the entry point the guerrillas had chosen for their latrine.

Blue Bandana leaned against the cookhouse, clutching his belly. He shouted for help, but everyone had his own problems. The Uzi slid off his shoulder as he leaned over to puke.

"Let's go."

Acadia was up on her feet like the goddamn Energizer Bunny. "About time."

Zak kicked open the door and motioned to Gideon, who did the same. A few of the men gave them bleary looks as they converged, then ran across the clearing. One even reached weakly for his weapon, but that was the extent of their interaction with the escapees.

Miracle of miracles, her plan had worked.

As he ran, Zak helped himself to a machete from one guy, an Uzi from another, and several clips and half a dozen sets of plastic handcuffs from a third, then jogged over to the twins, who were sprawled close together. Zak undid the stainless steel band of his watch from Blue Bandana's scrawny wrist and quickly fastened it on his own. The man looked up at him with pain-filled eyes, then rolled his head to puke.

"Payback's a bitch," Zak told him, with no small amount of satisfaction. Quickly, he stepped over the man's supine, twitching body, grabbed the other twin by his hair to lift the dead weight of his head, pulled the silver chain he'd recognized earlier over the bastard's neck, and let Gold Tooth's head thump back to the ground.

He stuffed the long chain and medallion into his breast pocket for safekeeping.

She'd better get herself a harder-working patron saint. So far, old St. Christopher hadn't given her anything even remotely close to safe travel. The thing about relying on anyone or anything was that they'd eventually let you down. Saint or person, they were all fucking fallible. Some more than others.

Except for Gideon—his brother had always been there, and no way was Zak going to let him die in this shithole. Not, he thought grimly, that a busted rib was a death knell, but Zak damn well wanted to make sure that was the extent of the injuries today.

He jogged over to join his brother and Acadia near the tree line.

Acadia, jaunty ponytail swinging, had an Uzi strap slung across her shoulder. Zak had never seen a more incongruous sight outside of the movies: a sexy blonde wearing an automatic as a fashion accessory. Gideon had gone shopping among the writhing bodies as well. He was loaded for bear with a machete, an Uzi, and God only knew what else. Zak shot him a grin, indicating with a jerk of his chin that they should get moving.

With Acadia between them, they ran for the cover of the trees and dense foliage. He and Gideon had decided they'd enter the jungle here, circle around the clearing, and start their trek toward the river several hundred yards out from their entry point.

They hacked at the undergrowth only as much as they

had to, preferring to push and crawl their way through so as to leave as little evidence of their passage as possible. Even a mediocre tracker would know their direction, but for the next couple of hours, no one from camp would be in any position to do any following. After that the jungle would have closed around them and blurred their passage. Or so their theory went. Zak sure hoped to hell they were right.

Acadia had gotten over her anger surprisingly quickly. Jennifer had always managed to sustain hers for days, sometimes weeks.

Gideon was in the lead, Acadia in the middle, Zak in back. Which left him in the perfect position to watch her curvy ass sway in front of him.

Damn.

He had a vivid memory of rubbing his cheek on the soft firm pillow of her ass before flipping her over to bury his face against the fragrant curve of her belly, then . . .

He'd slept with other women since Jennifer, but he'd never been *this* distracted by their very presence. He dropped back, letting the murmur of Gideon's voice and Acadia's soft response fade into the jungle ahead of him.

ZAK HAD DROPPED BACK again, letting them move ahead. Acadia knew he was walking two steps for their every one as he kept circling around to make sure they weren't being followed.

She picked up her pace to catch up with Gideon, who was wielding the enormous machete to clear a path.

Feeling a little queasy, she pressed a hand to her roiling tummy as she walked. Nerves. Stress. Heat. Too much action. No food . . . The list went on. Since the two men were in exactly the same boat, worse because they'd both been hurt, she didn't bitch about the situation. Now that they were relatively safe, or as safe as humans could be in an animal's natural habitat, the adrenaline overload was seeping away. She was dying of thirst and would have killed for gallons of ice-cold Diet Coke. Gideon pulled aside a large branch he'd just cut, and a spider with long, skinny legs and a black, hairy body practically leaped onto his shirt. He flicked it off with barely a glance. She felt it prudent not to point out that it was an aggressive and highly venomous Brazilian wandering spider. Acadia shuddered as she took a giant step to avoid it as it scurried into the thicket.

"That Visine thing was damned well brilliant," Gideon told her, his voice low. "You're a font of useful information."

"I'm the manager at Jim's Sporting Goods. It helps to remember all the warranties, and the inventory levels, and when to reorder and what bills to . . ." She paused as she caught herself rambling. "Anyway, having a good memory is my superpower. That and being crazy organized."

"Well, we wouldn't be here if you weren't. Thank God for your organizational skills, Jennifer would've—"

"Jennifer? Zak's wife? What was she like?" Acadia looked over her shoulder to make sure Zak wasn't behind her.

"Beautiful, fearless . . . Jesus, that woman went where

grown men feared to tread." Gideon paused. "She was also fucking bat-shit crazy."

Poor Zak. "Mentally ill? Or just . . . you know?"

"As far as I know, there wasn't a medical diagnosis," Zak's brother admitted as he ruthlessly sliced away a dense tangle of vines blocking their path. "But she was loud, theatrical, and a congenital liar. One never knew if she was acting or not, she was that good at BS. I've never met a more selfish, self-serving woman in my life. Jennifer wasn't just fearless, she was reckless, and she endangered anyone stupid enough to try to protect her from herself." He paused for a moment, breath rough as he had to use more muscle to cut through a large branch. "Zak never saw any of it. For some inexplicable reason she was the love of his life. I never got it."

Acadia helped him drag aside the branches he'd cut. "You didn't like her." She stated the obvious. She felt sorry for Zak, because even loving his wife as much as he had, it couldn't have been easy living with someone like that.

"I didn't like who *Zak* was around her. He—" He abruptly stopped talking. His shoulder-length dark hair snagged on a branch as he turned to flash very white teeth in her general direction. But he was looking behind her. "You okay back there, Zak-attack?"

Zak put a finger to his lips and motioned for Gideon to continue walking and lower the volume of their conversation. Acadia didn't speak Starkese, but she didn't need to. Someone was behind them.

That was why Zak had insisted his brother lead. With

Gideon hurt, he'd intentionally placed himself between them and anyone coming up behind them. All right, maybe he didn't want to be a hero, but he was watching out for his brother.

Despite his snarling sarcasm, that knowledge made her estimation of his character climb a few notches. The fact that he'd lost the love of his life was really sad. Gideon might not have liked Zak's wife, but the brothers were obviously close. They watched out for each other. Cared. Like family was supposed to.

Like her family used to, before everything went to hell.

She'd always wanted a sibling. A brother, maybe, like Gideon. Staff Sergeant Dad would've loved having a son instead of the girlie-girl daughter who'd had zero interest in wilderness survival or combat training. Although, come to think of it, both skills would have come in pretty damned handy right now.

Gideon took her arm and propelled her forward, slashing the machete faster and bringing her along in his wake. "So you know all about sports equipment and camping, right?" He kept his voice low, but if it seemed like nonsense to her, Acadia suspected it was to give Zak time to fall behind whoever was following them.

"I'd better. I've worked at the store since junior high." She lowered her voice to barely a whisper. "Are you sure we should be talking?"

"They heard us already," Gideon whispered in return. "If we stop, they'll know we're on to them. Keep talking. Zak will deal with them."

"For a guy who claims not to be a hero, he's doing a fair impersonation of one." How many men were back there? Had Piñero returned early to find her men dropped and her prisoners gone? Acadia's adrenaline did a sharp spike. Zak was back there alone . . .

Gideon slashed at thick vegetation, jungle sap clinging to the blade. "He had a . . . situation a few years back. Doesn't want anyone to depend on him."

"His wife was killed in Haiti, right?"

As much as she wanted to hear all about Zakary Stark and what made him the man he was—hell, as much as she wanted to hear about anything that took her mind off this mess—her ears were tuned to the sounds around them. The rustle of the leaves, a scratch of claws on bark as small animals scurried nearby, bright eyes watching their progress.

Waiting for the sound of automatic gunfire to erupt behind them, every cell in her exhausted body was braced for the impact of a bullet in her back. "She was a war correspondent for CNN, right?" she continued, shoving a tangled clump of leafy vines aside like a curtain.

"She took unnecessary risks . . . Look, if you want to know, ask Zak. He was the Jennifer Stark expert."

Acadia wasn't Zak's type. Gideon didn't have to say the words aloud for her to get that message. Putting up his hand, he stopped. *Thank God.*

It didn't seem right, anyway, to talk about her one-night stand's dead wife in the middle of a jungle escape. Or maybe ever. She lifted her hand to shove aside another thick green vine, and it reared up and looked her in the eye, then opened its yellow mouth and flicked its tongue at her.

"I'll wait here," Acadia whispered after she'd jumped back, hand over her heart, and managed to get her breath back. Her heart was beating overtime with fear. As much as she didn't relish being left alone, she said softly, "Go back and help him."

She stomped her feet as a winding army of red ants started an organized march over the toe of her boot.

"He doesn't need help, sweetheart. Zak can handle himself just fine."

"But why should he when we're here?" she asked reasonably, scraping the last four clinging ants off her boot with a leaf.

"Know how to use that?" he asked, voice very low. She glanced up from her feet to see he was indicating the Uzi slung over her shoulder. "It can be a bit unruly." Not waiting for an answer, Gideon pulled one of the hand-guns out of his belt. "Know how to use this?"

Acadia accepted the gun. Her father had always meant to take her to the range, but never had. And it was one thing to show a customer a gun's features in the store, another to shoot someone in cold blood. She swallowed hard. "I'm a crack shot," she lied through her teeth. In this instance, *in theory* was good enough, and she figured motivation would help her aim considerably. "Go."

He reached over and clicked off the safety, then used the blade of the machete to lift the barrel to chest height. "Not Zak or me. Point and fire." One minute he was beside her, the next just the movement of the foliage indicated he'd been there at all.

Indecisively, Acadia stood dead still for several minutes. She listened intently, her palms growing damp and slick. Every crack of settling branches, every whisper of moving foliage, even her own heartbeat, gathered like a slick knot of paranoia and fear in her gut.

A six-inch, emerald green lizard watched her from a nearby branch. The red ants marched in a wide, serpentine swath up the rough trunk of a nearby tree. A bird called. Leaves rustled as some small, unseen animal darted over and around protruding roots.

It sounded like . . . nature.

No voices. No gunshots.

God. Acadia's heart almost stopped. Were Zak and Gideon dead? The locals must know of ways to kill their prey without making a sound. The very thought that the two men were dead, and that she might be all alone, with no one close by to call upon but raping, pillaging guerrillas, chilled her to the bone. And the small scared part of her brain wanted to yell, "What about me?"

Because being *alone* in this vast greenness terrified her, and her panic level was escalating by the second.

Stay? Go?

She hefted the gun and cautiously followed the path of slashed branches back the way she'd come, struggling not to imagine feral hunting cats or—worse, probably— sweaty guerrillas behind every shrub.

Zak met her halfway, Gideon behind him. The relief she felt at seeing the two men was profound. She searched Zak's face and body for any signs of injury. Other than the bruise on his temple, he looked like the same cranky, hot and sweaty, preoccupied guy. And, God help her, incredibly sexy. He'd taken off his shirt and stuffed it in his waistband. Sweat trickled down his broad chest and sparkled like diamonds in his chest hair, which narrowed in a line down toward—

Acadia dragged her attention back to his face. "What happened?"

"Just a jaguar."

She let out a huff of a breath. "Oh, if only you were referring to the car, and not some ravenous wild animal looking at us as a potential snack."

Gideon barely hid a smile. "She was just curious. More scared of us."

Acadia took another deep breath, the arm holding the gun shaking. "No one from the camp is following us?"

"Not yet," Zak said flatly. "But they will. If Piñero does come back tonight, you can bet your ass she'll be on us like white on rice. The more miles we can push between now and dusk, the better our chances will be."

He glanced at the gun in her hand. "Know how to use that?"

"I work in a sporting goods store. What do you think?"

His eyes said exactly what he thought. He made a twirling motion with his hand and said to her back when she spun on her boot heel, "Just don't shoot yourself in the foot. I'm not carrying you."

Maybe the jaguar would get him.

TWO GRUELING HOURS LATER, Zak called a break. Gideon clearly needed medical attention, and Acadia was flagging, although neither had complained. He consistently checked their direction, both on his watch GPS and on the small handheld GPS Acadia had brought with her. At the rate they were going, they had six or seven grueling hours still to go before they reached the river. Zak knew they couldn't continue after dark. He added the time for them to stop and make a rudimentary camp. But the longer they were in the jungle, the higher the risk of the guerrillas' catching up with them.

How much longer could Gid go on? Skin gray, he was clearly in a lot of pain, and favoring his side more and more. Cracked ribs were bad enough. But what if one was broken? Gid could puncture a lung before they reached civilization. And the more time Zak spent with the ever prepared Acadia Gray, the more he realized just how fucking scared he was that this would go south at any second. That Piñero's men wouldn't be given the same constraints to stay away from her a second time. They were out here, hundreds of miles from civilization, with determined bad guys closing in, in a jungle filled with deadly animals, snakes, and insects. They were fucking lunch on the run.

The only thing ensuring Gideon's and Acadia's safety was himself.

He didn't fucking want the job.

"There's water here." He indicated a fast-running trickle of golden-brown water running through a mossy crease and disappearing into the foliage. "Let's drink our fill, and catch our breath."

Acadia hesitated. "I have a SteriPEN to purify the water, but I don't have a container big enough for all of us to drink out of."

Of course she did. "Then I guess we'd better hope our shots protect us, because this is the only game in town."

"I also have iodine tablets."

"If we want to wait around thirty minutes for them to take effect? Take a risk, or go without a drink. We're not hanging around here that long."

She drew in a breath. "Right." Then she sank to the ground and leaned over, cupping her hands. The long golden swath of her ponytail fell into the water beside her face, but she didn't seem to care, just kept drinking.

Jennifer wouldn't have touched that water without someone ensuring it was purified, and preferably bottled and chilled. His wife had thrived on danger and difficult conditions, as long as someone made sure she was safe and had all her creature comforts. She'd sought out filthy places, but hated getting dirty. It was a strange dichotomy Zak had never understood.

The difference between the two women, he thought, feeling a heavy sense of disloyalty, was that Jennifer, while wanting to be here, would've expected someone else to tote her shit, expected someone else to protect her, and expected that when she was tired, Zak—or someone—would make a comfortable camp for her.

Acadia just assessed the situation and kept going.

She was wise to have low expectations with him around. And he knew those expectation were at ground level . . . for now. Give her a few more hours of trudging through impenetrable vegetation with the very real possibility of getting shot, and the bitching would start. She was like waiting for the other shoe to drop, Zak thought sourly.

He observed how gingerly his brother knelt beside her, favoring his right side as he bent and giving a little involuntary grunt of pain. Acadia put a slender, dirty hand on his arm. "Hang on."

She rose and felt down her right calf almost to her ankle.

Zak crouched beside the stream. "You're a regular Girl Scout," he said sarcastically. "Got a water bottle in there?"

"Zak," Gideon cautioned, giving him a puzzled glance.

She ignored the sarcasm. "I wish." Acadia dug in an unseen pocket and pulled out a little silver triangle and popped it open. A folding cup. Of fucking *course* she had a *cup* on her. She dipped it in the water and handed it to Gideon.

Gideon lowered himself carefully to the ground, a hand on his ribs. Once settled, he accepted the water and drank, then dipped the cup back into the stream and gave her a grateful smile. "You're incredible."

"I'm *prepared*." She dipped her fingers into the stream

and rubbed them on the back of her neck with a sigh. "Although quite frankly, it never crossed my mind that what I packed would be this necessary. My friend Julia booked the river tour, but there were three nights of camping included, and I just . . . Well, you never know when you'll need—"

"A folding cup?" Zak muttered, annoyed with himself for letting her slip under his skin. Gideon was a likable guy. Of course she'd be attracted to him. The fact that she'd had that sassy mouth all over *him* just hours ago was beside the point. The friendly light in her eyes diminished when she looked at him. Fine. Zak wasn't trying to fucking make friends here.

This was a life-and-death situation, and he was the one responsible for the safety of all three of them. He didn't want the goddamned job, he hadn't asked for the goddamned job, hell, he wasn't qualified for the job, but no one else had stepped forward.

"Or eyedrops," she said pointedly, then pulled out a foil-wrapped bar from a pocket on the side of her right knee. "Protein bar." Then she went back for another and sat cross-legged on the spongy ground, lifting her hip to rearrange whatever was in a back pocket and using her teeth to tear the wrapping from each bar. She broke off an inch of each, then handed Zak and Gideon the balance.

"All right," Gideon said as he leaned against a tree trunk and stretched out his legs. "Now you've got me curious. What else is in your magic pockets, sweetheart?"

While Zak knew that his brother was just as determined as he was to get the fuck out of all this green, he looked like he was settling in to score points with Acadia. Something about that made the hair on Zak's neck stand up. They didn't have time to sit here at all, let alone loiter around chatting like they were in a damned pickup bar.

Gideon was using *that* voice. The voice he used when he wanted to get into some attractive woman's pants.

Sorry, bro. Been there, done that. And, God help him, he wanted to do it again.

Why the hell did *he* feel like a third wheel?

"I'm just happy you have them," Gid answered—referring, Zak presumed, to her magic pockets. "And that you're along for the ride." Gideon grinned as he shoved a hank of long hair over his shoulder and repositioned the webbed strap of the Uzi across his chest. His eyes were shadowed and his skin looked pale against a day's growth of beard. "Believe me, if I ever go on another survival adventure, I'm taking you with me."

"I don't need another adventure, thank you. This trip was something my friends coerced me into doing to put a little spice in my life. I think even they'll admit this is going way farther than any of us intended." Holding a piece of protein bar between her teeth, she made a "wait" motion with an upheld finger.

She took a tangle of rubber bands out of a breast pocket, untangled one, and handed it to Gideon. She closed her lips over the piece of protein bar and chewed as his brother acted like she'd just given him the keys to the castle and scooped his too-long hair back and secured it.

"Marry me, woman."

"No thanks," she replied cheerfully. "I suspect you two live life a little too far out on a limb for my small-town-girl tastes. I presume you were going to jump the falls with your brother?"

"This week, jump the falls; next week, Alpine ice climbing."

Acadia shrugged. "Ah, see there? This week, *see* the falls; next week, back to refolding pup tents at the store. We're just too different."

Jump the falls, his ass. She was a terrible liar. "*See* the falls?" Zak queried silkily, and raised an eyebrow as her laughing gaze met his.

Zak ate the dense chocolate bar, glad to have it. For all he knew, Acadia, the pole dancer who *wasn't*, had a six-course gourmet meal secreted somewhere on her. "Right. When you kids have finished flirting, we need to get mov—"

He froze as all the ambient noise in the jungle suddenly ceased. Gideon and Acadia looked at him intently, Gid shifting quietly to get access to one of the handguns at his waist.

Zak pointed, held up a hand for them to stay put, and went to investigate. He was in the mood to beat the shit out of someone.

Marry me, Zak thought as he picked his way carefully back the way they'd come. Gideon had never been married. He thought it was all fluffy fucking clouds and roses. He thought once the "I do's" had been said, the love just grew and deepened and it all became some magical fucking fairy tale and ended with happily ever after.

Zak hated to disillusion his older brother, but real-life marriage wasn't sprinkled with fairy dust.

A wife would get under his skin. A wife designed to love the thrill of adventure as much as he and Gid did wouldn't be able to help herself; she'd climb into his head and twist him around, make him doubt himself. Make him face himself, stare down mortality in a way that had *nothing* to do with extreme adrenaline and everything to do with his own helplessness as she died in some fucking war-torn country without him there to save her. Like Jennifer. *Fuckit.* Gid would find out if he survived. Right now, Zak needed to concentrate on that.

The birds had stopped singing. Now the jungle was a silent wall of dripping, humid vegetation as every living creature lay low. This wasn't your standard *oh, shit, a jaguar* silence. Humans were present. The jungle recognized the difference.

And so did he. They weren't even trying to be subtle.

Two men shoved their way through the undergrowth, coming straight toward him. Pug Face and Shorty. Neither looked up to see him standing right there in their path, feet spread, Uzi held over his shoulder like a baseball bat.

The men looked like shit. Pale and sweaty, and not too steady on their feet. Hardly a fair fight, but Zak wasn't feeling particularly fair at that moment.

They stood between him and a steak, a cold beer, a colder shower, and a clean, *empty* bed.

Instead of ducking out of sight, Zak charged. He swung the metal stock of the Uzi at Pug Face like a club before the man saw it coming. The flat edge hit him head-on in the nose with a satisfying crunch and spurt of blood, and drove bone and cartilage through the soft tissues. Up into the guy's brain. He dropped like a rock, dead before he hit the ground.

Zak stepped over Pug Face's prone body while Shorty was still fumbling to get his weapon in a position to fire. The electrical tape holding the grip assembly to the rear magazine well was firmly in place, but the ratchet on the bolt-retracting slide was giving him trouble in this humid heat. His sweat-slick, shaking hands tried to unlock the bolt so he could fire.

At this close a range, just three feet, Zak knew a 9mm Parabellum round would make a sizable hole in him, if Shorty ever got his shit together. He flexed his knees. "That's why I hate guns," Zak told the man in colloquial Spanish, straightening his back. "Never ready when I'm ready. Now, this?" He bent from the hip socket. "*This* is ready."

Using a baseball grip on the sixteen-inch barrel of the machine gun, he swung it like a golf club. As every pro said, it was all about the follow-through. Golf was a boring-as-hell game, but Zak had found a more creative way to use his skill. Just as Shorty switched gears and pulled the Taurus from his belt, the stock of the Uzi slammed up into his chin, knocking him on his ass.

A bullet discharged from the handgun and scared the crap out of a flock of red-and-green parrots, causing them to catapult through the treetops, shrieking and flapping their wings. Zak's heart rate hadn't elevated in the slightest. Maybe Jennifer had been right. He was dead, he just didn't know it.

Even when he staggered back in reaction to the bullet that slammed into his shoulder, he didn't feel anything, emotionally or physically. But that round of fire was exactly what he'd been trying to fucking avoid. Might as well have sent up a here-I-am-come-and-get-me flare.

⟡ SIX ⟡

Zak picked up his shirt, which had dropped during the scuffle, shrugged it on and hastily did up the buttons, then hoisted the Uzi back onto his shoulder.

Just in time; when he glanced up, Acadia and his brother stood waiting for him, and this time his heart did a little skip. Delayed reaction, he figured. He bent down to the first man to hide the blood already seeping into his shirtfront. He checked for pulses. Zip. "Both dead. Help me hide the bodies, then let's get cracking. That round of fire will pinpoint our direction."

Surreptitiously he snatched the bandana from Shorty's pocket. Christ only knew what kind of crap was on it, but it was better than nothing. He shoved it between his skin and his shirt. The webbed strap of the Uzi would keep it in place until he had time to see how bad it was.

"Were you . . . ?" Gideon indicated the blood on Zak's shirt when he straightened.

"Shorty's nose. I'm fine." No point worrying him. Zak had been shot before. It was going to hurt like hell soon enough, and whining wasn't going to get the bullet out.

Gideon helped him shove the bodies under a clump of dense foliage.

"We have to split up." Gideon gave Zak a hard look as he straightened. "Yeah, they *will* keep following, but we'll reduce the numbers if they have two trails to follow."

Zak didn't need to see the color of Gideon's skin to know he was in serious pain. "No. We stay together; safety in numbers."

"I'll swing back, way back, cover your ass while you get Acadia to safety."

Gideon wasn't listening. A common complaint Zak had about his brother. They were both strong-willed and stubborn, but Gid took the prize. "We don't have time to debate this. Two now, more right behind them if our luck doesn't hold. We stay together."

"We split up. Don't waste time arguing, Zakary. I'll travel faster by myself. We'll meet up in what? Two days? Gran Meliá?"

It did make a certain amount of sense. *If* both parties were uninjured. Fuckit. Gideon wasn't going to budge from this. If he said they had to split up, no matter how fucking ridiculous it was, he wasn't going to listen to any amount of logic.

"You take her," Zak ordered, resigned. "She'll be safer with you. We'll meet up at the Gran Meliá Hotel in two days, three at the m——"

Gideon cut him off. "No." He checked the clip in his sidearm, then glanced at Zak.

Zak turned to look fully at his brother. "Of course she'll be better off with you, Gideon. And you know it."

"Excuse me." Acadia took a step forward. "I get a say in this."

Both men ignored her. This was an argument that had been simmering for two years. Gideon was dead wrong.

"No," Gideon repeated flatly. "I won't take her with me. You'll have to suspend your fucking death wish until you get her safely to Caracas."

Zak's brain tangled at the thought of being alone with Acadia for even a moment. "Not that shit again, Gideon. Doesn't matter how many times you *say* it, it isn't true."

"For the last two years you've been doing everything in your power to join Jennifer. I won't let that happen, and I've just about killed myself trying to keep you around. Take the girl to Caracas. Use the time to talk yourself out of doing anything more stupid than you have to."

In his peripheral vision, Zak saw Acadia's gray eyes widen. God damn it.

Gideon pressed on grimly. "I've watched you, Zak, and I've talked until I'm fucking blue in the face. I can't seem to get through to you. You haven't just enjoyed all the extreme shit we're into; you've lived carelessly, irresponsibly, *stupidly*, and you've taken insane risks. You've done everything short of pulling a trigger on yourself. Maybe having to take care of someone else will remind you to live."

Zak's fists clenched. "Same shit, different day. Already fucking proven I'm lousy at the job," he snapped. "Want to risk her life to make your point?"

"Three days. Consider it an early birthday present."

"I'd rather buy you that Bugatti Veyron."

"Yeah. I know. Get to Caracas alive, and maybe you'll be able to do that, too." Gideon clasped his shoulder. "Take care. See you in there."

"Gid, this is fucking *insane*, don't—"

Unlike Shorty, Gideon had the third safety off as he aimed the automatic at Zak's chest. He stepped back. "I can help you out and end it for you here, or you can get Acadia back to safety. Your call."

Acadia didn't move a muscle.

Zak half laughed. "Jesus, Gid . . ."

Gideon's eyes, so much like his own, were hard and ice cold as he repeated, "Call it, Zakary."

A long, tense silence followed. Then, teeth clenched, Zak growled, "Fine." Gideon wasn't going to shoot him, no matter the provocation. But Zak didn't want to exacerbate the already volatile situation. Gid was injured. A scuffle, however well intentioned, would hurt him.

The muzzle lifted from his chest, shifted until it pointed safely at the ground. "Good," Gideon said quietly.

As he turned to go, Acadia stepped forward. "Wait a minute, here!" She pulled the stolen Uzi strap from her shoulder, rummaging in one of her many pockets with the other hand. "You can use this better than me," she said quickly, "and here's in case you, uh . . ." She hesitated as she pulled out a handful of magical mystery protein bars. "Protein will give you energy." She glanced over at Zak. "I'm giving your brother the GPS. You have one on your watch, right?"

"Yeah." Zak wished he'd thought if it himself. On the other hand, Gid wouldn't need a GPS if they all stuck together.

Gideon accepted the handful of stuff Acadia handed him, shoving things into his pockets, then nodded at her, his smile quick, and Zak felt as if he'd been kicked in the stomach when she smiled back. Gideon pushed off into the jungle, and for a long moment, all they heard was the rhythmic, muffled *thwack!* of his machete slicing and dicing foliage.

"Fuckit," Zak muttered.

Acadia's eyes were stormy as she spun to glare at him. "You tried to pawn me off on your *brother*?"

"It wasn't personal." The idiot had broken ribs. How long did he— Double fuckit.

"I *slept* with you," Acadia said tightly, color high on her cheeks. "That's pretty damned personal to me."

"He would've protected you better."

There were several beats of silence as she glanced at the wall of green where his brother had disappeared, then back at Zakary. "Too bad he *wouldn't* have shot you."

She sounded pretty sure about that. "You don't know my brother," Zak told her, only half in jest.

He'd never seen that expression on Gideon's face before. He didn't like it. Didn't like knowing Gid was worried about him. Didn't like that he'd been oblivious to that added layer of concern for years.

Didn't like—God damn it—that his brother might be right.

She cocked her head, gaze steady. "*Do* you have a death wish?"

Did not giving a shit if he was alive or dead count? "Why? You gonna make a run for it?"

"No. Because two of us have a better chance of getting out of here alive than one," she said tightly. "If it wasn't for you, I'd be sipping umbrella drinks with my friends right now. You got us into this freaking mess, you'd better get us out in one piece. At least now I have a heads-up. Let's go."

Now he not only had to worry about Gideon out there, hurt and on his own without anyone to watch his back, but he had to make sure neither he nor Acadia croaked, just to prove a fucking point. Great.

He started walking.

"Hey!" She grabbed his wrist. Her pale, slender fingers looked incredibly fragile against his tanned skin. He could break those delicate bones without even trying. The fact that she believed he had a death wish, and still touched him, intrigued him.

Worse, through miles of jungle trekking, through running, being chased, and God only knew what the hell else, he could still smell the faint delicate sweet musk of night-blooming jasmine rising from her skin.

"Aren't you going to bring the other Uzi?" She hung on with tenacity instead of brute strength. The hot pink of her flushed cheeks made her gray eyes seem almost translucent, and a stream of dappled sunlight from above lit her mussed blond hair into a halo.

Zak yanked his hand out of her grasp and continued walking when he could, hacking and shoving aside vines when he couldn't. "I don't like guns."

"You don't li— You shot that—"

"Clubbed."

"That's splitting hairs." She sounded breathless as she trotted to keep up in a clear section that allowed him to pass through more quickly. "You couldn't have taken out those men without it."

Leaves drifted to the lush ground around them. He glanced up to find three tiny black monkeys following them, swinging high above their heads, chattering as they leaped hand over hand from branch to branch. They weren't scared of him either. Did he want Acadia Gray scared of him?

Yeah, Zak realized, he sure as hell did. And had been doing whatever he could to foster that attitude ever since he'd woken up that morning with a cockstand and a gun held to his head.

He didn't need a shrink to tell him it was because she had a fucking way of knocking small chinks out of the wall he'd built around himself. He could feel the drafts. She talked too damned much, and she saw too much with those soft eyes that missed nothing.

She was like a fucking Weeble—he just couldn't knock her down. And while he admired her for it, the trait annoyed him at the same time. "Warranted," he told her, forging on. "Now our lives aren't in imminent danger. No guns. This'll do." He held up the wicked-looking two-foot-long machete, realizing that far from working out his aggression on those two yahoos, he was now more pissed than ever.

"I'm not crazy about guns either." She came up beside him and threw him a wary look. "But Piñero and her men could still come after us any minute, and at least we could fire warning shots to hold them off. Or something." She stopped dead in her tracks. "Can I at least go back for it?"

Zak's grip around her upper arm tightened as she pulled in the opposite direction. "Leave it."

"You are insane. *They* don't mind guns and have plenty of them. We *needed* that. How are we going to protect ourselves?"

"You have that." He indicated the Taurus revolver stuck in her belt, then held up the machete. "I have this. Get the lead out. I want to beat my brother to Caracas."

"Why do you do that?"

"What? You don't like honesty?"

"That's not honesty," she told him, shaking her head until her messy ponytail swung. "Why do you always turn into a jerk again? Just as I start to like you." She didn't say it with any level of heat, but he believed her.

And didn't like that it bothered him.

"You would've hated me eventually," he said, gaze straight ahead. "I just saved you time."

She wasn't easily intimidated, which was both damned irritating and, yeah, he allowed to himself, a little—*just a little*—intriguing. Shit. He didn't want to be intrigued.

He wanted out of this jungle, and wanted the gray-eyed tagalong out of his life for good.

He consulted the GPS on his watch, thought about the one she'd given his brother, and had to admit she'd pulled her weight, plus some, on this little adventure. He headed in the general direction of the river and decided to wait until the last minute to make camp.

Darkness was for feeding, and they were food.

Acadia's footsteps crunched behind him, and he thought about Gideon out there in the wet forest alone. Stupid bastard called *him* careless and irresponsible? Zak snorted. As far as he was concerned, Gideon was way out of line. The extreme sports they enjoyed so much made them *both* crazy thrill-seekers.

That was the way it had always been. It was the way they'd lived for most of their adult lives. Nothing had changed since Jennifer had . . . since Jennifer. She'd come along, as crazy for it as they were with her constant forays into war-ravaged countries, pushing her nose into dangerous shit for the story—or at least she had *said* it was for the story. But he knew.

He recognized a kindred soul. Jennifer had lived for the rush.

And died by it.

It changed nothing, he told himself silently. The brothers had always tackled the highest mountain, the steepest ice waterfall, the fastest track. Slash, slice, hack. And it sure as hell wasn't any different now as he chopped a path through the understory, his burning muscles fueled by hot anger. The machete was sharp, and Zak used it to good effect, hacking through the vegetation as fast as he could, leaving debris in his wake. He knew he might as well paint a fluorescent arrow behind them, but at this point, speed was more valuable than stealth. The bastards would catch up, he suspected sooner than later with a nice clear path to follow.

They knew the jungle; he didn't. But he was a hell of a lot more determined to stay alive than they were to kill him. He hoped.

Acadia's breathing was a little irregular, but she was holding her own and keeping up. He slashed through a tangle of vines as thick as his wrist, and a shower of small red spiders rained down on them. She cut herself off mid-cry, staying right on his heels as she brushed them off herself, then swept the little suckers off his shoulders and back while they walked. She was like a mother monkey picking fleas off its baby.

But Zak didn't tell her to stop, even after the spiders were long gone. He liked the feel of her hands on him, even if it wasn't sexual. Which was weird. And entirely unwelcome. But he didn't say anything as she took advantage of every opportunity and space to walk beside him.

Even though he was using his right arm to wield the machete, his left shoulder burned as if someone were holding a red-hot poker to it. Zak ignored the pain. Eventually the site would go numb; until then he'd ignore it.

She didn't shriek when they encountered a Colombian giant tarantula eight inches across, bobbing and wiggling its pink spiny legs inches from her face, or later, when they almost tripped over a python as thick as her own thigh hanging lazily from a low limb.

A dog-size tapir shot across their path, squealing as it ran through the heavy undergrowth. That was good news. Meant they were getting closer to water. At least they were heading in the right direction.

"We're cutting a map for anyone to follow us, aren't we?" Acadia suddenly asked, and he didn't have to see her face to know it was a rhetorical question. They hadn't spoken for half an hour; Zak suspected it was a record for his loquacious fellow escapee.

"No way to avoid it." And better him than his injured brother. *Damned idiot.* "If we're lucky, we're several hours ahead of anyone following us." He doubted the guerrillas would wait that long. Sick or not, they'd be on their trail before Piñero returned from making her ransom demands. Zak bet those guys would rather die puking and shitting in the jungle than face their boss when she come back to find the prisoners gone. As if reading his mind, a flock of tiny yellow-and-black troupials catapulted out of the trees and swooped overhead.

Birds flew *away* from danger.

Shit. Hadn't heard a damned thing. They'd shown up a hell of a lot faster than he'd anticipated.

Zak wrapped his arm about Acadia's waist and pulled her tight against his hip. Her eyes went wide. She didn't have to be told that the other shoe had just dropped.

⊶ SEVEN ⊶

Arm lassoed around Acadia's waist, Zak took her down behind a thick, spiky shrub covered in orange flowers. Not flowers, *butterflies*, which swooped up like tiny scattered autumn leaves at their movement.

They fell hard on the moist, spongy earth in a tangle of arms and legs, facing each other, hidden beneath the butterfly bush. Zak flung a protective arm over her head, holding her down and still, while the other tightened on her waist in warning.

This close she could see the small lines beside his eyes, and the dark bruise mottling the swollen skin surrounding the gash on his temple, distorting the old scar.

Obviously a man who liked to live dangerously, Zak had plenty of scars. And she realized with every passing second that she was a woman who didn't. With sudden, intense longing, Acadia missed her house just outside the army base, where she'd lived most of her adult life. She missed her local library, and her friends—*normal* friends—and she missed . . .

Her life. Her everyday, unexciting, fabulously uneventful life. This jungle adventure was an odd and too-dramatic segue between her normal life and going off to college at age thirty. And whining right now wasn't going to help. Her dad wouldn't ever let her sit around and complain. She was a smart woman. She had a strong man at her side—even if he didn't want to be there, she reminded herself—and now wasn't the time to be thinking about anything but getting to safety.

All right, so Acadia Gray, manager of Jim's Sporting Goods, should not be lying under a freaking shrub with a surly, scarred guy carrying a death wish and a machete. But she was. So she'd have to make the best of it.

The Swiss Army Knife dug into her hip, a branch poked her cheek, and Zak's leg was sandwiched between hers. His heavy arm slung across her waist brought back memories of the last time they'd been so close. And naked. Okay, so a surly, *hot* guy.

The voices came nearer. Well, *voice*. No mistaking the rotgut-whiskey tones of Loida Piñero. Over the bitching and complaining from their leader, Acadia heard the thud, crack, and rustle of the soldiers' footfalls heading straight for them.

Her pulse leaped. God, they were coming closer and closer, easily following the trail Zak had made for them. Moving just her eyes she was able to see the leaves and grasses near their hiding place vibrate with the passage of heavy boots. She held her breath, expecting at any moment to feel a gun barrel slam into the back of her skull.

One. Two. Three—

Pressure settled into the small of her back. Her whole

body flinched, but it was just Zak's hand, flat and firm and holding her in place. A silent order to remain still. She blinked to let him know she got his unnecessary message loud and freaking clear.

And then froze as her cheek tickled. Her skin itched, prickled, as something crawled s-l-o-w-l-y across her face. She gritted her teeth, not daring to move, not wanting to look. A deadly insect bite wasn't at the top of her I'm-peeing-my-pants fear list; that distinction belonged to the seven pairs of boots passing a few feet away from her nose. The guerrillas made no attempt at being stealthy or quiet.

When Loida Piñero had returned with her men to camp, she hadn't been happy. She was still pissed off.

Acadia didn't understand half of what she was yelling; all she knew was the woman was furious and that *cabezas rodarán*. A quick check through her limited Spanish filled in the translation: Heads would roll.

As the last pair of boots passed, one of the men assured Piñero that eventually the Americans *would* be caught and taken back to camp. Acadia's mouth dried as Loida Piñero vented her fury, and she had no problem understanding the gist when the woman said coldly, "We will hunt them until we find them. Understand? Kill one man on sight. I don't care which. Bring the other back to camp. The woman? You can have her, she is of no importance."

Acadia wasn't sure whether to be relieved or insulted. She opted for terrified.

Piñero's strident, gravelly voice eventually petered out as the group moved through the trees, shouting for their missing comrades. They'd passed the bodies hidden under the brush back on the path and not seen them.

Acadia strained to hear them as their voices faded.

The jungle was eerily quiet, as if holding its breath. No birdsong. No susurrus of insects. Her own erratic, overly loud heartbeat was the only musical score to the drama surrounding her. Hers, and . . . She shifted her eyes to the side as she realized the echoing thud near her ear was Zak's heartbeat, as rapid as hers despite his utter stillness.

A few minutes later the miniature butterflies flocked back in a riot of orange, lighting soundlessly on the glossy dark green leaves overhead.

She must've moved slightly, because Zak gave a slight shake of his head. While she waited for whatever was creeping across her face to creep back off, she tried to order her chaotic, panicked thoughts into some form of rational process that wasn't motivated by bone-deep fear. Being afraid all the time was just exhausting. Hard to sustain. She couldn't imagine what Zak and his brother did all day, chasing their thrills for hours.

When she opened her eyes again—because she couldn't not know what was happening—Zak's face was just inches from hers. His white teeth flashed in a grin.

She stared.

My God, the crazy man was *enjoying* this. It was the first time, the *only* time, she'd seen a genuine smile from him all freaking day. It was so . . . *inappropriate*, so insane, she couldn't believe what she was seeing. She shook her head, a tiny involuntary movement of incredulity.

His face was filthy. Chocolate-frosting-colored mud streaked his stubbled cheek; his hazel eyes looked more green than brown as they reflected the verdant vegetation surrounding them, and the gleam in them was impossible to misinterpret.

He was having fun. *Fun!*

Despite being kidnapped. Despite almost being killed. God help them, despite being in the middle of a damned jungle without a map or transportation, the maniac was having a blast.

It was so much the opposite of what she was feeling that Acadia couldn't wrap her head around it; she felt disoriented. Which was probably why she was charmed as she lay there squished against him, a twig poking into her cheek and a *thing* strolling across it.

He slid his hand up the small of her back in an insidious caress, and she felt just how damp her clothes were against her skin, and just how warm his fingers were through the fabric. She gave him a fierce scowl.

The ground was wet, and things moved all around her. Big things and little creepy-crawly things. She shivered. "I'd like to get up," she whispered firmly. "They're way far away now." Indeed, the birds and other chirpy, squeaky, trilling denizens of the forest were back in full voice. And her entire right side was saturated with . . . she'd go with *dirt*.

The good news was that the bug had flown off her cheek, but she still had the urge to touch her face to make sure. Changing her depth perception brought Zak into focus. She could see each individual eyelash, and the darker green band surrounding his irises. His sensual smile deepened the groove in his cheek, and the devil danced in his eyes, tearing away all thoughts of bugs and sanitizers and . . . This was a ridiculously insane time to show her he could be anything other than serious, or to show off a hidden dimple.

The flutter in her tummy became a gallop as the silence between them thickened, punctuated by water dripping off a nearby leaf, the croak of a small tree frog, the rustle of leaves as *things* moved around them.

The jungle came to life, and he didn't move or say a word as his gaze dropped to her mouth.

His brother was right. Zak Stark was certifiably insane, and he *did* have a death wish. Neither of which made her not want him in every way there was.

Again.

The naked hunger in his eyes shocked her. But more alarming was her own instant response, swift and needy in a way she wouldn't have expected from herself. So who was the crazy one?

"Give them another couple of minutes." His quiet voice sounded rough, his breathing uneven; his pupils dilated, and he lightly curved his big hand around her nape, making Acadia shiver. And in spite of the fear skittering inside the rational fringes of her mind, she shuddered in response to his touch. He cupped her damp neck and, with a little pressure exerted by his thumb at the base of her head, tilted her face up.

His long, lean-muscled body touched hers from her shoulder to toes, his mouth an inch away. *Dirt*, she told herself frantically. *Guerrillas, jungle. Bugs!*

Then he closed the gap.

Acadia's eyes fluttered shut as his mouth took hers in a hot, hungry, devouring kiss that catapulted her back into that seedy hotel room where this had all started. She hadn't thought then, and she couldn't think now.

The kiss wasn't slow or tentative. It was a kiss between partners who'd already kissed every part of each other's body in a tumultuous, all-night sexathon. It was the touch of a man who knew exactly how she melted like warm honey when he kissed the shell of her ear, and who knew exactly how to dip his tongue into the sensitive hollow behind it for maximum effect.

Drunk on his hunger, goaded by it, Acadia matched it with a voracious need that blindsided her, giving no quarter and not expecting him to give her any. She'd never felt such intense attraction before in her life, and she had a feeling she never would again. Everything about Zak turned her on. He smelled so good: clean sweat, the soap he'd used in the shower they'd shared so many hours ago, wintergreen mint, even jungle earth. Zak had his own smell, and she knew she'd recognize it anywhere.

She reached up to touch his scratchy, unshaven jaw as his tongue avidly dueled with hers. His mouth was bold, take-no-prisoners, a pirate plundering and taking without asking.

His fingers slid up her hot scalp to tangle in her hair. She heard the tiny snap of the breaking rubber band as he fisted his fingers in the damp strands. She shifted to wrap an arm around his neck and press her other hand against the steady thump of his heart. He slid his knee up tighter into the junction of her legs, and she tightened her muscles hard against the pressure.

He breathed a muffled curse against her throat as she squirmed against the damp ground, trying to get more contact as his lips once more covered hers. Her body remembered every decadent, deliciously devilish thing that had happened between them, and wanted more. Wanted so much that she arched, pressed her breasts to his chest; wanted so badly that her blood sang as his fingers tightened in her hair.

Suddenly he broke away. She stayed where she was, realizing that at some point he'd pillowed her head on his arm. Her body hummed with awareness. And sudden rationality, mixed with a healthy dose of frustration.

He was a labyrinth of contradictions. An attentive lover one minute and a total nut-job the next. His brother claimed he had a death wish, yet Zak held her so gently, it made emotions she couldn't define swell into a lump in her throat. Of course he could do all that and be crazy as a loon as well, she reminded herself.

He was complicated and dangerous, and she was used to simple and safe. A man like Zakary Stark would be a lot of work. The woman interested in him would have to *know* she'd never be the love of his life. Would never fill the hole where his heart used to be.

A woman would have to keep her eyes open wide, and her heart protected, at all costs.

She wasn't that kind of woman.

"They're not going to give up," he told her, keeping his voice low. Acadia was gratified to see that he wasn't as unaffected as he sounded. Sweat beaded his forehead, and his eyes held a glassy sheen.

Good. She didn't want to be the only one who'd forgotten where they were for those few minutes.

"We'll keep well back and turn the tables on them. Use their trail to make headway. Turn off closer to the river. Are you ready for a little cat-and-mouse?"

"What if I say no?"

Zak got to his feet and held out his hand. "I'll bribe you with half of that steak and a cold shower."

Acadia didn't think they had a snowball's hope in hell of finding the river at this rate. Not with a horde of determined guerrillas hunting for them. One leaf looked exactly the same as another to her. As far as she was concerned, Caracas might as well be on the moon, and they were just as likely to have dinner there.

But they couldn't stay put, either. "Make that my own steak," she said wearily. She reached up to take his hand, and noticed a dark stain on her fingers. More mud, more sticky sap, more . . . Her eyes flicked from her hand to his shirtfront.

The blue cotton on his left shoulder was stained red. She actually felt the blood drain from her head, knew she had gone pale. "M-my God. You've been *shot!*"

"I noticed." Zak's voice was dry. "You don't faint at the sight of blood, do you?"

Sick to her stomach, she shook her head.

"Good." He hauled her to her feet beside him. "Look. I won't lie to you, this isn't optimal right now. But it isn't as bad as it looks. Just one more scar to talk about when I get home."

It was probably *worse* than it looked. And not optimal? A gunshot wound? Talk about a freaking understatement. "To scar," she said brusquely, "one has to *heal*. We're in a jungle, Zakary! The worst possible place to have an open wound— Sorry. That wasn't very diplomatic, was it? Let me take a look."

He gave her hand a tug to get her moving. "I'll check it when we stop for the night. With any luck we'll hit one of those villages."

"It must hurt like hell. We have to clean it. You know how dangerous it is to have an open wound in this environment." She was already patting her pockets. This new development had wiped her brain clean and she couldn't remember where she'd so carefully and methodically placed each item in which pocket. "I know I brought—"

"I don't need anything. We don't have time to stop."

"God," she muttered, waving her free hand to move the tiny gnats away from her mouth as she talked. "Undo your shirt. Let me see what we're dealing with here." She shoved aside a branch covered in waxlike lime green orchids. "A *wipe* for a bullet wound?" she asked herself out loud, trying to think. What was the best way to treat the wound, and what did she have on her to do it with? "Do you have any idea how surreal this all is? Don't answer that. Of course you do. I've never seen a guy with more scars than you."

Zak kept her moving. "It'll have to wait. Gotta keep moving."

She pulled away. "Don't be a selfish ass! If you won't think about yourself dropping dead out here, at least think about what will happen to me if you pass out and I'm here all alone."

She glared back when he gave her a belligerent look. "We'll treat that as best we can and *then* we'll continue. Don't look at me in that tone of voice, Stark. I mean it. Stand still, shut up, and unbutton your shirt."

"Oh, for the love of—"

She gave him a hard look and stood her ground. "*Do* it."

Zak unbuttoned his shirt with his right hand. Rivulets of blood had trickled down his left arm and fingers, then dried into a crusty brown she'd mistaken for mud.

She sucked in a slow breath as he pushed the sides open so she could see where he'd been shot. Dried blood stained his shoulder and chest. A bullet wound bled, she knew that. But God, seeing all that crimson on his muscled, healthy body, just inches away from his heart, made her stomach twist in a tight knot.

He started to shift away from her. She gave him the evil eye as she patted her pants pockets. "Stay."

She found what she was looking for and removed the pack of gauze bandages. Ripping the packet open with her teeth, she dug around in her pockets until she found a ziplock bag containing Band-Aids and a small tube of the waterless antiseptic gel that had become so popular during the swine flu scare. Easily juggling the items, she selected a couple of gauze pads, put the bag back into the hidden pocket, and started to assemble a dressing for the wound.

There was no red on the back of his shirt, which probably meant the bullet was still in there, just under the ball of his shoulder. And while he was now wielding the long machete with grace and power, it was in his right hand because the bullet wound impinged on his dominant side. Ambidextrous? She wouldn't doubt it.

"We can walk while you're doing that," he pointed out.

"Fine." She gave in, too busy to argue. "Walk slowly and don't swing that arm until I figure this out."

Zak's lips twitched as he cast a look sideways, watching Acadia make some sort of dressing while walking, sweating, and avoiding hanging vines that could be snakes. She was a remarkable woman.

"We'll be okay," he told her. "Trust me."

"I do," she said absently, not looking up from her task. Which made her just as certifiable as he was.

Acadia Gray was a resourceful woman to have around—a good thing, since Zak knew she'd need every ounce of her ingenuity in the coming hours. He concentrated on putting one foot in front of the other, focused on staying, well, *focused*. But his mind was going a million miles a minute trying to figure out what would happen to Acadia should he pass out. Nothing good. He hadn't needed her to point out the obvious. If he passed out— fuckit, if he *died*—she'd be screwed.

She'd be stranded, alone. In a jungle this big, the chances of being rescued were slim to zero. Had Gideon managed to elude the guerrillas, or were they hot on his ass as well? Piñero hadn't mentioned a second group of searchers when she'd passed by.

Not breaking stride, Acadia doused the pad in the antiseptic gel and passed it back to him. "Clean it as best you can. Tell me when you're done."

"It can wait."

"Don't be a baby. It's better than nothing. You could get an infection and die. I don't want to be out here alone."

Zak's low laugh sounded a little pained to his own ears. "Since you put it that way . . ." While he walked and cleansed the wound, he saw that Acadia was spreading more gel on the thick pad she was making. The blood flow wasn't stopping, but it was slowing. Or maybe that was wishful thinking. He stuffed the bloody pad into his back pocket and took a look at his shoulder.

"Done," he told her. Nope. Still bleeding. Sluggishly, a mere trickle compared to earlier, but enough. Damn it to hell.

She paused to hand him the prepared dressing. She'd attached the biggest Band-Aids across the back so he could stick it over the wound. Admiring her ingenuity and quick thinking, Zak pushed that half of his shirt aside.

Her eyes widened when she saw the blood gleaming wetly around the hole high on his shoulder. "Damn it, Zak."

He slapped the dressing over the wound, pressed the sticky tapes down as best he could, then closed his shirt and buttoned it. "It looks worse than it feels."

"Liar."

Maybe. "Let's go."

Acadia nodded, and Zak once more pushed off into the jungle, silently admitting that even if it was just a padded Band-Aid, having the bandage in place made him feel better.

He shouldn't have kissed her. The woman was some kind of subversive siren. Problem was, he wanted to kiss her again. Damn, he wanted to do a hell of a lot more than kiss her. Since that wasn't gonna happen anytime soon, he kept the image of her pale, jasmine-scented skin right at the forefront of his brain, where he could take it out and look at it whenever he wanted.

It was going to be a long hike. There was fuck-all he could do about the pain now throbbing and burning like a red-hot poker in his shoulder, so he thought instead of burying his mouth against the musky heat of her wet mound, of her hands fisted in his hair as her hips arched off the bed . . .

Shit. Just thinking about her from last night made him intensely aware of her beside him now. Very much alive. His job was to ensure she stayed that way.

The insects seemed louder around them, and much thicker. It took several minutes for Zak's brain to compute that it wasn't the abundant insect life of the jungle. As the foliage fuzzed around him, he realized that he was experiencing the not-unexpected onslaught of dizziness and weakness. Blood loss. Just fucking great.

He'd been shot more than an hour ago, and the rapid blood loss was causing him to see black spots in front of him as he pushed through the trees. The guerrillas were still ahead of them, far enough to give them a little breathing room. But he and Acadia had left the path that the guerrillas had cut to angle off toward the river. Zak knew it wasn't a case of *if* he lost consciousness. It was a case of *when*.

Acadia fished another rubber band out of her magic pockets and coiled her hair up into a messy knot on top of her head. They'd found another trickle of water, drunk their fill, and followed it for several miles without a sign of Loida Piñero and her merry band of thugs.

And without, God damn it, another sign of the river.

Fuckit. Had he gone off course? He raised his shoulder to wipe the sweat out of his eyes, causing supernovas to flare in his vision. He angled his wrist to see his watch. Right course. Walking was just too damned slow.

The air was heavy, indicating rain any minute. Sluicing the sticky sweat and dried blood off his skin would feel great, but he needed to make some sort of shelter.

Not only from the deluge about to hit, but from the animals that would be coming out soon to hunt as the sun sank below the trees and night fell.

As much as he wanted to think about a naked Acadia doing energetic calisthenics while straddling him, Zak had other, more pressing, concerns. The guerrillas didn't seem to know that the brothers had split up, which he hoped meant Gideon was free and clear. A big relief.

But why did Piñero want either himself or Gideon alive at all? She'd gone off to make ransom demands and presumably had sent pictures to ZAG's corporate offices, and Buck, in Seattle. That was proof of life. Logic said that once all that had been done, she'd come back to the camp to kill them. So why one and not the other?

"Why are you scowling like that?" Acadia whispered. "How bad's the pain? Are we being followed again?"

He shook his head, then wished he hadn't as he had to catch himself on a handy tree trunk to keep from keeling over. "Just wondering why Guerrilla Bitch didn't insist we all be killed on sight."

"Maybe she wants one of you as insurance?" She dug into her pocket and brought out the mints.

"Maybe."

"You have no idea where we are, do you?" She offered the plastic container to Zak and, when he shook his head, helped herself to one and put the container carefully back in her pocket.

"Piñero's headed back to camp—we saw their path an

hour ago, and it clearly indicated they'd gone back." Zak was having trouble getting his tongue to shape the words. Fuck. "We're heading to the river; I've been watching the sun when I can see it and the GPS puts us on target. We'll find someone to sell us a boat, and we'll head back to civilization. You'll be in a cold shower in Caracas this time tomorrow."

"I hate to be the bearer of bad news, Zakary Stark, but you said that an hour ago, and an hour before that." She sighed. "I think we should stop at a gas station and ask directions."

He stopped, and she bumped into his side, jarring his shoulder. He gritted his teeth, but put out a hand to pull her closer.

"Oh, God. What now?"

He used his forearm to haul her flush against his body, the long knife fisted behind her head. "I want another kiss to keep me going."

She tilted her face up, and when Zak touched his mouth to hers he felt her smile shimmer its way deep into his chest. He just wanted a small kiss, something to keep his energy level from taking a nosedive. But she tasted of wintergreen mint and wide-eyed promises, and suddenly he was starving.

No. Bad idea. He needed his blood pressure to level off, not for blood to pump even faster in his veins. He let her go. "I'm not worried," he told her. "We have food and water, and the predators sleep during the day." Most of them, anyway.

"The people who kidnapped us are predators, and I

bet they aren't going to take a little siesta because the sun is shining."

"Point taken. Keep walking anyway. There are several small settlements along the river. Someone will be willing to take us to the closest town."

"How will we pay them?"

"We'll barter my watch if necessary."

"I have twenty dollars in my boot."

Zak huffed out a laugh. "Of course you do. Actually"—he fished in his breast pocket and took out her chain and St. Christopher medallion—"we also have this."

Her eyes lit up as he let the long silver chain pour into her outstretched palm. "You got it back for me. Thank you, Zak." Her smoky eyes glowed. "My dad gave it to me wh— We used to plan exotic vacations. None of which we ever took," she admitted, "but the planning was fun. This was the last gift he gave me before he got sick. I—" Her features softened, her gaze turning suddenly a little misty as she put the chain over her head, then tucked the St. Christopher medallion inside her T-shirt. "Thanks."

"Both your parents died? How old were you?

"Thirteen for my mom. Complications from surgery. My father died three months ago."

"Rough."

"Yeah. It was."

That was it? He was surprised she wasn't milking the story for all it was worth. Zak kept Acadia in front and a little to the left of him, keeping himself between her and anyone who might be following them. There was nothing to put between her and whatever animals they might encounter, however.

The jungle was filled with predators, both four- and two-legged.

So far, so good.

He could tell by the slump of her shoulders that she had already been pushed past her physical endurance, yet she hadn't complained once, nor had she asked to stop so she could rest.

Zak instantly felt a wash of disloyalty and regret, coupled with a surge of anger at once again being placed in a no-fucking-win position.

It had been his job as Jen's husband to love and protect her, and he'd failed miserably on both counts. They'd lived together for a couple of years. Marriage had been a given. But Zak had realized long before the wedding that he'd made a terrible mistake. At first he'd accepted a hundred percent of the blame for the failure of his marriage right from the start.

Marrying Jennifer had been the path of least resistance. He, Gid, and Buck had been so busy building the company there was little time for anything else. And he regretted that deeply after her death.

During the six years of their marriage she'd been bored, restless. Impossible to appease. She'd started going on trips alone. She'd gotten the job at CNN. Their lives separated, the gap widening more every day.

He'd suddenly noticed, and realized that if he didn't

put some work into it, the marriage was going to fall apart. But by then it was too late.

Gideon and Buck believed that Jennifer had been the love of his life; unfortunately, that hadn't been the case—not that Zak believed such a perfect union existed. No, Jennifer hadn't been the love of his life. But he had owed her his loyalty, and he had owed her his respect and devotion in public. The promises had been implicit in their vows. For better or worse. She'd been his responsibility. And no matter what she'd done, he'd failed her on every count.

"I'll take a mint." Shit, his voice sounded thready and weak. He'd give a fortune for a safe place to lie down for an hour.

Acadia dug the almost-empty container out of her pocket and shook two into her hand. "Good idea." She gave him a concerned look as she placed the small mints in his outstretched palm. "The sugar might help."

He was way beyond the help of a couple of candies.

And while Acadia doggedly kept putting one foot in front of the other, his strength was ebbing with each step. Sooner than he would have liked, dusk crowded out the little bit of blue sky visible through the dense foliage. It would be full dark within the hour. They had no shelter other than whatever he could jerry-rig together, an all but impossible task when it was dark. He kept an eye out for a likely place to stop. The dappled greens blurred ominously in his vision.

"We need to find a place to stop for the night." He

caught himself on a tree trunk, his vision wavering as though he were seeing everything underwater. His legs buckled. Not good.

"What am I looking for?" Her voice sounded far away, as if heard through a tunnel.

He frowned, trying his damnedest to focus. "Thick underbrush . . . Branches . . . Cove—"

·➤ EIGHT ➤·

Z ak?" Acadia glanced over her shoulder when he
    didn't finish the sentence. "Is something— Oh,
    crap, crap, crap!" His long body was sprawled
on the ground several yards behind her. Racing to his
side, she dropped to her knees in the spongy dirt. His
face was gray, his breathing labored, and he was clearly
unconscious. Her heart did a triple Axel as she frantically
looked around.

"For what?" she muttered under her breath. "A para-
medic?"

Pressing her fingers against the unsteady pulse behind
his ear, Acadia wished she knew which was good. Fast or
slow? What could she do about his pulse, anyway? What
could she do about *any* of this mess? Sitting back on her
heels, she cocked her head, straining to listen through
the constant sound of the jungle for any sign of the bad
guys. It wouldn't surprise her one bit if they jumped out
of the bushes now. Murphy's Law was in full freaking
effect.

Thank God the jungle was quiet. Relatively, anyway,
considering all the various squeaks and squawks coming

in stereo from the shrubs around them and the canopy above. Then she heard a heavy *plop*. Followed by a patter of large drops.

Rain. Rain? She tilted her face, anticipating a light, misting cool-down, but it was nothing so tame. Like an upended bucket, water sluiced from the canopy, a torrent drenching her to the skin instantly. "No. No. No, freaking no!"

Coughing at the unexpected mouthful, she quickly covered Zak's face with her body. Darkness descended faster than she could've imagined, turning the foliage into a spooky curtain. She could barely see the leaves in front of her face, and God only knew what those red eyes were looking back at her.

Acadia shivered, although she wasn't cold. She forced herself to think, logically prioritizing what had to be done in order of importance. Zak. He needed shelter, someplace dry, so she could tend his wound. Since she couldn't carry him, she had to produce a miracle from somewhere right where he'd fallen. She started by pulling some of the larger leaves that were at hand, making an impromptu tent over his face and over his shoulders to protect him from the downpour.

Dragging sodden strands of hair from her face and neck, she got to her feet, pulled a penlight from a pocket, and did a three-sixty to study the terrain. She needed to find the best spot to set up camp. Finally, luck was on their side. About twenty feet away was a dense curtain of thickly leafed shrubs, a decent hiding place and at least some kind of shelter from the storm.

She found a fallen stick, using it to poke and beat the bushes. Vigorously. A small capuchin monkey, its long, silky black hair waterlogged, raced out of the foliage. Acadia sprang back, biting back a shriek, and stared back at it as it sat looking at her before it darted up a tree trunk to observe her from a safer distance.

Pressing a hand to her rapidly beating heart, she addressed her audience. "You don't have the keys to a Jeep, do you?" The little guy tilted his white face and watched her with big, unblinking eyes. "How about a luxury suite with room service?" The monkey's tail curled around his body, and he cocked his head the other way. "No, I see," she said solemnly. "You're also shit out of luck as far as resources go." She paused. "What's that, you say? Hurry up before Zak drowns? Got it."

He scaled the tree and disappeared into the rain while she peeled open the flap covering a long, hidden pocket running down the outside of her right pant leg. Her friends had teased her mercilessly about bringing the tiny tent. It weighed only forty-four ounces, but that was added to the weight of all the other stuff secreted in her clothing. Really, she'd wondered if she'd need it, but brought it anyway.

Thank God she'd decided to err on the side of caution. Score another one for Acadia Gray. She stomped down a small area under one of the taller bushes, flattening small branches and leaves to make a softish spot big enough to pitch the tent. In spite of the fact that she sold camping equipment seven days a week, she'd never gone camping in her life. But she'd practiced pitching tents in her backyard so she could show customers how to do it. Rain or shine, every make and model number.

She could do this.

It wasn't as easy in the dark, in punishing rain, with the glow of animal eyes at various levels watching her. Acadia was all fingers and thumbs as she set up the thin, flexible arch pole and used her boot heel to set the stakes in place. The tent was small, even for one person, but it was better than braving the dark all night in the pouring rain.

After a few seconds of indecision, she shrugged, then unbuttoned her vest and took it off, then thought *what the hell* and stripped off her sweat-soaked T-shirt as well. Being free of the weight and the clinging fabric actually felt great. The rain felt like a warm shower set on pulse massage, sluicing the sweat and grime off her skin as she finished putting up the tent.

With the small penlight tucked into her topknot like a miner's light, she went back for Zak. He hadn't moved. When she bent to place her arms under his shoulders, his eyes flickered open, and he gave her a puzzled, upside-down look. His brow furrowed. "Give me . . . minute," he managed thickly, the words slurred. "Walk."

Seriously? He could barely lift his eyelids, let alone his entire body from prone to upright. But if he could try, maybe she could get him into place without any more damage to his shoulder. "That'll help," she admitted. "Let's see if it's possible."

She walked around so she could help him to his feet, holding his arm tightly against her body. His knees buckled and this almost sent her flat on her back, but she managed to spread her feet and brace him. Holy crap, he was heavy.

She used every ounce of strength she hadn't known she had left to hold him upright. The narrow beam of the flashlight danced across the raindrops and illuminated several pairs of small, red eyes watching their every move.

That tent suddenly looked like heaven. "All right, big guy, let's—" As he leaned heavily against her, something crept across the hill and valley of her breast. *Really?* She only glanced down when Zak's fingers skimmed lower to cup her rain-slick breast and pebbled nipple.

This had to be the least of her problems.

"Warm," Zak murmured, even as he nuzzled her ear.

The man could hardly stand, but here he was, rolling one callused thumb over her nipple with the precision of a surgeon.

The intensity of the storm, and possibly the danger as well, had heightened all of her senses, including touch.

And it felt good.

Acadia squeezed her eyes shut, the wild incongruity of the situation fighting with the warmth pooling between her legs. "Zak, you're going to fall over any minute—"

"Will you catch me?" His lips moved over her earlobe, and she jumped out of her sodden skin as his teeth closed over the sensitive flesh. "Nice landing. Soft."

Her breath caught as his palm cradled her breast, and her grip tightened on his arm. "Seriously," she breathed, and failed utterly to sound as resolute as she'd wanted.

"Am serious," he murmured as his lips traced a line of kisses across her jaw. The rain pounded over them both, warm and suddenly too damned intimate. Like an exotic shower. Or a tropical paradise.

Or trouble.

"You're weak from loss of blood," she told him. Her voice strangled in her chest as his fingers squeezed her erect nipple, his other hand sliding over her wet nape.

"Prob'ly," he agreed, entirely too cheerfully given how heavily he was leaning on her. His mouth teased at the corner of hers, and she shuddered.

"You have—" She turned her head to look into his eyes, to check to see if his pupils were dilated—that was a sign of a concussion, wasn't it?—and knew she had made a mistake as his lips closed over hers.

The rain covered them, glued them together, as his grip at the back of her neck held her still. His mouth caught at her lower lip, teased and nibbled until her own lips parted on a sigh. Eager, with a whole lot more energy than she would have given him credit for, his tongue swept into her mouth to taste her.

A dip. A flick. She felt more than heard his groan as his fingers tightened at her nape. "'S nice," he murmured against her lips.

More than nice, she realized. And even worse, completely insane. He was hurt! Somehow, she didn't think St. Christopher was equipped for this kind of stuff. Taking his wrist, she extricated his hand from her breast. He sounded drunk. The heavy weight of his arm around her shoulders made it hard to walk. But it beat trying to drag him bodily to the tent.

"All right," she said with as much asperity as she could muster. "It's time for you to lie down, Zak."

"Don' think this is the right time, sweetheart," he mumbled as Acadia, panting from the exertion, leaned him against a broad tree trunk and started unbuttoning his saturated shirt.

Now he decided to be sensible? "That's because you have a one-track mind, big boy." Dried blood—the *only* dry thing around—had stuck the fabric to his wound despite the gauze she'd used. She let the rain beat on it for a while, then reached for his belt buckle. "We don't want to sleep in wet clothes, right?"

He gave her a sexy, lopsided grin. "Sleep naked."

So did she. But if he were in her bed, she wouldn't be sleeping. That thing she'd just set up was a one-woman tent. Somehow, she was going to have to share it with him. She knew at least one of them wasn't going to get any sleep.

Crap. She got one arm out of the sleeve, no easy feat when the soaking wet fabric clung to him like a second skin. "Good to know," Acadia told him dryly as she picked a fat bug off his chest and flicked it off her fingers into the darkness.

"God, you're pretty. Sunny. *Happy*, for crissake. Don' get it," he mumbled.

She reached up to gently push his dripping hair out of his eyes. "*You're* pretty darn irresistible when you're out of it and forget to be a jerk, Zakary Stark."

Reaching out, he traced his thumb over her lower lip. "Sexy. Resourceful. Sexy . . ."

He was apparently making a laundry list of her attributes, she thought, amused. He wasn't this chatty when he was his normal self. She wondered when last he'd *been* his normal self. According to Gideon, not for a while. His wife must've been a paragon of wonderfulness to make a man like Zak not want to go on without her.

Acadia felt a pang of envy. She couldn't imagine what it would be like to be loved by a man that much. "That's me," she told him, keeping her voice cheerful as she tried not to imagine what might be surrounding them right now. As flimsy as the small tent was, it was a layer of protection between them and the critters. "Sexy and definitely resourceful."

One hand on his chest, the other fumbling for his belt buckle, she realized his pants wouldn't come off over his boots.

In spite of the rain, she was sweating as she straightened and began carefully working the fabric away from his injury. He bent over to drop a kiss on top of her head. The flashlight fell out of her hair and she sighed. "A little cooperation would be nice. Can you just stand still for a sec while I get the flashlight?"

"Lie down. Better."

"In a minute, okay? Let's get these clothes off first."

He unsnapped the top button of her pants, his touch unerring. Acadia choked back a laugh. "Okay, then." As long as it got him into the tent, she'd try just about anything.

Hard, driving rain was as good as a shower. Almost. And maybe once she got Zak situated, she'd take off the rest of her clothes and stand out there in front of God and those red eyes and use some soap.

Or maybe she wouldn't.

He slapped his hand not so gently against her cheek, his fingers clumsy. "Your skin is so soft. Smells like . . ."

She had to tilt him to get his other arm free, and hated knowing how badly she was hurting him as she did so. "Sheer, unadulterated fear?" she offered, tossing his shirt in the general direction of the tent, which she could barely see.

She went for his belt, tugging the slippery leather from the buckle, pulling it free from the prong. As she pulled the zipper down, he suddenly pressed her hand against an impressive erection. "Yes," he whispered, listing toward her. His skin was like a furnace under her fingers, even through his briefs. His penis was rock hard and in no way affected by a bullet wound to the shoulder or by standing in a tropical downpour in the dark.

With a smile and a shake of her head, she put her hand on his uninjured shoulder and gave him a little shove back toward the support of the tree.

"Not going t—"

He cut off her protest beneath his lips. As kisses went, this one didn't have much finesse, but what he lacked in technique he made up for with enthusiasm. After a few seconds of frying Acadia's mental circuits, he fell back against the tree trunk. "Need . . . lie down."

She sighed. "Got it. Stay right there and wait for me, okay? Zak? Don't move. I'll be right back."

She crouched down to work on the wet knots in his boot laces. Like her, he'd dressed hurriedly and had gone commando. Eye-level with his erect penis, she was tempted to— No. With a muffled laugh, Acadia picked up the penlight, stuck it back in her hair, and finished untying his shoes.

She stood up and steadied him with one hand braced on his chest. "Step out of this boot . . ." She nudged his leg with her knee. "There you go. Now, the other one . . . Good job." Carefully avoiding the penis that stood hopefully at attention, she managed to pull Zak away from the tree and toward the tent, then maneuvered his tall body into the small opening. Made him scoot all the way in under his own erratic steam. It took a while.

Before climbing in herself, she took off her own pants, bringing the garment inside and leaving the rest of their soaked clothing outside. They couldn't get any wetter. The tent was barely big enough for him, but she managed to squeeze in beside him.

His eyes were closed, his breaths deep. Asleep, she hoped, not unconscious. Using the narrow beam of the flashlight, she scanned it across his entire body while she looked for other injuries. Plenty of raised scars, but nothing more recent than the bruise and gash on his temple and a freaking gunshot wound.

Acadia removed the gauze from his shoulder and saw that the hole was still bleeding sluggishly. The skin around it was red and hot to the touch. Not good. Not good at all. Worry ate at her, but she didn't have time to indulge it. Zak was totally dependent on her. She didn't have time even to think about falling apart.

She was organized. Her friends always said so. Accordingly, she made a mental note to fall into hysterics in two weeks.

Feeling better knowing that she had a breakdown scheduled, she methodically emptied all the pockets in her pants and vest beside her hip, sorting through her supplies. She methodically and carefully cleaned and redressed Zak's wound, then covered him with the foil blanket. He'd need water when he woke up. He'd appreciate clean clothes, food . . .

As exhausted as she was, she crawled backward outside and set to washing their clothes with a little sliver of hotel soap, then left them spread over branches to rinse. They'd dry in no time once this damned rain stopped. Or be carried off by some wild animal, leaving them to finish their trek back to civilization naked.

If that was the case, she'd deal with it tomorrow. Right now she could handle only one thing at a time.

Feeling vulnerable and terrifyingly exposed standing naked in the dark, Acadia quickly washed herself and let the rain do the rest. She was exhausted by the time she crept back inside and pulled the zipper down, almost to the ground. Reaching out, she picked up the leafy branch she'd left there, propping it up against the front of the tent before she finished zipping the flap closed. It wasn't the best camouflage job in the world, but it was better than nothing. She hoped.

Zak slept on his side, leaving a narrow space for her to slide in and stretch out beside him. He slid his arm under her head as she settled, gathering her against his chest. His heart beat steadily under her ear.

ZAK KNEW THEY SHOULD move into the shade. The tropical sun was baking his body, and it was too bright for him to open his eyes. But damn, it felt good to relax here on the beach with nothing better to do than listen to the susurrus of the nearby waves and anticipate what was coming next. It'd been a while since they'd had nothing to do but each other.

He remembered all the good things with a wash of forgotten tenderness. God, he wanted those feelings back.

She cupped his face in her small capable hands. Odd. Jen's large, bony hands had been her Achilles' heel, yet now they felt so small and delicate against his skin. He liked it. Remembered that he'd once loved her more than he'd thought possible.

The scent of jasmine mingled with woman's musk made him hard as a rock. Zak was glad she'd gotten over the Obsession kick. Jasmine smelled much, much . . . Weak with longing, Zak slid over her, resting his hips on hers because he was out of breath with lust and the enervating heat wrapped around his body like a damp wool blanket.

Shade . . .

"Make love to me, sweetheart." She lifted smoky gray eyes to his, smiled, slid her hand down between them to close over his erect penis. Zak uttered a guttural moan, bent his head to her breast, and flicked his tongue across one distended tip.

"Zak, *please* . . . You're going to hurt yoursel—"

Arms straining as he braced his body over hers, he positioned himself over her damp heat and murmured, "Cady." And sank home.

BY MORNING ZAK WAS feverish, he wouldn't or couldn't swallow the water Acadia tried to drizzle between his parched lips, and she couldn't cool him down, no matter what she tried. And she tried everything.

Too bad she hadn't known this was going to happen; she would have given Gideon less of her aspirin supply back at the guerrilla camp. Zak's feeble calisthenics during the night probably had done him more harm. He'd been out of his mind, and quite determined to have wild jungle sex. Fortunately, he'd been too weak. She'd easily been able to restrain him. Besides, the tent was too small for two people to move about without doing serious bodily harm to each other.

But boy-howdy, he'd been determined.

The wound was red and angry-looking. It was infected, and she was running out of the only antiseptic she had. The hand sanitizer. She sponged his body from his head to his feet, then fanned him with the little battery-operated fan until the batteries died. There was no cross-breeze through the mesh windows. The still air hung thick and pregnant with more rain. Zak sweated profusely. He rambled. About his brother. About Jennifer.

About his car, and about his dog, which as far as she could piece together he'd named Mouse.

Their clothing had steamed dry, and she brought it inside the tent, folding it neatly into little squares, which she used to pillow Zak's head.

She ate half a protein bar and made a small cup of bouillon with collected rainwater and one of the small packs of powder she'd brought along for her friend Amber, who was always hungry. She made a mental note to thank Amber, because she was able to dribble the drink into Zak's mouth periodically. Acadia tended to him as best as she could, then went foraging.

She didn't know what the hell she was doing, so she stayed close by as she looked for fruit to supplement what she had with her. Monkeys chattered in the trees; birds sang as they also foraged for food around her. Insects buzzed and created a low hum that filled the still air.

At least there was no sign of the guerrillas, although Acadia never forgot that she and Zak were being hunted. She said a prayer of safety for Zak's brother, and one for her and Zak while she was at it. She hoped St. Christopher was listening. Maybe he only worked for Catholics?

Because of the rain, water was plentiful. Every hour on the hour she irrigated Zak's wound, then redressed it, and every hour it looked worse. She had to get him help, but she had no damned idea how to do that. She couldn't carry him, and even if she could, she had no idea in which direction to go.

The face of his watch was cracked, and water had

seeped inside. According to him they'd been heading toward the river.

She didn't even know how close they were to it or, if she found it, how quickly she'd find a town or village. She'd settle for a tiny one-building settlement with any sort of medical treatment. Not for the first time in her life, Acadia felt helpless, hopeless, and so frightened that she had no idea what to do next. At least with her father there'd been the Internet for reference, and people around to help. Here there was no one but her.

She'd wait one more night, but if he wasn't better in the morning, she'd have no choice but to go find help. Brushing his hair back from his forehead, she whispered, "Life's not done with you yet, Zak. Come back to me."

"YOU LOOK LIKE HELL." Zak coughed, shocked to hear the weak timbre of his voice. Acadia sat with her legs curled to the side to squeeze into the small space beside him. She wore a small, pale-colored T-shirt and, as far as he could tell, nothing else. She held his hand clasped between her breasts, her mouth touching his knuckles as if she was in prayer.

He realized they were in a small tent, the dim interior like a sauna set on high. Maybe because the lightweight nylon encasing them was a muddy color, or maybe because her pale skin looked bloodless with exhaustion, she looked jaundiced. Strands of her hair had escaped the lopsided coil on top of her head and hung like limp flags of surrender around her glistening face and neck.

At the sound of his voice, she opened her dazed eyes. It took a moment for her gaze to meet his.

Then her face crumpled and she burst into tears.

"Jesus," he rasped. "What is it?"

"You're awake!"

"Yeah. Apparently. How long was I asleep?" He stretched slowly, noting the weakness in his muscles and, as he shifted, the fire in his shoulder.

Gripping his hand in both of hers, she let the tears dry on her flushed face. "You've been unconscious for *days*." It was more an accusation than anything.

"No way . . . days? Last I remember, we were headed for the river." She was stroking his hand as one would a frightened animal. It was cute. Hell, she was . . . "Wanted to beat the rain." God, it was fucking hot in here. Maybe if he went outside . . . Rain pounded the canvas overhead. Rain would be cool . . . Yeah. Outside.

"You passed out. Stop moving around and lie still. The bullet's still in your shoulder."

"Feel it." God, it was hot. Claustrophobic. Noisy . . . Zak blinked her into focus. "You okay?"

"Peachy," she said on a hiccup.

He liked the way she was holding his hand to her face, liked the feel of her soft, damp mouth against his knuckles. "Where's Gideon?"

"Probably waiting impatiently for you at the hotel in Caracas." She sounded impatient, her face flushed. "You were out for two days, Zak."

"Shit. Any sign of the bad guys?"

"Not since you were shot."

Small favors. "What happened to my clothes?" The frightened look on her face haunted him in ways he couldn't describe, so he teased lightly, "Did you rip them off and have your wicked way with me while I was lights out?"

Her smile glimmered, but only faintly. "You bet. No foreplay, of course, but these were extenuating circumstances." She sobered again. "There was a lot of blood . . ." She swallowed hard. "I washed them while you were sleeping. They're dry now, and your head is resting on the pants. If you want, I can tuck your shirt under there, too."

Zak tightened his fingers around hers as she moved. "Thanks for taking care of me."

She shrugged. "I'm lousy with directions. I can't find my way out of a paper bag. I need you to find our way back to civilization."

He smiled with effort, not letting go of her hand. "Where'd you find the tent?"

"It's our best-selling one-person. Weighs just under three pounds, so it's easy to carry. Waterproof, easy to pitch . . ." She placed her free hand on his forehead and frowned. "You're still running a temperature. I've cleaned your shoulder as best I could, but you have to see a doctor. You lost a lot of blood, and the wound is infected. Do you think you can walk? I've made a walking stick for you out of a branch I found."

"What time is it?"

She glanced at his watch, which he noticed with exhausted amusement was strapped on her slender wrist.

"Six fifteen. Or it was when it stopped. The glass is broken. I think it's closer to noon."

"Give me my clothes and pack up camp. We need to make tracks. We'll find some civilization and I'll call the hotel where we're meeting Gideon."

Hell, even talking wore him out. Never happened before. Zak knew he had a fever, and knew he'd be fucking lucky to make it anywhere before he passed out again. Or, hell, died. He had to get her to safety before that happened.

"*You're* meeting your brother," she corrected. "I have to contact my friends and let them know I'm all right. Then hook up with them either here or at home."

"Not here. You have to go back to Kansas, Dorothy."

"Fortunately, you aren't the boss of me. As soon as we hit a town, you're on your own, Rambo."

"As soon as I know you'll be safe, you can be on *your* own," he told her, closing his eyes. "Until then, consider me your bodyguard."

"Who's been guarding whom for the past two days?"

Ah . . . hell. "Your point." Black sparklers obscured his vision as he opened his eyes. "What can I do to help?"

"I'll know what you can do when you try to do it," she said briskly. She let go of his hand, making Zak feel strangely bereft, and handed him a folding cup filled with something lukewarm and disgustingly salty.

He made a face. "Trying to poison me?"

"Damn. Why didn't I think of doing that while you were sleeping?" Acadia slipped her hand under his head and lifted it, touching the cup to his parched lips. "It's beef bouillon. Drink it or chew on a protein bar. I saved you half."

"Any water?"

She deposited the folding cup on his bare chest and reached over to bring a little plastic box to his lips. It tasted strongly of wintergreen, and was merely a small sip, but it was wonderful.

"More?" she asked.

"Please." Just that one word wrung him out.

Another hard surface brushed his mouth. This time it was a little more water. He drained whatever she gave him. The movement sent the black sparkles in his vision into a flurry. He kept his eyes focused on her face until they cleared. She tilted the cup to his lips, and Zak drank greedily, his mouth and throat parched. The water was lukewarm, and absolutely delicious. He drained the cup, wanting more. A gallon or two would maybe put a dent in his overwhelming thirst. The fever, he supposed.

"More?" she asked, still cradling the back of his head. He was inches from the soft mounds unfettered beneath her thin pink T-shirt. He had a vague memory of lifting the cotton and licking her warm breasts. He suspected that was more wishful thinking than reality.

Fever dreams.

"Please." His voice faded annoyingly. He had to get his shit together. The hand supporting his head felt cool. Couldn't be, they were in a steamy tropical jungle, but compared to the temperature of his skin, her fingers soothed his hot flesh like nothing else. Not even the water.

"You really are a Girl Scout." Zak was surprised at how weak he sounded. He cleared his throat. "How come some Boy Scout hasn't snapped you up?"

She shrugged. "My father was sick a long time . . ."

She tilted the little folding cup to his mouth, letting him drain that too before getting him to sip the bouillon. She gently lowered his head to the pillow she'd made out of his folded clothes. "Sorry. The bouillon makes you even thirstier, I know, but you need the protein to get better. There's plenty of water, the containers are just small."

A swimming pool would be too small, but she was clearly exhausted, and the frown between her pretty eyes seemed to be permanently etched there.

She'd been talking about her father. "There are places he could've gone—"

"Never." Her eyes flared. "I dated. Had a couple of fairly serious relationships. But in the end"—she shrugged—"different kind of lifestyle than you're used to, I guess. Junction City is pretty quiet and low-key. *I'm* pretty quiet and low-key."

"Bossy as hell." He wasn't sure how the words sounded more like a caress than an accusation.

"I have more containers outside," she said without her usually sassy comeback. "I'll get those so you can drink your fill. I wasn't able to get you to do much swallowing yesterday; that and the fever have made you dehydrated. I think you'll feel better when you can drink more. I'll be right back."

She maneuvered out of the small tent backward,

taking the containers with her. He had a nice flash of her pale, bare ass.

Acadia Gray was a remarkable woman, Zak mused, closing his eyes against the throb in his head and arm. God only knew what else she carried in all those hidden pockets, but he'd help her as soon as—

Darkness fell on him like a dense black fog.

"Okay," Acadia said as the tent rustled, "there's plenty more water. If you can come outside, I'll take down the tent, and we can be on . . . Oh no!"

Zak heard her voice as if through a dark tunnel and struggled to surface.

"Zak?" His name was accompanied by a small slap to the cheek. "Come on, Zak. Wake up."

He forced his eyes open. The pale oval of her face was a blur. "Out of here."

"Yes. I know. But maybe you need to rest one more day."

"No. H-help m'up."

"Lie still. I'll get everything ready and see how you're doing."

"'M good."

Acadia smoothed her cool fingers across his burning hot cheek. He wanted to press his mouth against her palm, but her hand moved to his forehead for a too-brief moment before falling away. "I see that." She let out a shaky sigh. "Close your eyes. I'll be back in a few."

Since he didn't have any choice, he let his lids drop. God. This was bad. Really bad. He was too weak to move, his brain too fuddled to hold on to any one cohesive thought. The only thing Zak knew was that they were both screwed.

THEY WERE IN BIG, big trouble.

Acadia wrapped her arms around her drawn-up knees and stared at a tangled forest of green. She knew she hadn't moved for a while, because when she was in motion the jungle went silent. Now small black-faced monkeys chattered to one another as they scampered from limb to limb overhead. A large yellow-and-brilliant-blue parrot perched on a branch directly over their small tent. Its plumage sported white circles on its head that looked like eyes, and it watched her, head cocked. A black spider the size of a tennis ball, with a garish red mouth, waited right in the middle of its giant web for a buzzing, shiny-winged bug to land.

Business as usual in the jungle.

Early-morning sunlight filtered through the treetops high overhead, and the moisture on the leaves from yesterday's rain was evaporating in tendrils of mist that hung low to the ground like diaphanous wisps of pale chiffon. She knew she should put out the empty containers to gather whatever water she could, that she should check on Zak and do whatever else she could possibly come up with to even pretend to help. But she was paralyzed with fear, her thoughts running like rats in a maze. Sweat trickled down her temples and gathered in the small of her back under her already damp T-shirt.

Zak wasn't going to walk out of the jungle on his own. Absently she scratched several red bites running up her arm. She couldn't carry him. She was back to square one, only now getting him to medical care was even more imperative. His dull eyes and flushed skin were clear signals, even with her novice medical skills, that he wasn't getting better on his own.

"I suppose I could sit here feeling sorry for myself for another day or two," she told the monkey, who ignored her. "His health would be taken out of my hands for sure. If he doesn't get proper medical attention, he's going to die. I could just wait until something comes to eat me. Or shoot me, or until the kidnappers come back and hold me for ransom again. I could do any or all, or . . ." She rubbed at her forehead. "Damned well nothing."

But that wasn't her, either. Acadia got to her feet, and the jungle fell silent around her. "Or I could leave my pity party and go in search of help," she told the suddenly hushed air. Because any and all of the things she was scared of could still happen, but in the meantime at least she'd be proactive.

"Right?" she asked the parrot, who gave her an unblinking stare. "Glad you agree." She dusted twigs and leaves off her butt and looked around. She'd leave everything with Zak. First, water. He'd wake up and be thirsty again.

She filled the various small containers and set them in a row along the wall of the tent within easy reach. Then she placed the last half of a protein bar, broken off into bite-size chunks, where he'd see them *when* he opened his eyes. She added the long machete as well. She didn't know how to use the damned thing, and it was much too heavy for her, even when she'd tried hacking at branches with both hands.

The Uzi joined the machete. Even if she knew how to use it, she wouldn't want to waste what strength she had toting it.

After refreshing the leaves she'd used days before to hide the tent from prying human eyes, Acadia stood back and surveyed the camp. She didn't want to leave him. The very idea was scaring her beyond anything else they'd been through so far, but she couldn't help him by staying. She wasn't helping herself by staying either.

She wished to God—not for the first time—that she were a different kind of person. Oh, she was organized, and certainly resourceful, but she wished she were braver and more daring. The most daring thing, aside from this trip, that she'd ever planned had involved moving out of Junction City to begin college at thirty years old. Up until now, the scariest thing she'd considered in her future was sitting next to a bunch of nineteen- and twenty-somethings.

Boy, did she have it wrong.

Jennifer Stark would have aced this test, and baked brownies at the same time. Too bad, she wasn't Jennifer Stark. But poor substitute that she was, Acadia Gray was the only game in town.

She crawled back inside the tent, delaying the inevitable. The flaps were open, but there wasn't a wisp of a breeze coming through the fine mesh, and Zak's naked body gleamed with sweat.

"I'm going to get help," she told him, taking out a couple of wipes to run over his body to cool him down. "You have water, food, and the machete, right here, okay?" The area around the wound was red and hot to the touch. Redder and hotter than yesterday? "I won't be long. Bandages. Only a little alcohol gel left, so don't have a party while I'm gone. I'm taking your watch so I can use the GPS—don't go wandering off without me."

Acadia bent down to place a lingering kiss on his mouth, running her fingers through the wet strands of dark hair clinging to his cheeks and strong brown throat.

He had to be all right. She'd make sure of that.

She kissed him again. Faster, this time, as if sipping from that font of strength he seemed to carry within. She removed the chain holding her St. Christopher medallion around her neck, cupped the coin in her palm, and squeezed her eyes shut. *Please*, she thought, and then didn't know how to finish. Carefully, she slipped the long chain over Zak's head.

"This'll keep you safe." Her fingers shook a little as she straightened the medal where it glinted amidst the dark hair on his chest. "I'll be back before you know it."

The alternative was unthinkable.

❧ NINE ❧

As it turned out, Acadia had pitched the tent less than a mile from a settlement. Unfortunately, it took her the better part of a terrifying day to stumble across the small Yanomami village, and that was by accident, not design. No one spoke English, and her rudimentary Spanish wasn't enough for easy conversation.

Still, through gestures and the very real threat of hyperventilation, she managed to instill a sense of urgency in the locals and got four men to follow her back to where she'd left Zak. It took only an hour to return, as the four men weren't slowed down by the wildlife, indecision, hunger, or thirst. True, the men did exchange some comments that she suspected weren't entirely complimentary, when it became obvious that she'd gone in circles at least twice, but they knew how to cut through her vague directions, and that was what mattered.

She was so damned happy to see the tent—to know she'd made it back—that she would've cried if she'd had any moisture left in her body. Unzipping the front flap, she crawled halfway inside.

"Zak? Zak! I brought back help. You're going to be— Oh, my God." Heat sizzled from his feverish skin, elevating the already stifling temperature inside the tent. He was unconscious and still as death.

Conveying the situation was easy. Her frantic gestures and facial expressions might have been convoluted, but Zak's physical state required no translation. She mimed what she wanted them to do, and within minutes she'd broken down the tent and gathered their meager supplies. The village men quickly formed a stretcher out of the tent fabric and poles they chopped down with their machetes and loaded Zak carefully on top, using one of the tie lines to keep him in place.

Acadia, so exhausted she was tempted to just toss what was left of her emergency rations into the woods, put everything back in its proper spot. The extra few pounds felt like cement bricks.

Zak lay ominously still in the curve of the stretcher. Acadia walked alongside when she could and dropped back when she couldn't, never letting him out of her sight. His cheeks were wildly flushed, but he wasn't sweating. Fever and dehydration: just as deadly as an infected wound in the jungle.

The men cut through the vegetation with ease, long machetes slicing through tangled vines and knotted plants much faster than she and Zak had managed. But instead of taking her back to their village, which she presumed was near a river, they went in the opposite direction.

"No. Wait! *Espera*—" She dashed ahead to the two men in the lead, reached out to grab a naked, oiled arm, thought better of it, and dropped her hand. "Don't we . . . *¿no debemos*—?" Crap, she needed a translator. "Are you taking us to a hospital? *Hos-pi-tal?*" They looked at her, faces blank and without any recognition for the word, despite her saying it loudly and as slowly as she could.

She felt like an idiot as they continued walking without breaking stride. Wherever they were taking Zak, they were taking him there quickly, and without any interruption from her. Giving up, she returned to her position beside him and took his hot, dry hand in hers.

She didn't know exactly how long they traveled, but eventually they emerged from the trees. This new village was a little bigger than the one where she'd found the men, but not by much. And the buildings were mud brick with corrugated iron roofs, not thatched huts.

"Doctor? *¿Un médico?*" she asked hopefully as they emerged from the trees onto a dirt track. It wasn't a paved road, but at least it indicated civilization.

"Padre Araujo," one of the men told her firmly.

Zak didn't need a priest. She didn't want to even *consider* that he'd need a priest. What he *needed* was a doctor. Maybe the priest knew where to find a doctor.

Jungle encroached on the rural village from all sides, pressing in like a living wall. If they were near the river,

Acadia couldn't see or hear any indication of it. And she didn't see any vehicles of any sort.

She didn't like not knowing exactly where she was, and she was so exhausted, she felt as though she'd been lost in the jungle her entire life. Right then, she would've given just about anything to be able to click her heels and get back to Kansas. Even glancing at the little GPS didn't help her. It was now working sporadically, which gave her hope they were near civilization, but without a map, it was just a bunch of numbers; *you are here.* The middle of nowhere. Big help.

She already knew that.

A handful of men watched their progress. Zak's bearers didn't acknowledge them, and the locals didn't call out a greeting. It was kind of creepy, as if they were in a somber, invisible bubble.

Acadia rubbed her upper arms, chilled even though the sun was shining. The savory smell of meat and onions cooking made her salivate, and her stomach rumbled. Counting back, she realized she hadn't had more than a few mints and a protein bar in days. Once Zak was in good hands, maybe she could barter something she had left in her pockets for food.

She'd need enough for two. The alternative was . . . unacceptable.

Eventually, the men slowed in front of a cluster of structures that had seen much better days. They stopped before a building with boarded-up windows covered with mold-stained plywood. If the walls had ever been painted, the color had faded and flaked away long ago. A rusting corrugated roof sagged on one end, and was supported on the other by several old fifty-gallon fuel barrels piled one on top of the other.

An elderly woman with snow-white hair clipped close to her scalp appeared on the narrow covered porch almost before they got to the front door. She was dressed in knee-length khaki shorts and a luridly floral short-sleeved shirt, her darkly tanned skin weathered and tough. Waving them all inside, she spoke rapidly to the men, leading them down a dim hallway to the back of what appeared to be her home, but as they passed beds in each room, Acadia realized it seemed to be a clinic of some sort.

She could have kissed the men on the lips in sheer gratitude.

The woman instructed them to place Zak on one of four iron-framed beds in an otherwise empty room that smelled of disinfectant and cheap cigar smoke. She shooed at them impatiently and they melted away before Acadia could thank them.

A loud *riiip* brought her quickly to the other side of Zak's bed as the woman—a nun, Acadia guessed from the rosary hanging about her neck—used both hands to tear his shirt off him. Buttons pinged across the tiled floor. With her head tilted like a curious capuchin monkey's, the woman ran her gaze over Zak's chest, taking in the dried blood and the glint of the silver chain from Acadia's St. Christopher medal.

The woman made the sign of the cross, closed her eyes, mumbled something Acadia couldn't hear, then picked up the cross at the end of her rosary and gave it a quick kiss. "Hmm." She glanced over her shoulder with sharp black eyes that belied the white hair. *"¿Su esposo, no?"* The dialect was unfamiliar, but Acadia got the gist. What if she admitted she *wasn't* Zak's wife? Would he not get treatment? Would the sister insist someone with authority give permission?

Probably neither of the above, but Acadia wasn't taking any chances. She lied without a blink. *"Sí."*

"This. *Tiene una herida de bala."* A gunshot wound. It wasn't a question, of course. The sister wasn't into listening, apparently. She was like a tiny steamroller in her pink Hawaiian shirt, baggy shorts, and sporty, green plaid high-top tennis shoes with the toes cut off for ventilation.

Too tired to think beyond the here and now, Acadia nodded, her attention on Zak. "We were kidnapped," she said in English. The whole kidnapping saga was beyond her grasp to tell in Spanish, and the sister wasn't paying her any attention anyway.

"We were held— *Oh!"* She flinched, even though Zak was too far gone to do it himself. His breathing, labored and shallow as it was, didn't even hitch as the nun tore the bandage away. "Shouldn't you have maybe *soaked* that first?"

The bleeding on Zak's shoulder started again. The wound smelled— Oh, God. It smelled putrid.

"This infection," the tiny nun said in English. "Here. Here." She pointed, but it was obvious even to Acadia's untrained eye that the swollen red skin around the entry wound was infected. The question was, was this woman equipped to deal with it? And if not, then who would be? "Will take out bullet," the nun informed Acadia as she walked over to an old-fashioned buzzer on the wall, jabbing a blunt nail against it several times. "Come back tomorrow."

"*Tomorrow?* No. I'm not leaving him . . . my *husband*," she clarified, just in case there was any doubt. "Are you a doctor?" She took a moment, translated it in her head first, and said stiltedly, "Ah— *¿Es usted médico? ¿Mi esposo necesita una cirugía?*"

The woman gave her a sharp look. *"Yo soy mejor que un médico."*

She winced. "Not to be rude, and I'm sure you *are* better than a doctor, but I think we need a *real* doctor here."

There followed an exchange Acadia couldn't hope to win. From the bits and pieces she could pluck out of the lightning-fast rejoinders, Acadia learned that Sister Clemencia was in charge of the mission clinic while Father Vicente Araujo was in Caracas. And since the good father wouldn't be back for a week, the sister was going to dig the bullet out of Zak herself, whether Acadia liked it or not.

She had no time for fluttering wives, and suggested— ordered—that Acadia leave, get food, rest, and come back tomorrow.

Acadia stepped out of the way.

Two men appeared and took charge of the patient while she stood helplessly against the wall. No matter how uncertain she was about putting Zak in the hands of the unusual nun, he looked frighteningly bad. And she was out of options.

The nun removed the St. Christopher medal and handed it to Acadia as the men stripped Zak and covered him with an old but clean-looking sheet, then swiftly wheeled him out. Sister Clemencia followed them down the hall, giving orders as she went, leaving Acadia alone in the room.

She stared blankly at the chipped, stained, age-yellowed walls and the rusted metal bed frames. The exchange with Sister Clemencia had been so quick, so fraught with language barriers, so freaking one-sided, that Acadia felt unsure if the nun was even *qualified* to perform surgery. Acadia was damned if she did, and damned if she didn't. She didn't know if Zak would have been worse off in the tent or down the hall, at the sister's mercy. She looked up at the wooden crosses on the walls and wondered if praying would help.

Maybe. But she doubted it. Shaking her head, she told herself that she should be grateful that she wasn't still lost in the jungle, looking for anything even remotely like help.

She wandered over to look out of the window while she waited. There was just the one main street running between buildings that looked as though they'd been there a hundred years, with only a dozen or so still more or less intact.

The clinic was the biggest building in town. Across the narrow street, three men sat on straight-backed chairs outside what looked like a bar, dozing in the early evening sunshine. A chicken and a mangy black dog wandered between their feet, ignored.

She didn't want to leave Zak here unprotected. But Sister Clemencia had made it abundantly clear that she wasn't going to let Acadia anywhere near Zak until she was done taking out that bullet, and Acadia couldn't just stand there for the duration.

They'd need transportation to Caracas. They'd need money. She needed a phone. Food was at the top of the list. She walked outside into the humidity and white sunlight to look up and down the street.

The smell of frying onions was stronger now, and Acadia could almost taste the steak underneath a heaped pile of golden-brown fried onions. A big baked potato. Heavy on the butter and sour cream. A tall glass of ice-cold Diet Coke.

She sighed, her stomach cramping uncomfortably. As Staff Sergeant Dad had always said, it was good to want things.

And God, she suddenly missed him. The dad she'd known as a kid. Funny, stern, resourceful, and—*there*. Always present for whatever she needed him to be there *for*. He'd baked cookies for school; he'd gone with her to buy her first bra, and sat patiently while she tried on dozens of potential prom dresses.

It was after that that he started to stop being the dad she knew, no longer consistently present. And then one day, he'd been there, but not present at all.

He'd watched her from puzzled gray eyes so like her

own and not known who she was. A couple of times he'd called her by her mother's name, Sylvia. And for the last five years of his life, he hadn't called her anything at all.

But she knew what he'd have said in this situation.

Acadia straightened her shoulders and told her rumbling tummy to shut up. It was good to want things. Meant she was still alive, and eager enough to want.

Didn't mean one got what one wanted.

The scrawny mutt trotted across the dirt road, all bony ribs and floppy ears, long tail wagging, and met her halfway.

"Hi, boy." He was probably full of fleas, but she bent to give him a scratch behind one droopy ear anyway. He pushed his wet nose against her hand as she asked the three men if there was someone she could report a crime to.

One old guy laughed, which was gross, because his dentures smiled at her from the arm of his chair, while his own smile was full of blackened gums. He thumbed over his shoulder. "*¿Policía?* José Fejos . . ." He said more, but the dialect was hard enough to understand without the added impediment of no teeth. Stepping back out of range as he literally spat out the words, Acadia hastily thanked him and pushed open the door, the dog a shadow at her heels.

The good news was, they had someone who passed for law in town.

The bad news was that the law in Venezuela was so corrupt that police and criminals here were practically one and the same. In her research, she'd read that more than twenty percent of the crimes committed in the country were committed by police officers. She had a feeling the bar wasn't the police station, and had an even sicker feeling about finding the *policía* in a bar, but she went in anyway.

The place was dimly lit. Not for ambience, but because the only light came through a shuttered window at the far end, where three men sat playing cards. A bar made of the same oil drums that held up the roof of the mission, topped by several stained sheets of plywood, held a few dirty glasses, an empty bottle, and a broken broom handle. An old-fashioned paddle fan missing one blade made a weird sighing *thrup-thrup-thump* as it turned lazily overhead. Small as it was, the cantina smelled like a lot of booze, and was also the origin of the tantalizing aroma of grilled onions. Her mouth watered. Maybe she was in time for dinner.

Clearly not that interested in a stranger in their town, the card players only glanced up when she walked in. None of them said anything, so her booted footsteps sounded very loud on the cracked tile floor as she walked up the narrow room to the back. The only clean spots on the floor were where things had spilled, and her boots made sticky noises with each step.

"*Buenas tardes*, gentlemen." The dog sat beside her when she stopped beside the scarred, beat-up oak table. "*¿Quién de ustedes es el oficial policía?*"

"I speak English." The man closest to her slung a beefy arm over the back of his chair and looked at her from beneath the rim of a grimy black-and-orange baseball cap with a roaring tiger emblazoned on the front.

A faded black short-sleeved shirt pulled across his large belly, exposing a lot of thick black hair on his barrel chest and the fleshy "smile" where his shirt parted from his pants.

Acadia kept her eyes on his face. Small, close-set, dark eyes. Heavy jowls, black five-o'clock shadow. Honest to God, he looked like every bad cop she'd ever seen in a movie. His accent was very heavy as he said proudly, "I am Police Chief José Fejos."

Of course he was. "Police Chief, my name is Acadia Stark. My husband is at the mission right now, fighting for his life. He was shot by kidnappers—"

He leaned forward, popping two buttons off the bottom of his shirt in the process. "You are *American*?"

"Yes, we—"

"You have seen the Bengals?"

She frowned. How had the conversation switched? "Are there tigers here?" Not that she'd ever heard.

"Cincinnati."

"Cincin— Oh!" The penny dropped. "The Cincinnati Bengals *football* team. No. I've never seen them."

"Eh. Who shot your husband?" Now he sounded disappointed, and certainly not interested in her shot husband.

She took a deep breath. "We were kidnapped from our hotel room by a woman named Loida Piñero. Have you heard of her?"

"No." He turned back to the game and picked up his cards. "You have papers, to be in my country?" He didn't look at her as he asked the question, instead reaching for an unlit, soggy-tipped cigar in an overflowing ashtray beside him.

The dog leaned his thin body against her legs, as if lending her his trembling courage, and she stroked his head. "No," she told the asshole police chief. "I told you, we were *kidnapped*. With just the clothes——"

He picked up a pink Bic lighter from beside the ashtray and swiped the cigar a couple of times with the flame until the end glowed red, then gave a couple puffs to get it going.

The choking stench drifted over her face. God, was he smoking manure? Disgusting. The stink obliterated the yummy fragrance of onions, not to mention any desire she'd had to eat.

He turned his Bengals cap her way and blew out a foul cloud. "*Por la ley*—by law—you must carry your passport and *tarjeta de ingreso*—your entry card—at all times."

"*Sí*," The guy to his right agreed. Bald as a billiard ball, he wore paint-splattered blue coveralls, was missing both eyeteeth, and had a tattoo of an openmouthed snake crawling up his thick neck. Lovely.

"*Por la ley*," Acadia said tightly, glancing back at the portly police chief, "Americans shouldn't be kidnapped in the dead of night and held for ransom. Sh—stuff happens. No, I don't have any papers. I would like to report the kidnapping, and then I need your help to get back to Caracas as soon as my husband is well enough to travel. In the meantime, I'd like the use of a phone to call——"

"You have American dollars to pay?" He gestured with his cards for the man to his left to play his hand.

"To pay for *what* exactly? A new entry card?"

The tall, skinny man on Fejos's left looked to be a hundred years old. His shoulder-length white hair was as fine as dandelion fluff, and his deeply lined face was baked dark brown by the tropical sun. Seemingly oblivious to the conversation, he tossed in a few coins and kept staring at his cards.

"How will you pay for Sister Clemencia's"—the chief shot an inquiring glance at the guy seated across from him—"hospitality?"

As with the guerrillas she'd thought she'd left behind, Acadia would not like to bump into any of these men in a dark alley. She'd particularly not like to bump into the last guy, even in broad daylight.

In fact, if she had her way, she'd actively avoid him.

He looked about thirty, fighting fit, with bulging muscles and an attitude that dared anyone to try to knock the chip right off his linebacker shoulder. Probably just to kill the offender stone cold dead.

He looked like a prisoner, a gangster, and a nightmare all rolled into one. His dead black eyes ran over her like a creepy caress, lingering on her mouth before sliding a greasy visual trail to measure her breasts. She restrained herself from shuddering with everything in her body and looked back at the chief and said firmly, "I'll send her money from Caracas."

"How much money?" Fejos wanted to know.

"It depends . . . Look. If you can't help me, just say so. But is there anyone in this town who can or will help two Americans get back to Caracas? We'll pay well."

"You can use my *teléfono* cellular," the chief offered, taking a brand-new iPhone from his breast pocket. She was so tired, Acadia didn't even blink at the incongruity of seeing it in this setting.

Almost weak with relief, she reached for it. He snatched it back. "Five hundred American dollars."

"Come on—" She modified the anger in her voice. She was blond, she was relatively attractive. She'd catch more flies with honey. Relaxing her shoulders and smoothing out her crimped features, she dug up a smile. "Help me out here, guys. I don't want to buy your phone, and honestly, I can't afford five hundred dollars." *You opportunistic dirtbag.*

Fejos grabbed her left hand, and she almost screamed the rusted ceiling down because she a), hadn't braced herself to be touched, and holy crap b), did not want to be touched by him. "Where is your wedding ring?"

"The kidnappers stole all our jewelry. Everything." The lie slid effortlessly from her tongue. Zak's watch was tucked inside one of her pants pockets right beside the St. Christopher medal. "And it was a beautiful—"

"How much money you got?"

"I don't have—" Lightbulb. It flashed behind her eyes and she said quickly, "I have twenty American dollars. I'll go get it for you. Then can I make a call?"

He waved his sausage fingers like he was the freaking

King of Siam and blew out a cloud of noxious smoke on the word "Go."

Acadia went. The dog kept up as she jogged across the street, went inside the mission, and returned to the room Zak had been in. With a quick glance around, she unlaced her left boot, tugged it off, and removed the folded twenty she'd tucked inside a century or so ago.

Staff Sergeant Dad had been right. A girl always had to have a little mad money with her.

She and Zak had exactly twenty bucks between them. But with one phone call to her friends, she could have money here—wherever "here" was—within hours. Or at worst, by the next day.

She and the dog returned to the bar.

Acadia held on to the twenty and extended her other hand for the phone. "Thanks, this is so great of you to let me use your phone."

Fejos plucked the bill out of her hand. Serious misgivings swooped in her stomach like dive-bombing pterodactyls. She didn't trust him any further than she could throw his lard ass, which would have required a crane, but she needed that phone.

"One phone call."

"Right." Fortunately, she remembered the number of the hotel, since she'd confirmed her early reservation. Twice. Her friends would be there. Worried out of their minds, rallying the police. Sending out search parties . . .

The phone rang. And rang. And rang.

The men at the table watched her, and she could

almost read their minds. She wished she couldn't. She half turned her back.

Pick up. Pick up. Pick up.

The dog growled low in his throat as suddenly the phone was plucked from her fingers mid-ring. Fejos was standing right behind her. *"Sólo una llamada telefónica,"* he told her roughly, tucking the phone into his pocket, then falling back into his chair. He picked up his cards. "You understand? Only one phone call. My telephone is only for police business." He waved her off as he tossed her twenty into the pot. "Go back to your husband. Where you belong."

With an iron ball of dread pitted in her stomach, Acadia left the bar, crossed the narrow street, and reentered the clinic.

With nothing left to do, she curled up in the bed Zak had been placed on what felt like hours before. She leaned against the hard metal headboard, causing it to clank against the wall every time she moved to pet the dog, who was curled up on her feet. "We are well and truly screwed, Dogburt. But I'm resourceful. I got us here, didn't I?" She glanced at Zak's watch, now strapped to her wrist. It was way too big, and the face kept sliding under her wrist, but it seemed to be working now. There were scratches and signs of wear all over the cracked face and strap; it reminded her of Zak. Plenty of scars, plenty of stories.

She wondered if she'd ever get to hear any of them. "He's been in surgery for over an hour," she told the dog, whose cold, wet nose was pressed against her bare foot. "Why's it taking so—"

The door to the room crashed against the wall, scaring the dog to his feet on the thin mattress, and Acadia bolted upright. The man, in a terrifying bloodstained apron, his eyes wild, motioned her to come. *Quickly.* *"Señora, señora, dale prisa, su marido está muerto."*

Acadia sprang off the bed. "God—what—"

He gestured wildly. *"¡Rápido! Entre por aquí!"*

Muerto. As in . . . Her knees buckled, and she dropped back onto the hard, saggy mattress to stare at him with dull eyes. "Zak is . . ." Her mouth dried to bitter cotton. *"Dead?"*

⊰⊱ TEN ⊰⊱

Still raining.

Zak opened surprisingly heavy lids. No. Inside. Not rain. Hard, narrow bed.

Unfamiliar.

Jennifer?

He waited for the typical heavy sensation of loss to lodge in the pit of his stomach; waited for that cold knot to crystallize as it always did on first waking.

Two beats. Three. It didn't come.

He blinked rapidly, but his vision was still blurry and he couldn't figure out how he'd gotten wherever he was. Had the three of them done the jump from Burj Khalifa's Spire in Dubai?

Yeah, a while back.

Zak frowned. Tibet, about to kayak down the Sanpo River? No. He remembered that trip with Gideon, and several more extreme sports trips the two of them had gone on afterward.

He flipped through memories like old postcards. Jennifer in Dubai, dark hair blowing, laughing into the wind. That last trip with her. Turkey . . . smile tight, eyes hard . . . Haiti—

Tangled honey-blond hair and soft, smiling gray eyes. The sweet, soft fragrance of night-blooming jasmine . . .

Something inside him lightened, flew free.

Acadia. Venezuela.

Got it. A surge of relief relaxed his limbs as his brain sluggishly ground into gear, moving him into the present. Not the cell. Not jungle. Tent? He blinked rapidly, his vision slamming back into focus. The smell— disinfectant? A hospital, then. His brain connected the dots.

Shot.

From the neat white bandage across his chest and his immobilized left arm, he had to be in a medical unit of some kind.

What hurt? Nothing.

The IV hooked to the side of his bed, dripping into his left arm. No pain. Well, that explained his oddly subdued emotions. But it still didn't tell him where the hell they were. Caracas? Had Acadia actually gotten them back while he'd been out? Impossible. She was good, in a Girl-Scout-be-prepared sort of way, but not *that* good.

"Hey?" he said into the semidarkness. No one answered, and he turned his gaze back to the bathroom, where someone was showering.

Bathroom door ajar, shadowy figure behind a thin plastic curtain, the medicinal smell of cheap soap and chemically treated water. He closed his eyes while he gathered his strength and tried to put the sequence of events together.

Acadia. His eyes sprang open. Was she——?

Through the partially open door he saw a quick flash of the curve of her ass, the slope of her back. White-gold skin shimmered in the light as she half turned under the silver streamers of water and light haze of steam.

He took a deep breath. She was here. Somehow—God only knew how—she'd managed to bring him to a hospital. Primitive, but someone had dug out the bullet and bandaged him up, hooked him to the IV . . .

No pain . . . Tired.

His lids drifted closed. Exhausted. Brain still not fully engaged, but not willing to disengage completely.

She confused the shit out of him with her sassy mouth, inexplicable humor, and annoying but endearing preparedness. He'd thought her pockets full of camping trinkets amusing, until their lives had depended on them. Hell, it only proved once again, he was no hero.

The curtain slid aside as she turned to face him, arms raised above her head, hair and hands covered in white foam. His gaze tracked a blob of lather as it slowly inched its way down the slope of her left breast. His dick stirred beneath the thin sheet.

Acadia tilted her head under the spray; her hair, slickly darkened by the water, conformed to the shape of her back in a sweet S curve that made Zak's fingers flex on the sheet. She turned slowly, and the islands of white suds slid over her shiny wet skin in slow motion.

Down the slopes of her breasts, suspended for a breath-less moment on the soft apricot tips of her nipples, then over, clinging to the plump slope before trailing down the gentle curve of her belly to converge in the soft light brown nest between her thighs.

Suddenly painfully hard, Zak kept his gaze on Acadia as he slid his hand beneath the sheet. He wrapped his fist around the hard, silken spear of his cock.

Vaguely he heard the rattle of the pipes when the shower cut off. His hand moved; not optimal, but— She stepped over the edge of the tub. Everything in him froze with . . . lust? Hell, yeah. But more.

Yearning.

Watching her made him feel alive for the first time in—God—longer than two years. A lot longer than two years. He'd been sure Jennifer had killed anything soft and loving inside him. Until Acadia had walked into that cantina wearing a flimsy dress and an open smile . . . Zak suddenly realized he hadn't felt a genuine emotion in a long, long time. He sure as shit hadn't been *happy*.

He doubted he could ever express how much he appreciated her saving his ass. She was nothing like Jen. Not only was she genuinely brave, she owned her behav-ior, had spunk in spades, was loyal to a fault.

In another time and place . . .

The minimum-wattage lighting wrapped her wet skin in a veil of sparkling liquid gold. Zak's fingers tightened as she bent over, exposing her heart-shaped ass when she wrung the water out of her hair. God, he loved a woman with a sweetly rounded ass.

At the hotel he'd gripped it in both hands, fingers digging into her soft flesh as he pounded into her from behind, flipped her, and took her from the front, her silken legs bracketing his head, his— Zak's hand moved, up and down. Fast. Faster. His head dug into the flat pillow as his hips arched off the thin mattress. Didn't want to close his eyes, but Jesus—

SHOVING A PLASTIC BUCKET under the rusty faucet, Acadia turned on the taps again. With hardly any water pressure, it would take a while to fill. She wrapped a threadbare, once-white towel under her arms. It was too small to overlap, exposing a wide V of skin down the front. Leaving the bathroom light on, she walked into the dimly lit room. God, it felt good to be clean. Half an hour before, she'd sat at a spindly table in the mission kitchen with Sister Clemencia and inhaled a spicy meal of *pabellón*— stewed, shredded meat accompanied by rice, black beans, and what looked like a banana. Filling and delicious.

Zak lay as she'd left him an hour ago. *Sleeping.* Thank God. "He scared ten years off my life dying like that," she whispered to Dogburt, who lay with his nose on his paws beside Zak's bedside, where she'd instructed him to keep guard. The dog's eyebrows moved as he tracked her progress to the side of the bed. "And he *did* die." *Flatline died. Heart-stopped died. Drastic-measures died.*

For a single, eternal second, her world had tunneled into raw, choking fear. And grief—God, she never wanted to watch anyone die ever again.

She'd done it too many times already.

"Okay, so jumping on him like that wasn't my finest hour."

She hadn't gone that crazy even when her father had died. Zakary Stark was a pain in the ass. An arrogant, mirthless robot of a man who had a powerful death wish. "But not on *my* watch!"

She'd almost lost him. She shuddered, rubbing goose bumps of residual fear on her arms. Padding over to one of the beds, she dropped the towel on the scrolled footboard and drew on a man's clean white dress shirt, supplied by Sister Clemencia. It smelled of lye and sunshine as she buttoned it over her damp skin.

The bathroom was crude and primitive, and not remotely clean. She hadn't cared. The tepid shower had gone a long way in helping her stay awake and restoring her spirits. The straight-backed chair shoved under the door handle would do the rest.

The idea of lying down was almost like the freaking Holy Grail, but Zak needed attention before she shut down for a few hours of well-deserved rest. When she was done washing him, she was going to drag one of the other beds beside his, so she could touch him and know if he needed anything in the night; then she'd sleep until someone woke her. Preferably for breakfast.

Preferably *not* by kicking in her makeshift lock and kidnapping them. Again.

Back in the bathroom, she turned off the tap and lugged the half-filled bucket of warm water, with a small piece of strong-smelling soap, to Zak's side and pulled the sheet down to the end of the bed.

His body was tanned all over, and perfectly proportioned from his broad shoulders down to his lean hips.

Acadia grinned, dizzy with exhaustion but amused to see that Zak had his fingers cupped around an impressive erection. "Naughty boy, even dead you want attention." She carefully moved his hand out of the way, then sluiced the washcloth in the water and rubbed the bar of soap into the fabric.

"You're going to be *so* sorry when you wake up tomorrow and find out that you missed participating in a sponge bath from a half-naked nurse." She kept her voice as low as possible, so as not to wake him. She ran the cloth over his forehead, inspected the bump and bruise in the iffy light.

"You could've died *then*. When that goon hit you over the head with the Uzi. Good thing you have such a hard head, Zakary Stark. And now you'll have one more scar to show off to the ladies on your next adventure."

She didn't like the idea of other women. At all. She kept talking, remembering reading an article somewhere about how even unconscious patients reacted to the soothing sound of a familiar voice. She wasn't his brother, or his beloved late wife, but she was the only voice around right now.

"That's a guy fantasy, right? Playing doctor?" She ran the cloth over his eyelashes, across his nose, and down first one cheek, then the other. His face was prickly with several days' growth. Even asleep he looked like a guy who could walk down a dark alley knowing nobody would mess with him because his whole demeanor screamed, "I don't give a shit if I live or die, so get your ass over here and give it your best shot."

When a man wasn't afraid to die, people knew not to mess with him.

No wonder he was covered in dings and scars.

Being careful of Sister Clemencia's dressing, Acadia washed away the dried blood on his throat and long arms; his tough, ropy muscles flexed under her ministrations, looking lethally strong. He had a powerful chest, and she ran her fingers over it lightly. When they'd had their wild marathon of lovemaking back at the hotel a lifetime ago, they hadn't taken the time to learn. To explore in the dark. Sex had been hard and fast and often.

She considered it a luxury to be able to look her fill.

There wasn't an ounce of fat on him. His pecs were solid iron, covered by soft, crisp dark hair that ran down between his impressive abs to form a dark nest for his erect penis. Acadia smothered a very un-nurse-like giggle. *Holy crap. I mean, wow.*

She turned to the bucket on the rickety table beside the bed, rinsed out the cloth, then turned back to keep on going with Zak's sponge bath. She took a moment to admire the length, breadth, and sheer scope of him again. *Seriously. Wow.*

Without warning, his right hand shot out, his fingers closing around her wrist. Startled, Acadia let out a little shriek and met a pair of gleaming, wickedly hazel eyes not looking in the least bit sleepy.

"Either stop petting it," he murmured thickly, "or do something about it."

Her gaze shot to his face. His cheeks were flushed. Not with fever, she realized, but with *lust*. His eyes picked up shards of golden light from the bathroom as he gave her a knowing look.

"You're awake," she accused, trying to tug her hand from his implacable grip.

"And horny as hell."

"I see that. But we can't— You shouldn't." Her brain short-circuited as his heated gaze slide like a caress over her. *"No."*

The corner of his mouth quirked in a wicked grin. "Put your knee on the bed."

"Absolutely not," she told him indignantly. "Two hours ago you were *dead*, Zak. It took a lot of work to bring you back. You have an IV stuck in your arm. You're . . ."

He stroked his hand down her thigh, then curled his fingers in the sensitive area behind her knee. Delicious and compelling, his touch raised a shimmer of goose bumps on her skin and completely scattered her wits.

"The harder you make me have to work for it, the more likely I am to rip out this IV, not to mention my stitches."

"That's childish," she chided. "And as compelling as your sob story is, I'm *not* having sex with you until you're IV free, and able to walk out of here under your own steam."

"I'm horny now."

"And you'll be horny again," she told him unsympathetically, running the warm soapy cloth down his left leg. Scar on his knee. Scar on his thigh. Scar on his big toe. "Imagine how traumatized I'd be if we were having sex and you died right in the middle of it. I'd be ruined for life, and there I'd be. In my prime and *celibate*. Think of what a waste it would be if I could never enjoy sex again because my last lover croaked while we were doing it. No thank you."

She moved to the other leg and noticed that his erection was no longer so prominent. Although, with Zak being so large, it was hard to tell.

"So just relax, knowing no matter how you plead your case, it isn't going to happen." She tried to keep her touch impersonal and finished washing him in record time, then pulled the sheet up to cover him.

"Spoilsport." His voice was sleepy.

Acadia carried the bucket back to the bathroom, dumped the water, and turned off the light. Stark white moonlight illuminated the room and reflected off the white walls.

Zak caught her hand as she stood looking down at him. "Stay."

Acadia smoothed his dark hair off his forehead. "I'm not leaving you for a second," she assured him softly. "Let go so I can drag the other bed next to you."

"Share."

The beds were far too narrow for two adults to lie side by side, especially when one of them was hooked up to an IV and several beeping monitors. She pulled the second bed up flush to his good side and climbed onto the mattress.

Dogburt immediately jumped up to curl at the foot of the bed. Acadia stretched out, then slid her hand into Zak's. His breathing was even; his hand felt cool to the touch. The monitors beeped steadily on the other side of him. He wasn't—thank God—dead. She sent up a little prayer of gratitude, then lay there staring at the moonlit ceiling.

She was wide awake, wired with residual adrenaline and waiting-for-the-other-shoe-to-drop fear. Where were Piñero and her men? How soon could Zak be moved? How was he to be moved? Where was she going to find the money to pay someone to—

"Stop thinking so hard. I can practically hear your mind doing wheelies."

"Go to sleep."

"Your thoughts are keeping me wide awake."

He wasn't wide awake at all. His voice was a little thick. Understandable under the circumstances; he was being pumped full of antibiotics and other drugs after his death-defying stunt this afternoon. "Talk to me."

Acadia rolled over to face him. "Tell me how you got this scar." She touched the small scar on his temple gently. The cut beside it—where he'd been knocked unconscious—was healing, the swelling had gone down, and the whole area was bruised yellow and blue.

"Wake-boarding in Bulgaria. An awesome ride that unhappily ended on the rocks. Worth it, though. That one gave me a few of the dings on my legs as well."

"Crazy man. Why do you do it?"

He smiled. "You never feel more alive than when your

heart goes manic and you stand on that fine line, challenging fate to a duel. There's a rush, a feeling of euphoria that's hard to describe."

"Why does your brother think you have a death wish?" she asked softly, sifting her fingers through the silky strand of hair at his temple. "He gets the same rush as you do."

"Jennifer . . ."

What about Jennifer? Acadia was dying to know who this woman had been to have such a strong hold on her husband years after her death. "How long were you married?"

His eyes were closed, his lashes casting dark fans on his cheekbones. Just when she thought he wasn't going to answer, he said flatly, "Six years."

She could tell by the way he said it that he'd loved his wife very much. Her chest felt tight and constricted. One day she'd have a man love her that much. "She was a reporter for CNN, right?"

"Freelance. Jen liked extreme wars as much as Gid and I liked extreme sports. She was fearless."

Of course she'd been fearless. A man like Zakary Stark wouldn't love a woman who wasn't as kick-butt and adventurous as he was himself. "Beautiful?" A given.

"Striking, rather than beautiful. Black hair, blue eyes. Men turned to look. Hell, women, too." He was quiet for so long that Acadia thought he'd fallen asleep. Good, he needed it. "She was killed by a car bomb in Haiti two years ago."

God—— "Were you there with her?"

"Gideon and I were kayaking around Cape Horn; she was supposed to go with us, but she wanted to see the quake devastation for herself. Someone rigged a car bomb in her rental. We got the news when we landed in Cape Town the next day."

"Oh, Zak—"

"There's a shitload of guilt mixed up with a bunch of other crap," he said, with what Acadia suspected was understatement. "We'd fought about her going. Haiti had already been dangerously volatile before thousands of people were killed and lost their homes . . . Jen went where angels feared to tread. She lived for that kind of adrenaline fix, and eventually it killed her."

"I'm so sorry, Zak."

"Yeah. Me, too. Lots of unresolv . . ."

She waited for him to finish, then saw his chest moving with his even breathing. He was asleep.

Acadia's eyes stung and her chest felt constricted as she tucked his hand beneath her chin and closed her eyes. Poor Zak. No wonder he didn't think he was a hero. He hadn't been able to stop his wife from going to an already war-torn country.

Zak was going to be well enough to leave tomorrow. But unless they planned on walking to Caracas, Acadia had to figure out a way to get money fast. She'd been an idiot to trust Fejos and his crooked buddies with her last twenty. No credit cards. No passports. The village was so tiny that there wasn't even a phone, let alone a bank.

Somehow, she didn't think the locals would shower her with money if she told them today was her thirtieth birthday, either.

She assumed that if Zak got to civilization, he could walk into any bank with lint in his pockets and get a cash advance on his good looks alone. He'd certainly float her a loan until she got home and could repay him. But to get from where they were to a place big enough to have a bank was going to cost several hundred dollars. Which they didn't have.

Beside her, Zak slept on. His color was better, the swelling and redness on his arm pretty much gone. She lightly pressed her palm on his forehead while he slept a healing sleep. Cool, no temperature. He'd wanted to leave hours ago. It had taken her all her powers of persuasion to convince him to stay one more day. "You are one determined guy, aren't you, Zak Stark?" she asked quietly. "And so damned far out of my league it isn't even funny. Would you have looked at me twice if we'd met at the church bake sale? Not in a million years." His kind of woman dived into other people's wars and sent back the reports she saw on the ten-o'clock news every night. Jennifer Stark had been a doer, just like Zak. While Acadia—She suddenly realized she'd been a doer, too, in the last week.

She'd not only participated one hundred percent, she'd helped. A lot. The thought actually stunned her. She'd. *Helped.*

Hot damn.

She smoothed down the sheet and moved the glass of water closer, in case he woke up thirsty. There was absolutely nothing for her to do. She'd cleaned what could be cleaned, including herself and Zak, and she'd tidied what could be tidied. Selfishly, she wished he'd wake up so she'd at least have him to talk to.

Instead, she pulled the straight-backed chair over to the open window and watched a few women coming back from the market. Two very old men sat under a broad shade tree playing chess. She waved away a fly and rested her elbows on the peeling paint on the windowsill as three men strolled down the street toward the cantina. One of them was Police Chief José Fejos, and with him were the toothless guy and the muscled biker. They were smoking fat cigars and laughing as they pushed open the doors and disappeared inside.

Acadia narrowed her eyes as a plan formed. Her last thought before she plummeted into sleep was that Zak's striking, fearless wife had been an idiot to leave him.

THE ROOM WAS FILLED with late-afternoon sunlight when Zak woke. He was disappointed to find himself alone. "Acadia?"

No answer. Zak gingerly got out of bed and carefully stretched. The sister had detached him from the IV at his insistence when she'd come in to check on him earlier. She had not been happy, and her mouth had pinched up like she'd sucked a lemon. She'd checked his temp and changed the bandage before she was willing to undo the IV.

Nun or no nun, he needed his strength back sooner

than later. Gideon was going to be frantic when he got to Caracas to find Zak hadn't shown up. He wouldn't know where to look. He'd think the worst. Zak might not give a flying fuck about himself, but he hated to worry his brother. And what if Gideon took it into his head to come back and search the jungle for them? Zak wouldn't put it past him.

He felt a hundred percent better than he had the day before. Much as he hated to admit it, he was glad he'd allowed Acadia to convince him to stay the extra twenty-four hours. He went into the bathroom, which looked shockingly clean, and guessed it was Acadia's handiwork. Ignoring his reflection in the stained mirror, he took a leak, brushed his teeth, then enjoyed what he could of a long, tepid shower. It took effort to keep his left side dry, but aside from the occasional splatter, he managed by draping the plastic shower curtain over his shoulder like a toga. It pretty much did the trick.

Sister Clemencia was entering the room when Zak returned, wrapping a towel around his waist. She held a tray with two covered plates. "*Buenas tardes, señor.* You are looking well."

Zak smiled as he picked up his watch to get it out of her way, strapping it to his wrist as she put the tray down on the wobbly table. He blinked as a flashing streak of brightness impacted his vision. It lasted a second, then was gone.

The sister gave him a worried look as he flattened his hand against the footboard. "You are dizzy? Sit down. Sit down."

"No, I'm fine. Much better, thank you for your care, Sister. Have you seen my wife?"

She got a pinched look on her homely face. "Elvis saw her go into the cantina *two hours ago*. Your wife, she has a drinking problem, *señor*." The nun crossed herself. "I have prayed for her."

"*Gracias*. I'm sure she needs all the prayers she can get." Elvis was the unlikely name of one of the elderly men who'd assisted her with his care.

As for his errant *wife*, it wasn't wise for Acadia to wander around on her own, especially at night, especially here. *Where are you, woman?* Fuckit. It wasn't safe out there, Acadia knew that as well as he did. What if one of the locals had tipped off Piñero for a reward? What if, while *he* was lying about, Acadia had been hauled back to Guerrilla Bitch's base camp?

Zak glanced through the grimy windows. The setting sun had disappeared behind the trees, creating a surreal violet twilight that seemed otherworldly.

He was worried about her, and yet she'd been the one to save his life. Several times.

Zak felt an icy shiver, a sensation of having been snatched from the jaws of death by the scruff of his neck and in the nick of time.

He had *died*.

The thought of croaking, in theory, had never bothered him. If it had, he'd never have been able to indulge himself with all the extreme sports he enjoyed. But now that he *had* died, the very thought of never seeing Gideon again, or Acadia, shook him to the core.

The urge to see Acadia, to hold her, strengthened, and he flicked the flimsy curtain to look out on the street. He let the curtain drop. He couldn't go rushing after her like he had a right to demand her company. Fuckit, he'd already asked more of her than he could possibly repay. Once this was over, and it almost was, they'd go their separate ways. The thought should've pleased him. It didn't.

He turned back to Sister Clemencia, who was straightening the already neat-as-a-pin covers on his bed. "Thank you, Sister. I appreciate all you've done for me. For us."

And he'd make sure that she and the mission would be amply compensated for their trouble. Hell, he'd build her a whole new hospital if she wanted one.

The shadows lengthened in the room. and the busy take-charge nun turned on several lamps, which didn't make a whole hell of a lot of difference in the dimness. Finally, with nothing else to tidy, she snatched one of the covered dishes off the tray as if it were the last wafer. "I will take this back to the kitchen. Have your wife come and find me if she is hungry."

"I'm sure she'll—" His vision darkened for a moment, and he sat down hard on the edge of the bed as he mentally caught a streak of jumbled lines. Closing his eyes and pressing his thumbs to his lids, Zak waited for his vision to clear. It didn't. The lines formed letters—no, not the alphabet. Numbers. A string of numbers tearing across his vision like the crawler at the bottom of a newscast on fast forward. He blinked several times.

Still there. Hallucination?

"¿Señor Stark?"

Zak raised his head, rubbing at his temple as his normal vision returned. "I'm all right." His vision was just fucking fine. If he wasn't seeing the numbers superimposed over the bottom ten percent of whatever he happened to be looking at. If he had to hallucinate, he could think of a million things he'd rather be seeing than the same numbers crawling across his vision in a never-ending stream.

He wasn't all right, but he wasn't dead. If his brain kept going on the fritz, he'd hit a specialist once he got home. But first, he'd follow the plan.

Get to Caracas to meet up with Gideon.

Find whoever had orchestrated their kidnapping and make them pay.

⤙ ELEVEN ⤚

Acadia squinted against the last of the tropical sun as it reflected blindingly off the light-colored buildings. The street was deserted, except for the chicken nesting on the remaining rung of an empty rocking chair outside the cantina. She'd left Dogburt guarding a sleeping Zak.

Heartbeat pleasantly elevated with anticipation, she yanked open the door to the cantina. As soon as it swung shut behind her, the room was plunged into shifting shadow. She doubted the atmosphere, or the decor for that matter, was deliberate. The useless fan overhead did its lopsided, uneven rotation. *Thrup-thrup-thump. Thrup-thrup-thump.*

The place stank of booze, cheap cigars, American cigarettes, and body odor. Overwhelming it all was the pungent stench of burned meat. She found the men in the back of the room at what was apparently their usual table. Acadia mentally rubbed her hands with glee. *I am going to kick your ass, Mr. Police Chief.*

The bartender, a tall man with lanky, greasy hair and a filthy, lime green T-shirt riding up his enormous belly, gave her a startled glance from behind the stretch of ply-wood that passed as the bar before scurrying through a thinly curtained doorway, leaving her alone with the foursome at the poker table.

None of them looked up. *Oh, you know I'm here, you jerks.* She deliberately walked with heavy steps as she approached the table and ignored the squelching pop-ping sounds her boots made on the liquor-sticky floor.

Police chief, con man, and extortionist José Fejos was about to deal, but when she didn't go away, he glanced up, deck in hand, fake-startled to see her. "Ah! The American. You are still here?" His tone said *go the hell away.*

"*Sí*," she said with a slight shrug. Where did he think she could go with no money and an incapacitated hus-band?

"Señora Stark. *Qué sorpresa maravillosa.* How is your husband?"

"Much better, thank you." She smiled and brushed a tendril of hair back behind one ear in a deliberately feminine gesture. "Asleep, actually. I hope you don't mind me intruding, but I'm so bored I could scream." The last time she'd been this sweet and girlie was when she'd conned a mother-made school lunch out of Skip Thomson in ninth grade by convincing him that the school bullies had threatened her and stolen hers. He'd had a turkey sandwich, cut-up apples, and a Ding Dong in there, for pity's sake.

She'd even managed a few tears, if she recalled cor-rectly. Poor Skip; he hadn't had a chance. It had gotten her a mom-made lunch then, and it was going to get her the money she needed to get out of town now.

"No. No. Not at all. This is, after all, a place that people can go, yes?" He glowered at her. He wore the same clothes he'd had on yesterday, and had what looked like the same disgusting, smelly cigar smoldering in the filled ashtray beside him. The tortilla chips beside the ashtray were liberally scattered across the rounded table of his hairy belly.

She suppressed a small shudder. A hairy belly and food should never be thought of in the same sentence. She tried to maintain eye contact. "Hmm."

"I would not recommend Teo's food," he warned, close-set eyes shadowed by the bill of his cap. He tap-tap-tapped the deck of cards on the table in an irritated fashion as he talked. "You are better off eating over at the mission."

No kidding. Eating here would probably give her some deadly intestinal disease. "Thanks for the warning," she said cheerfully, giving him a beaming, open smile. And waited, looking pointedly at the cards and the poker table. "I'm not hungry, anyway." She cocked her hip out to one side and smiled shyly.

Police Chief José Fejos looked at her expectantly, lifting the cards in a subtle *we'd like to get on with our game* gesture.

"Oh! Am I interrupting you?" She put a hand to her mouth. "I'm sorry, it's just that I love watching men play cards," she explained, sliding her fingers casually into the pockets of her khaki pants as if she hadn't a care in the world. "My daddy used to let me stay up once in a while and watch him and his friends when I was just a little girl. He's been gone eight years now, and I still have great memories; it was such a rare treat to see men who really knew how to play well."

Chips dropped from his shirt like golden snowflakes as he sighed. She was familiar with that sigh; it wasn't the kind of sound that suggested he thought highly of women in general, and her specifically. "Do you play poker, Señora Stark?"

Acadia laughed softly. "Well, I wouldn't say *play*. It's been so long, I don't really even remember the rules. But I used to enjoy watching. May I . . . ?"

His smarmy smile was almost as repulsive as his fat, hairy body. Oral hygiene was another thing not high on his grooming list. "But we play for money, *querida*, and you are without funds, not so?"

Because you swiped my last twenty, you dishonest, unchivalrous, disgusting pig.

She faked disappointment, then brightened, digging in her back pocket. "I have this. It's real silver." Placing the chain on the table, she arranged the medallion carefully.

The care wasn't fake. Her father would have enjoyed the hell out of what she was about to do. St. Christopher had better step up to the plate.

Acadia smoothed it with her fingertip. "Is that enough for a round or two?" *Or twenty.* Depending on how fast they decided to take it and send her on her way.

Cigar between two fingers, he picked up the chain on the nail of his pinkie. "This is worth nothing, *señora*. What else you got?"

Thank you so much for asking. She gave a disappointed sigh. "Nothing here, I'm afraid." She brightened. "But I have plenty of money back home. I just won the Kansas lottery, you see, just in time for my birthday!" Her smile widened. "Which is today, in fact. So I thought maybe I'd try to see if I could play, to celebrate. But of course, I don't have access to the lottery money here . . ." She trailed off, leaving the bait lying on the water like her father had taught her.

"You won a lotto?" Fejos's heavy jowls quivered, his piggy eyes bright. "How much?"

Acadia cast a nervous glance to the biker guy and a tremulous, hopeful glance at the old man, and smiled shyly at the bald man, who was all but levitating out of his chair with glee. "I won ten *thousand* dollars," she told them in a conspiratorial whisper filled with awe and excitement. They'd take her for ten. They'd kill her for five hundred thousand. "Can you believe it? I wish I could get my hands on some of it. But it's the weekend, and besides, there aren't any banks nearby."

"You give me the bank and numbers and I will take care of everything," Fejos assured her. More tortilla pieces rained down as he puffed up his already puffed-up chest. "I'd be honored to help you. *Feliz cumpleaños, señora.*"

Happy birthday to her. He wanted to rob her blind.

She opened her eyes wide at his cleverness. *Snap* went the trap. "You *can?* Well, if a girl can't trust the chief of police, who *can* she trust?" She smiled happily. "Just take out . . . how much do you think, to keep me playing for a couple of hours until my husband wakes up? Maybe five hundred dollars? No. Make that a thousand." She made damn sure her smile went all the way to her eyes. "I feel lucky. Okay. Take out a thousand dollars. Oh, this is so exciting! I'll write down my account number for you.

"Do you have— Thank you." Acadia took the pencil and piece of notepaper they'd been keeping score on, flipped it over, and wrote the bank account number she'd used for her father's medical expenses. Barring any recent bank fees, the balance was still holding at seventeen dollars and eleven cents.

After a brief bit of business with multiple speaking glances among the men, Fejos motioned for the skinny old guy to bring over another chair from one of the nearby tables. Acadia didn't have to guess where she'd be placed. Between Darwin and the rotund police chief, where she'd be on the dealer's left. Which meant she'd have to place the first bet.

"Oh, this is so cool." She scooted the chair closer to the table, all bright-eyed and eager and as girlie as she could be. "Thanks, guys."

Darwin's dark, wrinkled face scrunched up into a grin. Lots of teeth there. Big teeth. "*¿Conoce usted el juego de cartas* Texas hold 'em?"

Acadia shook her head, her ponytail, intentionally high and ingénue, bobbing on her shoulder as she gave him a wide-eyed look. "Just tell me the rules. I'll learn as I go." She turned to give Fejos a self-deprecating smile guaranteed to make him believe her IQ had just dropped another ten points. "I don't want to slow you down or anything. But can you try to not take all my money too quickly? I'd like to play awhile—at least until my husband wakes up!"

The police chief gave her a spotty recap of the rules, leaving out a few pertinent details. Of course.

If she'd been Dogburt, she would've wagged her tail. Subtly, of course. Just because the cards weren't in her hand yet didn't mean the game didn't begin now. Her poker face came wrapped in an airhead smile.

"I will be generous and lend you twenty American dollars, yes? Ladies first," Police Chief Fejos told her expansively. Everyone anted up, and he dealt each player two cards. Acadia glanced at her red cards. Not bad. A ten of diamonds and a ten of hearts. A pocket pair.

Fejos ran his thumb over the pile of banknotes in front of him. As her daddy used to say, an obvious tell. He was anxious to bet. *Bring it on.*

She could afford to lose several hands before she had to win a little to stay in the game. Three or four hands should be enough to read the men and learn their tells. She'd lose this hand; she frowned at her cards.

"I'm not so sure about these cards." she asked timidly, clutching them too tightly against her chest. "What do you call it when you don't want to bet?"

José looked up at her. "Tap the table and say 'check.'"

Acadia awkwardly tapped the table twice as if she wanted a second drink at a bar. "Check!"

The chief threw the equivalent of five dollars into the middle of the table. Darwin and gangster-prisoner Gomez followed and muttered, "Fold."

Fejos glanced up and looked away. Oh, yes. The slime

bucket had a decent hand, as well. He threw another five dollars into the pot.

Her turn. "I guess I'll call?" She looked up innocently. José dealt the flop and put three cards faceup on the table. King of hearts, queen of spades, and ten of spades. Acadia noted the twitch in his lip and concluded he had either kings or queens in his hand. A pair, unless she was misreading the signs—and she knew she wasn't.

Her heart twinged. God, she missed her father; he and his poker pals would be howling with laughter if they could see her now. Gomez threw the equivalent of ten dollars into the pot.

The chief leaned back in his chair, feigning disinterest while he stroked his stack of bills with his sausage fingers. "I'll see your ten and raise you five." He took a puff of his cigar and blew out a cloud of smelly smoke.

Acadia turned a cough into a sigh of frustration. "I don't think I should bet this hand." She threw her cards faceup so that the whole table could see them.

Gomez smiled at the perfectly good three of a kind she'd thrown away and glanced up at Fejos, whose eyebrows rose in surprise. "Next time, *señora*, throw your cards facedown," he said with irritation.

"Oh! Sorry!" She reached over and flipped the cards over, giving him a sheepish look.

Alberto folded, the openmouthed cobra on his neck looking on a little too realistically, and the chief raked in the first pot. She felt a pang as her St. Christopher medal was swept up into a pile of crumpled banknotes, bits of chip, and cigar ash.

She played several more hands, carefully reading her opponents, noting their barely suppressed excitement. She held on to her very small winnings, feigning surprise and pleasure when she won and frowning with disappointment when she lost.

The chief dealt her a five and a four. Frowning, she shook her head, ponytail bouncing. "How come I keep getting such horrible cards?" Everybody bet a dollar all the way around.

The police chief's pupils dilated in pocket-ace excitement. Oh, she'd seen that look before; he had a decent hand. Too bad she didn't. Crap.

He dealt out three more cards. Acadia's heart raced, and she struggled to look deflated. A ten and a two. Nothing by itself, but matched with the other three twos on the table, she knew she had it. "Check."

Alberto bet five. Darwin and Gomez both called. The chief called and raised. Acadia just called, knowing she had to look weak. One more card.

An ace.

The police chief draw in a telling breath. He had aces, and everyone else at the table had— Her mind raced, calculating the cards she'd already seen with the probabilities of folded hands—a possible full house.

The four men played each other with bluffs. The pile of money in the center of the table grew and grew.

There was one last community card to be dealt. The fifth card, the river card, make or break. The jack of spades.

Alberto checked.

Darwin checked.

Gomez checked.

The police chief rolled his cigar from one side of his fleshy lips to the other, the saliva shiny on the outside of the tobacco. He could barely contain himself and pushed all-in.

Acadia called without hesitation. But she made sure her eyes were wide and guileless as she did so. Alberto paused and called. Darwin called. Gomez called.

With an innocent look, she asked the chief, "Is it okay if I see your cards?"

His grin smeared from ear to ear as he turned over his aces. "Aces over deuces. *Completo*." Full house.

Alberto couldn't beat the hand. He folded. Darwin and Gomez folded.

Fejos stared at Acadia, who maintained a serious, if slightly puzzled, expression with some effort. She wanted to punch the air.

"What do you have, *señora*?"

She slowly turned over her ten. "I'm not sure . . . I think I might've have won?" God, she loved seeing the dawning realization that she'd wiped the floor with all four of them.

Beginner's luck, or skill? They'd never know.

Acadia plucked a stained bill from the pile of cash she pulled closer and set it in front of him gleefully. "What a *fun* birthday. Here's the twenty you fronted me, Chief. Thanks for letting me play!"

His eyes narrowed. "Your other card, *señora*."

With a wide grin, she flipped over the ten and slammed down the two. "Yes," she said with a good deal more cheer than maybe she should have, "I do believe I did." She scooped up the pot and shoved the notes into her pockets. "Thanks, guys, that was really fun! We'll have to do it again. I better go check on my husband now, I bet he's waking up and cranky at being cooped up inside."

Shoving away from the table, she picked up her St. Christopher medal and dropped the long chain over her head, then strolled past the table.

Apparently old Saint Chris had ducked out for a coffee break. Hard fingers snapped around her wrist. Acadia's heart plummeted into her stomach.

"*Un momento, señora,*" the police chief said, silky except for the underlying threat in every syllable. "I think you are mistaken."

"No," she began slowly, eyes darting to the three other men at the table, who stood with deliberate intent. Oh, crap. Did she really think it would be that easy? Her lashes flared, wide as she could, as she asked uncertainly, "I won, right? That's how people win." *Assholes.* "Right? And I paid you back, so now you don't even have to withdraw the money from my bank account," she added brightly, to remind him he had plenty to gain by letting her go.

The fingers on her arm were brutally tight, but the expression on his face changed. He had forgotten the bigger prize. He held on as he decided if he wanted both the cash *and* the lotto fortune, which didn't take long.

But before José Fejos could say or do anything more, the doors behind Acadia slammed open.

"¡Señora!" The shrill old voice sliced through the cantina like a rusty saw blade. Acadia watched the chief's eyelids flinch. *"Durante una hora, su esposo ha estado buscando a usted, y ahora ¿le encuentro aquí, en la cantina?"* Sister Clemencia strode across the uneven cantina floor like a miniature soldier in Hawaiian blue. Her beady little eyes were pinned on Acadia as she pointed at her, her tirade reaching a crescendo. *"¡Bebiendo como una borrachera! ¿Jugando las cartas?"* she spat. *A drunk, playing cards. "¡Usted es una mujer ingrata!"*

Acadia winced. She was *not* an alcoholic, ungrateful wife. She was getting them money to get her impatient *husband* the hell out of here! Still, she gritted her teeth, bowing her head. "I'm sorry," she said plaintively, and slid José a sideways glare. "I was just going back to the mission, if Police Officer Fejos is done."

Sister Clemencia fired off a rapid spurt of Spanish that had José's lips tightening to a thin, pale line. *"Sí,"* he all but growled, letting her go. Perhaps he'd settle for the lotto fortune after all. He gave the other men a quelling look and, turning his face away from the fierce little nun, a knowing smirk.

Acadia, shoulders hunched, dutifully moved to the old woman's side as Clemencia shook a gnarled finger at all of them. She didn't catch all of it, but she got enough to know that the diminutive nun didn't think highly of men who encouraged a young wife to sin.

She flinched as the nun rounded on her. "Your husband," she said flatly. "He is awake and seeking his wife.

You go. Be a good wife." *Or else* hung in the air just long enough for Acadia to march beside the nun across the bar and toward the door.

The men watched her all the way out into the evening light.

As the door swung closed behind Sister Clemencia, Acadia sucked in a breath, whispered, *"Muchas gracias,"* and ran like hell across the street back to Zak.

Happy birthday to her. She'd just won safe passage out of there.

5583623285967562535556558362328596756253555655583623285
96756 . . .

Zak saw the same unending sequence of numbers moving continuously in his mind's eye with crystal clarity, streaming left to right like some goddamned securities exchange ticker.

They weren't going away. In fact, they seemed to be permanently lodged in his head. Day or night. Lights on, lights off. No matter where he looked, the numbers were superimposed over the bottom edge of whatever he was looking at. If he closed his eyes, he saw them just as clearly. The only time he *didn't* see the damn things was if he was asleep.

Morse code? Some sort of algorithm? An encryption?

Fuckit. He had to stop trying to make sense of something that was a figment of his imagination.

He never got sick. Hell, he rarely went to doctors for anything short of the required travel vaccinations or getting a broken bone set, but he'd get on this shit quick.

It was both distracting and cause for real concern. He didn't like it, even though he imagined—hoped like hell—it was some sort of temporary hallucination. It *looked* damn real to him. Maybe it was a lingering sign of fever? Or the knock on the head back at the hotel where this had all begun must've knocked a screw loose.

Wouldn't Gideon find *that* amusing?

He and Acadia sat in a long *curiara*—a wooden dugout canoe; an elderly Pemon man and his grandson were taking them down the Orinoco River as far as Ciudad Bolívar.

The sky was a deep blue. Not fully dark yet, but several stars were popping up in the vast overhead canopy. The trees lining the riverbank were filled with flocks of red, yellow, and blue squawking parrots, and hundreds of large black-and-orange troupials, with their long tails and bulky bills, swooped and dived, feeding on the insects swarming the water. A heron stood on one leg and watched them skim by. A log or alligator lurked between the tall grasses on the bank. Zak kept an eye out for any quick movements.

"I'll miss him," Acadia said as the kid stood on the riverbank waving madly, the skinny dog at his side.

"He probably gave us fleas."

"Nah." She waved back just as enthusiastically, causing the canoe to list. "Not Dogburt."

"Sit still before you tip us over. Pace your excitement, it'll be a while."

Even in the wilds of the rainforest, anything was possible when one threw money at it. Acadia and the kid had shown up at the mission clinic within minutes of one another. The kid was there to retrieve his dog. Acadia, flushed and heart-stoppingly beautiful as she'd bounded in, had surprised the hell out of Zak by emptying pockets full of cash.

It was like providence. The kid's uncle's brother's second cousin—he was sure he'd missed something in the colloquial translation—had a boat. He was also unafraid of the police chief whom Acadia had relieved of his cash.

Something Zak didn't share, not with her cheeks flushed and eyes sparkling and hands full of money, was that he was scared shitless that Piñero would finally track them down. He wanted them out of there, immediately. Zak had ignored Sister Clemencia's admonishment that he wasn't well enough to leave. He'd *died*, she reminded him. Several times. God had a plan for him.

Yeah. Meet with his brother. Uncover who the fuck the kidnappers worked for, get back to his life. It was a fine plan. But he couldn't hold a candle to Acadia—the woman planned everything down to the last peso. He wished he'd seen her playing poker against the crooked police chief and his cronies.

She was an intriguing female.

"What do you think happened to Piñero and her men?" Acadia stared at him like she wanted to see inside of his head. No, thank you. Too damned cluttered as it was.

The old man and his son paddled them into the center of the river, where the water was clear and deep, and the current helped move them along briskly. "Maybe she just gave up."

She huffed out a breath, shifting to get comfortable on the hard bench seat across from him. "With sixty million U.S. dollars up for grabs? No, she didn't."

Loida Piñero *hadn't* given up. And if she hadn't given up, where *was* she? Zak scanned the lush vegetation on either side of the riverbank, as if Guerrilla Bitch might suddenly appear like a jack-in-the-box from among the trees.

While he didn't have the itch on the back of his neck he usually got when shit was about to hit the fan, he had a distinct waiting-for-the-other-shoe-to-drop feeling lying like a stone in his stomach. Sixty million American was a shitload of ransom to give up on. And Piñero hadn't looked to Zak like a woman who gave up easily, if at all. No, she was after their asses.

She just hadn't sprung out at them. Yet.

Another possibility—one he didn't even want to consider—was that they'd caught Gideon, and would use his brother as bait to get to him. But Gideon was smart and resourceful, so that scenario was as unlikely as it was unwelcome.

"What are you going to do?" Acadia asked. "You and Gideon."

"Turn the tables, and hunt her down like the bitch she is. She has answers we want, and I sure as hell don't like having to look over my shoulder. Something tells me she didn't instigate the kidnappings. But dollars to doughnuts she knows who did. Gideon and I are professionals at shaking bushes and rattling cages."

"You could just go home to . . . ?" She left it hanging, waiting for him.

The muscles along his jaw flexed. "Seattle," he supplied, "and not just no. *Hell*, no. Not until this is over."

"Okay, then." She trailed a finger in the water. "Are you going to recover physically before you hare off on this wild scheme? Or are you hoping to push yourself until you're really sick, and you——" He noticed she caught herself before she asked him if Gideon was right, if he really did want to die. *Again*.

"Until you can't do anything but lie in bed flopping like a——like a beached tuna?"

God, she was funny. A beached tuna? Where the hell did she come up with this shit? His lips twitched. "I'm plenty recovered." Except for the annoying numerical crawler in his brain, he actually felt surprisingly *great* for a guy who'd died recently. "Get your hand out of the water," he added. "Things bite down there."

Her eyes widened and she snatched her fingers back into the boat so quickly, he had to double-check that something hadn't taken them already. "Then why are you scowling?" she demanded, with a scowl of her own.

He rubbed his eyes with one hand. "I'm not."

"You have a headache, don't you?"

He watched an anaconda swish through the water a few feet from the *curiara*. Thing was as thick as his thigh, and six feet long if it was an inch. "Even my mother never gave a rat's ass if I had a headache." His tone lashed. "Don't mother me, Acadia; I don't need it."

"*Everyone* needs mothering once in a while." Her gray eyes were calm, mouth set in the lush line he was coming to recognize as Acadia Gray at her most determined. "What happened to yours?"

"Twenty questions?" His shoulder ached, and he shifted to ease the dull pain, annoyed and out of sorts that he couldn't help with the rowing. He tried to figure out what the numbers could be. A bank account number? Safety deposit? Hell, random numbers with no rhyme or reason? There were a lot of fives . . .

She did some ultra-feminine thing with the high ponytail and twisted it into an untidy nest on top of her head. Her nape was going to be feasted on by mosquitoes. Zak reminded himself he wasn't *her* mother either.

She dropped her hands to hold on to the sides of the canoe. "Got anything better to do?"

He could think of a few— *Whoa.* "Has anyone told you that you talk too much?"

"Strangely, no." She cocked her head, and the muted light streaming across her clear skin made her eyes look almost transparent. They got dark and smoky while she was being fucked. And hazy and foggy when she was limp and replete in his arms afterward.

"Okay, yes," she admitted with a rueful smile that pleasantly kick-started his heart. "Once in a while. And do you know why?"

"I probably don't, but tell me anyway." He liked listening to her talk. Liked hearing how her agile, funny mind worked, how her brain ticked through problems, and how she came up with solutions in her own convoluted way.

"It's a nerves thing, I mentioned that once." He remembered. "But it was also to get a little attention. My parents loved each other to distraction, usually to the exclusion of anyone else around. They waited ten years to have me—went through in vitro, and so on. When I finally arrived, they loved me to distraction as well, but they were pretty set in their ways, and sometimes they didn't notice me waiting to be noticed."

Her gaze drifted past him, out to the lush jungle bracketing the river around them. The noise was different out here; muted, somehow, but no less full. The sudden slap of things skating under the surface, the rustle of animals—even the birds harangued them from all sides.

And yet, aside from the blaring trail of numbers in his brain, Zak was momentarily at peace, and fascinated by all things Acadia Gray.

Her fingers trailed over the boat's edge again before she caught herself and tucked her hand around the curve of her thigh. He wondered what she'd do if he asked her to tuck it into his. "I'd talk a lot," she continued quietly, matter-of-factly, "and really fast, so I could tell them about my day or whatever before they lost interest."

He forced his mind to get into gear. "And they live in Kansas City?"

"My mom died—" She paused, and Zak frowned as something soft and squishy welled up in his chest. Sympathy?

Hell . . .

"A pretty routine surgery, but she never woke up." Her mouth twisted. "Breast reduction, actually. So you can imagine—or maybe you can't," she added wryly, "but I was terrified my breasts would get so large that I'd have to deal with the same issues she had. I'd just turned thirteen."

Tough for a teenage girl. Zak felt compelled to say something, anything, and settled for the first thing that popped into his brain. "Your breasts are perfect in every way." He loved it when her eyes crinkled up in amusement. "And your father?"

The amusement faded. "Died a month before I won the lottery, as a matter of fact."

Jesus Christ. "I'm sorry."

"Thank you." Acadia drew her knees up, resting her chin on them. The canoe wobbled and splashed water around their feet. She shot the father-grandson team an apologetic look over her shoulder. *"Lo sentimos!"* Then she said to Zak, "Me, too. He was a wonderful man, and I adored him. I guess you could say I had about thirteen awesome years with both of them. Then my mom died, and my father started getting . . . strange. I thought he was absentminded with grief. They'd been so close—It was years later that he was diagnosed as early-onset Alzheimer's. It was a slow, scary road. But those first years were . . . magical." She smiled. Not sad, not *woe is me.* A quiet smile filled with love.

She scooped up a handful of water and let it drip off her fingers. Behind her, the old man shook his head. But he didn't say anything. "I hope one day to have the same kind of marriage my parents did. They were so happy together." She paused. "Although I fully intend to pay more attention to my kids. What about you and Gideon and your folks? Close?"

"Not even geographically," Zak admitted. "Crystal gave our father what he wanted. A couple of heirs to the empire he'd built up around him like some kind of kingdom. She never professed to like kids. Which was fine," he added quickly, seeing her eyes go all soft and dewy. "We had sexy nannies, a stellar education, world travel, and absolutely no boundaries."

Her sympathy only deepened. "No wonder you both dare fate for kicks. What about your dad?"

"Unless he needed us for a photo op, we were pretty much invisible to him." His father had been an egotistical ass. Filled with self-importance. It had chapped his hide that Zak and Gideon had started ZAG with Buck and a few grand they'd managed to scrape together as seed money.

He'd always had Gideon. His brother had been his real family. "His indifference would've been better. It was just Gideon and me." And for a while, there was Jennifer, but he definitely wasn't going there.

"I'm sorry about your wife. That must've been so hard. At least there weren't children?"

Christ. Another fucking can of worms. "We were about to adopt. I stopped proceedings when Jen—" He hadn't wanted to do it. Jen's idea of family hadn't been that much different from his own. And her idea of mothering had been to get nannies and continue her wild ride of life unimpeded. His lips moved in a grimace he couldn't control. He'd not only lost his wife the day Jennifer died. He'd lost a child as well. Nobody had known that.

"She wanted six, she always said. Six multiracial kids."

Acadia frowned. "You didn't want to adopt, or you didn't want multiracial kids?"

"I didn't give a flying fuck *what* color my kid was, but I thought starting with one and seeing how that went made more sense." He didn't mention that the subject of children had been dropped the year after they were married, or that he and Jen had had sex for the first time in six months a few months before she'd been killed. She'd been barely three months pregnant and had called him in flight on his way to Cape Town to tell him.

He'd felt a surge of joy mingled with a surge of disgust. Divorce was on the table. Her timing couldn't have been worse.

God *damn* these fucking numbers! He pressed his fist between his eyes in an attempt to block them.

In fact, he was pretty much done with the sharing-life-stories business, so he made a big deal of rubbing his forehead. "I'll just close my eyes for a bit and rest." *And not let you drag my life story from me one painful oar stroke at a time.*

⤚⦿ TWELVE ⦿⤙

They arrived on the outskirts of Caracas at full dark. With his thanks, Zak paid the man most of Acadia's poker winnings, and the small boat disappeared into the gloom of the shadowy river.

"This isn't exactly civilization," Acadia pointed out. It was a rural area with a few buildings and several shops lit against the night. Dozens of people milled about the streets. All of them stared. She moved closer to Zak's side.

"Close enough." He dragged her into a nearby tobacconist and asked to use their phone. After a rapid-fire exchange, the skeletal man behind the counter handed him a rotary phone. Zak paid him with the rest of their money.

The tiny shop smelled strongly of tobacco and was filled with smoke from the three old men standing nearby, puffing at foul-smelling cigarettes as they watched her. Acadia leaned against the glass display counter and only half listened to Zak's conversation.

With his thanks, Zak slid the heavy black phone back across the counter, then took her hand, leading her outside. "The concierge at the Gran Meliá Hotel knows Gideon and me; we've stayed there many times. She's sending a car."

Acadia didn't miss the "she" and suddenly wondered if it wasn't just Zak's reputation alone that made everything within reach of a phone.

"How's Gideon?" The first question he'd asked the woman at the hotel.

Zak's jaw clenched, and she knew the answer before he said grimly, "Hasn't checked in yet."

Twenty minutes later, the luxury sedan that had been sent to pick them up was met at the five-star Gran Meliá Hotel by a stunningly beautiful young woman whom Zak quickly introduced as Carina García-Ramírez. "Has my brother—?"

"Not yet, señor. I'm sorry." Carina whisked them to the presidential suite. "I have tried to anticipate your needs, Señora Stark," the concierge told her, ushering them into a luxurious suite decorated in golds and cream. Acadia didn't want to walk on the pristine, plush cream-colored carpet with her jungle-dirty boots, so she paused just inside the doorway to unlace them and place them side by dirty side near the door. Didn't seem to bother Zak any as he strolled in like he owned the place. For all she knew, he did.

It wasn't until she'd padded into the suite after the other two that she realized the woman had just called her "Mrs. Stark." She got a fluttery feeling in her tummy, which was silly. It was just a form of address. An accident. Which Zak hadn't corrected.

Zak went immediately to the phone. He was calling his partner, she knew. Checking to see if Gideon had called, updating him on the situation.

Carina indicated the laden coffee table between two gold brocade sofas. "I took the liberty of ordering a light meal, Señor Stark, but should you require something more substantial, please let me know." She smiled. "Your toiletries are in the bathroom, *señora*, and I have chosen some garments I thought you might require overnight. If you would like to give me an additional list of your requirements, I will make sure everything is brought to your suite by morning."

"Thank you. That's—" Pretty freaking amazing. "Great." The opulence—hell, the cleanliness—after where they'd been was stunning, disorienting, and surreal, to say the least. Acadia walked to the windows while Zak talked quietly on the phone.

The wall of ceiling-to-floor windows framed a spectacular view of the lights and high-rises of downtown Caracas and the dusty outline of the mountains in the distance. She watched the two talk, reflected in the windows. The concierge leaned in just a little. She liked Zak. Liked him a lot. She touched his arm. He shook his head.

Acadia dragged her gaze away. Jealousy was an emotion she'd never felt in her life. The fact that she felt it now was . . . *stupid*.

She glanced around. To the left, separated from the rest of the room by a waist-high sideboard, was a highly polished dark wood dining table that seated eight. To the right, a living room area. The place was as big as a luxury apartment, a huge contrast to the squalid cell they'd shared just a few days ago. For that matter, it wasn't anything like anywhere she'd ever stayed; it was something out of a movie, not her version of real life.

The coffee table had been laid out with half a dozen covered serving dishes, several large pots of coffee, and a platter of artistically cut fresh fruit.

Zak turned to her with a tired smile when he heard her soft footfalls. "Yeah. Wherever he lands first," he said into the phone. He held out his right hand, and Acadia slipped her fingers into his. Her heart swelled with cautious emotion, but she ruthlessly tamped it down.

Zak put the phone down. "Piñero made her ransom demand a week ago. Buck's been frantic. He hasn't heard anything since." He scrubbed a hand across his jaw. "No word from Gideon."

"Because he's on his way."

"From your lips . . ." His eyes refocused as he looked at her. He reached out and tucked a strand of hair behind her ear. "Hungry?"

Acadia was starting to feel a little fuzzy around the edges. Exhaustion crept up on her in increments. The cessation of danger and drama and not knowing what scary-as-hell thing was going to happen next, the horrifying realization that Zak had died and then the total relief when he'd come back, had all combined to zap what energy she had left.

"I'd love a shower first. Then food."

"Shower's through there." Zak indicated a wide doorway into another room. "All the lotions and potions you need. If not, dial eight. Carina will take care of it."

"Right, okay." She didn't want to let go of his hand. She suddenly felt like a kindergartner on the first day of school. Right then, Zak was everything safe and secure.

And that was a problem.

She untangled her fingers. "Thanks." She turned to go through the bedroom, but Zak snagged her elbow as she passed. She stumbled, and he wrapped his free arm around her waist. Hazel eyes scanned her face. God. She must look a mess. Her hair was all over the place; her face was probably filthy.

He used a gentle finger to push a strand of hair off her cheek and said very softly, "Thank you for saving my life."

Her breast brushed his fingers, imprisoned in the cheap black sling across his chest. "You're welcome."

"You don't have to be on guard anymore, okay?" Zak told her gently, as if he could read her mind. "I'll take care of you for a change."

"Great."

He tilted her chin up on his finger. "Acadia Gray, warrior woman? At a loss for words?"

She lifted her eyes slowly to meet his gaze. "Funny, huh?" Her chest felt shuddery and tight. It wasn't just the shocking realization of his wealth. Or that she stood on a carpet three inches thick, surrounded by the fragrant aroma of freshly brewed Colombian coffee and the lush, civilized smell of hothouse flowers scattered about the room in cut crystal vases. Well, yes, it was all that. But more, it was the stunning realization that this Zakary Stark was as far away from Acadia Gray's lifestyle as Alpha Centauri from the sun.

"You're safe here. You can let down your guard," he repeated.

Wrong. Her guard was up and unbreachable. Self-imposed, but way up there. She had no place in his world, and he'd be bored out of his mind in hers. "Wow," Acadia said brightly, looking around at the expansive and exquisitely decorated suite. The original artwork, the gold brocade sofas, and the tasteful antique furnishings were all top of the line. "We've gone from the ridiculous to the sublime."

"You'll want that shower," he murmured, a smile in his voice, his gaze hot as he looked at her mouth.

She gave him a narrow-eyed look and saw him through a sparkling shimmer. "Now, that's just plain rude, Zakary Stark; you aren't any cleaner than I—"

She hadn't realized just how close he was until he hooked his hand around the back of her neck and pulled her around and against his bound arm.

A fluttery leap of anticipation made her tilt her face up to his. "Be careful of your sh—"

His hungry mouth silenced her. He didn't bother to warm up, or ask permission. His mouth was hot and demanding and impatient. The kiss was like dying of thirst all day and then sinking into a lake of cool, crisp water and drinking her fill. The flutter became a tidal wave of need. Of greed.

To resist would be futile, and damn stupid. Who would she be fooling? Mature, well-reasoned intentions be damned. She wanted him in any way she could get him. Acadia wrapped her arms around Zak's neck, fisting her hands in his hair as he kissed her with single-minded intensity that bordered on a territorial imperative. Her tongue met his, voracious and just as needy as his own.

His hand went down her back, and he started tugging her shirt free of her pants as she matched him in intensity, tilting her head and going up on her toes to better reach his mouth. She wanted him so badly that it never occurred to her to say no. Or wait. Or— Her mind went blank.

The next thing she knew, the small of her back hit a solid surface. The supporting arm around her left for a second as he swept a huge arrangement of fresh flowers, and several useless gold boxes, off the sideboard to crash to the floor. She felt a splash of cold water on her socked foot as the vase and flowers scattered on the plush carpet. Then she was flat on her back, legs dangling on either side of the mahogany cabinet, Zak wedged between her thighs.

His elbow digging into her chest.

Acadia started to giggle. The whole situation was crazy.

He dropped his forehead onto hers. "I've never had a woman crack up when I'm putting my best effort into seducing her." He sounded amused.

Since his free hand was trying to undo the zipper on her vest, he wasn't supporting himself over her, so he was extremely heavy. She liked the jut of his erection pressed intimately against her, and the weight of his hips pinning her in place. She started yanking his T-shirt from the back of his pants.

"We could take a lovely hot shower," she suggested, kissing his throat and jaw as she glided her fingers up his bare back. His skin was hot, smooth, and very touchable. "With *soap*. Then we could put on whatever your friend left us to put on—"

"Nothing."

"Okay. We'll sit and eat dinner naked. We'll have a glass of wine, and then we'll come back in here and—"

"Excellent idea, with one modification."

"What's that?"

"We finish what we started here first. *Then* we'll follow through with your most excellent plan."

All his hard places were aligned with all of her soft, moist places. A win-win as far as Acadia was concerned. Heat suffused her entire body, and moisture pooled between her thighs.

He whipped the sling off over his head, tossed it across the room, and concentrated on attacking her zippers. He almost didn't wince at the obvious pain in his shoulder. Big brave macho man that he was. "Zak! You'll pull out your stit—"

He crushed her mouth under his in a kiss so hot, so explosive, she forgot what she'd been trying to say. She'd have words with him later when she called the doctor in to sew him back up. Silly, silly man . . .

With three hands frantically trying to undo zippers and get her T-shirt off, Zak gave up and just took one side of her vest in his teeth, the other with his hand, and ripped. She gasped. "I'll buy you a dozen," he growled. "Get it off, it's in my way."

She didn't get it off. She got the zipper down and her T-shirt bunched up. And while she was doing *that*, Zak was running his mouth from her throat to her navel. "That's very ahh . . . distrac—"

He undid the top button of her pants with his teeth, which was a nifty trick, then yanked down the zipper with his fingers, spreading either side of the khaki pants with one large hand, fingers stretched wide. "Commando again. This saves time." He nuzzled his nose into the juncture of her thighs. "God, I love the way you smell. Earthy. Sexy. Hot for me."

Acadia cupped her breasts, since he was busy and *someone* had to do it. Her nipples were tight little buds, hard and begging for attention, and so sensitive her lightest touch was enough to send her skyrocketing into a massive climax.

All the lights in the room were on. The drapes, should anyone out there in one of the tall downtown Caracas buildings close by care to look, were wide open, and she was flat on her back straddling a piece of fine furniture. All firsts.

In no way hampered by having use of only one fully

functioning arm, Zak dragged her pants down her legs and instructed, "Lift," while his mouth was pressed against her.

She arched her back and lifted, pressing herself firmly against his open mouth. He hummed his pleasure, which vibrated straight through her. The smooth wood beneath her bare skin was warming up, but it was still hard as she settled her behind down again.

"Maybe we could go into the bedr— *Ahhh!*" She practically levitated off the hard surface as he opened her with his tongue and unerringly found the swollen bud nestled in her folds.

Her hands tightened on her breasts as he swirled his tongue across the knot of nerves and gently, deliberately, closed his teeth around her.

The climax rolled through her in wave after wave after wave of glorious, Technicolor sensation, so that she couldn't tell one from the next. The fireworks explosion at the end left her deaf, dumb, and blind as her sensory-overloaded body splintered into a thousand pieces.

"Good?" Zak asked, now standing between her limp, spread legs.

Her lashes fluttered up. "W-what?"

He slipped his forearm under her knees and slid her down to the very edge of the sideboard. "Just checking to be sure that was good for you."

Acadia lifted a weak hand. "You need to ask?"

Zak chuckled as he wedged his narrow hips between her spread knees. "Ready for more?"

"N— Are you insane? I can't breathe, let alone— Oh. My. God. Z-Zakary!" His penis was hard as a rock, thick and sleek, as he flexed his hips, plunging so far inside her in one powerful thrust that she shifted up the sideboard when she came again. He pressed a splayed hand on her quivering belly and kept pumping as she struggled to gather her scattered wits. Impossible.

The next climax rolled right behind the first until she couldn't tell if she was coming over and over or if it was one giant climax that was going to kill her with pleasure. But what a way to go.

She came again, hard, and the lights did pinwheels around her as she felt the pounding of her heartbeat in every pulse point.

With a guttural cry, Zak collapsed on top of her, stealing the last sip of air from her already collapsed lungs. She didn't have the strength to gasp for him to move.

Sweat glued their skin together, and he was still deep inside her. Acadia had never been more satiated. If she'd had an ounce of energy left she would've pulled up her pants and run far and fast, before he ripped out her heart and threw it over the edge of some distant killer mountain.

Right before he intended to snowboard the damn thing.

"Shower?" His voice was muffled against the hot, sweaty curve of her throat as he kissed her.

"Minute. Can't walk." *Can't breathe. Can't talk. Can't think straight.*

"I'll carry you."

Acadia choked out a laugh. "Oh!"

Zak lifted her with his good arm and tossed her over his bandaged shoulder in a very efficient fireman's lift, her bare ass right next to his lips. "Time for that shower."

Since she was suddenly dangling down his back, she tasted his damp skin as she tried to push his pants all the way off his hips. It took a while before they made it to that shower.

·∾ THIRTEEN ∾·

Zak left Acadia sleeping and followed the dim light to the living room. Seated at the large mahogany desk, he picked up a pen and held it poised over a piece of hotel stationery.

The shadowed suite smelled of sex and the crushed flowers he'd stuffed back into the vase after picking them up off the floor. He smiled. He might just buy that credenza thing and have it shipped home to Seattle.

Although he played sports ambidextrously, could even manage to brush his teeth or fire a weapon with either hand, writing with his right hand was a laborious process. But the damned number thing hadn't allowed him to sleep.

He was worried sick about his brother. Had that bitch captured him again? Was Gideon even now back in one of those stinking cells in the middle of fucking nowhere?

Zak rubbed his forehead. What had she said to her men the other day? "Hunt them until we find them. Kill either one on sight. Bring the other back." He pressed two fingers into his eye sockets, trying to get rid of the numbers so he could concentrate.

Loida Piñero had ordered her men to kill *one* of them.

Why not both? She'd had proof of life. The ransom demand had been made. Why keep one? Kill the other?

Zak didn't want to think the worst, but he and Acadia were several days late for the rendezvous. Gideon could be having difficulties obtaining transportation out of the jungle. He, too, might have sought medical attention, for his broken ribs. Injuries festered in the hot humid climate . . . And if there'd been any internal bleeding . . . Fuckit. He couldn't even think about it.

Christ. Zak's brain was cluttered with what-ifs.

He picked up the phone and dialed Seattle to see if Buck had heard from Gideon yet. Zak looked at the clock on the wall and let the phone continue to ring. Anthony Buckner was one of the calmest men Zak knew. Nothing alarmed their partner, even at 5 a.m. and woken from a deep sleep, and God knew there'd been lots of those calls over the years.

Buck cut him off neatly. "Before you say anything, no, God damn it, I still haven't heard from Gideon, *or* the kidnappers. And yes, I realize we have a policy, but I'm paying the ransom anyway. I'm in the middle of liquidating personal funds to cover it."

Zak closed his eyes for a moment, his gratitude profound. A few years older than Gideon, Buck had been in on the ground floor when they'd had the idea for a revolutionary new Internet search engine. Buck had worked his ass off side by side with them to form ZAG Search, now the biggest search engine in the world. It was a hell of an accomplishment, and one that had made all three of them wealthy beyond their wildest dreams.

Buck enjoyed the day-to-day grind, and Zak and Gideon had been happy to hand that off to him. The brothers worked hard, but they also played hard. What the hell was the point of all that money if they couldn't enjoy it?

At one point, at the beginning, they'd matched each other in being workaholics. Long hours, longer meetings, code-grinding, and the legalities of it all had made for caffeine-fueled sessions that didn't stop for hell or high water. But they had thousands of people to do the grunt work now.

The arrangement worked.

Buck was married, with two great teenagers and a very hot wife. He, Nikki, Zak, and Jennifer had been very close when Zak and Jen were first married. When their marriage had started falling apart, Nikki had taken Jen's side, and Buck had stuck to Zak. Zak knew that his marriage difficulties had put a strain on his friend. And here the man was, paying multimillions of dollars out of his own pocket.

Christ, that showed Zak the kind of guy Anthony Buckner was—had always been. Zak heard his friend getting out of bed as he took the phone into the den of his lavish Queen Anne home in Seattle to talk without waking Nikki.

"What did you expect? Fuck the policy. It's just money—you and Gid are more important. I've liquidated the sixty mil; picking it up later today."

Zak clenched his fist. "Gideon didn't leave a message on your home or private office line you might have missed?" He was grasping at straws. If his brother had contacted Buck in any shape or form, his friend would've said so. "Look, Gid could stroll in here in the morning none the worse for wear, but it might be good to have the money ready just in case. You should have used the company money."

"I didn't want you screaming about breaking company policy—and as your partner, and friend, I know you're good for it. I'll have the cash hand-delivered to you at the hotel. We'll need to bring in security people," Buck said. "We can't mess around with a kidnapping. Especially not in Venezuela, where it's considered a national pastime. If these guerrillas have Gideon in their clutches again . . . Shit. Sorry. You've gone through the variables yourself a million times, I'm sure."

"At least." Zak heard the chink of pottery as Buck poured himself a mug of coffee in the kitchen. He knew Buck's house as well as his own.

"Try not to worry. I know exactly who to call. Zak, waiting for if or *when* Gid shows up at the Gran Meliá might be too late. Think about it. Let me liberate the cash and pull a team in, send them to you, just in case? An insurance policy. Okay, buddy? And then if you don't need them, you and Gideon can use the company jet to come home."

Zak and Buck discussed logistics and what assets could be liquidated immediately, then hung up. Buck was nothing if not efficient. He'd have their security people arrive in one of the corporation's aircraft by nightfall. Cash in hand. Ready to hunt the guerrillas down if Gid hadn't shown up by then.

It was a sound plan. Zak prayed he wouldn't need to activate Buck's security people. He wanted desperately to believe that his brother would amble in, with his too-long hair and that cocky, self-satisfied look that always meant he thought he'd won.

The competition between them had kept their close relationship lively. The Stark brothers had been best friends, confidants, all their lives. The ten-month age difference had forged a deep friendship and love that Zak was terrified to lose. Hell, he didn't have a single childhood memory without Gid in it.

An insurance policy, he told himself. That was all the precautions were. An insurance policy. Because if he didn't see the whites of his brother's eyes within the next twenty-four hours, he was marching back into the jungle to track that bitch down and retrieve his brother himself.

The wheels were set in motion. Buck would be calling the bank manager and getting his ass out of bed right now. There was nothing Zak could do but wait. Pressing his fist between his eyes, he wrote down the numerals—625355565—as they scrolled through his mind in a continuous crawl.

What the *fuck* did they mean? Or was he trying to make sense of something that was completely irrational and nonsensical? He joined those numbers to another clump, although in his mind they all ran together like a fucking ticker tape.

5583623285967562535555565

Too many late-night stock market number crunches all coming together in a concussion?

Ridiculous.

He used the pen and slashed the numbers into twos, then stared at them. Nothing came to mind. He rewrote them and broke them up into threes. Again nothing.

Frustrated, he tore the top sheet off the small pad, then started tearing the paper into small squares.

He heard Acadia's soft footfall on the plush carpet and reached out his arm to tug her in close. He'd instructed the concierge to stock the bathroom with jasmine-scented products, and the fresh, familiar scent of Acadia's skin made him horny as hell. He couldn't get enough of her. He felt remarkably calm and centered around her. Relaxed and comfortable in a way he'd never felt in all the years he'd been with Jennifer. One-handed, he untied the loosely belted tie on her white terry-cloth robe, then slid his hand between the fabric and her incredibly soft skin.

"Couldn't you sleep?" she asked softly, leaning her hip against his arm and running her fingers gently through his hair as she peered over his shoulder to his doodles and bits of ripped-up notepaper. "What are you working on?"

Zak hesitated. Somehow, having Acadia know about his hallucinations didn't bother him at all. He had a disloyal thought—that he'd never have told Jennifer about it. In six years of marriage, they'd actually never had that level of trust. Jen would've somehow figured out a way to use what she would've perceived as a weakness to bring him to his knees, and she would have done it in such a way that it would've taken a long, long time for Zak to realize he'd been razor-cut and was bleeding out.

"I have sequences of numbers running through my brain."

She took the information in smoothly, soft eyes searching his face. "When did that start? After you were hit on the head before we were taken? God, Zak I knew you had a concussion! You still have a bump, and the bruise—"

"You'd think it was a concussion. But not unless it was a delayed reaction. No. The numbers started at the mission."

"After you died."

Zak huffed out a laugh. "Actually, after I came back to life. Okay, this *is* odd, but it isn't some newly developed sixth sense or anything woo-woo like that. I think it might be a hallucination. Or some sort of brain malfunction. Maybe I need a reboot. Or a shrink."

She gave him a worried look. "Have Carina call a doctor. Preferably a specialist—"

"If I still have the problem, I'll see someone back in Seattle."

"Are you . . ." She sighed. "Yes, I see you are. Okay, for now let's try to figure out what it is." Her fingers kept lifting, then dropping, strands of his hair as she leaned against his good shoulder. "What kind of numbers?"

He skimmed his palm down the satin-smooth skin of her hip, releasing the scent of night-blooming jasmine. He inhaled deeply before answering, "No idea."

"I'm pretty good with numbers. Want me to look?" She slid around to perch on his lap.

"You don't think I'm nuts and hallucinating?"

"Yes to the former, but that has nothing to do with these numbers," she replied, a smile in her voice. "And grounds for concern if the latter," she teased, shifting to get comfortable, thereby making him extremely *uncomfortable,* as she was sitting directly on his erect dick. He slid his hand inside the open robe to cup her breast.

"No hanky-panky. Let's take a look. What's the confetti for?"

"I thought if I wrote each number on a separate piece of paper, I could move them into groups. See if anything emerged that made any kind of sense."

"Do we have them written down as you see them?"

He reluctantly uncapped his fingers from the velvety softness of her left breast and flipped the page so she could see.

Her lashes fluttered against her cheeks as she read the numbers. Then she looked up to meet his eyes. "How do they appear to you? What do they look like?"

"They run across the bottom of whatever I'm looking at, like the crawler on a news program, or a ticker tape."

Chewing her lower lip in concentration, she

nodded. "Look at that wall over there. How big are the numbers?"

"They take up less than ten percent of what I see."

"Is there a beginning, a middle, and an end?"

Zak slid his hand back to stroke her breast again. Like a worry stone. *Or a freaking addiction.* "Far as I can tell it's on a continuous loop."

She picked up the pen and tapped it as she considered the numbers in front of her. Her hair tickled his lips, and the smell of jasmine would forever remind Zak of her. "Social Security number? Bank account number? Swiss bank account number?" She rubbed the top of her head on the underside of his chin. "How about a long-distance phone number card and PIN code, or house number? Somewhere you lived growing up?"

"I didn't think of a house number—but no, not that. And I don't know all my account numbers off the top of my head, but I can take care of that with one call to my financial adviser in the morning."

He buried his face in the silky strands near her neck. While Acadia was as complicated as a string of unrelated numbers running through his brain, she was considerably easier to distract. "It's not pi." Or a dozen other improbable theories.

"As in apple?"

She glanced over her shoulder and gave him a smug and sassy grin. "Pi is a mathematical constant whose value is the ratio of any circle's circumference to its diameter in Euclidean space," she rattled off easily. "The same value as the ratio of a circle's area to the square of its radius— What?"

"You memorized that?"

"Wiki. I read it just for kicks. But yes. I pretty much remember weird stiff like pi." The pen tap-tap-tapped. "Having problems with any circles lately?"

"Would this be considered a circle?" Zak pinched her nipple lightly between his fingers and felt her whole body shudder. She pressed down on his swollen dick and shifted enough to make him grit his teeth.

"Not in this instance, no. We need a computer."

"Yeah. The hotel would supply one, but I thought I'd wait till morning and go buy one instead."

Acadia twisted around until she straddled him face-to-face. The robe accentuated her lithe body and beautiful, perfectly sized breasts. Just looking at her made Zak catch his breath. "In that case, since it's the crack of daybreak . . . let's go back to bed and get some sleep." Bed, good idea.

Sleep, not hardly.

"I bet in the morning Gideon will be here," she continued softly, "starving and ready to rumba. And with proper rest, maybe your brain will reboot and the numbers will go away." She reached up and slid her fingers along his lips as he opened his mouth to argue. "And if that *isn't* the case, then the three of us will figure out your number problem, no sweat."

ZAK'S BROTHER DIDN'T CHECK into the hotel during the predawn. And neither did Zak's brain reboot. He was still seeing the scrolling numbers. Acadia could tell he was loath to leave the next morning, but he needed a phone and a computer. And though Carina had supplied Acadia with a pair of black pants and a crisp white shirt, and the clothes fit fine, she needed clothes of her own if she was going to stick around with Zak for a few more days while she waited for her paperwork to go through. If it could even be done within a few days. She had no idea how long it would take: weeks, months? She had no identification on her at all.

She had to go to the American consulate, and she needed to access her bank account. Now that they were back in civilization, she didn't expect Zak to pay her way. She wouldn't have accepted it before she'd won the lottery; she didn't need it now. She didn't bring up her need for her own money and her own clothes, because she knew he'd argue with her, and she wasn't in the mood to fight.

She wanted to enjoy his company for as long as they had left together, however short a time that was; then she'd pull up her big-girl panties and mope when she was alone. But until the second she was, she was going to enjoy every minute in Venezuela with Zak.

"When Gideon gets here, he's going to be exhausted, filthy, and hungry," Acadia told him reasonably as they ate breakfast in the suite. "He won't want to sit down and compare notes. Let's go out and do our errands and come back in a few hours to give him a chance to recuperate."

They hit the U.S. consulate first. Fortunately, Zak's fluent Spanish, and his forceful, polite insistence that they would *not* be returning to the scene of the crime to file a police report for their stolen papers, finally sank in. Acadia didn't think she wanted to hear one more time that no papers could be filed unless accompanied by a police report detailing the how, where, and why of the loss of their official papers.

Zak methodically, and patiently worked his way up a very long food chain until he received the correct answer.

They were to return in forty-eight hours to receive their paperwork. Acadia hoped that meant passports, because she couldn't leave the country without one. But passports, they were told, could take up to two weeks. They had to come from the States. Zak assured her that with the correct bribes he could shorten the time. But first they had to obtain the papers.

They hit a bank next. There, fortunately, Zak knew the bank president, who was called at home and would be there to attend to whatever Zak might need, within the hour.

Which Zak told her meant at least two hours in Venezuela.

"I'm starving," Acadia told him as they stood in the bright sunshine outside the ornate marble-and-gilt bank. "Should we go back to the hotel for lunch and see if your brother's there?"

"We'll call Carina, see if Gid's arrived. Otherwise, no. Let's not waste time. I have a long list of purchases I'd like to make before we head back."

Acadia smiled. "With nothing but your good looks to pay for things?"

"I got some walking money from Carina. We'll charge what we need to the hotel. It's already set up with her."

They could walk into a store, charge whatever they purchased to the hotel, and that didn't seem at all strange to Zak? "Okay," Acadia tucked her hand in his good arm. "Let's go shopping."

There was a computer store conveniently located next door to a women's boutique. They split up at the door to the dress shop and agreed to meet in half an hour. Acadia wasn't much of a shopper. She either liked something or she didn't. It fit or it didn't. She could afford it or not. However, in this case, Zak came back and gave the store manager whatever information she needed to charge Acadia's purchases, then had her purchases sent to the hotel.

Zak's expression when he took in her new chocolate-and-cream wrap dress and high-heeled sandals made her heart leap with anticipation. The heat in his eyes, as his gaze did a slow trip up and down and up again, made her pulses skitter and dance. She hadn't had much time, but in that time she'd shopped like a madwoman and bought and applied makeup. She felt like a new woman.

He brushed the backs of his fingers across her cheek, his attention unmistakable. "You look . . . amazing."

"Thanks," Acadia gave him a slow, sexy smile filled with promise. With heels on, she was eye level with his mouth. He had a scrumptious mouth. Firm, and well shaped, and . . .

"You bought this dress to drive me to distraction, didn't you?" Zak accused, voice rough. His open hand slid from her face down her throat, until he got to the deep V between her breasts. He crowded her a little until Acadia's back was against the store's window, then ran a lazy finger up one side of the edge of the V and down the other.

He was tall enough to block out the sun, but it glinted off his hair and his strong brown throat. "You're aware we're standing on a busy street." Because he was like a magnet, she found herself leaning in, hand on his chest. "In public," she murmured as Zak dipped his head. "In broad dayli—"

Acadia's lips were there to meet his as his mouth brushed hers in a too-brief kiss that left her wanting more.

He smiled as he straightened. "Your eyes cross when you're horny, know that?"

They didn't cross—she didn't think—but it did take a few seconds for her vision to clear. "They do not." She gave him a light punch to the arm. "You overestimate your charms, Mr. Stark. Who could possibly be horny standing in the middle of one of Caracas's busiest shopping districts?"

"You? Me?"

Yes and yes. "Didn't you find what you needed?" she asked, tucking her hand around his bicep. She'd never been big on PDAs, but with Zak she was afraid that public displays of affection could easily become the norm.

When he touched her, everything and everyone else disappeared.

"Got a computer," he told her easily as he started walking. "Sent it back to the hotel. Here, hold this." He handed her a small white bag with the familiar Apple logo on it. "I got you a phone. It's fully charged, and has my number and the concierge's number at the hotel. I also programmed in the numbers of my partner, Anthony Buckner, and my personal assistant, Debra McGuire, in Seattle. If, for any reason, we get separated, or you need anything while we're here, contact Deb first."

They *were* going to be separated. Soon they'd go their own ways. She doubted Zak would want her to contact his office *then*. "Thanks for the phone." Acadia removed the iPhone from the bag, sliding it into an outside pocket of the purse she'd just bought, the strap secured across her body. Plenty of pickpockets in Caracas.

She fought off a pang of separation anxiety. Despite the danger and uncertainly these last few days, she'd never felt so alive, or had so much fun, ever. Even if the fun was fraught with danger and mayhem. And no matter how much Zak protested about not being a hero, she trusted him with her life.

AFTER A LEISURELY LUNCH, Zak took Acadia back to the bank, where he secured a cash advance for her. It was unnecessary for her to know that the banker, Landro Méndez, did so only on Zak's signature. She was an unknown entity with no identification, whereas Zak had done business with Méndez on several occasions and had dined at his home on his last visit. Gideon had hauled Zak's ass on a trip to climb Pico Bolívar, in the northernmost reaches of the Andes Mountains, six weeks after Jennifer . . .

It had been too soon, the trek and subsequent climb, not nearly challenging enough for the way Zak had felt at the time. He'd spent the entire trip in a morose silence, although God only knew he appreciated his brother's attempt to distract him when he thought about it later.

Jesus, Gideon. *Where the fuck* are *you?*

Méndez offered Zak the use of his car, which he'd accepted gladly. Renting a vehicle without identification, while not impossible with the right bribes, would have been time-consuming. And Zak could all but feel time, like an hourglass, running out around him. The scrolling numbers hadn't stopped, even after a few hours' rest earlier this morning. They didn't change. They didn't speed up. They didn't slow down. Zak was almost getting used to the monotonous intrusion, except that something about them seemed . . . critical.

Acadia settled back in the luxurious black leather seat of the borrowed Mercedes, clicking the seat belt across her lap. "Back to the hotel?"

"No," he told her, voice grim, jaw clenched with tension as he pulled into a break in the traffic. "I need your expertise. I'm taking you to your home away from home."

Zak had been on the phone with the hotel five minutes before. Gideon was still MIA, although Carina had

Gideon's room ready, with clean clothes and a doctor on call in case Gid needed one. Zak had given her both his and Acadia's cell numbers and instructions to call the second his brother showed up.

Zak had a bad feeling. Gid shouldn't be taking this long to get to Caracas unless something had gone drastically wrong. He gave Acadia a quick glance as he wove through the traffic, noticing how the silky fabric of her dress separated across her thigh as she crossed her legs. "What are you wearing under that dress?"

"The appropriate underwear. Why?"

His fingers tightened around the leather-covered steering wheel. "Take off your panties."

"There's a bus right next to us." But she didn't say no.

"Now."

"We'll never see those people again, right?" She slid the skirt of her dress up higher, exposing a mouthwatering length of smooth, lightly tanned skin. She leaned against his arm and lifted one cheek to hook her thumbs into what Zak fleetingly saw was a sheer scrap of aqua. There wasn't much of it, and his dick stood to attention as she arched her back to slide the panties down her legs.

"Happy?" She stuck the wisp into her purse.

"I like knowing there's nothing between what I want and where I want it, *when* I want it."

"Well, you aren't getting it driving seventy miles an hour in traffic, Mr. Stark."

"But I know how much you enjoy being well prepared in case of emergency."

She laughed. "You think sex is an emergency?"

"With you? Yeah. Knowing that you're in commando mode again will keep me motivated until we get back to the hotel."

She settled back into her seat and recrossed her legs, letting the dress slide all the way against her body, not exposing anything, but firing Zak's imagination so that he almost drove into a pickup truck filled with pigs as his libido went haywire.

Twenty minutes later, Acadia was in her element, in the sporting goods store. She dragged him around for one circuit, then got a cart. "Surely you won't walk back into the jungle alone?" she asked as they waited for a clerk to go in back and return with ammunition for the weapons Zak had loaded into the cart, with no questions, no ID required. "It's too dangerous, Zak. Especially while you're still healing."

"Buck's sending a security team with jungle experience. They'll be here tonight. Can you locate a map while I'm waiting?"

Acadia went off in search of a topographical map of Canaima National Park. He watched her stride off, filled with confidence and high energy. God, she was hot and so sexy in that dress, with her long legs and high heels, he practically had to wipe the drool off his face. Knowing that she was bare under that thin layer of fabric made his heart pound and his pulse race.

She was sweet and honest and funny and peppery and sassy. He knew the taste and texture of every inch of her body, and just looking at her bare ass lovingly outlined in chocolate-colored silk made him hard. Her sunny blond hair was loose down her back, and looked as shiny and soft as it felt when he crushed it in his fingers.

Damn. If only they'd met in another time and place . . . if only he'd been a different person.

The clerk returned with his arms laden with boxes of ammo. Zak piled them in the cart, then checked the list Acadia had jotted down in the car. With each selection he prayed that he was wasting his money. That Gid would be back at the hotel, waiting impatiently for him to show up.

But if that were the case, Carina would have called him.

A few minutes later, Acadia handed him a folded map and dumped an armload of khaki into the cart on top of the boxes. "SCOTTeVESTs for both of us. Very handy in the jungle, as you know."

Zak's heart ricocheted into his throat, and unexpected fear tasted unfamiliar and unwelcome in his mouth. He stepped right into her personal space and grabbed her arm. "You're *not* going with me."

Acadia put up both hands. "Down, boy. You're damn right I'm not." She flattened her palms on his chest, so he shifted out of her way. A place he'd very much have liked to stay in if they hadn't been in the middle of rows and rows of weapons and pup tents. "But you owed me a new vest. I'm collecting."

Zak opened his mouth.

"Sshh!" She pinched his lips closed with two fingers. "*One* vest. Not a dozen." She pulled the list from her pocket. "Okay, what else do we need? I'm starting to get hungry again."

He was hungry, too. He wanted his mouth on her, and his hands on her, and then he wanted to bury himself to the hilt in her hot, wet, silky heat.

Pretending to be oblivious to his thoughts, she was an efficient drill sergeant, collecting things Zak thought he might need, vetoing things she knew were inferior products and unnecessary because she'd found something that did the job of three. She certainly knew her stuff, and saved him time as well as weight as she loaded the cart with essentials.

They were soon on their way back to the Gran Meliá in the late-afternoon commuter traffic, which was slow going. Zak checked his phone to see if either Buck or, please God, his brother had called. Neither had. He stuck the phone back in his pocket. "Hotel or restaurant for dinner?"

"Hotel. You'll want to be there when your brother arrives. We can work on your number thing, and go over the map to pinpoint where the guerrillas held us." She paused to give him a sultry smile. "Then you can indulge all those fantasies you've been having all afternoon."

"While shopping for supplies?" he asked, pretending puzzlement.

"True," Acadia murmured. "*Most* inappropriate. I'm sure you didn't consider sliding your hands under my dress to fondle my bottom when I bent down to look at the hunting knives in that case back there. I'm positive you didn't calculate to the last nanosecond how quickly you could untie this one little bow at my waist to get this dress off me. Or wonder if my new bra was as sheer and pretty as these." She twirled the postage-stamp-size thong under his nose. "I'm positive none of that crossed your mind at all."

He shot her a feral smile, because she was dead-on, and there'd been plenty more one-second inspirations all afternoon. "*Nervous*, Miss Gray? Because you're going to have to run like hell when we get to our floor. I'm not sure we'll make it to the room before I see for myself."

"Oh. Did I forget to mention I talk a lot when I'm so hot I'm about to explode without your help?"

"Spread your legs," he ordered thickly as he pulled into the tree-lined parking lot adjacent to the hotel.

"Absolutely not!"

"It'll stop you from coming without me."

She eased her knees apart and he could smell her musky warmth. "Don't touch me, Zak," she grumbled, voice strained. "I mean it, I'm hanging on here by a thread."

HAND IN HAND THEY raced into the suite, slamming the door behind them. It was dusk, the sky outside the panoramic windows a deep indigo, sparkling with city lights. Acadia barely noticed the heap of packages on the coffee table as Zak stripped off his clothes and hauled her through to the bedroom at warp speed. They'd paused, barely, before coming to the suite, to check in with Carina in person and inquire again if Gideon had arrived while they'd been out. He hadn't.

"I'm going to take a shower," she said breathlessly, laughter bubbling up inside her as Zak flung himself naked on the bed and motioned her with one finger and a cocky smile to come to him. God, he was irresistible, though she saw the pain in his eyes, and the worry he was doing his best to hide. And even with that, this was the most relaxed she'd seen him since they'd met, what felt like a lifetime ago, in a small, noisy cantina.

"I'll shower with you." He caught her hand and gave a little tug. "Later."

"I'm hot and sweaty."

Not smiling, he tugged a little harder. "And about to get a lot hotter and a hell of a lot sweatier. Put your knee right here." He patted the mattress beside him with his free hand, and winced as if his shoulder hurt.

"You're going to tear out your stitches if you aren't careful."

"Then you'll have to do the heavy lifting." He exerted a little pressure on her hand, and Acadia bent her leg and rested her knee beside his hip.

"All things considered, I've already done all the heavy lifting, Stark." She smiled, her body practically vibrating with anticipation. The sight of his hard body laid out for her viewing pleasure made her throat close and her lungs tighten. He was fully, impressively erect, lying there like some sort of pagan god waiting to be serviced.

"*I've* been *your* hero for days on end," she told him sternly, her nipples hard beneath her clothes. Moisture pooled between her thighs as she looked down at him. "You should be parading around naked and feeding me peeled grapes in gratitude for being so resourceful, so helpful, so ably equipped to repeatedly saving your life."

"So true," he told her soberly and, she saw on his face, with utmost sincerity. "I am naked, but not parading at the moment. However"—he gave her a wicked smile—"I plan on repaying you by being your sexual slave for many glorious hours. Then I'll order a *vineyard* of grapes as soon as we're done, and we'll start on fulfilling your every fantasy. Swing your leg all the way over." His voice was rough, slightly uneven.

Her body blocked him from the city lights shining in through the window, turning most of him into a forbidding shadow.

Acadia gave him a stern look. If he touched her right then, even the lightest of touches, she'd go up in flames. "You are completely out of your mind, do you know that?"

The wicked grin widened. "Do it."

Acadia straddled his narrow hips, but didn't sink down on his erection. She folded her arms under her breasts and scowled fiercely. The man was certifiable.

He motioned to the bow at her waist with his chin, holding her gaze with his own. "Untie that."

The skirt of her dress pooled on the mattress around her hips, but under the dress she was bare, and exquisitely aware of it.

She'd felt naughty and bold and delicious sexy all afternoon, knowing that he knew she was naked under the perfectly proper dress. His thick penis stroked her inner thigh.

After a few moments of nonverbal, eyeball-to-eyeball communication, she tugged slowly at one end of the sash and the bow fell apart.

"God." Zak closed his eyes as if in pain. "You mean that's all it would've taken this afternoon to get you naked?"

She still didn't lower her body, although they were both almost breathless from wanting her to. "I would have expected grapes."

He wasn't touching her, just lying between her spread knees as she straddled his hips . . . waiting. "I told you. A vineyard." His eyes glittered.

"That's a little extravagant, isn't it?" Acadia couldn't pull her eyes away from his. The two sides of her dress parted, leaving an inch of skin exposed between the edges.

"No." His hand slid between her legs and brushed the dewy petals of her damp folds, sending a zing of electricity through her entire body. "You're very wet." Working a finger inside her, he growled, "Keep going," with a jerk of his chin at her still hands.

She shrugged and the dress fell off one shoulder, revealing a chocolate-brown satin demi-bra. He worked two fingers into her wet passage and stretched her wide. Her back arched as delicious tremors and hot shocks of pleasure streaked through her body.

"God," he said thickly, eyes as deep and dark as the jungle at night. "Look at you." His gaze caressed her, traveling over her body to rest where his hand had disappeared between her legs.

Eyes heavy-lidded, he murmured, "I want to taste every delectable inch. Lick you like an ice cream cone . . ."

Wanting desperately to impale herself, Acadia started lowering her hips.

"Not yet." Naked fire burned in his eyes.

His heated look inflamed her blood, and a film of perspiration covered her skin. She tried to fill her restricted lungs, but there wasn't enough air in the room.

"Leave the bra on." He moved his fingers deep inside her. Acadia's gaze was drawn to his hand moving between her legs. His penis was huge, jutting past his belly button, a network of veins distended in stark relief along the length. His wrist rubbed up and down his long shaft with each stroke of his fingers inside her.

He was stroking himself while he was pleasuring her.

Knees weak, she let the dress slide off her shoulders, then slipped her arms free and tossed it aside. It landed with a soft plop on the floor beside the bed.

Zak pushed another finger inside her as his thumb found her clit. "Pull the cups down and touch your nipples."

Her nipples were hard tight buds, aching even as she hesitated. "Zak . . ."

"Lightly."

There wasn't much to the bra cups, just a curve of satin and a little lace. She pushed the fabric down, then cupped her warm breasts and tentatively ran her thumbs across the erect tips.

"How does that feel?"

Better if he were doing it, but, "Good," she said hoarsely. Really good.

"Just use your fingertips and pinch them. No, don't close your eyes. Look at me." Zak's hand was saturated with her juices as he moved his fingers in and out of her, until she wiggled and ached for more.

He plucked the sensitive hood of her sex between his thumb and forefinger and she shuddered, gasping with need, and tightened her fingers around the globes of her breasts. She could feel her own heart racing beneath her fingers, feel the rising temperature of her damp skin.

It was hard to focus. She squeezed her nipples hard enough to elicit a moan. She did it again, harder, tighter. Her head fell back, so that she felt the cool, wet glide of her long hair caress her naked back. The restless heat building up inside her made her crazy with sharp longing. "Zak!"

"Do you want me to kiss your pretty nipples, Cady?"

She opened dazed eyes. Squeezed her breasts, feeling the hard points of her nipples press needily against her palms. "Y-yes."

"Lean forward."

She didn't want to take her hands off her breasts, but she wanted his mouth on her more. "I—"

"Brace your arms on the pillow . . . Yes. Like that."

She curled her fingers into the pillow on either side of his head and lowered her breasts to his mouth while his fingers kept up their relentless assault. Her hair made a wall of golden silk on either side of their heads. His hot mouth closed on one nipple, sucking it inside the wet cavern of his mouth.

"I can't stand this. Zak, *please* . . ."

His teeth closed not so gently on the engorged tip, and her back arched as he nibbled and licked until her body was one giant sensitized nerve ending.

His fingers slipped out of her. She lifted her head and moved her hips to regain contact. "Damn it, Zak, don't torture me . . ."

His damp hand slid up her back, telling her without words where and how he wanted her positioned, straddling his hips. The prod of the thick, blunt head of his penis demanded entry against her slick folds. She let out a strangled cry as he pushed himself slowly, inextricably, deep inside her, his hand tangled in her hair as he brought her mouth down to his in a kiss that stole her soul.

Acadia's sheath tightened around him and she sucked in a shuddering breath at the full and exquisite sensation of him deep inside her. She quickly found a rhythm, her hips rising and falling against him until she crested and climaxed, far too quickly. While she shuddered and her internal muscles clenched, he came inside her, his entire body tensing in the aftermath of the massive climax. Feeling his body buck beneath hers, she went into liquid free fall and came again.

How—Acadia wondered, as her body still shuddered with aftershocks and the sweat on their skin cooled— how was she ever going to go back to a normal life after this? After Zakary Stark?

❦⚬─⚬❦

WHILE ZAK WORKED AT his new computer, Acadia sat on the floor nearby, with bags of their purchases beside her. Dumping everything out beside her, she started sorting, then systematically filled Zak's SCOTTeVEST pockets with things she thought he'd need on the trip back into the jungle. *If* he returned to the jungle. Which she was praying very hard he wouldn't have to do.

First the shirt, then the pants. She wasn't a religious person, but with each item she stuck in each of his twenty-eight pockets, she said a little prayer to keep him safe.

Last, she took her St. Christopher medal and stuck it securely in the breast pocket right over his heart.

Zak had generously replaced everything she'd lost or used in the jungle, and since there wasn't anything else to do while he looked for numbers to match his numbers, she filled her new vest with items. Not that she was ever likely to wear the clothes. But they were a nice souvenir of the— No, she didn't want to think about it.

Getting up off the floor, she lugged the extremely heavy garments into the bedroom and placed them on one of the chairs. Hers she'd pack before she flew home. If it took longer than a couple of days, she'd find an inexpensive hotel while Zak left to look for Gideon.

Zak would wear his when he went in search of his brother. Because, as much as she hated to even think it, she knew Gideon Stark wasn't finding his way to the hotel in Caracas. He was still out there.

Going back into the living room, she pulled a dining room chair up to the desk beside Zak at the computer. There were four other suites on the floor; a connecting room was reserved for Gideon. Every now and then she heard the faint ding of the elevator, or the subdued sound of voices passing by. But no key card snicking in the lock. No Gideon.

"Anything?" Acadia pulled her bare feet up on the rung under the seat and leaned against his good arm.

"Not a bank account. Not anything financial."

"How about—hell, I don't know—let's just throw stuff out until something clicks. Fibonacci series?"

He shook his head. "They're not in the right integer sequence." He flipped the sheet where he'd written the numerals, 55836232859675625355565, for her to see.

"Not even close. Okay. How about . . . Golden Ratio? Are the numbers the *size* of something? No? How about prime numbers?" She stirred as he typed up a list of numbers to look at. "How about another cup of coffee and a some of that—what's it called? *Bien me* something?"

"*Sabe*," he finished absently, fingers tapping.

Acadia went to the table where their finished meal had been laid out. She put the dirty dishes back onto the serving cart, then dished up two servings of a sponge cake bathed in liqueur, layered with coconut cream filling, and topped with meringue.

"I'm going to wheel this out into the hallway," she called to him, pushing the cart in front of her.

Unchaining and unlocking the door, she used her hip to hold it open, then pushed the loaded cart to one side before going back in.

Collecting the two desserts, she carried them back to Zak, placing them on the desk beside the computer. "How about we give the number thing a rest for a bit? Let's spread out the map over there, and see if we can find where Piñero's hangout i—"

A thunderous explosion rocked the building. Seconds later, a violent column of flames and black smoke shot up from the parking lot eighteen floors below.

·ᴥ· FOURTEEN ·ᴥ·

W ow. That was loud," Acadia uncurled her legs
and rose to her feet. "I wonder wha—"

Familiar with the sound, Zak jumped from
his chair. "Car bomb!" He grabbed her by the arm and
spun her toward the other room. "Get dressed. Now."

He'd heard car bombs in Ireland, in Yemen, hell, even
in Bangkok. There wasn't a doubt in his mind that the
other shoe he'd been waiting for had just dropped with a
very loud percussion and a billow of smoky flames.

She gave him a startled look but didn't ask questions.
She turned on her heel and sprinted so fast, he glimpsed
long bare legs as her robe flapped behind her body like
wings. Zak clicked off the desk lamp, then raced over
and switched off the two other lamps, plunging the living room into semidarkness.

It stood to reason that since he'd just been kidnapped
and held for ransom, and his brother was still MIA,
Zak was the target. His gut told him to stop messing
around and move before whoever was behind the bomb-
ing crashed into the suite to finish what they'd started
once and for all. His best guesstimate was that he had

less than five minutes before they'd have uninvited guests.

One alive. One dead. Did this mean they had Gid, and wanted Zak silenced? Or had Gid evaded them and now they were after Zak instead? He hit all the lights. Click. Click. Click. Once an assailant's eyes adjusted to the difference in brightness from the outside hallway, it would be easy enough to see with the illumination from the city lights streaming through the window. Zak would have about fifteen seconds before their sight adjusted and he lost the home-team advantage.

Grabbing two chairs, he flipped them on their sides, leaving them in the middle of the room, then dragged out an ottoman as well. Everything low to the ground, more an obstacle course than a trap. Anything to slow them down. For good measure, he dumped out the two bowls of mushy dessert into slippery puddles in a couple of places on the floor. Adrenaline sped through his veins as he saw the computer, screen lit and displaying the research they'd done.

Slamming the computer closed, he didn't bother crawling beneath the desk, just yanked the cord to unplug it, then tucked it under his arm like a football. Once in the bedroom, he closed and locked the door. Another flimsy deterrent that wouldn't keep anyone out, but might add the few precious minutes he and Acadia needed to get free.

Acadia sent him a brave grin as she shoved her feet into her boots and then slammed a clip into the SIG-Sauer they'd bought that afternoon. Both her pants and her shirt were unbuttoned and flapping open over her nude body.

"Good girl," he whispered, tossing off his robe and hastily pulling on his pants and shirt. Thank God Acadia was such a methodical woman; she had distributed the weight evenly, and his movements weren't hampered at all. He stuffed his bare feet into his boots.

He grabbed up several more guns, tucking them into the back of his waistband and one cargo pocket, then added the rest to the bag and shoved the computer into an outside pocket. He hated guns, but he'd never had more reason to carry one. Or two. Or three. "Take only what we can carry," Zak whispered, although there was no one to hear him. Yet.

She nodded, then held up a hand in a *wait* motion. Grabbing the pillows and their robes, she formed lumps on the bed under the pulled-back covers, then threw the comforter over everything. Her shirt still hung open, and she gave him an inquiring look just as a sound alerted him to the presence of someone breaking down the front door. Zak carefully opened the door into the adjoining suite, slipped inside, and held it open. "Shh," he breathed, letting Acadia duck inside under his arm before silently closing and locking it behind her.

Ear pressed to the thick wood, Zak heard stumbles and curses as his obstacle course tripped up at least one member of the hit team. Acadia's fingers tightened on his arm as she listened.

Next, the bedroom door was kicked in, and Zak heard at least couple of footsteps. Immediately followed by two distinct pops.

Silencer.

Acadia's eyes went wide.

"Make sure the wife's dead." The voice was male. And American.

"*Sí, jefe.*"

The bed was on the wall beside the door to the connecting suite they'd reserved for Gideon. The sound of the covers being drawn back was indistinct, but the American cussing was loud and clear. "You goddamn dickhead. You said she was in the room."

"*Sí. Sí.* She come to take out the *carrito de alimentos.* The old food, *¿sí?* I see her."

"Well she's not here now, you fucking moron! We got the car they borrowed, so wherever she is, she's meeting up with Stark. Obviously he knows we're after them, but they'll be on foot. Let's go."

Zak kept Acadia standing by the door in the dark room for a good twenty minutes, until he was sure the two men were long gone. Not a hundred percent sure, but they couldn't stand there forever.

Zak figured Buck's security specialists should've landed about now. They'd show up at the hotel to find him gone. He added, to the growing list, calling Buck to give him their new location.

He indicated her undone clothing. "Finish getting dressed. Don't forget your bootlaces; we're going to have to run." And run like hell.

The sound of emergency vehicles, fire engines and police cars, was faint but unmistakable, even eighteen stories above the street. The cavalry had arrived—although, in this neck of the woods, the cavalry was just as likely to be in cahoots with the bad guys.

He finished buttoning and zipping. "Empty most of that crap out of your pockets; it's going to slow you down."

For once, she didn't argue. He noticed she looked paler than usual, but with thin-lipped determination, Acadia laid the SIG on a nearby chair and quickly started emptying some of her pockets. She tossed the heaviest item—the tent—behind the upholstered chair in the corner. "I need everything else I'm carrying."

"Sounds like whoever hired the guerrillas is American. And they aren't happy to find us alive and well and not here."

"Did you hear what the American guy said? 'Make sure the *wife* is dead.'"

"Yeah. Got that." That little bit of business added yet another unpleasant layer to the miasma that was this whole clusterfuck. Who else would know about his "wife" except hotel staff, the sister at the mission, and the son-of-a-bitch chief of police she'd beaten at poker?

She took a deep, steadying breath. "That Spanish voice, that was one of the guerrillas."

"What? Who?"

"The kidnapper in the hotel room who sounded like he had a cold? That was him in there. I recognized his voice. Kind of high," she explained, "like he had to talk through his nose."

Or has a nasty coke habit, Zak thought. Damn. If it was

the same guy, and Zak was inclined to believe it was, then Loida Piñero had finally caught up with them. *How* she'd found them, he had no idea.

"Okay. We're going to slip out, turn left, and haul ass down the hallway to the emergency exit. Don't stop, no matter what happens. If we get separated—"

"We're not getting separated."

"If we get separated," he repeated, fighting the inane urge to smile, "I want you to find somewhere to hide. Then call Buck and have his security people meet you. They'll make sure you get back home. Promise me."

"Fine."

Zak grabbed her by the front of her shirt and kissed her quick and hard. He touched his fingers to her soft, warm cheek. "Don't do anything stupid. You hear me, Acadia Gray?"

Her chin came up, eyes shadowed. "Ditto, Mr. Stark."

"Keep that gun pointed, and be ready to shoot without asking questions. These assholes mean business. I don't want any extra holes in you, got it?" Her lips twitched as if she found that amusing. She nodded.

Zak eased open the door, hand held up to keep her behind him. There was no one in the hallway. The floor indicator showed that all the elevator cars were in the lobby. He waved her out. Together, they stuck close to the wall, running toward the exit sign. No one stopped them, but Zak waited for a tap on the shoulder at any minute. Or, worse, the muffled report of silenced gunfire.

He eased open the door to the stairwell, and Acadia passed through. He closed the door behind them, then peered through the small window to see if they'd been followed. No one out there.

"Eighteen flights," he reminded her. "Pace yourself."

SHE NEEDED TO RENEW that gym membership. Eighteen flights of stairs at a jog just about gave Acadia respiratory failure by the time they reached the bottom. Her knees ached. Her legs were rubbery, and she felt lightheaded.

"Catch your breath," Zak said. He wasn't even breathing hard. They were in a small area at the foot of the stairs, still inside, but the metal door was marked *Salida*. "I'm going to get transportation."

She held her hand to the stitch in her side. "I-I n-eed a-air."

Zak hesitated, then pushed open the door onto the muggy night. They stepped outside into a narrow alley, where flashing red and blue lights of various emergency vehicles bounced off a nearby wall in a disco effect, but thankfully they were hidden behind a low outbuilding. "Okay. Stand right here." *Here* was comprised of two large, noxious-smelling trash bins. "Stay put."

Hands on her knees, head down, she grunted an affirmative. She felt the brush of his hand on her neck. "You're a hell of a—" Suddenly Zak's phone beeped. "Jesus—"

Acadia would've liked hearing the rest of that sentence. She straightened as Zak turned on the phone, saying a brisk "Yeah?" He paused, his features relaxing while he listened to whoever it was. "They are? Good to know.

Where's the jet?" Zak listened for several seconds. "The kidnappers broke into our hotel room. Yeah. No, we're both fine. Have the pilot stay where he is. File a new flight plan. I'll be there in twenty. Yeah. Thanks, Buck." He disconnected.

"The security guys are on the ground," he told her. "Plane's being refueled as we speak. Wait here. I'll be right back." He lifted her chin and gave her a searching look. "You okay?"

"Terrific. Oh, wait!" She reached out and cupped his face with both hands. Standing on her tiptoes, Acadia kissed him with all she had left, a longer and wetter kiss than the one he'd given her upstairs, but she was a whole hell of a lot needier than he was. And she knew it.

It was still too quick. She released him and smoothed her palm down his crumpled shirt. "Hurry back."

His grin said he would, especially if more of that was on the way. He melted into the darkness, and she was alone. Adrenaline was pumping hard and fast in her system, making her temples throb. This, this right here, was the reason she and Zak were never going to be together. He took it all in stride—the car bomb, the gunmen, being on the run—as if he were getting a cup of coffee and reading the Sunday-morning paper.

A cat meowed plaintively nearby. A sheet of newspaper, teased by the hot breeze, fluttered down the alley where she waited. A car horn bleated in the distance. And the voices of the emergency personnel over on the other side of the building were crystal clear as they tried to figure out whom the car had belonged to and if there had been any occupants.

Thank God, no.

Wheels crunched loudly on gravel, and she backed against the wall as a police car, lights off, pulled up in front of the trash bins. If she could see the vehicle, the occupants could obviously see her. Oh, shit. Shit. Shit. Another adrenaline spike made her dizzy for a moment, and she pressed her sweaty palms to her temples. *Breathe, Acadia, breathe; this is not the time to pass out.*

The passenger door popped open. "Get in!" Zak straightened from opening the door as she jumped in and slammed it behind her.

"Oh my God!" Acadia stared at him in awe. "You stole a *police* car?"

He turned on the lights. "No one was using it," he said dryly, driving at a sedate pace down the alley, away from the public parking lot on the other side of the buildings and the growing assortment of officials. "Buckle up."

"They're going to miss this sooner than later."

"Probably. We'll blow up that bridge when we cross it. Keep the SIG on your lap and take the safety off. We won't dick around should anyone give chase. Be ready to use it."

Acadia swallowed hard, then curled her fingers around the butt of the gun. "Where are we going? Airport?"

"The company plane." His jaw in profile was tight, his fingers white-knuckled on the wheel, and he kept a close watch in the rearview mirror as he drove. Acadia was doing the same in her readjusted side mirror.

The police radio crackled with incessant Spanish.

"Buck instructed the pilot and two security men to stay onboard," Zak explained. "The rest of his people are on their way to meet me at the hotel with the money. As soon as you take off, I'll have Buck coordinate with the security team, then I'll take them back with me to find Gideon."

A neat plan. One that excluded her completely. Well, of course it did. Acadia knew that. Her time with Zak was finally at an end. But still, she wanted to help. "Want me to show you what I figured out on the map at the hotel?"

"Yeah, sure."

She reached over and slid the folded map from Zak's breast pocket, then took out a small penlight from her own. The map was enormous, but she folded it to the area she needed to make it more manageable, then traced a line from the hotel near the falls where they'd been taken to the approximate location of the mission, then made an educated guess as to where they'd been left after they'd gone downriver. Then drew a line with her finger to Caracas. She jotted down the numbered coordinates from each stretch on the white edge of the map.

"What do you have?"

"Hang on," she muttered as she found Angel Falls on the map. She finished writing the last digits and skimmed over her neat figures. "Okay, I have a list of coordinates of all our known locations, and then an estimation based on time and approximate distance traveled."

"Let's see it."

She handed over the list, which Zak held to the steering wheel, eyes dropping down periodically to her organized column of numbers as he drove.

His brow furrowed. "Acadia."

Her gaze flew to the rearview mirror. "Are they— What?"

"What's the last set of numbers?" Acadia checked the map. "Angel Falls, why?"

"Jesus! The coordinates are identical to the numbers I see."

She pictured the list of coordinates. Her mouth dropped open for a long moment before she said slowly, "The GPS coordinates for the area around Angel Falls?"

"I get it." He shot her a frowning glance. "But how—"

"Road!" she warned quickly, and he jerked his attention back to the traffic, swinging them back into their lane. The driver of the van they'd almost hit leaned on his horn and stayed on it, turning on his high beams even after they'd passed him. Acadia caught a glimpse of his face and was grateful she couldn't hear what he was saying.

"You concentrate on driving like a bat out of hell to avoid the bad guys, and I'll make sure." She returned to the map on her lap, double-checking her figures. "There's no doubt. They're the same."

"How's that possible?" Zak demanded. "Hell, why is it possible? And what does it mean?"

"Since we got to the hotel, have you been seeing the numbers continuously, or have they stopped occasionally?"

Zak smiled, his gaze sliding to her briefly. "Honestly, there were a couple of times that I wouldn't have noticed if the numbers were ten feet high and in neon."

She focused on not getting swept away in that smile. "When we're together, you mean? In the shower? In bed? Where?"

"I suppose . . ." His eyes flickered to the rearview mirror.

"Okay. Let's backtrack a bit. You started seeing the numbers precisely when?"

"At the mission."

"The second you woke up?"

"No . . . The nun came in to check up on me. I insisted she take out the IV. I took a shower. I don't remember seeing anything odd. Sister Clemencia came back in all pissy because you were out drinking and carousing . . ." Zak frowned as he took a right at the sign for Maiquetia Simon Bolívar Airport. Traffic was light at this time of night. No one was following them. Good. They were getting close to the plane. Even better.

But Acadia didn't relax her guard; her hand was still under the folded map, her fingers wrapped around the handle of the gun.

"She had a dinner tray. She put it down . . . No, my watch was in the way. I put it on to get it—" His frown deepened. "My watch."

"Take it off!"

"Hard to steer with my knee; you'll have to undo the strap."

Acadia reached for his wrist, then paused, her hand on the steel band. "Are you seeing the numbers now?"

"Yeah."

She unsnapped the clasp and let the heavy watch drop into her hand. "How about now?"

"I— Jesus. No. The numbers are completely gone. Put it on me again."

She did so, laying the multifunctional watch over his strong wrist as he drove. She didn't even have it fastened before he said, incredulously, "And they're back. Jesus. This is just plain fucking weird."

Acadia plucked it off him and turned it over. She flashed her penlight on the underside, and read out loud, "'Gideon Stark. August 2008.' This is your brother's watch, Zak."

"Oh, shit." His voice was incredulous, his expression intent, as he juggled driving with wrapping his mind around the . . . visions? What were they?

Whatever they were, Acadia thought, it was unbelievable. "Do you each have the same one?"

He nodded. "Our maternal grandmother gave us each a watch for our birthdays that year. Mine in May, Gideon's in March. I must've grabbed the wrong one when we lit out of the guerrilla camp. Jesus, that's—" *Crazy?* "Stunning."

"What if your brother's watch is somehow giving you his GPS coordinates?"

Zak eyes narrowed. "How is this even possible?"

Acadia bit her lip. How *would* it be possible? Unless . . .

St. Christopher protected travelers; maybe he—or some other saint or power or, hell, she didn't know, the bond between brothers—protected him still? "Zak, I know this sounds . . ." She hesitated, staring down at the map. "Well, it sounds crazy. But I think when you died in surgery at the mission"—her voice cracked—"you flatlined and were pronounced clinically dead. I think when you were shocked back to life, somehow you developed this amazing new sense."

"Come on, that's ridic—"

Acadia leaned over, using both hands to refasten the watch on his wrist. "Say that again."

He blinked. The airport was coming up, a low white building brightly lit, with a full parking lot of coming-and-going traffic. And the numbers instantly materialized to move from left to right in the lower quadrant of his vision. "Read off the coordinates again," he demanded tightly. "Without the degrees or spaces."

Heart pounding with excitement, Acadia carefully ran one finger across the top of the map and another down the side. "558362328596756253555565? That's it, isn't it?"

He heard the numbers said out loud and mentally read them as they scrolled in his head. It was . . . God. He didn't know what to think. But . . . "Jesus, Acadia! I know how to find Gideon—we'll be able to go right to him."

She placed her hand on his thigh and squeezed, and Zak realized he didn't need to vocalize the amazement and heartfelt relief he felt. He didn't need to tell her that what he was experiencing was profound. Terrifying. Overwhelming. Inexplicable.

He knew he didn't need to say any of it, because she got it. All of it. She got *him*. And more amazing, she wasn't hysterical or crying or freaking out in the slightest. She just accepted him, as he was, without reservation.

Zak wished with everything in him that he didn't have to put her on a plane. Wished he didn't have to kiss her good-bye. Wished . . . Hell, he wished a lot of things; that didn't mean any of them were going to come true.

"Aren't we going through the terminal?" she asked, her palm stroking up and down his thigh in a comforting gesture that somehow soothed his soul. More, it calmed the fear he'd been carrying around inside him since Gid had insisted they split up in the jungle a lifetime ago.

"The company jet will be at the auxiliary terminal," he explained. "It's only about a quarter of a mile from here. Don't worry. No one followed us."

"I know," she said quietly. "It's not me I'm worried about."

"I'll be fine. Now that I know where Gideon is, I'll go and retrieve him right away, whether he's free or a prisoner."

"You have a propensity for getting into trouble, Zakary Stark. What are you going to do without me and my magic pockets there to help you?" She said it teasingly, but there was an undercurrent of fear in her voice.

Jesus, he didn't want her to go. Didn't want to be parted from her, but couldn't allow her to stay.

Zak was surprised to see that Buck had sent the Falcon. It was a small jet that seated only twenty.

Admittedly, twenty in absolute luxury. But not the plane he would've chosen to transport a bunch of ex-military guys and their equipment. Still, the plane was here, the pilot was onboard, and Acadia would have two trained, professional bodyguards to escort her home.

The situation he was going back to was going to be fraught with danger, even with skilled personnel on hand. He had no idea what condition he'd find Gideon in. No idea how many men Loida Piñero would have with her this time. The extraction was going to be a bitch, and he didn't want Acadia anywhere near it.

Or anywhere near him, when he hit the boiling point and bullets went flying. "But I'll be much better able to do what I need to do if I know you're home in the States," he added, and knew that wasn't a lie. "Safe and sound."

She glanced out of the window as Zak drove out on the tarmac to get closer to the Falcon. "I could wait here," she offered. "You said there are two guys plus the pilot. Look around. No one can get near the plane without us seeing th—"

"Acadia?" He pulled the police car up near the stairs, the interior lights turned on in warm, civilized welcome.

She glared at him. "What?"

Zak bit back a smile at her belligerence. "Does flying make you nervous?"

"No." She opened her door and got out of the car, and he followed suit, walking around to stand toe-to-toe with her.

He cupped her face between his hands. Even though it was a warm, muggy night, her skin was cool. Her gray eyes were dark and stormy as she looked up at him.

Zak stroked his thumbs across her cheekbones, his chest tight and constricted. Fuckit. He didn't like good-byes. "Then why are you scared?"

"Scared? Me? No, I'm not."

"Very chatty and lying."

She gave him a cross look, but brought her hands up to cover the backs of his fingers against her face. "Nobody has ever made me as nervous as you do, Zakary Stark."

He brushed a kiss over her soft, trembling mouth, and said against her lips, "You make me nervous, too."

"I make you nervous?" She huffed out a laugh. "There's nothing in this universe that makes you nervous."

He threaded his fingers through her hair as she stood on tiptoe to meet his mouth. "You'd be surprised." He couldn't begin to tell her how he felt; he was having a hard enough time admitting it to himself. So he let his kiss do what he couldn't: tease her, tempt her. Praise her. Thank her. His tongue touched the very corner of her mouth, slid over her lower lip, as she staunchly tried to remain unmoved.

He liked her melting in his hands, too, and backed her against the car. She shuddered, lips opening under his gentle assault, as he fitted her lush curves against his body, sliding his hands into her loose hair to deepen his kiss.

She tasted sweet and sad and like heaven all at once. The numbers slid through his mind, but all he could smell, taste, feel was the woman in his arms. He heard her uneven breathing, felt the rapid beat of her heart against his chest as her tongue rubbed sleekly against his. Or maybe that was his heartbeat.

Fuckit.

He reluctantly broke away. "The engine's running; they're ready to take off. Come on."

Acadia put her hand on his arm, her gaze steady despite the flush in her cheeks. "I'm a big girl. There's no need. Go find Gideon."

Zak wrapped his good arm around her waist. "Come on. I want to strap you in and"—*have a few more moments with you*—"get you settled. You can sleep all the way to Kansas." They walked up the stairs together. He didn't say he'd call her, and she didn't ask. Until he found Gideon, he couldn't and wouldn't think of anything else.

The door was open, and he wondered briefly why none of the men had at least come out to see why cops were parked out on the tarmac.

He ducked under the lintel and stepped inside the plane he'd been on dozens of times. Camel-colored plush leather appointments, polished teak. All the luxuries of home, thousands of feet in the air. The air-conditioning was on full, breathing a cold blast of air on their faces as Zak held Acadia right inside the door opening.

The hair on the back of his neck lifted as he noticed a faint reddish-brown handprint on the cockpit door.

Tightening his arms around her, he pivoted and dragged her back down the short flight of metal stairs in a flat-out and noisy run. "Get in the car! Go. Go. Go!"

Yanking open the driver's side door, he practically threw her across the seat, leaped into the car, and cranked the engine even before his door swung shut. He put his foot on the gas and hauled ass, the tires screeching as they raced across the tarmac.

"Zak? My God, what . . . I don't—"

She gave a muffled protest as Zak grabbed the top of her head and forced her down, her face on his thigh.

In the rearview mirror, the jet exploded. A ball of black smoke and orange fire rolled into the sky. Seconds later, the sonic impact slammed into the car.

⊶ FIFTEEN ⊷

Their vehicle levitated. The wheels spun with a high-pitched whine, then caught as they hit the ground with a jarring shudder. The police car slewed to one side, then skidded the other way before the tires grabbed traction on the tarmac. They sped across the runway like a bat out of hell.

Zak's muscles bulged and flexed as he fought the wheel, wrenching it into the spins. A quick glimpse at his feral expression and Acadia braced her feet and gripped the dash with both hands. He floored the pedal.

Shell-shocked and disoriented, Acadia turned to look back. It look just like it sounded. A *big* freaking explosion. "What— What the hell just happened?" Her voice was as unsteady as her heartbeats.

She dropped back into her seat and studied Zak. Jaw rigid, eyes intense, his entire focus was on the road ahead. He had both hands on the wheel, and he wasn't wearing the sling. The fact that he'd pull out his stitches if he exerted that much pressure and movement on his shoulder didn't seem to register. Or maybe—she caught her breath—perhaps this life-versus-death thing was just how he lived.

"I don't understand what the fuck's happening either," he growled, violence leashed in every word, "but I'm starting to, and— *Fuckit!*" He slammed his palm on the wheel.

Acadia didn't know what to do. How to help. She sat rigid and quiet, her heart beating too hard and too fast. Even when a pair of fire engines and half a dozen police cars with lights and sirens blazing came toward them from the terminal, she didn't say a word. Hadn't she just left the scene of another explosion and escaped another parking lot filled with emergency vehicles? It was some kind of terrible déjà vu.

Then her survival instincts kicked in, and she reached across the dash to activate the siren and lights.

"Good girl. Hand me the radio mic."

Acadia got what he was doing immediately and unhooked it from the dash. "Ready?"

"Yeah. Go." In fluent Spanish, Zak proceeded to inform his "fellow" officers that he was in pursuit of one of the perpetrators of the explosion, but that there had been three vehicles leaving the scene. He described two cars in detail with partial license plates. He assured the other officers that he would bring his man in, and then nodded for Acadia to switch the mic off.

She watched two police cars behind them suddenly peel off in the direction he'd indicated. "Very clever."

They were going over ninety miles an hour, past the terminal parking lot, onto the main road leading from the airport, then the freeway—a dangerous speed that had other cars swerving to get out of their way as they came careening up behind them, lights blazing and siren blaring.

Acadia buckled her seat belt and kept her eyes trained on the side mirror, her heart beating so fast she could feel it in her eyeballs. *Oh God, oh God, oh God.* She watched to see if any of the other police vehicles would choose to follow them, and their phantom perpetrator, or not.

So far, so good.

But then, she knew those were frequently famous last words. Especially around Zak.

Bracing one hand on the dash, she gripped the armrest tightly with the other as he increased their speed. She didn't look at the speedometer. She really, really didn't want to know.

She didn't talk, mostly because she didn't want to break his concentration for even a nanosecond at these speeds, but also because her mouth had dried up with sheer, unadulterated fear.

Not a fan of speeding cars or chaos in general, Acadia preferred having a plan to follow. This wasn't a plan. There weren't even loose guidelines here. She wanted instructions. In writing would be great, and in triplicate even better. Their stolen police car wove between two loaded produce trucks and scraped the center divider, sending sparks shooting off the side of the car like fireworks.

With a hard yank to the wheel, Zak leveled out to pass a pickup truck. "Get out your phone," he instructed, watching the road.

She'd rather find her *gun*, now that she came to think

of it. But she lifted her butt and removed the cell phone from her back pocket.

Zak twisted the wheel to pass a tourist bus, missing the back bumper by inches. "Ready?"

She turned the phone on, found the window with the illuminated keypad. "Okay."

Zak rattled off a number.

"I don't think that's an area code, Zak . . ."

"It is, trust me. Put it on speaker."

Acadia dialed the too-long number, sure it would have some sort of error message, but the phone rang.

Once. Twice. A man, not sounding happy, snarled, "This better be fucking good. It's four seventeen a.m."

"Zakary Stark. I have a situation."

Acadia held the phone up for him. *A situation?* She leaned over and pressed the horn on the steering wheel to prevent two cows from wandering into the road. Yes, indeed. It was certainly a *situation*.

"Where are you?" The man on the other end suddenly sounded wide awake.

"Caracas. Any second now we're gonna have the bad guys up our asses."

"Explain later," the man said briskly. "Got a vehicle?"

"Commandeered a police car."

The other man chuckled. "Conspicuous. GPS?"

"Yeah."

Acadia took her life in her hands, because she had to release the latch on her seat belt to turn on the GPS. Her stomach sloshed unhappily as Zak threaded the car too fast through the traffic.

The voice on the line gave Zak short directions, which Acadia programmed into the GPS as the vehicle rocked and whined and shuddered, passing other cars. Up ahead, the dome of light over the city brightened while they approached at full speed.

The voice asked, "Got that?"

Acadia tried to figure out spellings, took a wild guess, and finished punching in the unfamiliar street names.

"Yes," she told him, hitting Start.

"There's an alley at that street number. Blue Ford Taurus, license . . . Hang on. Ready?" Without waiting, he rattled off the plate number. "Key's taped inside the exhaust pipe. Change of clothes, cash, and a selection of toys under backseat. Lose the cop car. Lay low. Call me if you encounter any more difficulties." The phone went dead.

Acadia lowered the phone, but kept it in her hand in case Zak needed to call someone else. Her knuckles whitened as she tightened her fingers around it. "Who was that?" she asked, bemused that the man hadn't even bothered to find out what would happen to his car once they were done with it. Then again, she'd clearly entered some *Bourne Ultimatum* spy universe.

She was ready to leave it.

Zak frowned. "An old friend. Savin was a recruiter, back in the day, when I attended MIT."

Not a recruiter for MIT, she bet. "And he's where?" Because that wasn't a regular area code she'd punched in.

"Somewhere in the States."

That was certainly vague enough. "And he just happens to have a spare car parked in a Caracas alley?"

Zak's lips twitched, and she noticed that his shoulders weren't quite as tense as they'd been minutes before. "He's that kind of guy."

She waited for Zak to follow the GPS directions. She pushed her foot hard to the floor, where a brake pedal would be if she were driving, as he swung across three lanes of traffic to take the exit. Her heart stopped beating when a minivan, a flatbed truck, and a wandering llama were all barely skimmed by the car's fenders.

"What kind of guy is that?" she asked weakly when he took the off-ramp. At the bottom, he turned off the siren and lights, and her ears throbbed in the sudden silence.

"He wanted me to come work for him, way back. Black ops," he explained, and suddenly, it made sense. Military, or something like it. "We were working on ZAG. I declined. "

"If he can get us out if this mess, I think I love him."

"Married, kids. You'll have to look elsewhere."

Wasn't looking, but found you anyway. She kept her mouth shut.

The traffic thinned out around them as they entered the city and slowed to a normal pace. *Normal* in Venezuela, she was discovering, was pretty damned fast. She wondered if her hair had turned snow white since they'd left the hotel.

Ten minutes later, Zak pointed out the alley, then drove several blocks away and parked between two large delivery vans. It was a tight squeeze, and she held her breath, as if that would help him maneuver the car into the narrow opening.

"Let's go." He popped his door, then walked around the front of the vehicle to take her hand as she got out on her side. Slung over his bandaged shoulder was the heavy bag that they'd hastily packed; in his right hand was one of the guns she'd had on her lap for the drive to the airport.

"I know you're a guy with an aversion to guns," she said solemnly, "and I just want you to know that I'm very grateful you've put that aside for now." She thought she detected the hint of a smile, but he said nothing.

The engine popped and steamed, pinging loudly as the overstressed parts cooled.

Acadia interlaced her fingers with his. His hand felt big and solid in a world gone completely mad. The night was warm, but she realized her teeth were chattering and cold shivers traveled up and down her spine. Goose bumps of fear roughened her skin. She took out her little penlight and illuminated the cracked, weedy sidewalk.

"Why would your friend have us walking in the murder capital of the world in the middle of the freaking night?" Acadia demanded, voice low. She tightened her fingers in Zak's. "The murder rate in Caracas tops that of every other city in the world. There's one here every ninety minutes," she told him. Wishing she'd shut up, but too scared to stop herself.

There were no streetlights in this part of town. And while the city lights illuminated the black sky, where they were walking was dark and scary as hell. Caracas wasn't exactly a safe city to be wandering around at midnight. If she'd thought the street where they'd parked was dark, the alley, narrow and close, was darker. It smelled strongly of urine and feces, and they walked in the middle where there weren't as many filthy newspapers and other hard-to-identify things pushed against the walls on either side. She watched where she stepped and tried not to breathe. From time to time, she heard something scuttling close to the walls. Rats?

Three derelict-looking cars were parked halfway down the block. The blue Ford was in front. It was the only one with all four tires, but the back window had been knocked or shot out, and the side window of the passenger door was held shut with liberal use of electrical tape. Zak let go of her hand to crouch down by the rear bumper.

Acadia felt exposed and so freaked out she was about to jump out of her skin. Angry too, but her anger had nowhere to go. Zak had done everything in his power to send her home. And God, she wanted to be home in her small house outside the base right now. She wanted every light on, and the fresh scent of flowers from her garden drifting through the window.

Locking her knees, she wrapped one arm tightly around her waist and held the light for Zak.

She dragged in a shuddering breath as he ran two fingers inside the exhaust pipe. Something caught, tore, and he straightened with a key ring in his hand. Matted duct tape fluttered as he stripped it off his hand. "Get in on my side."

Acadia dragged in her first steady breath in hours as she crawled across the seat of their getaway car.

ZAK GOT IN AND started the car, headed north. He shot a brief glance at Acadia. Her long blond hair was wild and disheveled. She looked sex-rumpled. He caught a glimpse of the freaked-out look in her soft, gray eyes and the strain on her pale face, which reminded him that while he was used to life-and-death thrill-seeking adventures, she was not. And coming down off an unexpected adrenaline rush could be a bitch.

He wished with everything in him that she were thousands of feet in the air and winging her way back to Junction City, where she'd be safe. "I'm sorrier than hell for dragging you into this clusterfuck."

"Save it," she snapped. "You can apologize if we live through this."

The vehicle looked like a piece of crap, but the engine purred. Souped up, for sure. From the sound of it, there was a twin turbo-charged eight-cylinder under the hood. He hoped to hell he wouldn't have a reason to put it to the test. "You're okay, right?"

"I think maybe we should stop asking that question," Acadia suggested wryly. "Because anything either of us answers is going to be a big fat freaking lie."

Zak huffed out a pent-up breath. "Jesus. I was so hot for you I almost missed the signs."

"Signs?"

"On the jet. I saw, but my brain wasn't in computing mode." Because he was so consumed with nonverbal communication, so intent on getting her to safety without saying all the things on his mind, he'd almost gotten her killed. "There was a bloody handprint on the door going into the cockpit. It was small, just a smudge, but the image only registered as we were getting the hell out of Dodge."

It could've been a costly mistake. Thank God he had quick reflexes. The instant he'd felt the give of the carpet as he'd stepped off the stairs and inside the cabin, he'd jettisoned them back down the stairs and straight to the car.

A pressure-sensitive explosive device had done the rest.

Acadia was fading fast. The adrenaline, with nowhere to go, was going to knock her on her ass. His shoulder ached like a son of a bitch, and his thoughts were taking him in a direction he sure as shit didn't want to go.

They both needed rest; God only knew they hadn't had much in the last few days. He usually thought well on his feet, but if this situation was shaping up the way he didn't want to think about, his feet were going to be knocked right from under him.

He had to rest his body and get his mind clear before he started jumping to conclusions. Any conclusions.

Even the obvious one.

He started looking for a small, out-of-the-way hotel. One that wouldn't ask questions. Cold, hard cash was going to be their identification. Zak found a hamburger joint that was still open, navigated the drive-thru, then continued until he spotted a small hotel on the edge of a gentrified neighborhood. As far as he could tell, no one had followed them, but he circled the block a couple of times just to be sure. In the quiet middle-class neighborhood, it would be easy to spot a tail. Paranoia had saved his ass more times than he cared to count.

THEY CHECKED INTO THE Hotel Altamira Centro as Señor and Señora Montoya, took the elevator to the top floor, and didn't speak for all five stories as the elevator rattled faintly around them. Zak found the room number, opened the door, and ushered Acadia inside.

Slapping on the light switch, he locked the door with both locks, set the food bags down on a nearby chest of drawers, then slid the monstrosity across the room to block the door.

Acadia was still standing in the same spot when he was done. "Hungry?" he asked quietly, scanning her face. She looked scared and exhausted, and seeing her that way, because of him, twisted like a knife in his gut.

"I'm not sure," she mumbled, her lips barely moving. Definitely shock. "I think I want a shower first." But she didn't move.

Damn. This was bad. Zak crossed the gold shag carpet and cupped her face gently in both hands. Her silky hair covered his fingers. Her skin felt warm and smooth, but her eyes looked a little bruised, and her soft mouth trembled. "Want help?" he asked softly.

Her lashes fluttered heavily to make eye contact. Her mouth twitched in a small smile. "Can I eat in the shower?" At least she still had her humor. That was a bonus.

"I doubt that hamburger could stand up to dousing, but you can make it a quick one, okay?"

Turning on lights as he went, Zak wrapped his arm around her waist and escorted her into a small, clean bathroom. She leaned her butt against the sink and watched him with glassy eyes.

"Hot or cool?"

"Hot."

He turned on the shower for her. Anticipating her needs, he peeled the paper off a bar of soap and reached in to set it on the tiled shelf. The bathroom was rapidly filling with steam. "Need help getting undressed?" he asked, his pulse suddenly loud and heavy in his ears.

Her arms dropped limply to her sides as he tugged her shirt from her waistband. She had the prettiest breasts he'd ever seen. Small, and full, with delicate apricot-colored nipples that peaked as his hand skimmed across her chest to liberate the other arm.

He'd forgotten that her clothes were filled with all sorts of gear. He quickly undid the vest zipper, loving that she was braless. He eased the heavy vest over her shoulders, tossed it out through the open door, pulled off her T-shirt, then found the button at her waistband and eased that zipper down. Smiling, he said thickly, "It's never been *this* easy to get a woman out of her clothes."

"You have to have them kidnapped first, then try to blow them up a couple of times." Her lips curved. "Those won't come off over my boots," she pointed out as he eased the loose-fitting, pocket-laden khakis down her long, gorgeous legs.

Zak settled on his haunches to untie the laces on her boots. Acadia rested one hand lightly on his good shoulder.

"Then," she continued seriously, with a little more life in her voice, "you have to follow all that up with a death-defying, high-speed car chase. Try it again. You'll see just how accommodating women will be."

Using his last gram of willpower, Zak ignored the fluffy triangle guarding her womanhood directly in front of him, and bent lower to tug off her boots. She had a red blister on one of her baby toes, and he paused to kiss that before pulling off her pants. Then he saw the quarter-size bruise on her thigh. He had to kiss that as well.

He eventually stripped her pants off. Braless was excellent, commando was a slice of heaven.

She folded her arms under her breasts. Zak liked them all plumped up like that. A lot. But despite having a boner that wasn't going to go away without help, he refrained from grabbing anything.

She was exhausted; he'd put her through the wringer. She deserved to be left alone to take a private shower before getting some much-needed rest.

"I'll wait."

He lifted an eyebrow as he straightened. "For?"

"You to get naked," she said, and all the remaining blood left his head to plunge between his legs. Fuckit. Acadia plus hot, steamy water?

Two bombs couldn't kill him, but this had a *serious* chance of success. And there was no way he was going to argue with her.

"Right." He stripped in record time, tossing his clothes out into the bedroom. There was no hiding his erection, so he just stepped into the tub and held out his hand to help her climb in with him.

Soft gray eyes gave him a leisurely up-and-down, and her diabolical smile was deceptively innocent, her lashes fluttering back to his face as she stepped in beside him. "Your bandage is getting wet."

She wasn't looking at the damned bandage, and having her clutch his waist to keep her balance wasn't helping his good intentions. "It'll dry. Turn around, I'll wash your hair first."

With his help, she maneuvered to face the spray, bracing her hands on the tiled wall beneath the showerhead. She had a small cut on the back of her hand, and a bruise on her ring finger, which reminded him of what she'd been through and reiterated why this was supposed to be *just* a shower.

The view from behind was almost as luscious and spectacular as it was from the front. He'd never really thought about a woman's back; he'd always been a lot more interested in the front. But Acadia's was creamy and sleek, with a scattering of golden freckles across her shoulders he hadn't noticed before. Her tight ass was shaped like an inverted heart. He'd taken little nips and—

"Zak?"

With a noncommittal grunt, he dragged his attention away from her ass and poured shampoo into his palm, then lathered the long strands, running his hands through to the wet ends that hung halfway down her back.

She moaned as he massaged his lathered fingertips against her scalp. The moan made his dick grow like Pinocchio's nose after a big lie. He rinsed, lathered, and rinsed again. He should get a damned medal of honor for his commitment to duty in the face of almost certain death by blue balls. "Conditioner?"

"Hmm."

He applied the smoothing liquid to her wet hair, then reached for the soap. Lather, rinse. There was probably a washcloth around somewhere, but he used his hands. His hands and plenty of the glistening suds turned her skin into a play area with lifts, runs, and jumps he just wanted to dive into.

Zak gritted his teeth and kept his touch as impersonal as a doctor's. "Turn."

He had to hold her arm so she didn't slip. Holding her arm meant his hand was beside her breast. It needed washing. Lather, wash. Lather . . . a little more washing. *Concentrate, pal. And don't forget to breathe.*

"If you're going to keep that up, it would only be polite to kiss me first."

He smothered a laugh. "I don't want to get you worked up; you're tired."

"I'm worked up, I'm just too tired to show it by exuberant movements and wild cries of delight." Her eyes glinted from beneath a spiky fan of lashes. "I'm *quietly* worked up."

Jesus. How damned adorable was she? Very. Zak slid his soapy hands down her hips, then slid one into her soapy nest of curls. "I'm quietly worked up, too." The understatement of the century.

He rubbed his dick against the smooth, wet skin of her stomach and smiled against her mouth. "Hard to hide."

She nibbled his lower lip. "I have a perfect place. Nobody but us will ever know." With a laugh, Zak turned off the taps and picked her up, soapsuds, pouring water, and all, and carried her into the bedroom, a matter of a couple of feet. Stepping over their scattered clothing and boots, he dropped her on the mattress with a little bounce, then followed her down.

Their bodies were dripping wet, sliding erotically together as he shifted to rest between her sprawled legs. Acadia practically purred as she lazily wrapped her arms around his neck, entwined her legs around his waist, and shifted her hips to accommodate him.

Zak's penis slid into her tight, wet sheath without fanfare. He slanted his mouth to kiss her, loving her response, loving the feel of her arms and legs enveloping him. Loving . . . hell, loving it all.

Their lazy, almost dreamlike lovemaking made the intensity of their shared climax even more powerful when it struck them within seconds of penetration. Zak's muscles tensed unbearably as a rocket blast of power ratcheted his muscles and tendons and left him gasping for an unrestricted breath.

The climax went on and on. One rolling into the next.

He thought Acadia moaned his name. But his hearing was on mute, every ounce of focus on where their bodies joined.

It felt like a nanosecond, or a year, later when her legs fell limply away from his hips and her arms dropped from his shoulders. She dragged in a shuddering breath, lifted her hand weakly to touch him, dropped it back to the bed, and looked up at him with dazed eyes. "Death by sex."

"Hell of a way to go." He brushed a tangle of wet hair off her face and shoulder as she closed her eyes. "I'm sorrier than hell I got you into this clusterfuck. Do you wa—"

She let out a gentle, but unmistakable, snore.

◦◦ SIXTEEN ◦◦

Acadia yawned, her face buried in the lumpy pillow, decided she was awake, and cracked open one eye. Sunlight filtered through the cheap, uneven red curtains, and sounds drifted through a haze of half-awake consciousness.

Tap-tap-tap. Fingers on a keyboard. The hum of a cheap vacuum cleaner laboring up and down the hallway beyond the door. A distant dog barking.

Opening the other eye, she rolled over and stretched. Naked and well rested, she felt terrific, considering everything they'd been through in the last couple of days. Must be all the sex keeping her energy levels up. Whatever it was, she knew it had everything to do with Zak. She'd hated saying good-bye yesterday, and she was going to hate it again today. Probably more. Every hour she spent with him was making it that much harder to be cool and sophisticated about saying good-bye.

Dressed and freshly shaved, Zak looked both devastating and determined. A muscle worked in his jaw, and he was frowning, as he sat at the small table working on the computer.

"Don't you ever sleep?" she asked around another yawn.

At the sound of her voice, he turned around, resting his arm along the back of the chair. His expression made Acadia's heart skip several beats. Satisfied male, yes. But there was also a warmth and softness that she hadn't seen reflected in his eyes before.

More than likely just her own postcoital glow, she warned the butterflies swooping around in her tummy. Dangerously close to her heart.

"I only need about four hours." Heat flared in his hazel eyes as she stretched her arms over her head. He liked her body, she knew, and she held the pose as his smoldering gaze traveled in a leisurely fashion over her breasts and down her belly, paused at the juncture of her thighs, and lazily moved like a caress all the way to her toes. Then climbed unhurriedly back up.

"I need at least eight or I get grumpy." She arched her back and gave him a memory to keep after she was gone.

The skin across his cheekbones pulled tight as his gaze returned to her face, and a pulse beat in his jaw. Voice thick, he said, "You look like Aphrodite emerging from the sea."

He could probably make her come just by looking at her like that. "Ha!" She shifted, thrilled when his pupils flared. Teasing him turned her on all over again. The man was a sex whisperer. "You're just too polite to tell me I look like Medusa. I know, because I slept with wet hair." She pulled a face when she tried to run her fingers through the tangled mass. Flushed by the intent in his eyes, she sat up and curled her arms around her bent knees. "What's the plan for today?" *Get rid of the blonde, avoid bombs and kidnappers, cheat death, find brother.*

"For one thing, I'm sick and tired of playing defense." Zak's expression hardened. Acadia rubbed her shins with both hands. She wouldn't like Zak ever to look at her like *that*. "Time to go on the offensive," he said, more, she figured, to himself than to her.

"Excellent. I'm with you there. You're not wearing the watch? Numbers bothering you?"

"The strap should be replaced; it's starting to show signs of Gid's wear and tear. If I hadn't been so damned distracted, I would've noticed. He's a lot harder on his things than . . . Don't want to lose it. And no, seeing the numbers doesn't bother me now that I know what they are. In fact, they give me hope. I figure if I'm still seeing them, then he's still alive, and I'll find him."

He picked up the watch, which lay on the table beside the computer, and glanced at the time. "The embassy opens in eleven minutes. I'll call. See where we stand on our paperwork. If we need to cross a few more palms with cash to expedite this, then that's number one on our to-do list this morning. Getting you on a private plane is next; unfortunately, I can't get another one sent here before I leave. I *really* want you safe and on your way home before I hie off with Buck's security guys."

He absently strapped the watch to his right wrist, and she could tell by the telltale flicker of his lashes that he was once again seeing the scrolling numbers.

"That leaves a commercial flight, but without proper clearance, that won't fly. Literally."

The embassy had told them it could take up to two weeks to get a new passport. She didn't even want to know what kind of strings Zak must've pulled to get her on a flight. "You got me a flight out? Today?"

"*Tentatively*. If all the fucking stars align. Two twenty. You have a layover in Houston. You'll be home for a late dinner."

"Great," she said, keeping her voice upbeat despite the huge lump swelling uncomfortably in her throat. She was starting to feel like a piece of annoying lost luggage that kept getting rerouted. "I don't suppose there were any clean clothes in that bag we brought upstairs with us?"

The wreck of a Taurus had had a well-concealed compartment, revealed when the backseat was lifted, and last night Zak had brought both their bag and a duffel he'd retrieved from his friend's car up to the room with him.

"Boxers or briefs?"

"Boxers, for sure."

"Then you're in luck. You have several pairs to choose from, also a couple of large T-shirts and some cargo pants that would fit both of us together."

"That would make it hard to walk." She smiled, bunching her hair in a fist and holding it on top of her head. "Any progress on Gideon's exact location?"

"Yeah. I think between the computer, the map, and what's scrolling, I have a pretty damn accurate location. I talked to Buck last night while you were out like a light.

He was mildly pissed about the plane, and glad we're okay."

Mildly pissed? Acadia had no idea how much a personal jet cost to replace, but she was pretty sure it warranted more than "mildly." "You told him I'm with you?"

"Actually, no. It wasn't relevant."

She digested that for a moment. She'd been through freaking hell with him and it wasn't *relevant*? It annoyed her to realize how much the offhand statement annoyed her. "Odd. I feel very relevant," she said. Maybe he would've thought her relevant if he'd had to explain her demise to her friends back home. She slid her legs off the bed and stood. "I'm going to take another shower, and then I want to try and call my friends back home. I'll be ready to leave in fifteen minutes."

"Acadia . . ."

She washed efficiently, trying not to overreact, and got out of the tub. The only two towels in the bathroom were still wet, despite having been hung neatly on the rack. Tears smarted in her eyes, which was asinine. She dried off as best she could, then finger-combed her hair and blew it dry with the feeble blast from the dryer on the wall.

Zak had left several pairs of boxer shorts and folded-up clothes on the side of the counter when she was behind the cheap plastic curtain. He hadn't climbed in with her, as he'd done the night before; he hadn't even—

Shut up, Acadia. Just get over the drama of it all.

There was enough real-time drama going on around them without her having a hissy fit because she was hurt by what he'd said to a man she didn't even know. It wasn't like her to be so overly sensitive. She'd never been this way with either Tom or Jeff. Both long-term lovers. If they'd said anything obtuse, she'd questioned them, debated the situation, and it was over.

Acadia didn't like this new, insecure . . . *girlie* side of herself when she was with Zak. She was a prosaic, pragmatic, and down-to-earth woman. The truth of the matter was, she should be grateful that he was doing everything in his not-unlimited power to ensure she got home where she could go on with her boring, albeit safer, life.

She could either spend their last few hours together irritated that he hadn't told his friends about her, as if she were in junior high, or she could enjoy every second of what she had left and make the most of it.

She'd never before met a man like Zakary Stark, and she doubted she ever would again. It was her choice. "Choose wisely, Grasshopper," she whispered to her reflection.

She grabbed the first thing that came to hand—purple silk boxers—and pulled up her pants. She layered the black T-shirt under the pocketed vest and left it hanging open. Then went into the room. "Ready. Did you talk to the embassy?"

"They called while you were in the shower. Both our passports and our paperwork came through. I—"

"That's amazingly quick. But great. No need to hang around, then, right? We'll get my passport, and I'll be on a plane and out of your hair in no time." She found one of her boots under the bed and the other wedged under the dresser; she had to lie flat on her stomach to fish it out. "I'm due back at work the day after tomorrow, so this'll work out perfectly."

Carrying her boots, she plopped down on the side of the bed, her back to him. "Everyone is going to want to see pictures, of course, but I—"

"You can't stay with me," he told her, his tone belligerent and extremely annoyed. "I have to go get Gideon. It's too fucking dangerous for you—"

She looked at him over her shoulder and cut him off, because apparently she wasn't as mature or evolved as she'd hoped to be. Teeth clenched, she stuffed one foot into a boot and contorted her leg to put her foot on the bed beside her to do up the laces. "A, I didn't *ask* to stay here. B, I don't *want* to stay here. Frankly, I'm not that fond of Venezuela or for that matter being blown up. And C, unlike you, I don't thrive on danger and living one terrified minute to the next. Believe me, Zak, fun as this has been, I really, really want to go home now. I'm not cut out for the life of an adrenaline junkie."

He held her gaze. "You're scared."

"Any sane person would be. Which says a lot about you." She shoved her other foot into the other boot and pulled at the laces. Oh, yeah, she was scared. Scared that this man was coming to mean more to her than she'd ever thought was possible in such short a time. She was terrified that she'd crossed some personal line in the sand and she'd never recover.

She glanced at him over her shoulder again. "The last plane I boarded blew up." She had to undo the boot laces because she'd strangled her foot by pulling them too tight. "I hope like hell they don't try to blow up a commercial flight full of peop—" She scowled as he got up and stepped around the foot of the bed. "What do you think— Oh!"

He pulled her up, fingers digging into her shoulders. Up. On her feet. Into his arms. One. Two. Glorious three.

Sliding one long-fingered hand under her hair to cradle her nape, he lowered his mouth to hers. Her lashes fluttered closed as she drew in the familiar scent of his skin, which no soap could disguise. A soft brush of his lips had her heartbeat skittering in her chest. His tongue swept inside, and she welcomed it with a deft sweep of her own. His tall body felt hard and strong, and more familiar to her now than her own. Yet she felt the bulk of the dressing on his shoulder and knew that he wasn't invincible at all.

Her breasts, sensitive and needy, pressed against the hard plane of his chest as Acadia wrapped her arms around his waist, fisting the back of his shirt and standing on her toes to get closer.

His thumb stroked the sensitive skin on the back of her neck, his mouth slanted to explore what she so willingly offered. The man—she shuddered—knew how to kiss.

His lips withdrew by a breath, and her mouth followed, clinging to his. He moved again, until a fraction of an inch separated their damp mouths. His eyes were dark pools, the pupils obliterating the color.

"You're a dangerous woman, Acadia Gray." Picking up a tangled skein of her hair draped over her shoulder, he ran it back and forth over his lips, maintaining eye contact. "If it wasn't for, hell, *everything*, I'd hole up in this room with you for a month. We'd never get dressed, and they'd have to deliver our meals periodically so we could keep up our strength. But the only way I'm going to be able to find my brother quickly is by knowing that you're out of harm's way. Got that? I want you as far away from these people as I can get you. And *fast*."

ZAK FOUND A PARKING place a few blocks from the embassy. It was a beautiful, sunny day, not a cloud in the hard blue sky as they walked to the front of the building. He hadn't clarified his statement about wanting her to leave ASAP. Did he mean forever? For the time being while he searched for his brother? He didn't have her home address, although Junction City and the store wouldn't be hard to find. Still, it would ease the ache in her chest if she could be sure she'd see him again.

Acadia wished with all her heart that this were over. That Gideon were back in Seattle safe and sound, that Zak . . .

She wished she were back at home with Zak right now, wearing one of the feminine and pretty floral sundresses the women walking to work wore. A sundress and pretty shoes. High heels. And at least a freaking smudge of masca—

Abruptly he slammed his arm across her midriff, breaking her stride. "Omph!"

He crowded her back against the wall of the embassy.

"What's the matter now?" This high drama was exhausting, and she wasn't in the mood for it this morning. She wanted a smooth transition back to Junction City. Saying good-bye to Zak had taken all her emotional fortitude yesterday; she was *trying* to be mature about it again today. Practice wasn't going to make perfect. Especially if he kept putting his hands on her.

They had a plan. Zak was going to meet up with the security team later to get his brother as soon as she was safely on a plane back to Kansas. Suddenly he spun around and grabbed her by her shoulders. He cupped her face in both hands and pressed her back against the sun-warmed plaster. His eyes were open, too. And he was looking off to the right, his hands still holding her shoulders. Acadia gave him a little shove. "I enjoy kissing you, God only knows it shorts all my circuits, but would you mind telling me what *that* was about?"

Zak wrapped his arm around her shoulders and started walking rapidly back the way they'd come. "Loida Piñero and four of her men just went inside. They were wearing the green camouflage uniforms of the National Guard. The Guardia Nacional is a paramilitary force run by the Ministry of Defense to provide national security within the country."

"Okay." Acadia took two steps to Zak's one just so she could keep up with his long strides. Once they reached the Ford, he yanked open the door and practically threw her in through the driver's door. He got in, cranked the engine, and pulled smoothly into traffic.

"The fact that Piñero is here, in National Guard uniform, no less, is no fucking coincidence." He eased the car into the middle lane and kept a steady pace. To where, Acadia had no idea. "I thought when the embassy called first thing this morning that it was oddly efficient of them to have pulled the paperwork together *that* fast; they originally told us it would take forty-eight hours, and it's only been a day since we were there, believe it or not. I should've trusted my instincts."

"Okay, what am I missing?"

"Loida knows we can't leave the country without papers. We filed for new papers—our names went out to cyberspace, where she apparently looked for and found them." Zak sucked in a furious breath. "Okay. New plan. We go to the airport; I hire a plane and pilot to take you home. No middleman. Keep your eyes peeled for anyone following us." He reached into his breast pocket and handed her his phone. "Dial Buck."

Acadia put the phone on speaker and clicked on Buck's name. He answered before the third ring. "Zakary, my men will meet you at the airport in an hour. I chartered a helicopter to take you as far into the jungle as they can. The men are equipped to walk in the rest of the way. Can you get there in that time frame?"

"On my way now."

"Good. Listen, Zak, I don't want to be an alarmist, but I'd really like you to reconsider your position on this. Leave the extraction to my people. They're trained professionals. I can pull some strings, get you on the next flight out. Hell, you can be home waiting when the men bring Gideon home. "

"First, a commercial flight isn't going to cut it," Zak said tensely. "I don't have a passport and neither does Acadia. I saw one of the kidnappers at the embassy. No idea if she's in cahoots with someone there, but my gut tells me she was our welcoming committee. I'm going to hire a charter. Get Acadia on it, then meet your guys as soon as I see her safely on board. I know exactly where Gideon is, Buck. I'm gonna get him, and bring him home."

"You know— Thank God. Wait! *How* do you know exactly where he is?" Buck blew out a breath. "The kidnappers made contact? Where do we drop the m—?"

"No, they haven't. It's complicated. Just leave it as I know where he is."

"If you know, you know. Who's this woman, Zakary? This Arcadia?" Acadia flinched at the exasperated derision in the man's tone. "For God's sake, man. This is not the time to think with your dick. Gideon must be shitting bricks and wondering where the fuck you are. Does he even know you made it out? These bastards aren't above torture just for the sport of it. God only knows what he's enduring. Zak, can you really afford to have your attention diverted right now?"

"Her name's *Acadia*, and she's—" The tires squealed as he stomped on the brakes. Acadia shot out her arm to brace herself before she kissed the dash just as Zak shouted, "Fuckit!"

"Christ!" Buck yelled. "You just scared ten years off me. What's going on?"

"The entire airport is crawling with National Guard. I'll call you back."

Acadia disconnected the phone as Zak peeled a U-turn into oncoming traffic and drove out of the airport lot at the same speed as other motorists. "They knew we were coming," he said, his voice strained and tight.

Acadia gave an uneasy laugh. "I know you're a big deal, Zak, but I seriously doubt an entire police force would be waiting at the airport to rekidnap us."

"Check out the JumboTron over the door."

She looked through the rearview window. Her Junction City driver's license was up there with a Wanted, Armed, and Dangerous notice beneath it. Zak's was scrolling up next. The police were expecting them.

"Get out that map," Zak ordered tightly. "You're going to enjoy Caracas hospitality a little longer."

"I'd rather not. There must be another wa—"

"There isn't."

Stomach in a knot, Acadia refastened her seat belt. It didn't matter what the hell she wanted. She had to stay. "Should we call Buck back and have him send those security guys to meet us?"

"No," Zak said grimly. "I don't want *anyone* knowing where we are until we figure this thing out." Everything about this entire situation smelled bad. From the kidnapping, to their escape, to the hotel bomb, to the—hell, all of it.

"Do you have something in mind, or are we just driving around until we run out of gas?" Acadia asked after she'd been quiet for a good fifteen minutes.

Zak saw trees up ahead and pulled into the lot of a city park. "Let's take a walk while we think this through."

She crawled over the console and climbed out on his side. Zak took her hand to help her and, because it felt so perfect in his, kept hold as they started along a winding path that circled a small duck pond. A few young mothers wheeled kids in strollers, a shabbily dressed bum slept with a magazine over his face on a bench, and farther along, two old men played a lively game of chess in the shade of a gnarled broad-leafed tree. Several other old men stood around watching every play.

"Gideon's being moved," Zak said as the silence was broken by a kid's loud wailing on the other side of the pond, his paper sailboat sinking like a rock.

Acadia looked up at him with a frown. "The numbers are changing?"

"Yeah, slightly. I have to get to him, Acadia, and I don't know——" Fuckit. He ran his left hand over his face, and his shoulder ached like hell. God. He didn't even want to vocalize what he'd thought of in the early hours of the morning. But once the idea had taken hold he couldn't forget it.

Her fingers tightened in his. "Tell me. Let me help."

"Something about this last week seemed . . . off. I can't quite put my finger on it."

"I take it you're talking beyond the obvious? Zak, you think whoever is behind the kidnapping was targeting you. But what if they were targeting me?" She pulled him to a stop. "Hear me out for a moment. If they were after you, they wouldn't have brought a strange woman along for the ride. They would have gone to your room. Not mine. I would've been redundant. They had you and Gideon, and you're insanely wealthy and powerful. Why'd they drag me with you?"

"Because I was in your room, and you'd seen their faces."

She waved that away. "They could've shot me at any time."

"Do you have powerful enemies, sweetheart? Anyone want you dead?"

"I hope not. But that doesn't mean it isn't a possibility. We have to think of everything if we hope to get away from them."

"I don't for a second think that you were the target," he said with a firm shake of his head. "Yeah, it's *possible*, but probable? No. It's more likely that they followed me to your room from the cantina that night, and when they went to get me and Gideon in the morning, and I wasn't in my own room, they just went where they'd seen me last."

Acadia nodded grudgingly, but wasn't done making her case.

"If someone wanted to get my five hundred thousand dollars, and didn't know you and Gideon were ZAG Search . . . that's a *lot* of money to just about everyone who isn't a multigazillionaire."

"It *isn't* you they're after."

"That guy said 'make sure the *wife* is dead.' Clearly he wasn't aware that you don't have a wife." She swept her hair back over her shoulder and blew out an irritated breath. "So let's follow that thread for a minute. The guy didn't say 'make sure *the woman* is dead.' Or 'make sure *Acadia Gray* is dead.' He said 'wife.' The point was *wife*. And as far as I know, only two people believe we're married, right?"

"Sister Clemencia and the police chief you swindled."

"Yes, and a good thing neither of us is Catholic, or we'd probably go straight to hell for lying to a nun. And I didn't swindle him, I played him fair and square."

His lips twitched. "And I told Carina we were married to expedite matters. So someone from one or both of those sources believes we *are* in fact married."

"Exactly," Acadia said, sliding her hand through his arm as they walked. How very normal, she thought; normal, not death-defying. Her lips twitched, although this was no laughing matter. "I don't believe a nun posse is trying to kill us. And I don't think ninety-eight-pounds-soaking-wet-Carina-the-Concierge is trying to kill us either, do you?"

"Right, that's a no. But one of them did tell someone. Someone who'd kidnapped you and didn't care if you died."

Zak walked in silence, his fingers tightening around hers as the puzzle bits floated around in his mind like so much flotsam and jetsam. Between the numbers and the jigsaw and the warm, silken smooth texture of her palm against his, he couldn't think straight.

No. He really, really didn't *want* to think straight.

"Guerrilla Girl didn't refer to me as your wife," Acadia mused, matching her steps to his as they strolled casually through the park. "That only started after the mission and after we arrived in Caracas, right?"

"But they'd care if that wife was eligible to inherit my estate." Shit. He didn't want to go down this detour.

"Zak . . ." She hesitated. "What if this wasn't about a kidnapping at all? What if it's some sort of murder for hire? Who inherits if you die?"

He'd been thinking the same thing after the men had broken in the night before. The knot in his gut had been sure of what his brain didn't want to admit, and Zak didn't want to go there.

Going there meant he'd have to rethink every conversation he'd ever had with everyone he'd ever known. With his friends, with his business partner, with their associates—it was a long fucking list.

He blew out a hard breath. There had to be another explanation. A reason, somewhere. He'd find it. "Of course, it could be a murder plot," he admitted. "As a company, we've bought out failing businesses. People have lost their jobs when we've mashed businesses together for efficiency. Christ, we've done dozens of hostile takeovers in the last ten years alone. It's all business. Not personal . . ."

Her eyebrows rose, and he caught himself with a grim smile. "Yeah, to some of them, it must've been personal as hell."

Acadia nibbled at her thumbnail. She glanced around the park, studying every person around them with suspicion. He held on to her hand—just a normal couple out for a normal walk in the park—although he couldn't tell if it was to reassure her or himself. She shot him a smile, which didn't quite reach her beautiful, thought-ful smokey eyes. "How about a disgruntled employee? A business associate who feels . . ." She let go of his hand to gesticulate wildly in the air. "Who knows? But they're mad at you for whatever reason." Zak almost laughed as she slanted him a speculative sideways glance. "Okay, how about a spurned lover?"

He shook his head. "Don't you think I've considered all of this? I'd hate to think I pissed someone—*anyone*—off enough that they'd go to such elaborate lengths to kill me. And that would mean killing *me*, not my brother or a faux wife." Zak threaded his hands through his hair and cupped the back of his skull.

"Unless someone wanted what you have. Wealth. Power. A great lifestyle. My guess is that Gideon is your heir."

"The bulk of my estate and assets goes to Gideon, yeah. But he's already got all that, same as me." *Click.* Even as he said it, the knot in his gut tightened. "We're equal partners with Buck; we each own a third of the business. In the event of my death, my third would be split between Gid and Buck."

"But if you were married, wouldn't your third go to your wife? And say *you* inherited Gideon's share, then *you* died—then if you *had* a wife it would all go to her, and she'd have controlling interest in the company, right? But if she died, Buck would inherit everything."

Zak pressed his lips together firmly until they formed a flat line. "But I don't have a wife."

"Yeah, well, apparently people around here *think* that you do," she pointed out as she walked beside him. "We never let them in on the joke. So, for all intents and purposes, they want to kill you *and* your wife, because if *you* died, your money would go to your lovely bride, and if she were also dead, it would all go to your brother."

"Not all," he corrected quietly, "but certainly the bulk of it. So you think the plan was to kill either Gid or me—they didn't seem to care. That way, one brother inherited everything. Then the kidnappers hear that I'm married, which would trump my brother's inheriting. So, first they have to get rid of *you*, then either brother. The last brother standing gets everything? Except, that would imply that the person behind this elaborate plan is—"

"Not your brother," she finished quietly, sidestepping before a girl on an old pedal bike ran them down. The cheery *ring-ring* of the bell seemed harsh and grating. "It doesn't make sense to give himself a couple of broken ribs when he could just as easily push you off a mountain somewhere."

Zak's fists clenched, and she winced in apology.

"Sorry. But I do think it's the work of someone who wants something from you badly enough that they'd kidnap you, and set two bombs. One of you was supposed to die out in the jungle." She tilted her head and looked up at him, her expression earnest.

"And as butch and in charge as Loida Piñero is," Zak mused, his fingers shoved into his front pockets, "I seriously doubt she has the resources to pull all this off. Even here, bomb materials are expensive, not to mention the manpower it took to kidnap and transport us."

Acadia nodded. "There've been only a small handful of people who think we're really married. The crooked police chief—oh, *and* his three scummy friends—the nun, your friendly concierge, and your friend at the bank, right?"

Zak stopped on the path. The sun felt illogically chilly on his face, and his jaw ached as he said out loud what he didn't want to hear. "One other."

"Who?"

"My partner, Anthony Buckner," he said, his voice low and dangerous. Buck, the holder of 33 percent of ZAG Search, and the man who waved the Stark brothers off on adventure after dangerous adventure with a smile.

The man who stood to inherit it all.

∽ᄋ SEVENTEEN ᄋ∽

Acadia's soft, sympathetic gaze almost did him in. "There must be other possibilities."

No. No other possibilities. A ball of disbelief lodged tightly in Zak's gut, and he heard the derision in his tone as he asked, "Why, you think there's a long line of people who'd like to see me dead?"

He lived his life to the hilt, sure, but with conscious, scrupulous integrity. Hell, even when they did hostile takeovers, they made sure the owners were compensated far above what anyone else would have offered, and that people were taken care of fairly. There'd been a few glitches and a couple lawsuits along the way, but nothing that would warrant this kind of payback.

He couldn't think of one person who hated him enough to want him dead. There were plenty *greedy* enough to want him dead, but this didn't smell like a money grab. They wanted to make him hurt. This felt personal. All rational signs pointed to this being a plan enacted by someone close. Close enough to know where to find the brothers and be on top of them when they called. So close Zak had eaten in the man's kitchen.

Buck.

Fuckit. Zak had the *who* in the equation, he was sure of it; now he needed the *why.* It didn't make sense for Anthony Buckner to go to such elaborate lengths to dispose of the Stark brothers. Money couldn't be his motive. Buck was financially conservative by nature. He had more than he could spend in a lifetime, even with a shopaholic wife and a couple of great, but indulged and spoiled, kids.

"No, of course not," Acadia assured him, rubbing his upper arm in an absent gesture. "But I trust your judgment." She left her hand on him, light, but so strong and capable. Her touch helped more than she could possibly know.

"Let's move into the shade," she told him briskly, tugging on his arm. "We need to rethink this." Her brow furrowed in concentration as she walked a few yards to a patch of shade under a nearby tree. "What about that Savin guy? You say he tried to recruit you for his black-ops thing when you were at MIT? *He'd* certainly have the contacts and resources to pull off something of this magnitude, wouldn't he? Did anything happen between you that he might've *misconstrued*?" She shrugged helplessly. "Sometimes people perceive a slight when none was intended. Did you guys ever go on some bender where he told you something and now he has to kill you?"

Savin would certainly have the contacts and the resources. On the other hand, Buck had the resources to *make* the contacts. He appreciated her effort, but Jesus, he knew he was right. "Haven't seen or even spoken to Marc in—hell, must be ten or twelve years now. I was damned surprised that he even remembered telling me to call him if I ever needed help. It's not him, sweetheart."

Christ. Zak wished with everything in him that he had a more logical suspect than Buck. But things were starting to click in his brain, and as much as he didn't want to go down this road, there wasn't anyone else who fit the bill. Then again, *Buck* didn't fit the bill.

"It was Buck who suggested the Angel Falls trip," he told her, leaning against a tree trunk. BASE-jumping the falls hadn't been that high on their daredevil scale, not by a long shot. He rubbed his hand across his mouth. "Why else would he do it?"

"Because he thought you'd enjoy it?" Acadia suggested.

"Maybe." Zak considered it briefly, then shook his head. "But I doubt it. Within hours of my calling him, two people tried to kill us at the Gran Meliá. Within hours of *that*, the company jet blew up, right after I told Buck we were headed to the airport. And this whole thing started with someone *knowing* that Gid and I were in that small hotel; that info wasn't exactly available on Page Six."

"What about back home? Can you remember anything that might strike a chord?"

"Nothing big. Buck keeps the business running like clockwork. You and he would get on great."

"Not if he wants to kill you, Zak." She brushed her hair off her shoulder. "So, he runs the business. Was there something major he wanted to do? Something new he wanted to try, that you were arguing about?"

He hesitated. "We're in the process of doing a buyout of a small rival search engine company; the deal is being finalized next month," he said slowly. "But the sale has been amicable, and Buck has that under control. I don't know, Acadia. None of this makes sense. No matter how I look at it."

She reached out to touch him, offering whatever comfort she could without words. He didn't deserve it. Every passing second that left Gideon alone in the jungle with no backup was agony. Zak pressed his fist between his eyebrows for a second, his gut twisting as he noticed the small change in the numbers indicating Gideon's movement. God, there was a possibility that his brother had escaped. *He'd* done it; so could Gideon.

But the kidnappers had been caught unawares when they'd escaped, and incapacitated by Acadia's quick thinking and multipocketed clothing. Hell, half the reason they were still alive and walking around was her ingenuity. And pure luck.

Besides, Gid's ribs might be broken, which meant he'd be slower. Zak hated feeling so inept. So freaking *powerless.*

He refused to consider the alternative. That Gid was already dead, and someone else was wearing his watch. "Once you eliminate the impossible," he quoted bitterly, "whatever remains, no matter how improbable, must be the truth."

"Not necessarily," Acadia said very seriously. She

stopped speaking as three teenagers on skateboards rode toward them. They stepped off the path to let them go by. "Technically," she continued, shading her eyes against the bright sun, "anything *is* possible, therefore, nothing is impossible. Therefore, there is no impossible to eliminate. Therefore, anything *can* be true. Right?"

He crowded her against the back of a nearby bench. Then cupped her cheek, because he needed to touch her to feel grounded, if only for a moment. "Convoluted." He stroked his thumb across her sun-warmed skin, and she leaned a little into his touch, but didn't say anything.

Zak shook his head and stepped away from her. She was like a magnet and he a lodestone; he was so attracted to her that if she was in touching distance, he couldn't keep his hands to himself. He really needed to start learning how.

He stuffed his hands into his front pockets and stared off into the middle distance.

He had to find a safe place to stash Acadia. Where? He wasn't sure if the police and National Guard were after them because of the stolen police car or because they were on someone's payroll. Either way, the officials had her photograph and identification; there was nowhere she could hide and no way he could get her out of the country. And he could forget about the money. Buck would have made sure there was no access.

The longer he took to find a safe haven where he wouldn't have to worry about her, the longer it would take him to find Gideon. And the longer it took, the less chance of finding him—

His phone rang, and he snatched it out of his breast pocket. *Buck.* "Hey," he said by way of greeting. His throat closed and acid roiled up in his stomach. He'd known this man for almost half his adult life. They'd gotten drunk together when Jen had died. And again when Buck's teenage son had overdosed on drugs last year and almost hadn't made it. They'd built a business from nothing, and taken rare family vacations together.

Other than Gideon, Anthony Buckner was the one person on this planet he had trusted the most.

Zak couldn't even comprehend how it had come to this . . . or why.

"Buddy, my guys want to be wheels-up sooner than later. What's the holdup?"

"I have to keep a low profile; the cops were looking for me at the airport," Zak said, not quite lying. "I had to ditch the car, and I'm waiting to rent another one. Taking longer than I thought."

Acadia tapped away at the keyboard of her phone as he talked.

"Screw the rental," Buck said impatiently, then hesitated. After a moment, he said with more calm, "I'll have one of my men come pick you up; it'll be faster. Give me your location."

Acadia turned her screen so Zak could see the list of car rental places she'd ZAG-searched. He chose one as far from the airport as he could find and rattled off the street address, shooting her a grateful smile.

"Okay, bud, hang tight. I'll have someone there ASAP," Buck assured him. "We'll get Gideon, Zak.

Whether it takes a duffel bag of cash or they go in guns blazing. We *will* retrieve Gideon."

Sure you will. "Thanks, Buck. Appreciate your confidence." He took the phone from his ear and heard Buck ask casually, "What happened to the woman?"

Without answering, Zak disconnected, then stood there for a moment, looking blankly across the pond, where the little boy waited patiently for his mother to build him another paper boat. Ducks swam lazily on the reflection of a hard blue sky.

Everything around him looked so normal, yet his entire world was upside-down.

He needed help. Pissed him off, but he needed help and he needed it now. He dialed again. "Who are you calling?" Acadia whispered, and he held up a hand for her to hang on as the line connected.

"Marc?" he said into the phone. Acadia's expression cleared. "It's Zak Stark. Here's the deal." Quickly, he told him the whole fucking story from beginning to end.

After a silent moment, Marc sighed. "Hell of a clusterfuck. Give me ten minutes, okay? I'll call you back with the location of a safe house."

The line went dead, and Zak pocketed his phone. Next to him, Acadia watched the surface of the pond, her eyebrows knotted tightly.

"Don't look so worried," Zak said, tracing a finger over her frown. "He'll get us to a safe house and come up with a solid plan. Not as good as yours, but his weapons are bigger than a bottle of eyedrops."

Granted, he didn't know much about Savin aside from

what he'd told Acadia already. He might very well have just made a bargain with a man who could kill him without leaving a trace of his body. But his gut didn't agree.

"We'd better hope you weren't confiding in the wrong guy," Acadia muttered, once again reading his mind. "On the upside?" She tucked her arm in his as if they were a couple of dating kids on a Sunday afternoon stroll. "If he decides to kill us, he'll know how to make it *quick*." She shot him an impish glance.

It hit him like a rock between the eyes.

As if she heard the shifting of his heart, she swiveled on her toes to face him. She paused, as if wanting to say something, then shook her head and reached up to give him a swift, hard kiss on the mouth. She let go and took his hand, twining her fingers with his as they started walking back to the car. "Let's go see what a safe house looks like."

THE SAFE HOUSE LOOKED like a cheap hotel in a bad part of town. The sign read BATES HO L, featured a bullet hole in the middle of the O, and hung precariously by one rusted chain. Acadia gave it a skeptical look. "Are you sure this is it?" The building was squeezed in between other similar structures. They all desperately needed a coat of paint, and . . .

Who was she kidding? Paint wasn't going to do anything for them. No, they all looked like they should be razed to the ground and rebuilt. The plaster and bricks were crumbled on all the facades. Shutters hung askew, and most of the buildings had metal bars covering windows and doors. Garbage, feral cats, and filthy, far too skinny, ragged children were *everywhere*.

"That's the one," he told her. He waited with his back to her as she slid across the driver's seat to get out of the car. "Keep your eyes open, and step lively. Ready?"

"Ready not to feel as though I have a bull's-eye on my back?" Acadia cast a nervous glance at the swarm of mini criminals edging closer to the car. She instinctively moved closer to Zak. "Damn strai—" She suddenly noticed he had a gun in his hand. "God, Zak, surely you wouldn't shoot little children!"

"Move!"

As they ran across the street, the kids swarmed around them like locusts. They grabbed at her clothes and hung on her arms; one boy about eight slid down her leg and grabbed her around the top of her boots so that she had to run with the child as an anchor. Despite the gun in Zak's hand, three more kids were clinging to his duffel bag, dragging their heels on the pavement, to no avail.

The black door of the hotel was thrown open, and they spilled inside while an enormous bald man with a barrel chest and thick black mustache picked the kids off them like lice. The door shut with a surprisingly solid thump, and the man rapidly engaged several locks, then slapped his palm on a pad next to the door. When the tumblers clicked into place, he turned and gave them an assessing look.

"Don't feel sorry for the little buggers, Miss Gray,"

he said, with a faint Scottish burr. "They'd as soon slit your throat as look at you." He held out a ham-size hand to Zak. "Campbell Garcia, call me Cam. Manager of this here Bates Hotel." He grinned as he and Zak shook hands. "You doin' all right, lass?"

"If this is the rabbit hole, sure." She smiled when Cam gave her a broad white grin, then slapped her on the shoulder, almost toppling her. Zak grabbed her arm to keep her upright.

"Sorry about that, lassie. Just us boys here most of the time, I forget my strength around the ladies. Come through, I'll take you up to a room. We have your extraction team assemblin' as we speak. You'll be moving out in under an hour."

The vestibule was small, and paneled in a blond wood that was worn and peeling. The dirty black-and-white tile floor was dotted with cracked and uneven squares; a small reception area was tucked under the uncarpeted stairs.

"Had some food taken up, nothin' fancy, but you'll need something in your stomach, now won't you? This way." Cam started up the stairs, his footfalls so loud on the bare wood, Acadia was surprised they didn't splinter.

She met Zak's glance and made a what-the-hell face. He smiled, and she got a quick glimpse of his dimple. She much preferred seeing Zak with this expression than with the one of desolate betrayal he'd worn in the park.

The uncarpeted hallway, like the stairs, was scarred and battered wood. Acadia happily noted that the higher they climbed, the cleaner the hotel became. "First floor," Cam told them, rounding a landing with a row of six closed doors marching down the long corridor. "Should we ever be compelled to take in a real guest." He looked over his massive shoulder and winked at Acadia. "Which we rarely do. Only one more flight. You'll have a bit of time to wash up, eat somethin', and say your good-byes. I promise," he told Zak, barely taking a breath. "I'll keep your lady safe until ye get back. With your brother, is it?"

Their boots sounded extraordinarily loud clomping down the corridor. Cam shoved the door open, then stepped aside for them to enter. They saw twin beds, covered in striped, multicolored heavy cotton throws, shoved against the walls; a wide chest of drawers with two lamps on it between them; a reclining easy chair beside a floor lamp; and a partially open door leading to a bathroom. All the comforts of home.

A narrow table, with an open laptop computer on it, also held a tray of covered dishes. The smell of freshly brewed coffee and something spicy made Acadia take one of her first easy breaths of the day. "Thank you."

"Basic," Cam assured them. "But clean. No worries about vermin o' any kind in Cam Garcia's place. Before you dig in, I have to show you some of our special features, then I'll leave you two alone for a spell." He headed for the bathroom, but paused to point a thick finger at the computer. "Savin will be callin' in a few."

He led them into the bathroom—small and sparse, but clean. The once-white tile was cracked in places, but it smelled like cleanser and the pine air freshener hanging from the shower rod. Worn rust-colored towels hung on the rack.

"An escape route, if you need it," Cam offered cheerfully.

Acadia blinked at the man. "Um?"

He pointed to the towels. "Behind the rack," he explained, and beside her, Zak smothered a laugh. "Pull it toward you and hard to the right. It'll take you downstairs, right by the side door. That opens into a side alley."

No kidding? This was serious spy stuff, and Acadia's head hurt thinking about it. "Will we be using it?"

"Ah, I hope not, lass," Cam replied, clapping her much more gently on the shoulder. "But you never know. Now, eat up while you can. I'll just be leavin' you to it."

"That was . . . interesting," Acadia said a few minutes later, as the door closed behind the Scotsman.

"He's a character, all right." Zak crossed the room to lift the covers off several large platters. "Are you hungry? Looks like he thinks we haven't eaten in a year."

She shook her head. Any minute now Zak would be leaving. Her heart was beating—she knew it was, otherwise she'd be unconscious. But Acadia couldn't feel anything. She was numb. "I'm having separation anxiety," she admitted, her feet rooted to the area rug.

Zak crossed the room to take her in his arms. To her horror, her whole body shuddered with the contact. She couldn't control it; his touch had become so profound.

"You'll be safe here. Savin's arranging transportation for you. His people will ensure you get home safely."

"I know. And I appreciate it, but—"

Zak lifted her chin on his finger. "One thing at a time, okay?"

"Of course." He was already gone, and she couldn't blame him. His body was here, but his head was in the jungle, climbing the falls. Searching for Gideon.

She stepped out of his arms, which made the feeling of separation a thousand times stronger and the ache in her chest that much bigger. "Have something to eat and a cup of coffee," she suggested brightly. "You'll probably have a long walk ahead of you." She poured two cups of strong black java and handed him a mug. Neither of them sat down.

"I'll t—" Zak's words layered over hers as she said at the same time, "Promise me, you'll—"

"Stark."

They both turned to see Savin's face fill the computer monitor. "Savin," Zak said. "Appreciate your help." Marc Savin didn't look much different than he had ten years ago. His dark hair was no longer tied back, and he'd lost the diamond earring. A little older and wiser, but weren't they all?

"Grab a seat, and let's get some shit out of the way before the show starts." Zak sat on the foot of one of the beds; Acadia stood against the wall, out of camera range.

Marc launched into the plan with clipped efficiency. "First things first. I've assembled a team of four men and a pilot in an Apache helicopter to take you over the target. John Reith is team leader. We have him on speaker in case there's any breaking news," he added. "The men hired by Buckner took off from the airfield in a rented chopper seven minutes ago, after returning from the car rental place you sent them to. They weren't happy." Savin smiled. "Good thinking there."

Zak's gaze flicked to Acadia, who grinned at him.

"They have a ten-minute head start," Savin continued. "They'll be landing at the small strip near Angel Falls and walking in the rest of the way. We'll get you over the target and you and my men will rappel down, snatch and grab your brother, and return the same way."

Acadia didn't watch the screen. She watched Zak, memorizing every detail of his face, his stance, even the way his shoulders tensed as he listened to the plan. But it wasn't fear she saw setting in his suddenly rigid jaw. It was elation.

Rappelling from a helicopter? Busting in before the bad guys to rescue his injured brother, making the grand escape with bullets flying? Even she couldn't deny what a rush it'd be. But, whereas she'd be retching from nerves, Zak was eating it all up like candy.

You're leaving, she told herself. She just had to remember that.

Savin glanced down at what Acadia assumed were papers of some sort. "Intel tells us that Buckner hasn't been seen since seventeen hundred hours, shortly after you spoke to him this afternoon. Any idea as to his location?"

"Did he fly out?" Zak shrugged. "Hell. I have no idea. Follow the money."

"We couldn't find evidence of a large cash withdrawal

in any of Buckner's accounts in the last two weeks, Stark. However, prior to that, he made a withdrawal for one hundred million dollars from his account in the Caymans."

Acadia flinched. That kind of money couldn't possibly be real. But Zak, she noticed, appeared unfazed. "Before the kidnapping," he pointed out. "But it's money to do with as he likes."

"I'd be interested to see exactly what that kind of money can do, wouldn't you?"

Wouldn't he just? "You bet," Zak said dryly, not able to keep the resentment from his voice. "Like fund a well-armed group of guerrillas."

Savin nodded. "My thoughts exactly. It looks like he put a lot into this before you and your brother even left the States. A lot of cash, a lot of Russian-made weapons, and a lot of manpower."

"Buck's always been a hard worker," Zak said bitterly.

"Let's cover a few more bases. Give me the lowdown on Jack Flynn and Michael Cobb."

Zak narrowed his eyes. "You've certainly been thorough."

"I'm putting my men and my resources behind you, Stark. I'm dotting all my i's."

"Fair enough." Zak impatiently scraped both hands through his hair. "Flynn brought a nuisance suit over ZAG's so-called hostile takeovers. It went nowhere. That was in 2002."

"And Cobb?"

Ah, Cobb. A massive thorn in the company's side for years. "Cobb worked with ZAG Search in the design department. To be fair, he did a lot of the early usability and interface work on the website." Zak translated: "He helped make the website easy to use and accessible to all users, handicapped or otherwise."

"So?"

"So, he decided to make some extra money by selling his designs to a rival company. We found out, fired him, and he sued us for breach of contract in 2004." Zak shrugged. "He lost." It had all been part of doing business. "These are just regular people who got swept up in business deals they weren't ready to handle," he said. "I can't see any of them carrying out a personal vendetta against me, Gideon, or Buck." And especially not *with* Buck.

"Anything you haven't told me?"

"Probably quite a lot." Zak's lips twitched as he got to his feet. "But none of it pertinent."

"I have forensic accountants and a battery of lawyers going over every inch of ZAG Search's financials." The calm statement was like a punch to his chest. He forced himself to relax. It had to be done. "Personal *and* business," Savin added. "If you have anything to hide, Stark, anyone that could slither out of the woodwork, now's the time to share. I don't like sending you or my men blind into a situation like this."

ZAG Search was his baby, but he let the territorial urge slide. The company was nothing without Gid. "Find Buckner," he said. "And then find out *why*. None of this makes any sense at all. Yesterday I would have sworn beyond a shadow of a doubt that Buck was innocent of any wrongdoing, but today he's the only one who looks guilty as hell. And I still don't believe it."

"What do you know about Adam Paulson?"

All the air left Zak's lungs. Shit. Paulson. He hadn't thought about him since MIT.

"Zak?"

"Right," he said, frowning. "Adam was part of our little group back in the day. Used to sit around and shoot off ideas with us, but he wasn't willing to pony up the time or any cash to get in on the ground floor of ZAG. He thought we were nuts for ditching college, and he had plans to be a plastic surgeon. Said he'd not only be rich, but be up to his neck in tits and ass before we made our first million."

"Know what happened to him?"

Zak frowned. "Not really. Last I heard he was in his fifth year of medical school and about a hundred grand in debt with student loans." He shrugged. "Not sure about the tits and ass part. Why?"

"Nikki Buckner is his sister."

Zak collapsed back into the chair. "Fuckit. You sure?"

"Yeah, I'm sure. Buckner never mentioned it?"

"No. But I thought Nikki's maiden name was Hibbert."

"Half siblings. Different fathers."

"You think Buck's in this for Paulson?" That made even less sense than Buck doing it for his own convoluted reasons.

"Or Paulson thinks you three owe him and is using Buck as a scapegoat to bring you all down together in one neat little bundle. 'A house divided against itself cannot stand,' and all that bullshit."

"But how?"

Savin shrugged. "If Paulson and Nikki are close, she could be the one pulling the money out of the account," he suggested. "Setting up her husband. Or, hell, Paulson could be blackmailing your partner with dirt he's got on Nikki. God only knows, but offhand, I can think of half a dozen ways to wring money out of a rich man."

Zak thought about it, staring up at the ceiling. "I hate to say it, but it makes sense."

"I'll keep working on it from this angle. In the meantime, give us an update on those coordinates."

Zak rattled off the numbers. The last few numbers were changing very slowly. Gideon was on the move. Question was: alone, or under armed guard?

"They're moving him." Savin spoke to someone off-camera, then faced forward again. "Time to go. Your team is refueling, checking ordnance, and will be ready as soon as you get there." Savin stared straight at Zak. His eyebrows knotted over a stare so intense, it made even Zak want to stand at attention and salute. "We'll find him, one way or the other. Reith is downstairs waiting to take you to the airport. Good luck." The screen went dark.

For a long moment, the room was silent.

Acadia stirred. "God. Can he do that?" She stood, her voice shaky. "Just go digging into your life like that? Is that even legal?" She rubbed her upper arms, face pale and strained.

Zak didn't know for sure, but the man was helping him. So he shrugged. "I have nothing to hide, and
frankly, even if I did, if it means tracking down whoever
is responsible for doing this to Gideon, then I don't give
a fuck what he finds." Zak held out his hand, meeting
her wide eyes across the dim room. They brimmed with
emotion, worry. For him, he knew. And something softer.
Sweeter. His chest kicked hard. "Walk down with me?"

She slipped her fingers in his, and he brought their
joined hands to his lips, kissing her ringless fingers and
marveling that something so fragile-looking could be so
damned capable.

He stepped down onto the cracked black-and-white
tile of the lobby, then turned to place his hands on her
hips. She stood a step above him, so they were eye-to-eye.
"Don't talk to strangers." *Stay safe. Don't do anything fucking
stupid in the name of bravery. Be here when I get back.* But she
wouldn't be there. She'd be on her way home while he
went to get Gideon. Zak didn't say any of those things.

"I promise," she whispered softly, her soft eyes
clouded and lost.

She didn't say anything more either.

THE DOOR CLOSED BEHIND him with a soft, final click.
That was it. He was gone.

Acadia plopped down on the bottom stair as Cam
bolted the door behind Zak. Her vision blurred, and she
wiped her forearm across her eyes before the tears could
form. She'd known it was coming. She had no excuses.

A loud whistle pierced the air, making her jump.

"There, lass, just the kettle," Cam soothed. "Your man and his brother will be safe and sound before you know it. How about a cuppa tea in the kitchen before I take you to the airport for your flight?"

Acadia gave him a surprised glance. "If I'm leaving right away, why didn't I catch a ride with Zak and the other man?"

"Mine's not to ask the why of it," he said easily. "Hop on upstairs and get your things, lass. I'll have the tea steeped by the time you come down."

"Thanks, Cam. I'll be right back."

Acadia went upstairs, each step heavy with unshed tears and banked emotion. She wished she could stay here, holed up with Cam Garcia, until she saw Zak and Gideon safe and sound with her own two freaking eyes. But no one, particularly Zakary Stark, had suggested she wait. The fact that in a very short time she'd be on a plane and on her way home should've thrilled her. Instead, she almost wished she had had the guts to insist she be allowed to brave the jungle at Zak's side.

Pushing open the door to the room, she took out her iPhone and called Amber's work number. Her friend, a purchase manager for a trucking company, had been able to commit to only so many days before she had to return home. Acadia knew she'd be there now, worried, but having to keep on punching the clock.

Amber was out, so Acadia waited while the guy on the other end found a pen to take a message. By the time he got back to the phone, several minutes later, Acadia realized she couldn't put everything she needed to say into a message, so she made sure to say she was fine and that she'd be home the next day. She'd call Amber when she got there.

She picked up Zak's duffel from beside the bed. What on earth was she supposed to do with a bagful of bullets and silk boxer shorts? Maybe she should leave it here.

Better yet, she'd leave it with Cam. As she stepped out into the corridor, she heard a loud, *very* loud, thud. The odd sound stopped her in her tracks. "Don't overreact," she whispered as her heartbeat went into manic overdrive. "Cam dropped something, or—"

She strained her ears for another noi—

An explosion rocked the building. The walls shuddered, the floor pitched wildly, and she had to grab the doorjamb to stay on her feet.

Footsteps—punctuated by gunshots—echoed up the stairs as Cam yelled from the floor below, "Go! Go! *Go!*"

‑⊸ EIGHTEEN ⊷‑

Cam pounded to the top of the stairs. Without sparing a glance for Acadia, he shot out a hand to grab the newel post, then pivoted and continued firing down below. The sound of running feet and gunshots echoed and reverberated through the stairwell. She watched in disbelief as Cam shouted, without turning, "Catch!"

Something sailed over her head and clinked to the wood floor several feet behind her. She was afraid to look.

"Bathroom, lass," he shouted, splitting his attention between firing his weapon and keeping whoever was trying to run upstairs from doing the same.

Acadia scrambled to pick up the key.

"The escape route," Cam prodded. "Remember? Get downstairs and out the side door. Across the empty lot and two streets down, hit Juan Pablo South. Bank parking lot. Green Ford truck. Haul ass to the airport. Don't stop for anything." His entire conversation was punctuated by the rapid fire of a submachine gun pointed at whoever was answering fire below him on the stairs.

She gripped the key tightly. "What about you?"

"I'll do my job. Hold them off. Keep you safe. *Go*."

"Will y—"

"*Go!*"

Acadia ran back into the room and slammed the door. God. She was some kind of freaking bomb magnet! How could anyone know where she was? Oh, no. Zak? If they knew she was here, had they already— She flinched at the sound of gunfire. Close. Too close. Wood shattered; a high-pitched screech as if a bullet had hit metal.

Locking the surprisingly solid door, she quickly wedged the chair under the handle, then ran into the bathroom. Footsteps pounded up the uncarpeted wooden stair leading to the second floor. She slammed the bathroom door, pulling at the towel rack with the towels still on it.

Wait; if she just vanished, would they know to look for a trapdoor? She needed a red herring to delay them.

Window! A likely escape point. She ran to the small window and flung it open, then grabbed the towel rack again.

Pull forward, twist to the right.

A small door opened in the wall. It was plenty big enough for her to crawl into, which she did like a crab; then she kicked it closed behind her just as she heard the door to the room shatter with the force of a kick or a shot. She couldn't let herself think about Cam.

The tunnel wasn't big enough to stand in, but she

crawled as fast as she was able. It was dimly lit with small, motion-activated LED lights spaced at twelve-foot intervals. It was also dusty, dirty, and filled with cobwebs that clung to her hair, face, and clothes. She heard the men shouting to one another through the walls. Their American-accented voices sounded muffled and distorted through the tunnel.

Acadia breathed a sigh of relief as she heard footsteps racing farther away.

She took a short flight of steep steps down to the lower floor, another long crawl as she navigated a tunnel and another set of sharply descending stone stairs, until at last there was a door.

Holding her breath and her aching side, she cautiously opened the door into bright sunlight. She quickly glanced around—no guys with guns, no feral kids with a vendetta. She ran.

Gasping for breath, she sprinted across a weed-choked lot with a dilapidated building on it. Over piles of bricks and broken stones, over mounds of dry, cracked dirt, over blowing newspapers and empty bottles. Her breathing came in sharp pants; her lungs burned. She felt as though she had a giant bull's-eye painted on her back. If any of those men glanced out of one of the side windows, they couldn't miss her fleeing form. She'd be dead.

She turned the corner, heart manic. The streets were empty. It was hours until the city workers would start returning home. She was alone. Just her and the scraggly weeds. The hot breeze lifted her hair off her sweaty neck and cooled her cheeks. The stitch in her side gave an uncomfortably sharp pang as she ran around the corner and checked the street name. Juan Pablo.

There, across the street. Banco Central. Clearly not in business, with its broken windows, decayed facade, and trash-strewn parking lot. The green truck Cam had told her to find was the only car in the otherwise empty lot and Acadia squeezed the key until the teeth scored her palm. She forced her legs to pump faster as she ran across the empty street.

How long since Zak had left? Fifteen minutes? A little longer? Would she get to the airfield before they took off? God. He was *not* going to be happy to see her. She knew that. But there was nowhere else for her to go. Nowhere that she'd be safe. *If* she ever felt safe again, which was a pretty big if.

And what if she got there and Zak was gone? Or dead!

From thirty—twenty—ten feet away, the truck screamed *rusted piece of crap.* Her heart sank. It didn't even look as though it would run. No wonder it had been safe left out here. No thief was desperate enough to steal it.

It was also the only game in town.

Acadia sucked in a breath and pulled at the door handle, half expecting it to come off in her hand. To her surprise, the door was locked. She dropped the key trying to jam it into the lock, bent to pick it up, and shoved it into place on the second try. She yanked the rusted door open and slid across the cracked vinyl seat. The truck smelled of fried food and spoiled fruit. She'd open the window later. Right now all she cared about was putting as much room between herself and the not-so-safe house as possible.

Acadia had the key in the ignition even as she was slamming the door shut and locking it. The engine came to life with a powerful purr. More a Ferrari than a jalopy, just like the Taurus.

These black-ops guys were something else.

Gripping the wheel with both hands, she pulled out of the lot onto the street. The truck went from zero to seventy in seconds. As she paused a fraction of a second at a cross-street, she heard a massive explosion. An enormous plume of smoke and fire mushroomed into the sky behind her from the direction of the safe house. Acadia flinched. "Oh, God—Cam . . ." She couldn't think about him right now. "Don't look back, don't look back."

She put her foot down on the pedal, flattening it to the floor, and the truck leaped to 100 miles an hour. The body rattled alarmingly, and she was afraid pieces of it were going to come flying off, but that didn't stop her. She'd never in her life driven so fast that buildings passed in a blur.

Acadia managed a screeching turn onto the on-ramp, two wheels rising into the air, and she hurtled toward the *autopista intercomunal del aeropuerto*. If she remembered correctly—and she knew she did—the private airfield was three miles beyond the airport turnoff.

Acadia slowed down only enough to blend in with the other speeding commuters leaving the city, determined to reach Zak—if it wasn't too late. Her hands were damp on the wheel, and the speedometer was edging just over 102 when she heard the sirens behind her. At any other time, in any other place, she would've been thrilled to have the police right on her tail. But she didn't think those black vehicles closing the gap behind her were the police.

And even if they were, they sure as hell weren't going to help her. The last time she'd seen them, they'd followed her and Zak from the airport. The exit to the private airfield was up ahead. She pressed her foot to the floor and prayed that she didn't kill herself before the guys behind her managed to do it.

She shot a lightning-fast glance into the rearview mirror, and the truck slewed sideways. Three black SUVs closed in behind her. They had black tinted windows, police insignias, and flashing lights.

Ahead she saw a large black helicopter with lazily spinning rotors. There was no choice. Stomach in her throat, she slammed her sweaty palm down hard on the horn and headed straight for it.

AS THE RAUCOUS SOUND of a car horn echoed over the noisily spinning rotors, Zak looked up from strapping himself in. "What the—"

An old pickup truck was barreling across the tarmac, heading straight for the chopper. A quarter of a mile behind it, three black SUVs fanned out in a pincer movement to trap truck and helicopter. They were gaining fast.

As the deceptively junky-looking truck approached, Zak saw the pale oval of the driver's face.

Acadia.

His heart leaped and his hands went to his harness. Her features were blurred by speed, but he couldn't miss that silky blond hair, or the sensation of horror he felt seeing her here. Fuckit. Now what?

"Friends of yours?" Reith asked dryly, his weapon, an M-16, in the firing position, his eye narrowed as the pickup and the SUVs behind came straight at them at over a hundred per.

Zak gritted his teeth. "The one in the truck."

Behind him, the man who'd introduced himself as Spincher flagged down the chopper pilot. "Incoming hot!" he said into the mic. "We got bogeys closing in, get those guns warmed up!"

The chopper had massive artillery at its disposal. Enough to lay waste to a couple cars. And Acadia, if he didn't get out and get her. *Now.*

Zak swung down to the ground, head ducked. They'd equipped him with a fully loaded M-16 for the trip, and he had that with him as he landed on the tarmac in a crouch.

"Cover me," he shouted as the truck screeched to a stop, engine still running. He yanked open the driver's door and grabbed Acadia's arm. Over the rotors and gunfire, he yelled, "Are you hurt?"

The sound of a handheld rocket launcher canceled out what she shouted in return, and Zak made do with hauling her as fast as he could scramble back to Savin's Apache. A hundred yards away, the lead SUV exploded into a loud fiery ball of heat and metal. The guys on the chopper knew what they were doing. The heat and force of the blast swept over him, singeing his lungs. He staggered, but he didn't let go of Acadia, just pulled and supported her while they kept their heads down and their feet moving.

A flaming steering wheel slammed down a foot in front of her, then bounced. Tightening his arm around her waist, Zak lifted her over it without breaking stride and kept going. She was shaking and out of breath, hyperventilating, but as far as he could tell, she wasn't bleeding.

She was shouting, but he couldn't hear her. "They blew up the safe house." Zak read her lips as they reached the chopper; hearing was impossible with the noise. A second vehicle was hit and more flames shot high into the blackened sky, producing pillars of thick, oily smoke.

In the distance, he heard the faint sound of sirens. Or maybe the sirens weren't that distant; it was hard to tell with the cacophony of bullets firing and shit blowing the hell up in every direction. Bits of vehicle—a seat, a car door, part of an engine block—dropped around them like some sort of Salvador Dalí hailstorm.

He boosted Acadia inside as gunfire shattered the *whoop-whoop-whoop* of the fast-moving rotors.

Spincher grabbed her hand, hauling her all the way in.

Zak jumped after her, and the man yelled, "Go! Go! Go!" through his lip mic.

A bullet struck the side of the four-bladed, twin-engine Apache, pinging loudly as Zak pushed Acadia down and buckled her into a harness. Then he sat beside her and secured his own. The armor-plated door slid closed.

Normal conversation was impossible. Reith brought a pair of headsets back; Zak placed Acadia's over her head and hooked her up, then settled his own back on his head.

They rose at seven hundred feet a minute, taking fire to the body, but giving back worse than they received. The 30mm automatic M230 chain gun fired at something like 625 rounds a minute. It took out the last SUV and several police cars with it. Whatever personal vendetta Buck had against Zak, he'd just made it into an international incident. Fuckit.

He looked over Acadia's head as the vehicles exploded in another fiery display. The show had drawn a swarm of police cars, lights and sirens blazing.

Acadia trembled, her face white and streaked with dirt.

He touched her cheek. "Okay?"

Her eyes, fixed on the rapidly retreating tarmac, slowly swiveled to his face. Mutely, she shook her head and made a rocking motion with her hand. Zak pulled her into his arms and pressed her head against his shoulder.

They flew over downtown Caracas, and within minutes saw the smoke cloud over the safe house, now a big fucking hole in the ground. Jesus. No good deed went unpunished. Savin was going to have his ass. And Zak had a feeling he wouldn't be invited back to Venezuela anytime soon.

It would all be worth it if—*when*—he found Gideon. Alive.

THEY FLEW OVER THE camp where the military helicopter carrying Buck's security people had landed. There was nothing more than blackened earth from another massive explosion. Jesus—how much explosive did these assholes have? And why the fuck would Buck's people blow up a multimillion-dollar chopper? Didn't make sense. Fuckit. None of this made any sense.

Licks of flame leaped between smoldering parts of what was left of the Blackhawk.

"Any chance they're already on their way in?" Zak demanded, although the smell of the lazily drifting smoke told the story. Jet fuel, burning rubber, and charred human flesh.

"That bird was shot out of the sky," Reith told him grimly. "Nobody walked away."

"Or it was set up to look that way," Zak said grimly. Buck was a clever guy. Zak wouldn't put it past him to pull something off like an "accident" to misdirect his partner into thinking he had a better shot at rescuing Gideon.

"Pretty fucking expensive hoax," Spincher said into his lip mic.

The cost would be immaterial to Buck. "There's a big payoff." They left the smoking wreckage behind and flew low over the tree canopy as Zak gave them the coordinates again.

He drew in a deep breath, his focus on finding Gid. He'd deal with Buck when the time came, he suspected sooner than later, but for now his focus was on his brother's rescue.

Two of Savin's men would rappel down with him. The other two, with the pilot and Acadia, would remain in the air. The men would lay down cover fire when they found and extracted Gideon. The sun was a red-hot ball as it sank behind the treetops. Zak rested the fingers of his left hand over the face of Gideon's watch, a talisman, on his right wrist. Wearing a too-big bulletproof vest supplied by one of the men, along with a helmet and goggles, and strapped in on a cord, Acadia huddled beside him, her gray eyes wide as she tried to take it all in.

She slipped her slender, slightly damp hand into his, linking her fingers with Zak's.

He wished with everything in him that she wasn't there. This whole situation was as fucking precarious as climbing Everest without oxygen tanks. The variety of possibilities for maiming, failure, and probable death was mind-boggling.

He changed his depth perception and visually fuzzed out everything around him, a trick he'd learned years ago for when he had to concentrate and focus. He had to trust that the trained professionals would keep Acadia out of harm's way while he focused on his brother's rescue.

Zak hated depending on other people to do his job: protecting the woman he l—protecting Acadia Gray, an innocent caught up in his mess.

He'd failed once with a woman who'd counted on him to keep her safe. Even from herself. He wouldn't do it again. For a moment, Zak's conscience warred with his heart.

What if he *hadn't* developed a sixth sense after he'd officially died? What if he *did* have fucking brain damage and this was a hallucination?

What if he was responsible for dragging innocent people into this fucking delusion with him? Zak had to call it now. Time was running out. Rappel down and hope to God he found his brother? Or have the pilot change course and get Acadia to safety? The numbers in his head kept up their steady, uninterrupted scroll.

If he could believe them, Gideon was in the same position he'd been in an hour ago. That would make retrieval easier.

The chopper started slowing as it made its descent.

Acadia's finger's tightened in his. *Call it, Stark.*

Thirty-five years with a brother he adored, versus a handful of days with Acadia?

It shouldn't be a hard choice.

"Stark?" Reith said through his headset, indicating the chopper's GPS. Zak nodded. Correct coordinates. In fact, the numbers in his head were brighter somehow, more vivid the closer they got. Gideon was down there . . .

The other man flashed a five-second countdown with his fingers.

The chopper dropped another couple of hundred feet.

Acadia's fingers looked small and bloodless clutching his.

The sound of the rotors would be heard on the ground now, and soon enough the chopper would be seen. But there was nothing but thick jungle for miles in every direction. Whoever was with Gideon wouldn't get far.

Zak untangled his hand from Acadia's. She turned to smile at him. A small, brave smile that tore a hole in his chest, as though something had been ripped out of him. It hurt, empty and aching and brutal. The breath left him with a harsh sound.

Because he couldn't not touch her, he reached out and put two fingers across her soft mouth. Her lips brushed his fingers as she said softly, "Go get Gideon, Zak. Bring him home."

Before either of them did something fucking stupid, he got to his feet.

Reith slid open the door, and dropped the rope bags. Zak fastened the M-16 securely across his chest. Checked to make sure that the KA-BAR knife and side-arm weren't going to go on separate trips without him as he rappelled, and waited his turn as Reith disappeared over the side of the chopper.

Don't look back, Stark.

The air whistled past him, and he took a deep breath. It didn't fill the hole behind his heart.

Fuckit. He stepped over the side.

THERE WAS NOTHING SUBTLE about it. Zak, Reith, and Spincher saw the glint of firelight between the trees and went in guns blazing. Trying not to be distracted by the way the numbers were getting brighter and brighter, as if someone were turning up a dimmer switch, Zak fired the M-16, getting off the first shot at the two men unlucky enough to be the welcoming committee.

With a surprised shout, the first man dropped. Zak swiveled to drill the next guy, but Spincher got him first. That man also dropped to the recently cut vegetation, blood a crimson wash across his fatigues.

Repulsed, Zak was reminded of all the fucking reasons he didn't like guns. They killed, and they killed fast.

Two men flanked Piñero in the rough clearing, Uzis in their hands.

"Buenas tardes, Señor Stark. *Bienvenido de nuevo.* You missed our hospitality, I see."

Zak saw the hastily constructed shack out of the corner of his eye. Six by six. No windows, no ventilation. It would be like an oven inside. *"Gideon!"*

It was a fucking Mexican standoff, the six of them standing there with their weapons pointed at one another. Zak itched to shoot them. It'd save time, if they were fast enough not to get shot in return.

Not likely. "Drop your weapons," he told them coldly. God, he'd never felt such a strong desire to do violence.

"I think—" Piñero began haughtily, and Zak squeezed the trigger, firing a round close enough to the woman that he saw the whites of her eyes as the bullets whizzed by her ear. The man to her left screamed in fear and covered his head; his weapon sailed into the wall of green behind him.

"Drop them now," Zak instructed, firing another warning shot. *"Gideon?"* he yelled again. A parrot screeched and jettisoned out of a nearby tree. Zak lifted the barrel to point directly at the middle of Piñero's forehead. "Bring him out. *Now.*"

She didn't move, but whispered something to the guy on her right. He was medium height and dressed in boots and camo, his cap pulled low over his eyes. The man responded, and Piñero, clearly reluctant, threw down the Uzi. Without having to be told, she clasped her hands on top of her head.

"*All* your weapons," Spincher told them as he and Reith fanned out around them. A quick search showed the guerrillas were unarmed. "Go get him," he added to Zak. "We don't have much time." Reith walked behind them, and told the men to put their hands behind them. Loida Piñero did so, an unpleasant smile on her thin, homely face. Her men followed suit.

"Me da pena que él no puede caminar sin ayuda." Handcuffed behind her head, Piñero jerked her chin at the shack.

Zak turned for the shack. Suddenly a spray of bullets winged past them. Gunfire echoed from the surrounding vegetation, and Piñero laughed as she sprinted for the border of the clearing.

"Incoming!" Reith shouted, and added harshly, "Stark, go! We'll engage. Go, go, go!"

Ducking low, Zak sprinted for the shack, his heart in his throat.

He raced across through the tall grass and small shrubs, and crouched, desperately aware of the report of automatic fire behind him.

The narrow door of the shack was nailed shut. "Gid! Stand aside, I'm coming in!" One hard kick from Zak's booted foot, and the door ripped off its hinges and clattered to the floor inside.

"Ah, Jesus, Gid—" It only needed one large stride to reach the opposite side of the sweltering hot structure, where his brother was sprawled on the floor. His clothing was dark with sweat and covered liberally with blood. Zak didn't know where to touch him to see if he was alive. The numbers were pulsing and so bright he wouldn't have been surprised if anyone looking at him could see them too.

He crouched beside his brother and carefully turned his face. It was battered and bruised. One eye was swollen shut; his lower lip was split, already fat and puffy and crusted with dried blood.

"Gid . . ." Zak had to swallow bile and regret before he could go on. "I've come to take you home, you lazy son of a bitch. Rise and shine."

He heard a volley of shots outside as he placed his fingers on Gideon's throat. Holding his breath, he prayed harder than he'd ever prayed as he searched for a pulse. It was there, slow and thready. Zak thought Gideon was unconscious, until his brother slitted open one eye to give him a dazed, unfocused look.

"Z-zak." He barely got out the one slurred word. Clearly Gideon was too weak to even lift his head, let alone walk. God damn it, he wouldn't be able to climb up a fucking rope attached to a moving helicopter.

More shots were fired, and men's voices shouted warnings and instructions. Fuck. Now what? Zak hiked the M-16 across his shoulder, and shifted to pick up his brother. "I'm going to lift you. Don't try to help."

"S-s-sh." Gideon struggled to speak, his limp fingers weakly searching for purchase until they closed around Zak's wrist. "S-she . . . ba-ack."

"Hey. Hey, okay. Don't worry about anything, okay? I've got you." He grabbed Gideon's arm and did a fireman's lift. Knowing he was causing him untold pain by the movement, he went as fast as possible. Gideon's dead weight hung over his shoulder, limp as a rag. "You're going to be okay," he grunted. "You're going to be o—"

". . . ant you . . ." Gideon's voice was weak, but he plucked with surprising strength at the back of Zak's sweat-soaked shirt to get his attention as they went through the door.

"Yeah. I know," he muttered, concentrating on not letting his brother slide off his shoulder, trying to hold the M-16 in one hand, wondering where the fuck everyone was. "Buck wanted us both dead. He'll pay, Gid. He'll—"

A soldier stepped into the path, blocking his way. Zak lifted his weapon, finger squeezing down on the trigger as the guerrilla spoke in a low, deadly voice. "I see you haven't changed, you selfish bastard. You're still giving credit where it isn't due."

Impossible.

Improbable.

In the fucking flesh.

Zak froze. "*Jennifer?!*"

⤙ NINETEEN ⤚

"S urprised?" Jennifer asked, cocking her hip and readjusting her hold on an Uzi.

Zak stared at the woman's vaguely familiar face, which didn't go with the *very* familiar voice. She'd been the "guy" standing beside Piñero, the one who'd convinced the soldiers to drop their weapons. The only thing familiar about her was her voice.

"What?" Zak asked blankly, incapable of wrapping his mind around the fact that he was talking to a woman he thought he'd buried two years ago.

Dressed in camouflage pants and shirt, an Uzi strapped across her chest, a KA-BAR knife in an ankle holster—Jennifer just didn't fit. He was in another fucking dimension. Whereas once she'd been tall and slender, the sixty-plus pounds she'd packed on distorted her once-willowy frame. But it wasn't just the weight gain that had changed her features so as to be unrecognizable; it was also the drastic plastic surgery that had thrown him off. She was a grotesque, distorted Angelina Jolie impersonator.

Brows, nose, cheekbones. He tried to superimpose his beautiful and elegant Jen, with her small delicate features and slender body, onto the bloated, altered woman before him. "I buried you."

Jennifer's laughter was harsh. She tossed a long, greasy black braid over her shoulder. "Reports of my death were greatly exaggerated, Zakary."

No shit. "I went to bring your body home." Zak's chest ached at the bitter memory. "We buried an empty casket because there wasn't enough of you to take home." Two years of soul-eating guilt that he hadn't been able to save her, even from herself. Two fucking years of blaming himself for what had happened to her. Her death had colored his world.

"I must admit, faking my death in Haiti was a little complicated. But nothing a few thousand American couldn't expedite."

Gunfire erupted beyond the trees, but Zak kept his entire attention on her. "Why?"

"I was bored, bored, *bored*, Zakary." She took off her cap, keeping the weapon pointed at his chest. He didn't doubt for a second that she'd shoot him right there and not bat an eyelash. Despite the sultry heat, his skin felt cold and his gut twisted with impatience and revulsion.

"I thought you'd be much more exciting than you turned out to be. You told me no a lot. I don't like being dictated to. Marriage wasn't working. I think you knew that early on. But you're so fucking bullheaded, so sure you're always right, you kept on trying and trying and fucking *trying*."

"We'd made a commitment." Jesus. He had to get Gideon on that chopper— "I believed if we worked at it, we could make it work. I did my best to make you happy." And it had never been enough.

"Well it didn't, and I wasn't. You fell out of love with me before we even got married, didn't you? Yeah. I knew you did. But you were fool enough to hang on, flogging a dead horse, for six interminable years." She started as a troupial erupted out of a nearby tree, but even though she flinched at the sound and movement, her weapon was steady as she insisted he backtrack. "It was time to move on. I had other things to do, other places to go." She caressed her Uzi as if it were a pet.

He heard another series of rapid retorts of automatic gunfire beyond the trees, and the *whop-whop-whop* of the helicopter over the canopy. Sweat rolled down his temple. Gideon's thready pulse beat right over the bandage on his own bullet wound. He adjusted his brother's weight; the urge to turn his back on Jennifer and run like hell for the chopper was so powerful his muscles shook and his heart pounded. But an Uzi to the sternum, at such close range, was a strong deterrent. One bullet would kill Gideon with him.

A bone-deep ripple of revulsion swept through him. The loathing he saw in Jen's eyes was as unfamiliar as her appearance. He just wanted to get the hell back to the chopper. Jennifer and her fucking theatrics could go straight to hell.

"We could've divorced, as I suggested a few weeks before you went to Haiti," he said tightly. "You cried and begged me to give us another chance— What happened to the baby?"

She laughed. "Get serious."

"There was no baby." Of course not. He'd been talking divorce. The ruse had worked. He'd wanted to work things out.

"A divorce would've been a lot simpler than all this." And he could have gone on with his fucking life without all the guilt eating at him like a staph infection.

"I was still making *plans* for this." She swept her arm out to encompass their surroundings. "I wasn't going to walk away with a paltry five million when I could have it all." She'd been unpredictable and theatrical before, but Zak had no idea how to handle this Jennifer. Was this where she'd been heading, all those times before? What he'd thought of as moody . . . Christ.

"How did you know about the safe house?" Acadia could have died in the explosion. Fuckit. She could still die if a bullet hit the chopper.

"Your girlfriend made a call to the States." With the barrel of the Uzi, Jennifer motioned for him to step back. Back to the shack where she'd held Gideon. Back, away from the helicopter, rotors throbbing overhead. "With the help of the local police, I was tracking your cell phones within half an hour of you buying them. Almost got her that time. But it doesn't matter. It's not legal. You're already married."

"Why the car bomb at the hotel?" he demanded without responding to her jeer.

"To smoke you out. Jesus, Zakary. Follow the bouncing ball here, would you?"

He didn't give a shit why she'd done the bat-shit crazy things she'd done. Not anymore. And sure as hell not now. He tried for logic. "Gideon needs medical attention."

"I don't give a flying fuck," she shot back, voice cold, the fury in her eyes flickering like a blue flame. "I want him to die. Your precious brother's death will hurt you more than anything I could do to you. You've caused me a lot of trouble, Zak. I invested a fortune to pull off that kidnapping and to hire all those cops . . . I wasted a fucking *fortune* buying weapons and C-4, damn it!" The Uzi snapped up to his face, and he stared down the black barrel. "You two were supposed to be waiting when I got here. *Gideon* was supposed to die a week ago while you watched and begged me to save him. That woman you were fucking was supposed to be blown to hell on the company plane. You've never been predictable, Zakary."

"Then why tell your pal Piñero to keep one of us alive?"

"I *didn't*. I instructed that stupid bitch to keep *you* alive, my darling. I didn't give a shit about your brother once I discovered you were gone. He's been nothing but a pain in my ass for years." She smiled, a travesty full of taunting cruelty. "He served his purpose, I suppose. I knew you'd come and look for him. It was always you and your brother." She twisted two fingers together, then turned it into a shaking fist that punched her thigh.

Gideon's breaths came more slowly. Zak's sped up.

"Gideon this," she mimicked in falsetto, "Gideon that. I've been planning this for *years*." She gave him a hostile look. "I was building a nice little settlement back there. I wanted to come and visit you in your small, airless cell. I wanted to see your face when you first saw your dead wife come back to life. You think I want a piss-willy little five mil, when you're worth a hundred times that? Hell no. I want it all. You cheated me out of hundreds of millions I should have made as partner of your stupid fucking ZAG Search. And now I'm going to collect."

Bats darted low, directly over their heads. She didn't seem to notice. He didn't even try to make sense of what she was babbling. "You had a beautiful service, Jen. All your friends were there to pay tribute," he told her, keeping his tone moderate, though he felt anything but. "We all loved you. Your life was celebrated and you were mourned by everyone who cared about you." Zak, Gideon, Buck, and Nikki. Those were the mourners. And Buck and Gideon hadn't ever liked her, although they'd tolerated her for his sake. Clearly they'd never been blinded by her sex appeal and high IQ.

She gave him a cold look. "I'm not the wife you *pretended* to love. But I am the woman who's going to watch you die, by small, small increments. I won't be cheated out of that. I worked for it. I want it, and you can't tell me no, Zakary Stark. You will *not* tell me I can't have what I want. Ever. Again."

There was no reasoning with her. "Fine," he said, his voice flat. Sweat ran down his temples, small gnats swarmed around his face, and Gideon was starting to shift on his shoulder. His brother's body blocked Zak's access to the gun tucked in his belt in the small of his back. Could he shoot Jennifer? *Hell, yeah,* Zak thought savagely as she stood blocking his way to getting Gideon to safety. "Let's fucking do that. But first, let me get Gideon on board the chopper. Let him get the help he needs before you start hacking me limb from limb."

"Hell no. That'll impact what I get as your widow. I want it all, every last damned dime you have."

"You can have every last damn dime," Zak told her tightly. "Give me something to write on and I'll sign off, *after* we get Gideon to a hospital."

"When he dies, I'll have more."

"Not the way the partnership agreement works," Zak lied. "If Gideon dies, his shares, all of his money, goes to a distant aunt in Kansas City." The scrolling numbers, so bright in the chopper, were fading as if the dimmer switch were being lowered. He tightened his arm across the back of Gideon's knees. *Hang in there.*

"Fine." She waved a filthy hand airily. Her nails were chewed to the quick, and he saw part of a tattoo disappearing from her wrist and under her sleeve. "I'll have yours and Buck's."

"Buck will have something to say about that. But mine—"

"Buck had an unfortunate accident this morning soon after chatting with you, I believe. Home invasion. Knives were involved."

"Jesus! You had *Buck* killed?"

"I had to *delegate,* Zakary," she bitched, as if he'd asked her to take the garbage out and empty the dishwasher at the same time. "I couldn't *be* in two places at once!"

Jesus. It hadn't been Buck at all. It had been Jennifer all along. "Who did you delegate to?"

"Nikki, of course. She's at a lovely spa outside Los Angeles, having her facial reconstruction done, by Adam. You remember Nik's brother, don't you? Someone else you screwed on your way to the top? A great alibi. We got a twofer on that one." She aimed the Uzi at his heart, holding the barrel five inches from his chest, and smiled slowly, her dirt-smeared cheeks crinkling. "And before I let you die, *darling*"—she said it like a curse—"I'll be sure to blow up your fucking *new* wife once and for all. *After* I tell her that you already *have* a wife."

He *had* to get on that chopper. But there was no way she was going to miss him if she fired. "Nikki had her own husband killed?"

"We have that in common." She ran the tail end of her braid across her cheek. "We've loved each other for years, you know."

"You and Buck?"

"You're an egotistical idiot, Zakary, do you know that? Why does everything have to be about you and your goddamn dick? Drop that lump of patheticness, and get back into your cell where you belong. When the others get back, we'll take care of your homophobia."

How the fuck had they gone from murder to homo— "You and *Nikki*?"

"She's always been my soul mate." Zak's knees almost buckled as he took in the betrayal of his married life, of Buck's married life, of Buck's death. Christ. He couldn't take it personally, not right now. "Then I wish you both well," he told her calmly. "I'll set the two of you up forever and we can all live happily ever after."

"You don't get to live happily ever after! You"—prodding him with the Uzi so he had to take a step back—"*you* get to live *miserably, painfully, unhappily* ever after, and not for long."

Gideon was slipping off his shoulder. His brother's entire body shifted as Zak moved backward at every prod from Jennifer's weapon. Zak tightened his hold around his brother's knees, but Gideon kept sliding and twisting.

Suddenly Gideon dug his elbows in, grabbing the handgun from the strapped holder in the small of Zak's back. He twisted just enough to fire a shot that hit Jennifer at close range, square in the face. Her head exploded like a watermelon, spraying Zak and Gideon with gray matter and blood.

"Wel-come," Gideon slurred, dropping his head down to bounce against Zak's back. The pistol fell from his nerveless fingers into the grass.

"Christ!" The numbers in Zak's mind winked out. "No, Gid— Damn it! No!" Zak tried to will them back. Nothing. He tipped Gideon off his shoulder, laid him in the grass, pounded his chest with both hands. His brother's slack face wavered and blurred. "*Breathe*, damn you. Breathe!"

The rotors overhead whipped the treetops, and the burst of gunshots muted to background noise as Zak struggled to breathe for his brother. He tried mouth-to-mouth. He pounded on Gideon's chest, trying not to think about his possibly broken ribs. "Don't do this, Gid. We're going home now. Please. Don't. Die. On. Me."

He pressed two fingers beneath his brother's jaw. Nothing. Zak's head dropped to Gideon's still chest. "Damn it, Gid!"

"Stark?" It was Reith, out of sight. "Get your ass in gear. We gotta go. Now!"

ACADIA HAD DONE EVERYTHING but turn invisible to keep out of the way. But the helicopter wasn't very large real estate, and people were shooting at them, and the two men, dressed all in black, were firing some powerful-looking guns at the people on the ground.

The pilot was yelling that they had to get the fuck out of there ASAP, that they were getting hit hard. Yes. She'd noticed. The impact of things hitting the sides of the craft sounded like cannon fire from inside.

Below them, flames were erupting around the small clearing as trees caught fire. In other words, all hell was breaking loose and Zak and Gideon were in the middle of it.

Where were they?

"Down there" was mayhem. "Up here" was a pilot fighting to keep the helicopter steady so that he could beam the men on the ground back to the mother ship. And two men firing and loading some serious weapons. And one woman who was making the smallest footprint she could in order to stay out of their way.

"We have Spincher."

The helicopter dipped and swayed.

Good. Not the man she wanted to hear about. But good. Acadia held her breath, waiting, praying.

"Here come Reith and Stark. Hold your fire!"

"Thank you, God." She winced as a barrage of shots came from the ground. "Hurry. Hurry. Hurry."

Spincher was hauled on board and immediately turned, weapon in hand, to cover the man climbing up the rope. Zak? Oh, God, please . . .

Reith was yanked onto the floor of the helicopter, lay there for a few seconds catching his breath, then picked up his weapon and braced himself against the open door, firing down into the whipping treetops. By now the fires were reaching into the canopy, and the smoke further obscured the view of the clearing below.

"Find his brother?" one of the men asked through the headset in Acadia's helmet.

Reith fired another round through the trees. "Didn't make it. Drop a second line."

"We don't—"

Reith cut in tersely, "Drop the line! He wants to bring his brother home."

Spincher leaned over through the open door as another rope was quickly lowered. "Ordnance coming in hot. Son of a bitch is gonna get us all killed. Hurry the fuck up, Stark!"

A hailstorm of bullets hit the side of the helicopter. Acadia needed to get out of the harness, but Reith grabbed her shoulder as she started to undo the snap. "Nothing you can do, ma'am. Stay put. Speed things up, you two!" he yelled, gesturing at the men pulling what Acadia presumed was the rope tied to Gideon.

Beside her, Reith muttered "Shit" under his breath. *Oh, Zak.* Acadia's heart ached. To have come this close and lost his brother must be devastating.

"Here he comes!" Reith shouted, then answered fire, ducking against the inner wall. A bullet went all the way through one open door, and out the other. "Get ready to rock and ro— Oh, hell!"

"What? Acadia strained against the restraints. "Is Zak— *What's happening?"*

"No!" Spincher screamed down to Zak. "Keep climbing, you asshole. Keep fucking climbing!" He turned back and addressed Reith, although they could all hear him over the headsets. "The brother's tether was shot and severed, body's back on the ground. Help me pull Stark up, *fast.* "The men scrambled, hauling in the line hand over hand. *"Pull. Pull. Pull!"*

Between them, they pulled Zak onboard. He was furious.

The helicopter lifted higher in a dizzying climb that had Acadia's heart in her throat. She was strapped in, couldn't get to Zak, who stayed where he was, sprawled on the floor, as they climbed. The sound of the gunfire dropped away, leaving the echo in her ears and the heavy percussive sound of the blades spinning overhead.

"Everyone in one piece?" Reith asked over the headset.

Everyone answered in the affirmative. Except Zak, whose eyes were filled with such pain, Acadia felt it to her soul. Her heart swelled too big for her chest as she felt the pain coming off him in waves.

She wanted to crawl over to him and press his head against her breast. Wanted to rock him, or kiss him, or stroke his back. She wanted to take some of that pain and share it with him to lighten his burden.

All she could do was sit there like a statue and watch him struggle to deal with the loss of his brother. Tears blurred her vision, and she had to swipe her face against her shoulder.

The helicopter jerked right, and everything slid until the pilot smoothed the ride. The move brought Zak from his daze and he rolled over, pushing himself upright. He sat there, hands hanging between his bent knees. His skin seemed pulled too tight over his features, and his eyes were dark, sunken pools as he stared at nothing.

After several minutes, his chest rose and fell as he dragged in a ragged breath. "Piñero?" he asked hoarsely.

"Dead," Spincher replied evenly.

"Fly over the falls," Zak instructed, voice thick.

The pilot looked back and gave a grim nod.

A few minutes later, the helicopter hovered over Angel Falls. Acadia had to admit, it was beautiful. The water dropped over the edge of flat-topped Auyantepui Mountain to plunge almost three thousand feet to the valley below. By the time the water reached the Kerep River, most of it would've evaporated. A cloud of fine mist sprayed the windows, and gathered in rivulets to run like tears down the Plexiglas.

Instead of spending her thirtieth birthday looking up at its majesty and power from the river below, she was looking at it from a dizzying height, hovering above it a lifetime later.

Please, God, Acadia prayed, surreptitiously fumbling with the latch to her harness, *do not let Zak jump*. What she'd do if he tried, she had no idea. Wind buffeted the helicopter, and Zak held on to the open door, almost suspended over the spray, for several moments of heart-stopping fear for Acadia.

Zak whispered something, then drew his hand back and flung his brother's watch out into the mist.

He slammed the door shut with a final-sounding thud. "Let's go." Clearly not interested in conversation, he took off his headset, leaned his head back, and closed his eyes.

Two hours later, thanks to the mysterious Marc Savin, Acadia sat alone on a Learjet, winging her way home to Junction City.

⊸ TWENTY ⊷

Zak missed Acadia with an intense longing that had only grown stronger in the months since he'd seen her. During the wild time they'd spent together, she'd inextricably become part of his very soul. Her departure had torn Zak's tenuous tether to her and made him realize just what an asset she was. As he'd stood on the tarmac watching until the plane was a speck in the sky, something had unraveled inside him.

He was done waking in the night, reaching for her, only to find himself alone.

He'd gone to Venezuela seeking excitement.

He'd found her.

He'd found love.

He'd come to Boston to retrieve her.

Zak had sold ZAG Search, despite the crappy economy. But it had taken months to unravel the clusterfuck of events leading to his brother's and Buck's deaths.

He'd earmarked the majority of the money from the sale of ZAG to fund adventure camps all over the country for underprivileged kids in Gideon's name. The first would be breaking ground in Seattle soon. And he was in talks to construct a BASE-jumping camp near Angel Falls, also in Gid's name.

Angel Falls and Gideon would forever be indelibly linked in his mind. No one would ever know Gid the way he had, but the camps would keep his brother's adventurous spirit alive for hundreds of kids for a very long time. Gid would've loved what he'd done. But it could never be enough.

God he missed him. The loss was a gnawing ache in Zak's gut. He wasn't sure he'd ever get past the guilt that if not for his fucked-up marriage, and Jennifer's hatred of him, Gid would still be alive. Great, a new guilt to replace the old. He was trying to think of a better, more productive way to deal with it this time around.

It was almost as though he could hear Gideon's voice as the weeks stretched into months: *Find her. Bring her home.* *Yeah*, Zak thought, with a mental salute to his brother. *I'm on it.*

Cambridge hadn't changed. Everything looked the same as it had when he, Gideon, and Buck had attended MIT here. Jesus, they'd been young and idealistic, full of wild ideas and big dreams. An unstoppable trio, they'd buoyed each other along the way as they achieved everything they'd set out to do. And more. They'd parlayed a crazy idea into a groundbreaking company and made millions, not only by building the biggest, most powerful search engine on the Internet, but by keeping cool heads and making shrewd deals. They'd lived their lives to the fullest, and regretted nothing they'd given up to build the company.

The ridiculous amounts of money they'd made had merely been an entertaining way to keep score. But none of it meant anything now, not without Gideon and Buck.

He'd needed time to adjust to the loss of the two men who had meant the most to him. But once he made the decision to live again, he'd moved with determined purpose to achieve his goal. He'd utilized every second of the last ninety days in his haste to tie up all the loose ends before coming to see Acadia. It wasn't that he was done grieving; the hole in his heart would never completely close. He just assured himself that he was accepting that life would be different from now on. A new normal.

A new challenge. One with blond hair and gray eyes, who was the equivalent, in terms of both difficulty and accessibility, of scaling Mt. Everest. Only a hell of a lot more thrilling.

Zak pulled the rental car to the curb in front of Acadia's modern high-rise and touched the place beneath his shirt where her St. Christopher medallion rested. She'd slipped it into his pocket, he suspected, when he'd left Savin's safe house. At first, seeing the familiar scrolling numbers superimposed on the sky as her plane lifted over Caracas, his heart had leaped, and his first thought had been *Gideon*. But Gideon was well and truly dead. And then he knew—

Acadia.

Her medallion was his link to her. As long as he held it, Zak had known exactly where she was from the moment she'd made it safely home to Junction City. He'd "seen" her traveling cross-country by car, and he'd known to the exact coordinates when she'd arrived here in Cambridge, Massachusetts.

He'd traveled across the country to find her. The GPS location coordinates had been scrolling through his mind for weeks. Now the numbers glowed "hot," indicating she was right there, minutes away. He blew out a hard breath, letting go of his death grip on the steering wheel. The sun shone down from an ice blue sky, no warmth in it. He hadn't felt warm since they'd parted.

Carrying a large cardboard box, Zak strode confidently up the path, stepped through the glass doors, crossed the lobby, then hesitated like a lovesick schoolboy as the elevator doors slid open. He needed another minute—

No, he didn't. Months had already been wasted. He got in and slapped the button for the eleventh floor and concentrated on breathing in and out to slow his racing heartbeat. Which was ridiculous. He'd done more dangerous stunts in his quest for adventure than a Hollywood stuntman. He'd scaled the highest pinnacles, dived to the deepest depths, leaped from heights that had made even his equally adventurous brother quail. Yet here he was, sweaty-palmed at the mere thought of seeing the woman he loved.

The elevator ride was over before he could think of anything intelligent to say. Although he'd considered dozens of opening lines in the last few months, none of them now seemed right. Fuckit. Possibly the most important negotiation of his life, and he was tongue-tied. Gid would have laughed his ass off.

Zak got out and strode down a quiet, carpeted hallway. Staring at Acadia's front door, he waited through several heavy heartbeats before he was able to ring the bell. *Chicken.*

It was almost as though she had been standing with her fingers on the handle, because the door jerked open. "I was just— Zak!"

Ah, man. Acadia. His heart sang her name in three-part harmony. She was breathtakingly beautiful. Dressed in skinny light blue jeans that hugged her curves and a white cotton sweater that clung to her breasts, her honey-colored hair loose and silky around her shoulders, she looked even better than she had in his dreams. Cool, fresh, healthy, and—

Damn. She was gorgeous. Smelled like heaven, too. Night-blooming jasmine and Acadia Gray. He was as addicted now as he'd been thousands of miles and too many adventures ago, in Caracas. A feeling of euphoria swept over him, and he smiled. "Expecting someone?"

"No. Yes." She opened the door wider. "I thought you were the guys coming to pick up— Never mind. You're a long way from . . . wherever you've been." Her voice was a little frosty, her expression hard to read.

"Can I come in?" He'd hoped for a warmer reception.

She gave a noncommittal shrug and opened the door wider, then turned and padded in bare feet across the marble foyer, not waiting to see if he followed her. Thinking he'd follow her to the ends of the earth and back again, Zak bent to place the box he was carrying on the floor beside the hall table and surreptitiously pocketed her car keys in case she decided to make a run for it.

It wasn't an overwhelming welcome, but she hadn't slammed the door in his face, and he was profoundly grateful that she didn't hate him. God only knew she had just cause: putting her in danger, dragging her all over the jungle, nearly getting her killed, nearly dying on her, leaving her at the end. It was a long and damning list.

"Do you want something to drink?" Acadia tossed a glance at him over her shoulder as she led him into a living room. "I have— *Ohmf!*"

Zak spun her around, sliding his fingers under the silk of her hair to cup the back of her neck. Her body instantly melted against his. She felt deceptively fragile as she opened her mouth to welcome him. She felt achingly feminine in his arms, and he loved that part of her just as much as he loved her tensile strength.

He just . . . loved her.

Zak put everything he had into that kiss. Longing, need, regret, the apologies. Reaching into that raw, empty void in his heart, he desperately, silently tried to convey to her how he felt.

Her lips softened under his. Her lashes fluttered closed, and she sighed. After a few breathless moments he reluctantly lifted his head, and was gratified to see the haze in her wonderful gray eyes as she struggled to refocus.

He brushed his thumb over her smooth cheek and said tenderly, "How've you been?" *Have you missed me as much as I've missed you?*

"Fine." She was getting her bearings back faster than he was. But then, he reminded himself, poker was her game. "Busy." She pushed back, forcing distance between them as she smoothed her hands down her thighs. "Getting settled in my new place, getting ready to start school. How are you?"

"I can't sleep. I can't eat. Everything is in monochrome. Awful . . . without you," he finished. "My life is colorless without *you* in it, Acadia."

"Really?" She cocked a brow. "And yet I haven't heard a peep from you in three months."

"I've been busy."

"Really?" Her eyes narrowed dangerously. "So have I. In fact, I have an appointment in"—she glanced at her wristwatch—"twenty minutes, so say whatever you have to say, I need to get ready to go."

"I love you."

She didn't skip a beat. "You had a traumatic experience. You miss your brother—"

"Agreed. But that doesn't negate how I feel."

She folded her arms under her breasts and gave him a level look. "Is that it?"

Zak laughed. "You aren't going to give an inch, are you?"

They were standing four feet apart, in the middle of her living room. Zak felt an unfamiliar sensation of panic and ineptitude. He'd given symposiums to upward of twenty thousand people at a time, yet he couldn't effectively communicate with the woman who held his heart.

"Just because I picked you up in a bar and slept with you an hour later doesn't mean I'm available whenever you feel like showing up for a booty call. I'm worth considerably more effort than a few easy-to-say words, Zakary Stark."

Oh, that the words were easy, he thought with self-deprecation. "Seattle to Boston is a hell of a long way for a booty call."

"One would think."

His lips twitched at the asperity in her voice. Her eyes said one thing, her folded arms another. "Can we sit down?"

"No." Her look was unflinching, but he noticed that she let out a breath she seemed to have been holding. "Tell me what happened when you went back after I left."

"How—"

"I know you wouldn't leave Gideon there, Zak."

Because he felt touching her now wouldn't be to his advantage, Zak shoved his fingers into the back pockets of his jeans. "I went back at first light the next day. There was nothing to find." In the area where his brother had fallen, there were a few partial remnants of human bones scattered about. But not only Gideon and Jennifer had lost their lives there; there'd been half a dozen others who'd died that day. And although he and the men he'd taken with him had found bone fragments within several hundred yards of the kill zone, there'd been no bodies.

Remains were food. Animals and the voracious insect life had wasted nothing.

He found himself tenderly tracing a line to her chin, then the corner of her mouth, but didn't remember taking his hand out of his pocket. Touchable. Alive. Present. No matter how desperately Zak had wanted to bring Gid home for a decent burial, there'd been nothing left. And that would've been the way Gid wanted to go. Dangerous, and on the edge. Going out winning. Saving Zak's ass, knowing he'd leave behind an exciting story for others to tell in the aftermath.

Acadia covered the hand he had against her cheek. "I'm so, so sorry, Zak."

"Me, too." More than he could ever say, but he knew she understood. She moved her hand from his, and he tucked a strand of silky hair behind her ear and felt the small shiver that ran through her body at his light touch. "No more regrets, Acadia." Zak filled his senses with the smell of her hair and skin, filled the void she'd left where his heart had been. Now he felt filled to bursting with emotion. As if she were pouring liquid sunshine into his every dark nook and cranny.

"Tell me about Jennifer."

Zak almost groaned. She was the last person he wanted in the room with them right now. "Can I just hit the high points?" he begged, voice thick. God. He wanted—everything from her. *Everything*. And wasn't getting everything worth waiting for? Hell, yeah. But it was still killing him.

"Sure."

"She was behind it all. The kidnapping, the police, the explosions."

"Why? How?"

It had to be said, but Zak sure as shit didn't want to talk about any of it. "She claimed she'd always hated our marriage. Apparently she'd been in love with Nikki Buckner, Buck's wife, for years. I had my forensic accountants go back to the day we married and found that the two women had been funneling millions for years." They'd also spent most of their time together, while he and Buck had been working their asses off.

"You didn't notice the loss of 'millions' of dollars?" Acadia asked dryly as she ran the flat of her hand up and down his arm in an unconscious comforting gesture.

Zak shrugged. He'd noticed, he just hadn't cared. If Jennifer had wanted the money, she had been welcome to it. "It wasn't important. Of course, if I'd known what she was using it for, that would have put a whole different spin on it," he told her dryly. "She started putting things into place to stage a kidnapping just before her fake death in Haiti two years ago."

"She sounds very organized, but she couldn't have known you'd be in Venezuela at that *exact* time." Acadia's curious gaze met his. Was she playing with the shirt button, or undoing it?

"Because of our various business commitments, Gideon and I couldn't always coordinate time off simultaneously. It took considerable planning. We'd been talking about BASE-jumping Angel Falls for a while, so she knew we'd be there, eventually."

"A long-range goal."

His lips twitched at her sarcastic tone. "Let me get this on the table before I tell you the rest. I honest to God loved Jennifer when we first met. I thought she was everything I wanted. Bold and daring and ready for anything at any time."

She raised both pale brows. "A female version of you?"

Probably. "The scales fell from my eyes within months."

Zak wasn't willing to air every scrap of dirty laundry between himself and Jen. Not now. "And for the next six years I tried everything in me to make it work."

"If she was in love with Nikki, *that* wasn't going to happen."

"I wish I'd known that at the time. If she'd been honest, I would've wished her well and gone on with my life. Her subterfuge made both of us extremely unhappy." Her lies had gotten two good men killed. "She hired Loida Piñero and her men to kidnap us. It was all about the money right from the start. A divorce would have netted her half my assets, if that. We had a prenup. But she wanted it all. Christ. If I'd known, I would've gladly given her every last cent I had! Her plan was to kill Gideon so I'd inherit, then keep me prisoner at the first camp— Remember the place they were building? That was to be my home away from home for a few weeks while she taunted me with a laundry list of my failures and wrongdoings."

"The freaking *bitch*. She was a black widow patiently waiting in her web."

"Yeah. She and Nikki were responsible for a lot of deaths, not just Gideon's and Buck's. Gid shot her before he died."

"Good." Acadia's soft eyes filled with empathy, and she reached out to take his hand, twining her fingers with his. "He didn't want you to have to do it. Your brother loved you."

"Yeah, he did." The feel of her slender hand in his gave Zak hope. "I realized, standing there in the jungle, confronting my own mortality, when everything I knew and loved was about to blow up in my face, I knew what I felt for you was overwhelmingly . . . *different*. She was nothing more than a pale imitation of the real thing. You're the real deal, Acadia. As real as it gets."

She smiled a *Mona Lisa* smile, but she didn't move out of reach. "It's understandable you'd think that under the circumstances—"

"I've had three months, and I haven't been able to get you out of my head. Knowing where you were kept me doing what had to be done. Jennifer is dead. Nikki's awaiting trial for first-degree murder." She'd killed the father of her children. Zak had tracked down the hundred million she'd stashed in a Swiss account; that mess would take years to unravel. He'd set up trust funds for Buck's kids to attend whatever college they wanted in the world, buy themselves homes and have a healthy start in whatever career path they chose once they graduated, but it wouldn't be enough.

The strain was leaving her eyes, and her shoulders were a little less stiff. "How *did* you find me? Did you

ZAG me? Or was it through your spy network?" And she had reason to wonder, since she'd told all her friends and coworkers back in Junction City not to tell him where she was if he came calling.

"I used this." He pulled the chain and medal from beneath his shirt.

She smiled. "It kept you safe."

"Your St. Christopher medal brought me directly to you. But it did more than that. You're my lodestone, Acadia, in so many ways." Zak wanted to hold her. He wanted the conversation to be postponed so he could make love to her— God, he wanted to touch her so badly he hurt. It took everything in him to allow this to move at her pace. Because if things progressed at the pace he wanted, he'd have her naked and on the closest flat surface the moment she said yes. "But know this: I would have done whatever it took to get to you." This part he wasn't so confident about sharing. "The number thing wasn't just a link to my brother, Acadia. As soon as I held this, I saw *your* GPS location scrolling through my mind, clear as day. And the closer I got, the brighter and more vibrant the numbers became."

"You saw my GPS coordinates. Here?"

"Yes. But if my newly found skill hadn't worked, I would've turned the world upside down and shaken it until I found you, make no mistake. But it seems my new sense is here to stay. I'm going to use this . . . *skill* to help other people find their loved ones. In time—"

"Wait a minute," she cut in, shaking her head. "Hang on; just to be clear, are you saying that if you hold an item that belonged to someone, you can find them? It doesn't have to be a person you're related to, or someone"—she gave him a mischievous glance—"you love?"

"No. As long as I hold an item, I can track the person with this new sixth sense my near-death seems to have given me. It's a gift, Acadia."

She didn't look horrified, or appalled, or disbelieving. He should have known. He brushed his lips across hers. They clung for a second, and then she moved a little out of reach.

"So far it's only worked on Gideon and, you say, me."

"I tried it with a client of my lawyer's, a young mother whose son was snatched from his bedroom. Turned out it was her ex as suspected, but the guy was Serbian, so that's where they were looking. Instead he had the kid holed up in a small town in Greece. I was able to lead the police right to him. I'm not going to waste this skill, trait, magical sixth sense, internal GPS tracking system, whatever the hell it is. I'm going to turn something negative into something positive."

Acadia grinned. "You're a superhero."

He shook his head. "I'm no superhero. Just a man. I've sold ZAG Search. It was something for me, Gid, and Buck. It's time for a fresh start. A new company."

"In Seattle?"

"So far I have the name but not the location." He searched her face, but her expression gave nothing away. "The company is small. Just me. I'm calling this new venture Lodestone. Acadia, I can find people, I can find things—anywhere, anyone. I found you. Come back to

Seattle with me. God only knows I need your organizational skills. And the University of Washington has an excellent Architecture–Construction Management, dual-degree undergraduate program, if you want to go to school."

"I came *here* to go to school, Zak."

"Then I'll move here," he replied immediately. "Wherever you are is where I want to be. When I thought I had nothing left to feel, you taught me to love." He threaded his fingers through the silky fall of her hair.

Her beautiful eyes clouded. "Our worlds are nothing alike, Zak. I think you're confusing the heat of the moment with something else. Maybe . . . maybe you built what we shared into something bigger than it was." She bit her lip. "I'm just— I'm just me. I don't like heights; I'm not jumping from a plane unless it's on fire *and* I have two parachutes. Our time together was high-octane passion, but for me, it was almost like visiting someone else's life." She lifted her chin. "I like popcorn and television on Friday night, not being gunned down by guerrilla terrorists. I can't compete with all the bells and whistles, all the excitement you thrive on."

Zak's heart twisted. "I love *you*, Acadia. I love the way you plan your day, I love the way you stay true to who you are." He leaned in and kissed her until the protests he saw forming behind her delicate features vanished. "I love your passion, I love how meticulously organized you always are, I love that you're my center in a storm, and that you lie through your teeth when you're scared. I love your sense of humor, and your strengths, as well as the way you combat any perceived weaknesses. I love the whole Acadia Gray package."

Sunlight streamed through the uncurtained window behind her, highlighting her golden hair and the smooth curve of her cheek. Zak felt an overwhelming surge of love mingle with the intense lust.

"I—"

He pressed two fingers across her lips and smiled into her eyes. "I have some plans I think you can help me with."

"Help you . . ." She blinked. "*What* plans?"

"I'll be building a dozen or more adventure camps in Gideon's name for underprivileged kids all over the country. Exotic places like Angel Falls, as well. I'll need an enterprising, well-organized architect to stay on top of such an extensive project."

"Lovely." Her lips twitched. "A job offer before I even start school."

"More of a lifetime commitment."

"Do I say, 'Draw up a contract and I'll show it to my lawyer'? Or do I just keep it a simple yes or no?"

"Let's start with the simple yes; then if you feel the need to have an attorney, we'll get you one."

"Be very sure, Zak." She pointed to her bare walls. "Simple. Uncomplicated." Zak realized the place was painted stark white—the whole place was still in boxes, which surprised him. From the way she could pack a pair of pants, he'd figured her for a nester. She led them toward a plain beige sofa, which faced a small TV on a box. Hardly a home.

Heart in his throat, he seized the thread of her protests. "If 'simple' means bravest, strongest, and most daring, then yeah. You're simple."

She stopped before the couch and laughed, her fingers toying with another button on his shirt. "I was scared to my bones from the moment I met you in the cantina that night. But how I wanted you! Before that I'd never gone out of my comfort zone. I'm not brave. You made me brave."

"Bravery is doing what has to be done even when you're too terrified to do it." *Like now,* Zak thought with self-deprecating humor as she continued to undo his buttons, thinking he didn't notice. Oh, yeah, he noticed. And every button that slipped from its hole was another notch slipping on his limited supply of control. The fact that she was doing this gave him hope. Explosive, mind-bending sex was something they had in common, all right, but there was more. At least, he wanted it to be more. "I wouldn't be alive without you," he reminded her.

"You're too stubborn to die." She paused, then said softly, "No attorney. Yes."

"Yes?"

"That was your convoluted and rather obscure proposal of marriage, wasn't it?"

He wrapped her in his arms, resting his cheek on top of her head as he inhaled and let out a deep, contented sigh. "God, yes."

He felt her smile. "You've thought of almost everything."

"Not 'almost.' I've thought of everything. Over and over." He kissed the corner of her smile. "Name it, and it's yours."

Her hands were busily investigating his back under his untucked shirt. "There's something I really, really want."

He couldn't think of a single thing he wouldn't buy, or do for her. "Grapes."

She did a double take. *"Grapes?"*

"In the box I left by the door. Twenty pounds of seedless Thompson."

"Okay. I'll bite. *Why* did you bring me twenty pounds of grapes?"

"You told me once that you wanted me to parade naked while feeding you peeled grapes in gratitude for your being so resourceful, so helpful, so ably equipped to repeatedly save my life."

Her beautiful laughter poured over him. "You're a crazy man."

"About you." He started reversing her toward what he hoped was a bedroom.

No adrenaline rush in the world could provide him what she did with a single touch. A cool, rock-solid sense that no matter what happened or what he did, they'd be together. They'd have each other. Love and support and incredible sex; he couldn't ask for anything more. "Thank God," she murmured, walking backwards, her footsteps matching his as they kissed, shuffled, and talked their way to the bedroom. "I love you, Zak. You've taught me that love can be messy, and scary, and confusing. But above all, *amazing.* Thank you for accepting me for who I am, and who I want to be. You're everything I never knew I wanted." She paused to stand on her tiptoes to kiss him tenderly.

"I was in the process of packing up and moving to Seattle, where I was about to start stalking *you* until you came to your senses." She pressed her smile against his lips, and the heat and joy of it spread through him like sunlight.

As something in his heart eased, fluid and gentle, Zak knew he'd never again need the rush that had put him at death's door so many times. Her skin, her hair soft as silk in his hands, her smile, would be enough thrill for a lifetime. Here in Cambridge or there in Seattle, whether in exotic, dangerous Venezuela or calm and normal Junction City, wherever Acadia wanted to be was home.

Without breaking contact, Zak fumbled for the door handle behind her. "I love you, Acadia Gray."

Her arms tightened around his neck. "Thank God," she whispered, her eyes lifting to his. "Never doubt that you'll always be my hero, Zak. My light. My love. *My* lodestone."

He opened the door to the linen closet and, with Acadia's laughter filling his world, shut the door.

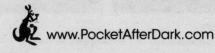

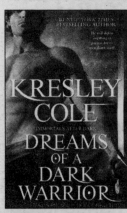

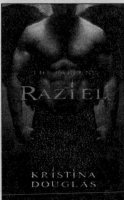